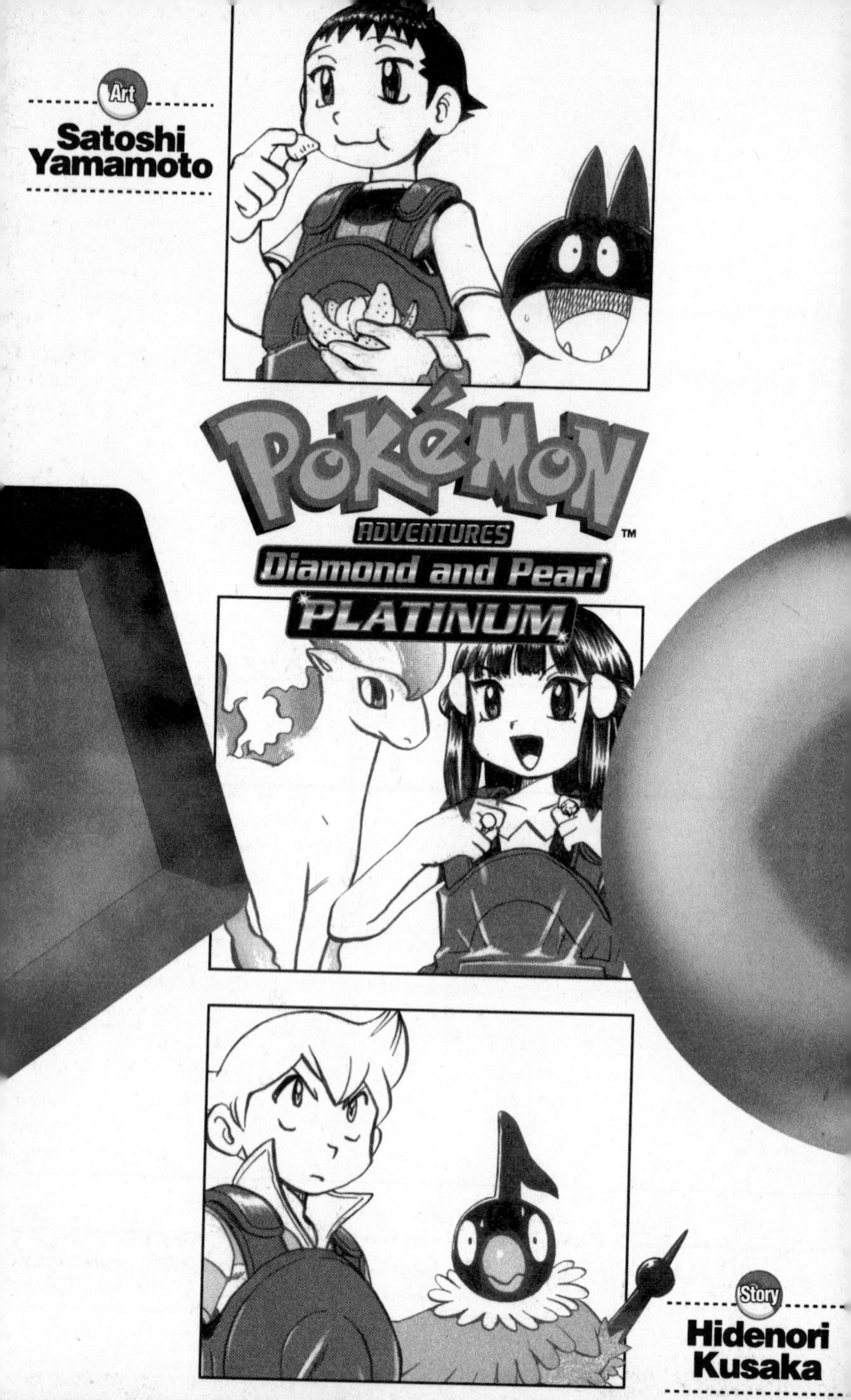
Art
Satoshi Yamamoto
POKéMON
ADVENTURES
Diamond and Pearl
PLATINUM
™
Story
Hidenori Kusaka

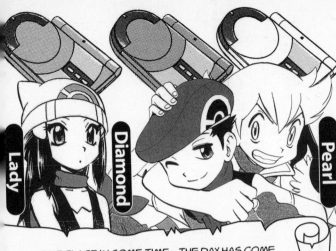

Lady

Diamond

Pearl

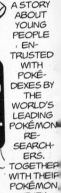

A STORY ABOUT YOUNG PEOPLE ENTRUSTED WITH POKÉDEXES BY THE WORLD'S LEADING POKÉMON RESEARCHERS. TOGETHER WITH THEIR POKÉMON, THEY TRAVEL, DO BATTLE, AND EVOLVE!

SOME PLACE IN SOME TIME... THE DAY HAS COME FOR A YOUNG LADY, THE ONLY DAUGHTER OF THE BERLITZ FAMILY, THE WEALTHIEST IN THE SINNOH REGION, TO EMBARK ON A JOURNEY. IN ORDER TO MAKE A SPECIAL EMBLEM BEARING HER FAMILY CREST, SHE MUST PERSONALLY FIND AND GATHER THE MATERIALS AT THE PEAK OF MT. CORONET. SHE SETS OUT ON HER JOURNEY WITH THE INTENTION OF MEETING UP WITH TWO BODYGUARDS ASSIGNED TO ESCORT HER.

MEANWHILE, POKÉMON TRAINERS PEARL AND DIAMOND, WHO DREAM OF BECOMING STAND-UP COMEDIANS, ENTER A COMEDY CONTEST IN JUBILIFE AND WIN THE SPECIAL MERIT AWARD. BUT THEIR PRIZE OF AN ALL-EXPENSES PAID TRIP GETS SWITCHED WITH THE CONTRACT FOR LADY'S BODYGUARDS!

THUS PEARL AND DIAMOND THINK LADY IS THEIR TOUR GUIDE, AND LADY THINKS THEY ARE HER BODYGUARDS! DESPITE THE CASES OF MISTAKEN IDENTITY, THE TRIO TRAVEL TOGETHER QUITE HAPPILY THROUGH THE VAST COUNTRYSIDE.

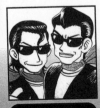

Paka & Uji

THE REAL BODYGUARDS HIRED TO ESCORT LADY.

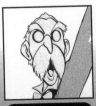

Sebastian

THE BERLITZ FAMILY BUTLER, WHO IS ALWAYS WORRYING ABOUT LADY.

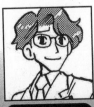

Mr. Berlitz

LADY'S FATHER, WHO ASSISTS PROFESSOR ROWAN.

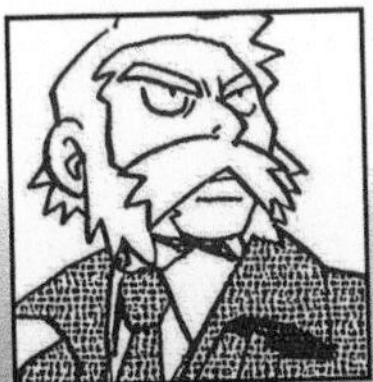

Professor Rowan

A LEADING RESEARCHER OF POKÉMON EVOLUTION. HE CAN BE QUITE INTIMIDATING!

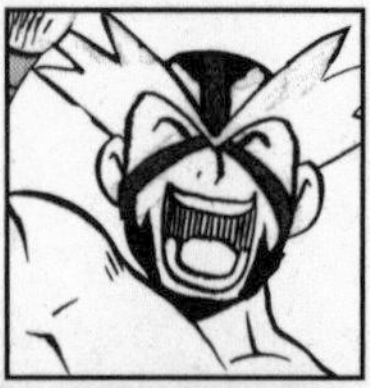

Wave

A MASKED WRESTLER FROM PASTORIA.

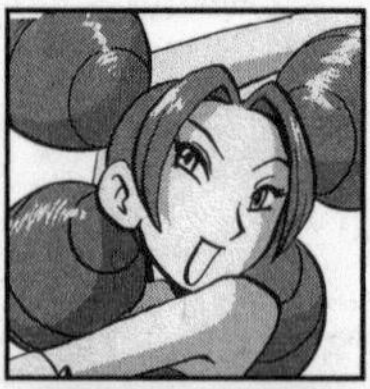

Fantina

THE ALLURING SOULFUL DANCER OF HEARTHOME.

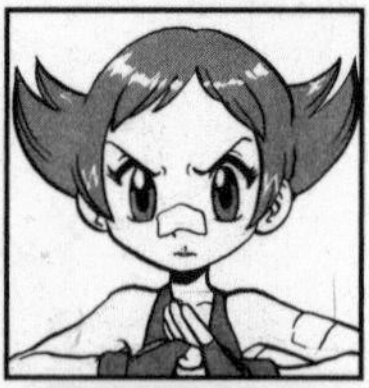

Maylene

THE ENTHUSIASTIC EAGER GYM LEADER AT VEILSTONE CITY.

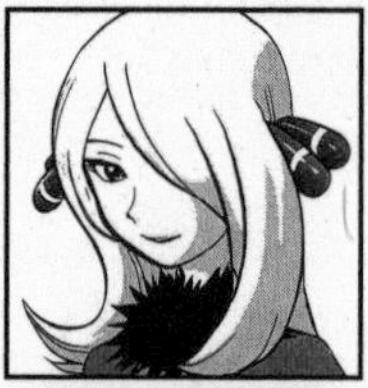

Cynthia

THE MYSTERIOUS WOMAN WHO SOLVED THE CASE OF THE KIDNAPPED BIKE SHOP OWNER.

THE TWO BODYGUARDS ENTRUSTED WITH ESCORTING LADY ARE AWARE OF THE MIX-UP AND SET OUT TO CATCH UP WITH DIA, PEARL, AND LADY. TO TOP IT OFF, MYSTERIOUS TEAM GALACTIC IS BUSY MAKING TROUBLE IN THE SINNOH REGION. THEIR DEVIOUS PLAN IS TO CREATE A GALACTIC BOMB. WHAT WILL THIS STRANGE DEVICE DO?

NOW, TO RAISE MONEY FOR THEIR NEFARIOUS PROJECT, TEAM GALACTIC HAS SET THEIR SIGHTS ON THE WEALTHY BERLITZ FAMILY! PAKA AND UJI FINALLY CATCH UP WITH DIA AND PEARL, WHO HAVE JUST ARRIVED AT VEILSTONE CITY. THE MISUNDERSTANDING IS CLEARED UP, AND THE FOUR WORK TOGETHER TO PROTECT LADY FROM THE ENEMY. HOWEVER, IN THE MIDST OF BATTLE, PAKA AND UJI GET SWALLOWED UP BY A MYSTERIOUS SHADOW...!

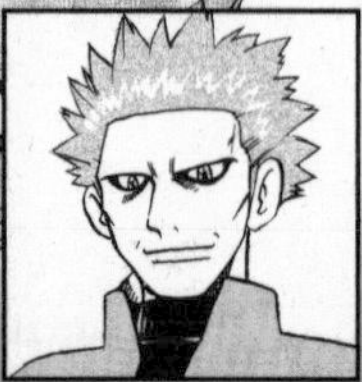

Cyrus

TEAM GALACTIC'S BOSS. AN OVERBEARING, INTENSE MAN.

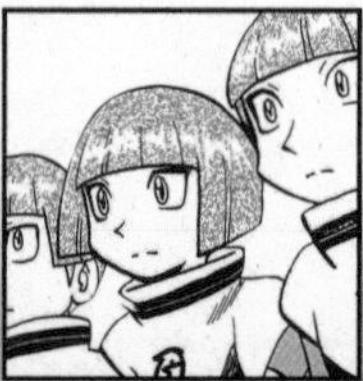

Galactic Grunts

THE TEAM GALACTIC TROOPS, WHO CARRY OUT THEIR LEADER'S BIDDING WITHOUT QUESTION. CREEPY!

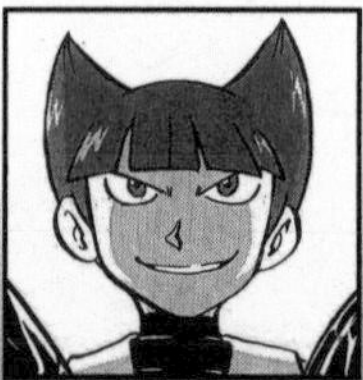

Saturn

HE IS IN CHARGE OF THE BOMB AND RARELY STEPS ONTO THE BATTLEFIELD HIMSELF.

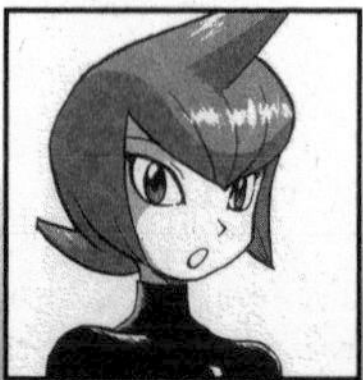

Mars

A TEAM GALACTIC LEADER. HER PERSONALITY IS HARD TO PIN DOWN.

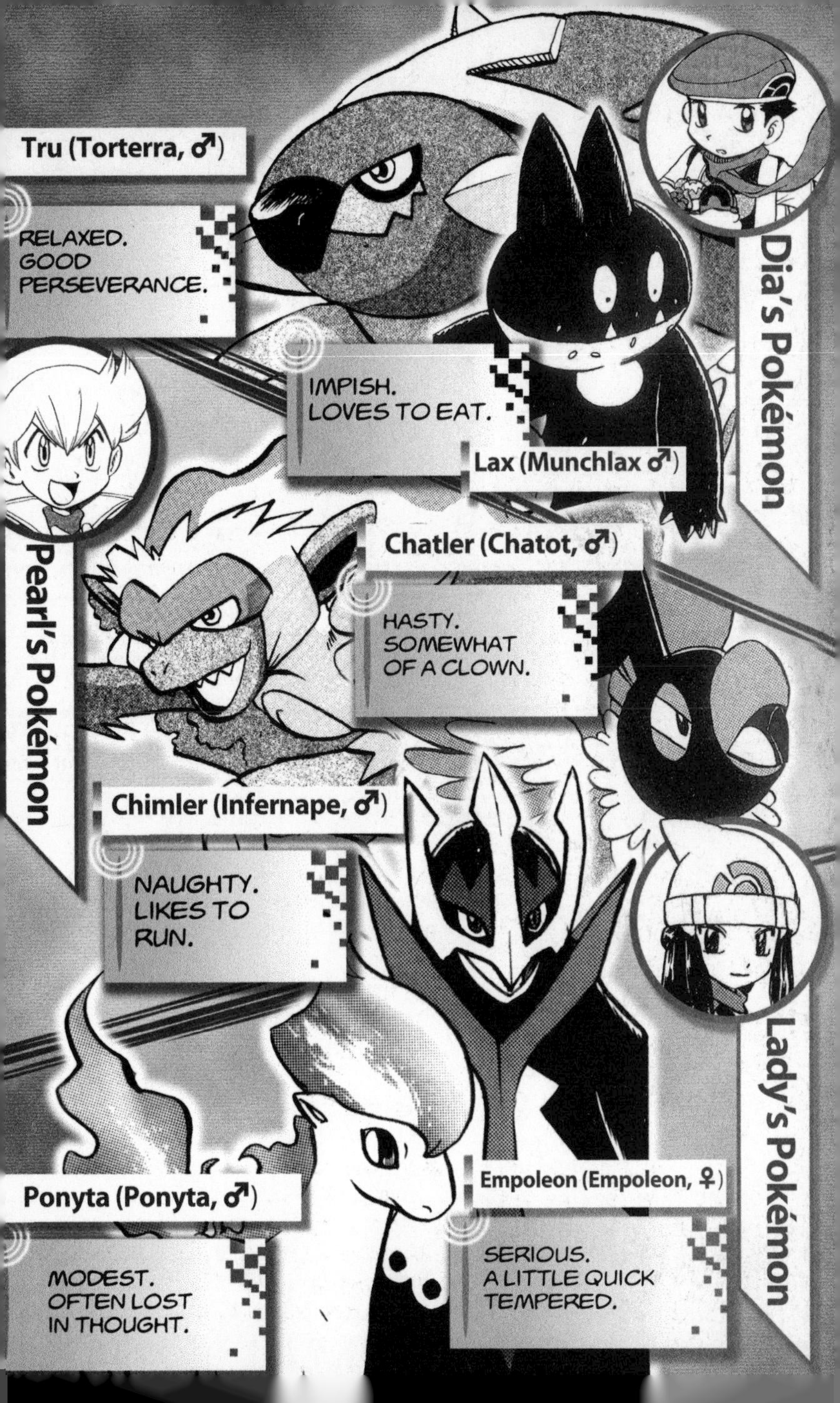

Dia's Pokémon
Tru (Torterra, ♂)
RELAXED. GOOD PERSEVERANCE.
Lax (Munchlax ♂)
IMPISH. LOVES TO EAT.
Pearl's Pokémon
Chatler (Chatot, ♂)
HASTY. SOMEWHAT OF A CLOWN.
Chimler (Infernape, ♂)
NAUGHTY. LIKES TO RUN.
Lady's Pokémon
Empoleon (Empoleon, ♀)
SERIOUS. A LITTLE QUICK TEMPERED.
Ponyta (Ponyta, ♂)
MODEST. OFTEN LOST IN THOUGHT.

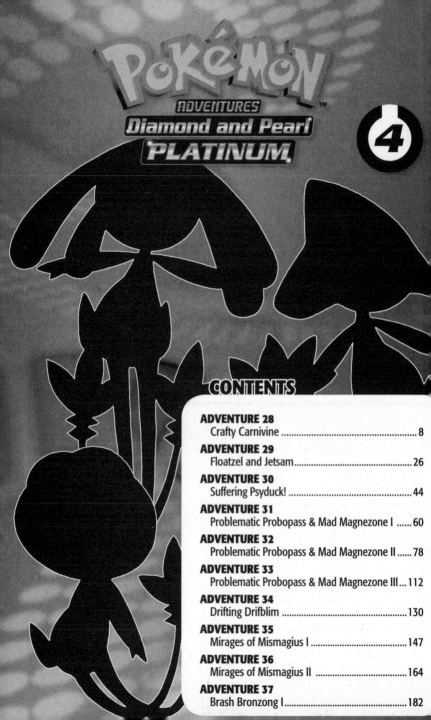

POKÉMON
ADVENTURES
Diamond and Pearl
PLATINUM

4

CONTENTS

28

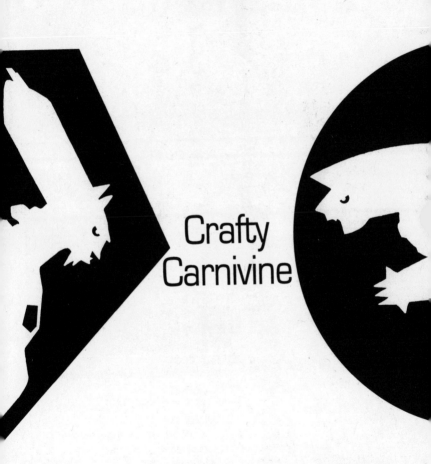

Crafty
Carnivine

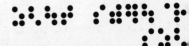

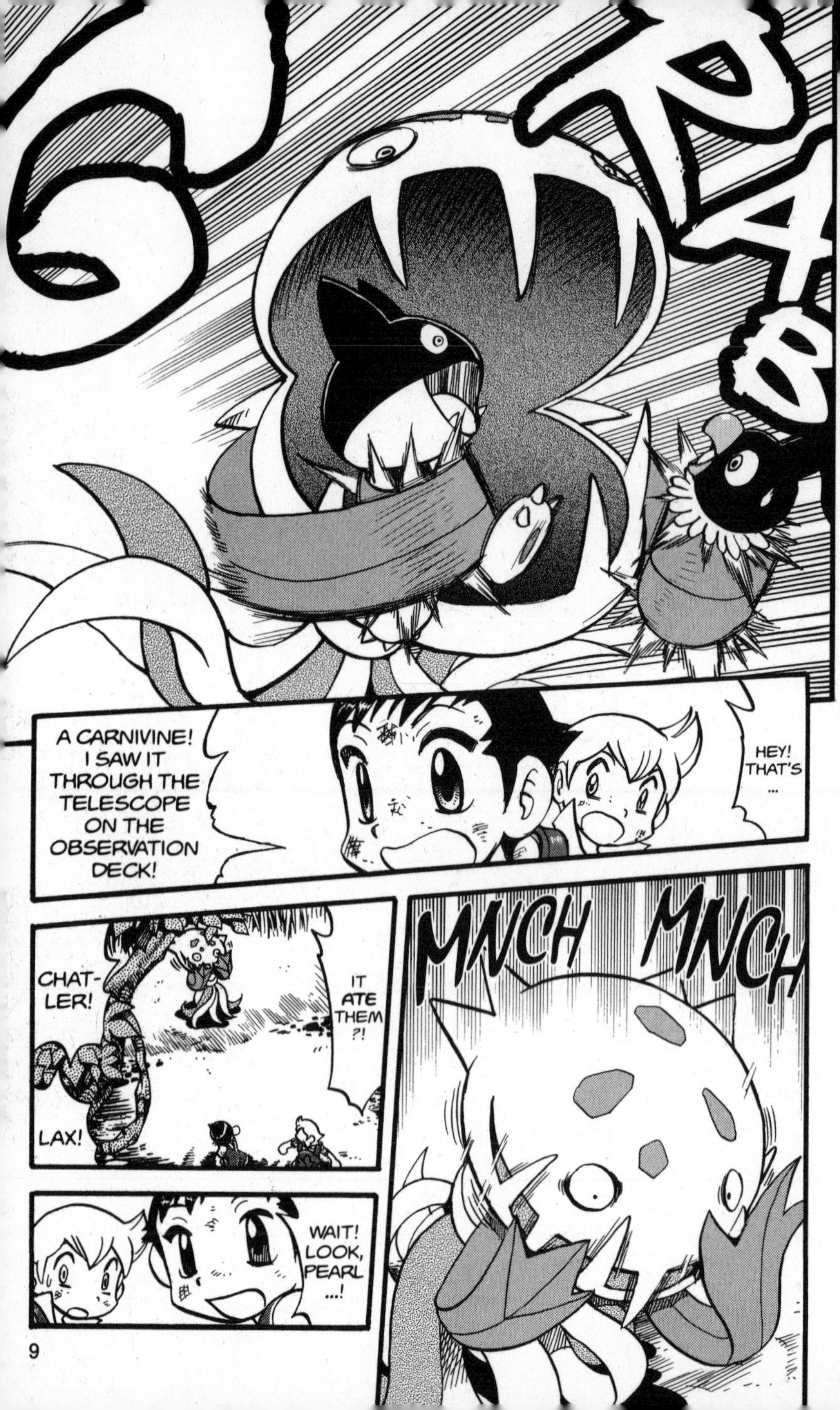
HEY! THAT'S ...
A CARNIVINE! I SAW IT THROUGH THE TELESCOPE ON THE OBSERVATION DECK!
MNCH MNCH
IT ATE THEM?!
CHAT-LER!
LAX!
WAIT! LOOK, PEARL ...!

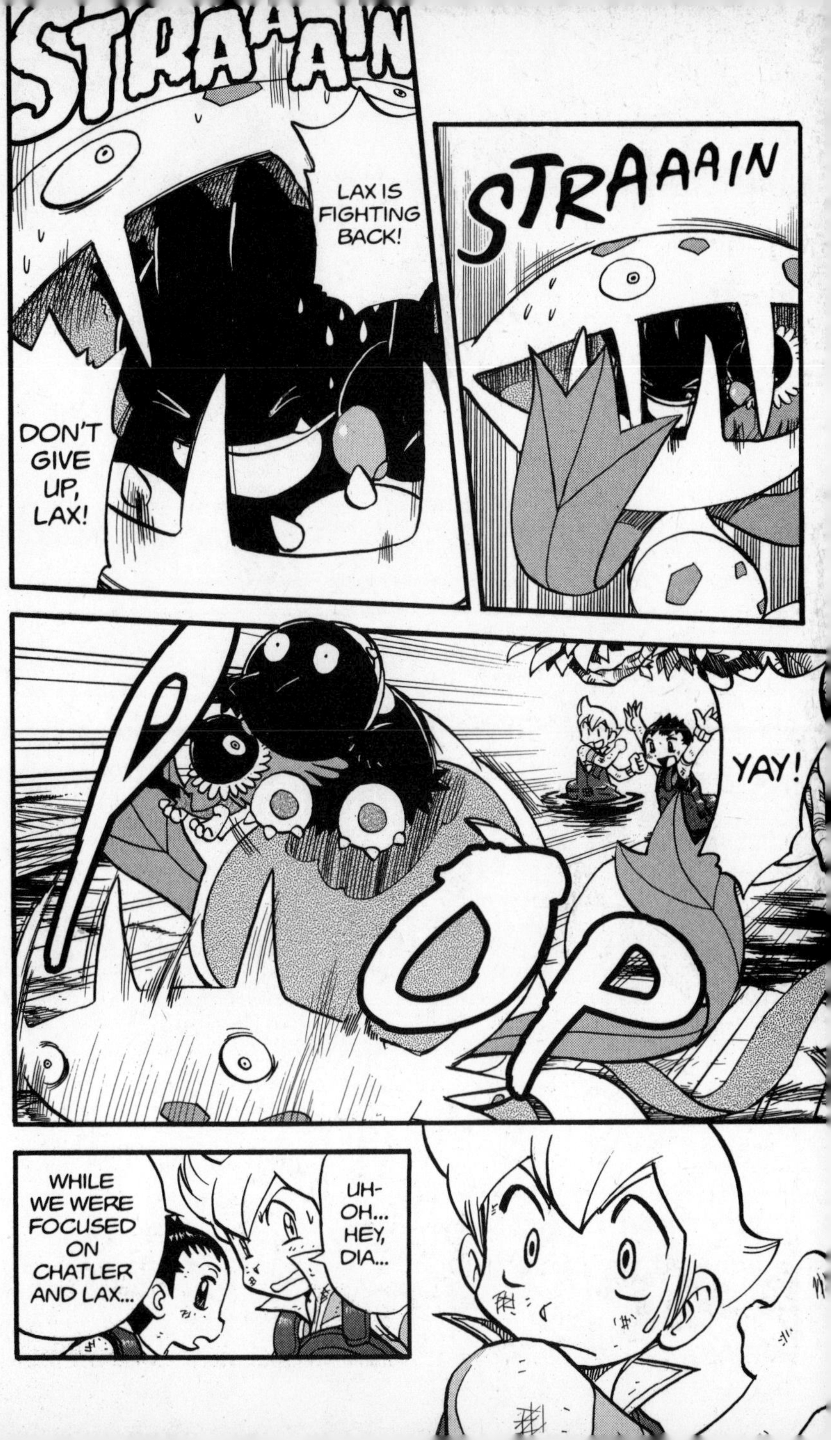

STRAAAIN
STRAAAIN
LAX IS FIGHTING BACK!
DON'T GIVE UP, LAX!
YAY!
OP
UH-OH... HEY, DIA...
WHILE WE WERE FOCUSED ON CHATLER AND LAX...

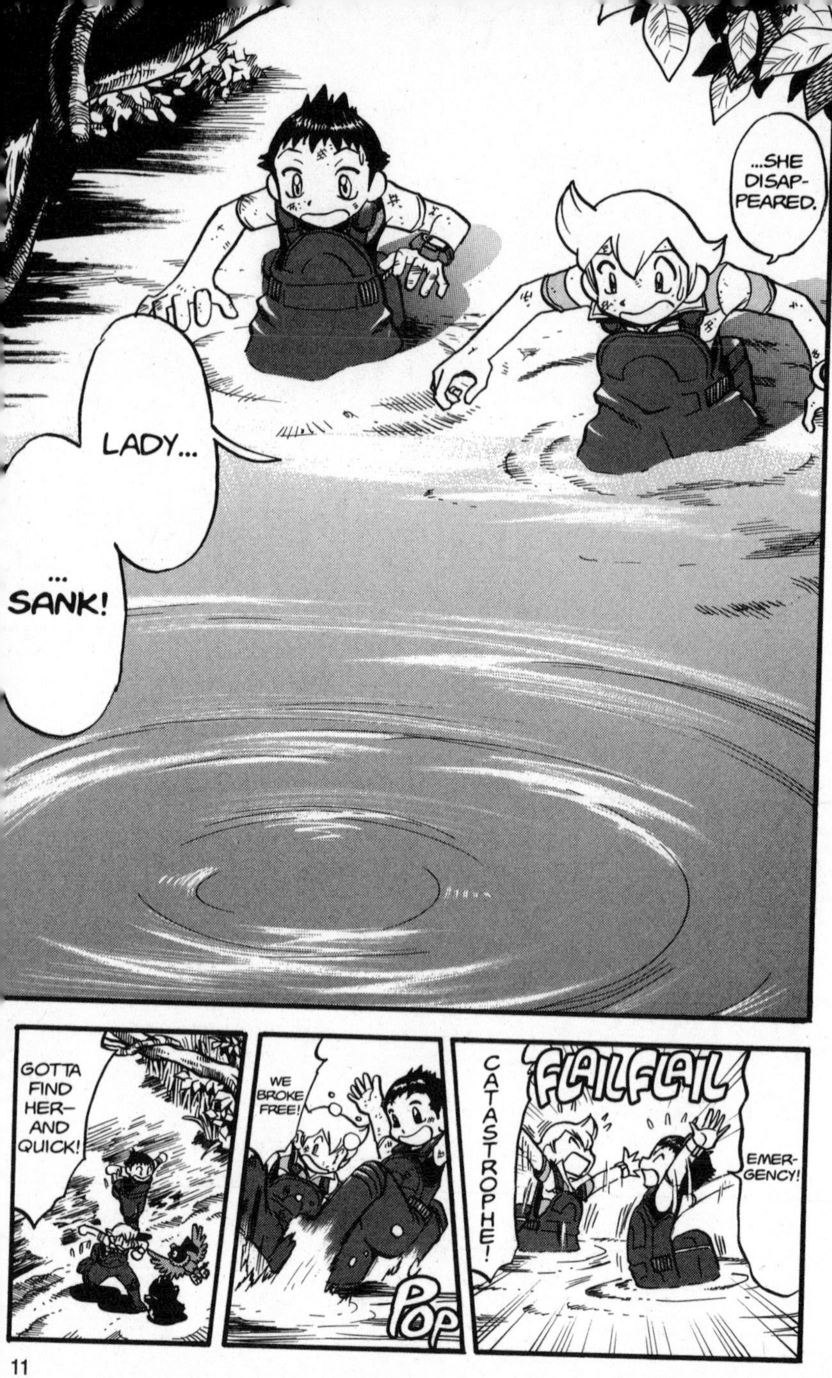
...SHE DISAPPEARED.
LADY... ...SANK!
FLAILFLAIL
EMERGENCY!
CATASTROPHE!
WE BROKE FREE!
POP
GOTTA FIND HER— AND QUICK!

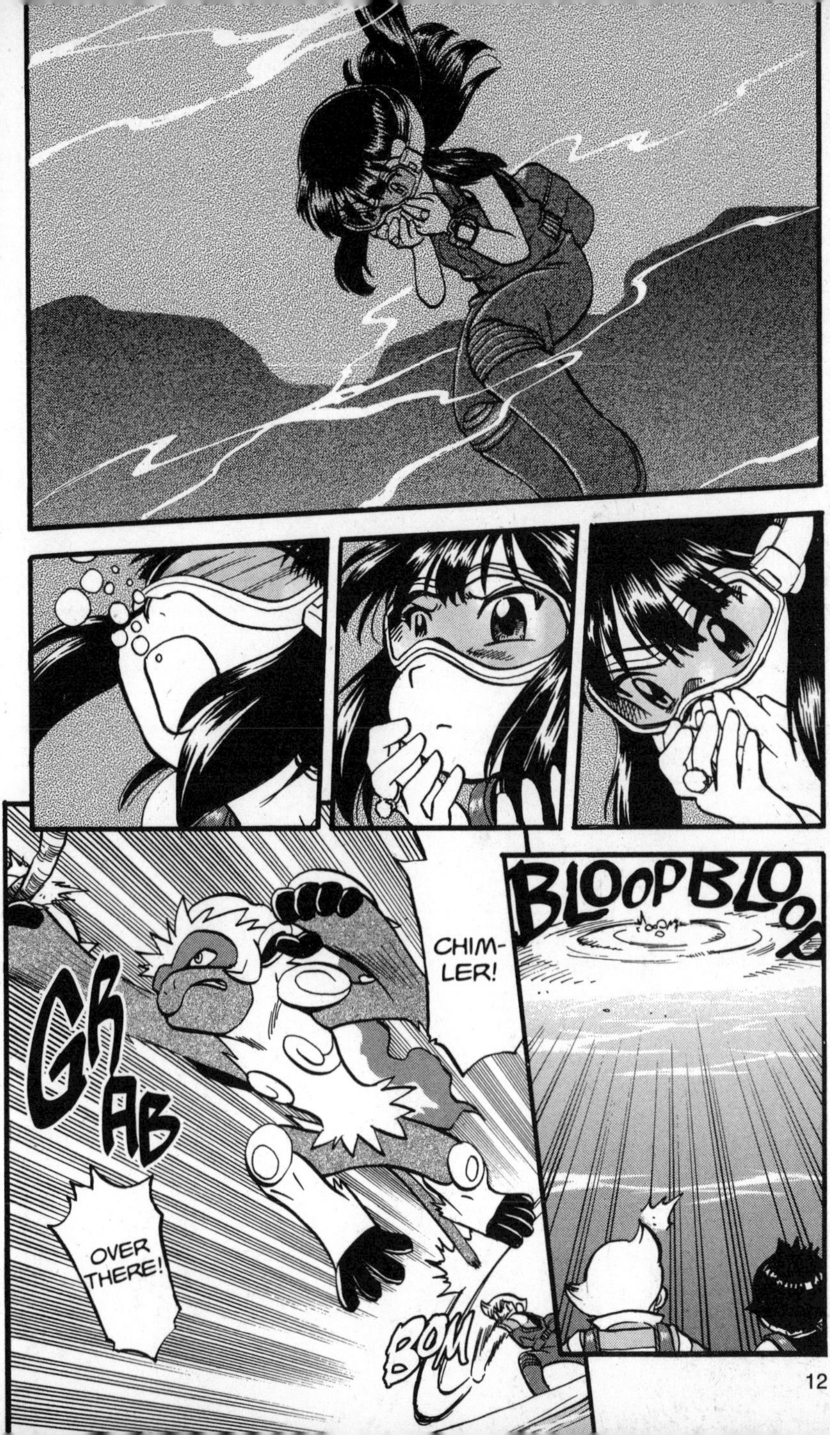
BLOOP BLOOP
CHIM-LER!
GRAB
OVER THERE!
BOM

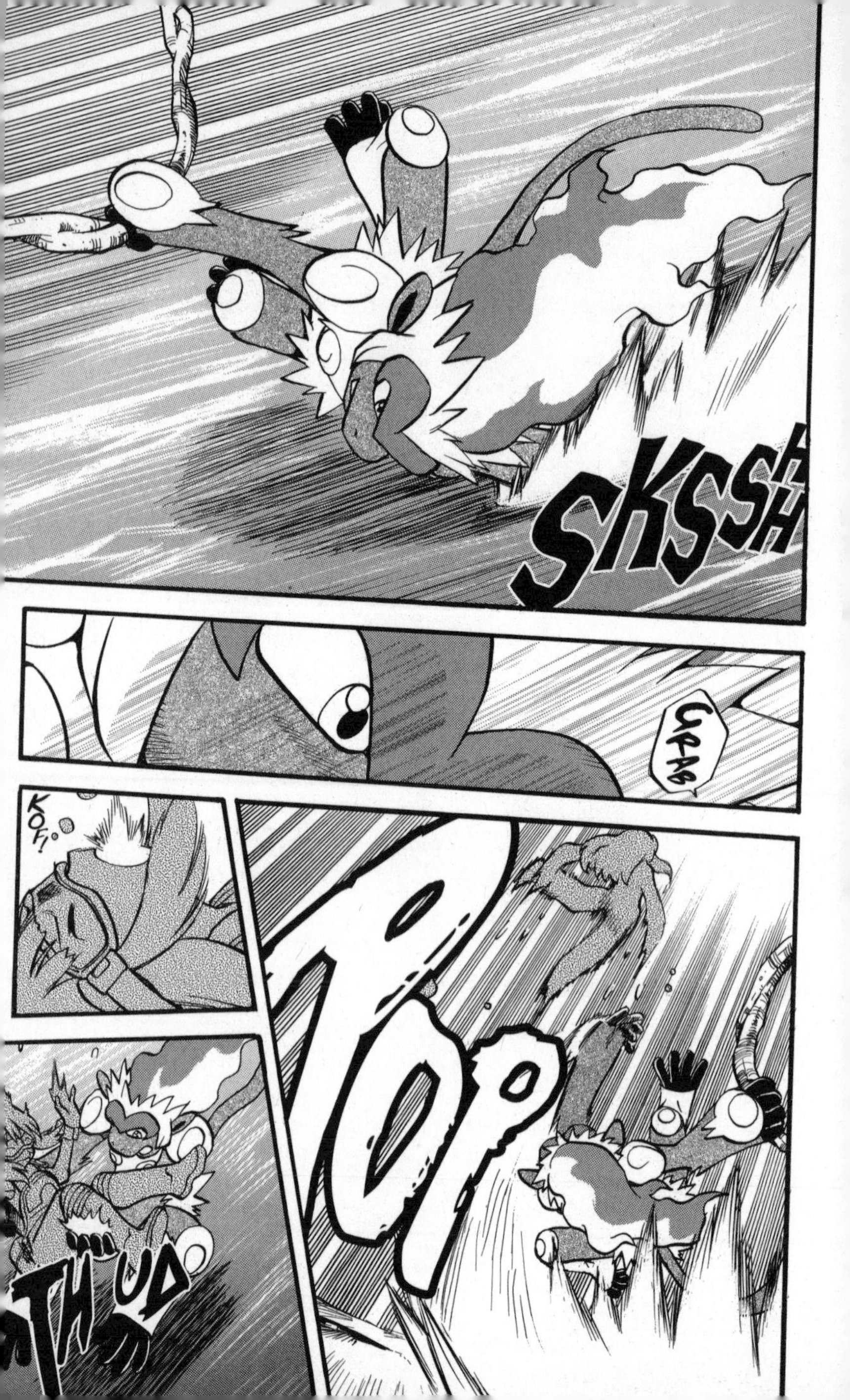
SKSSH
GRAB
KOF!
THUD

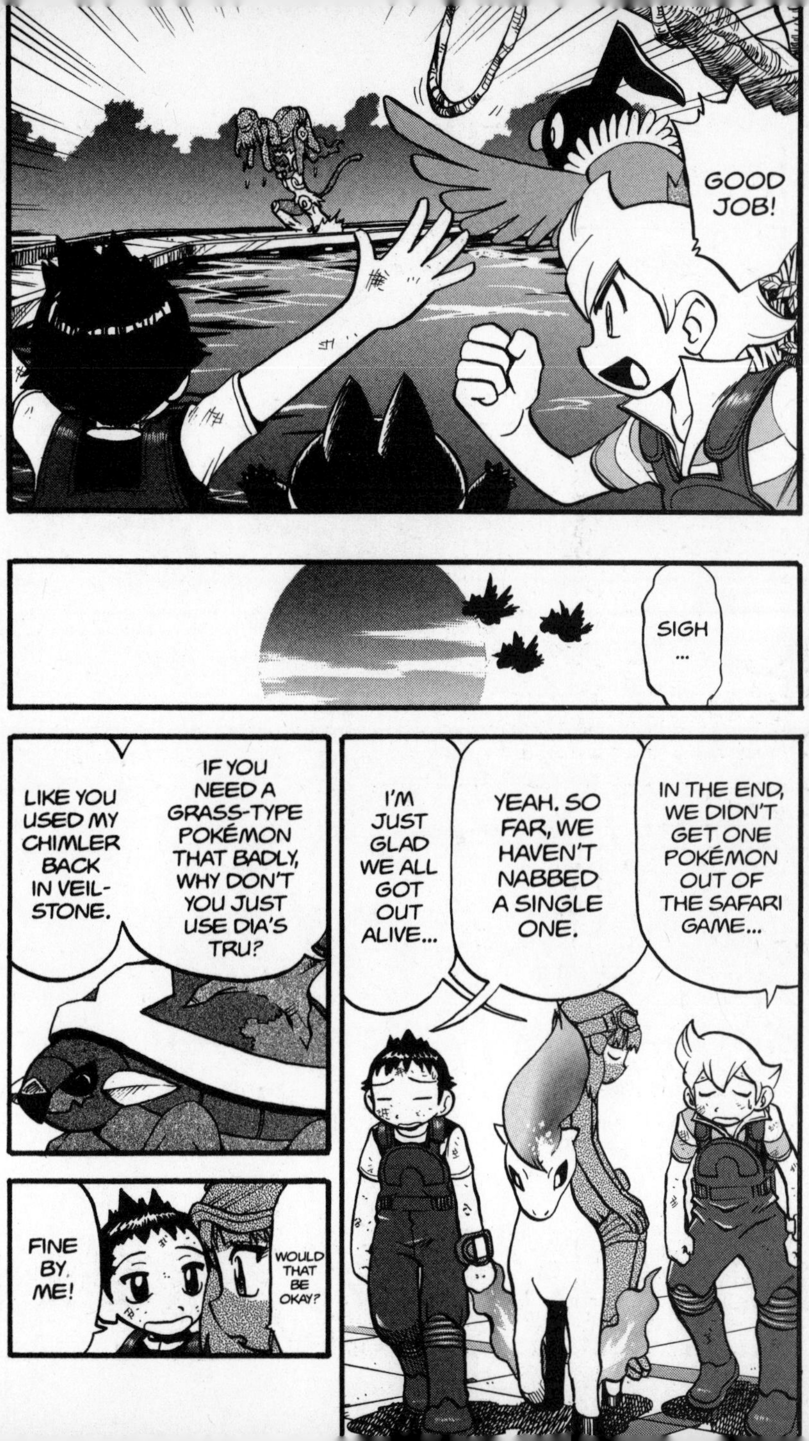
GOOD JOB!
SIGH ...
IN THE END, WE DIDN'T GET ONE POKÉMON OUT OF THE SAFARI GAME...
YEAH. SO FAR, WE HAVEN'T NABBED A SINGLE ONE.
I'M JUST GLAD WE ALL GOT OUT ALIVE...
IF YOU NEED A GRASS-TYPE POKÉMON THAT BADLY, WHY DON'T YOU JUST USE DIA'S TRU?
LIKE YOU USED MY CHIMLER BACK IN VEIL-STONE.
WOULD THAT BE OKAY?
FINE BY ME!

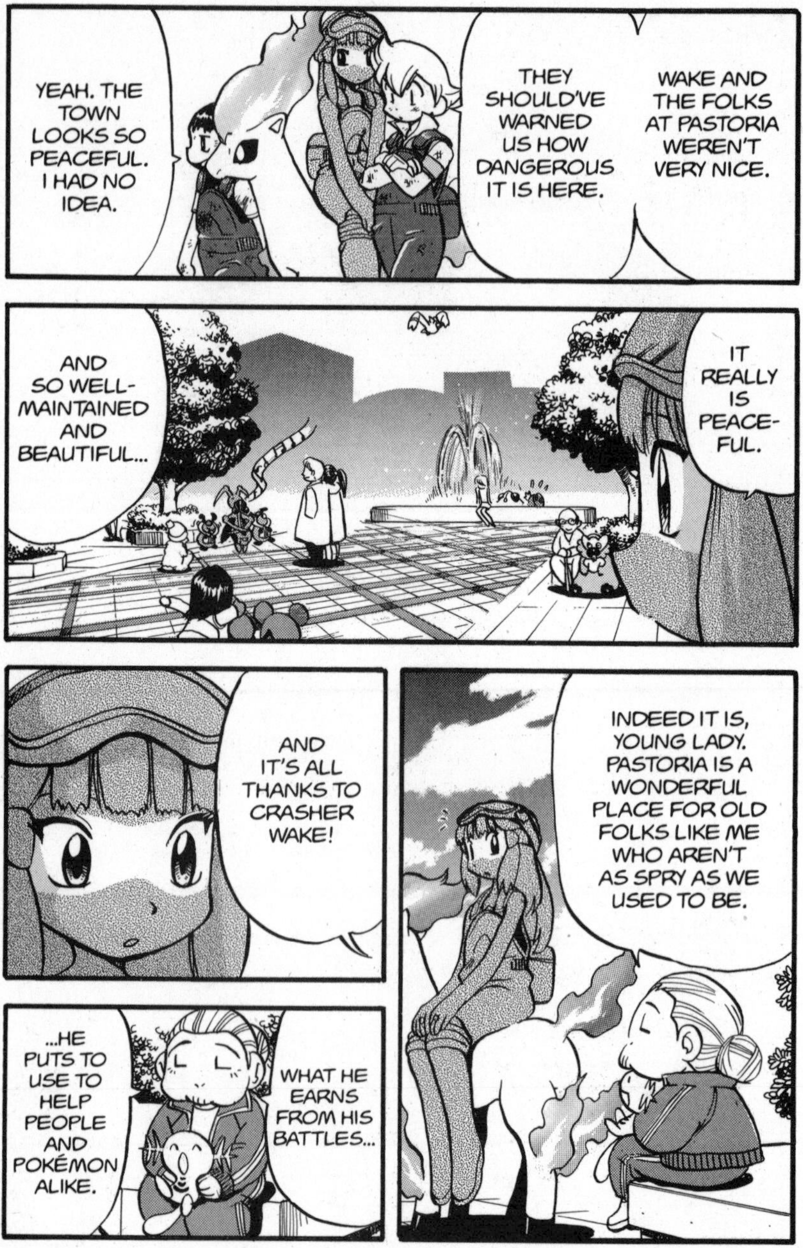
WAKE AND THE FOLKS AT PASTORIA WEREN'T VERY NICE.
THEY SHOULD'VE WARNED US HOW DANGEROUS IT IS HERE.
YEAH. THE TOWN LOOKS SO PEACEFUL. I HAD NO IDEA.
IT REALLY IS PEACE-FUL.
AND SO WELL-MAINTAINED AND BEAUTIFUL...
INDEED IT IS, YOUNG LADY. PASTORIA IS A WONDERFUL PLACE FOR OLD FOLKS LIKE ME WHO AREN'T AS SPRY AS WE USED TO BE.
AND IT'S ALL THANKS TO CRASHER WAKE!
WHAT HE EARNS FROM HIS BATTLES...
...HE PUTS TO USE TO HELP PEOPLE AND POKÉMON ALIKE.

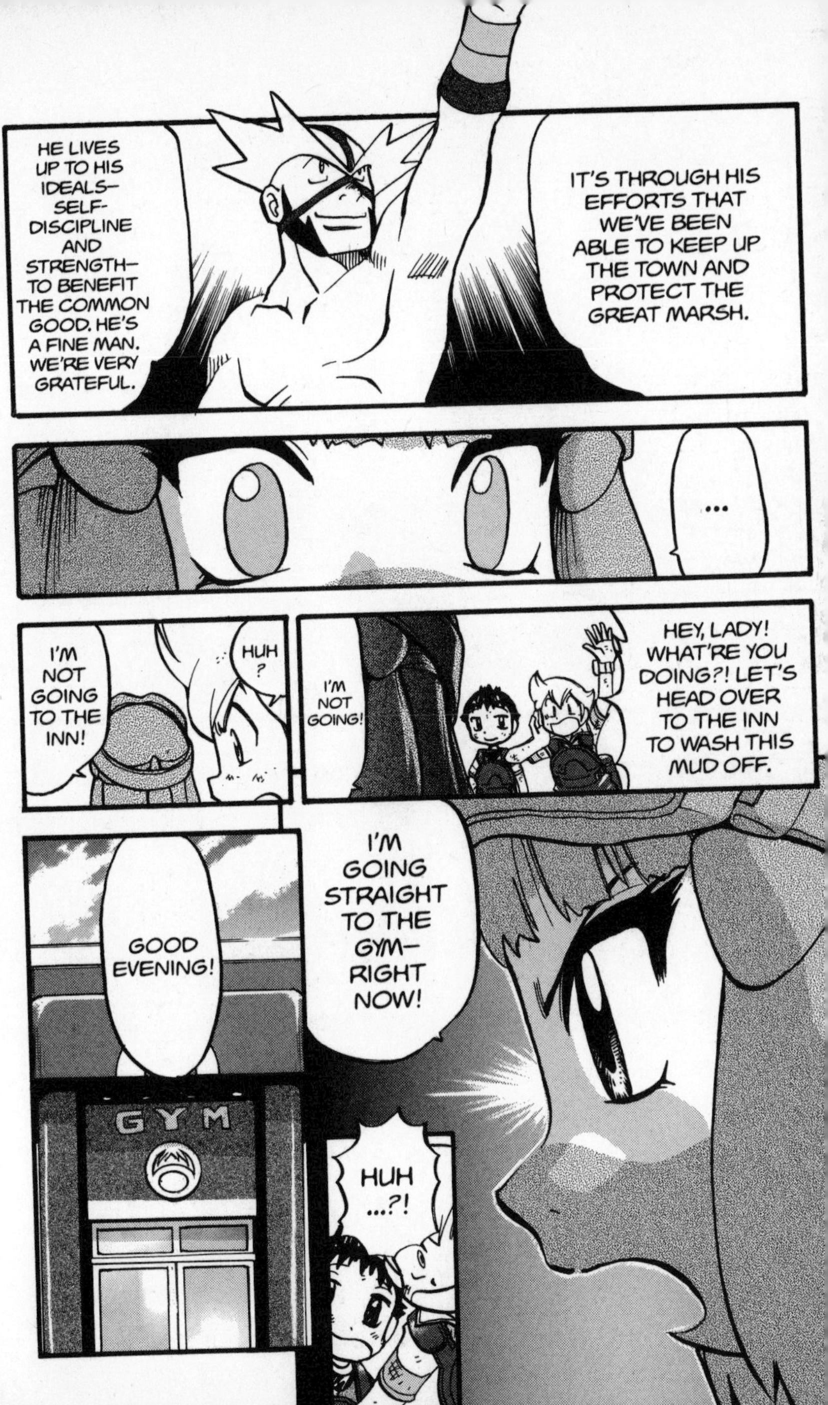
IT'S THROUGH HIS EFFORTS THAT WE'VE BEEN ABLE TO KEEP UP THE TOWN AND PROTECT THE GREAT MARSH.
HE LIVES UP TO HIS IDEALS—SELF-DISCIPLINE AND STRENGTH—TO BENEFIT THE COMMON GOOD. HE'S A FINE MAN. WE'RE VERY GRATEFUL.
...
HEY, LADY! WHAT'RE YOU DOING?! LET'S HEAD OVER TO THE INN TO WASH THIS MUD OFF.
I'M NOT GOING!
HUH?
I'M NOT GOING TO THE INN!
I'M GOING STRAIGHT TO THE GYM—RIGHT NOW!
GOOD EVENING!
GYM
HUH...?!

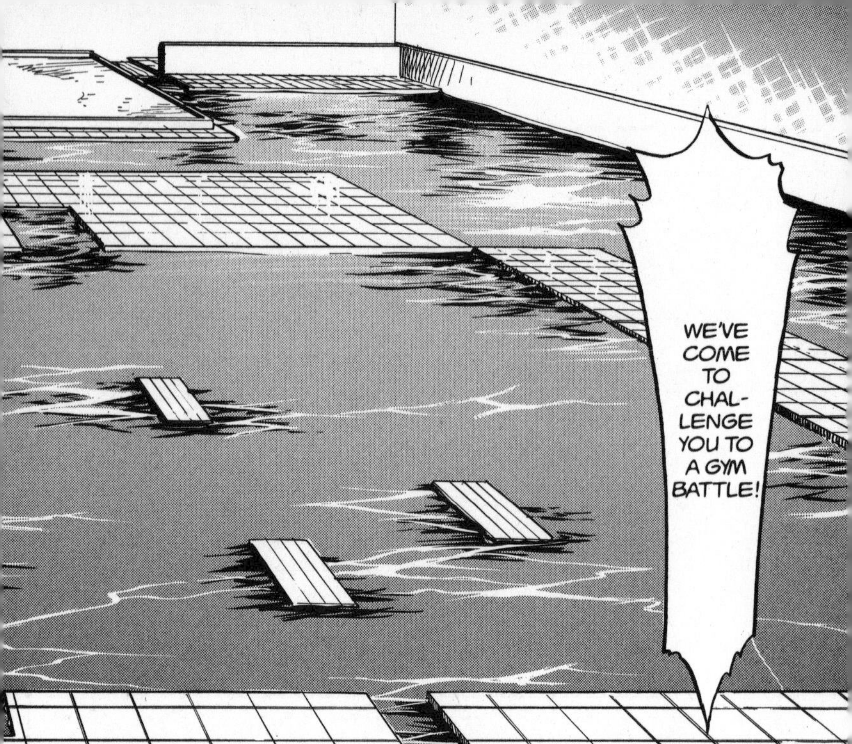
WE'VE COME TO CHAL-LENGE YOU TO A GYM BATTLE!
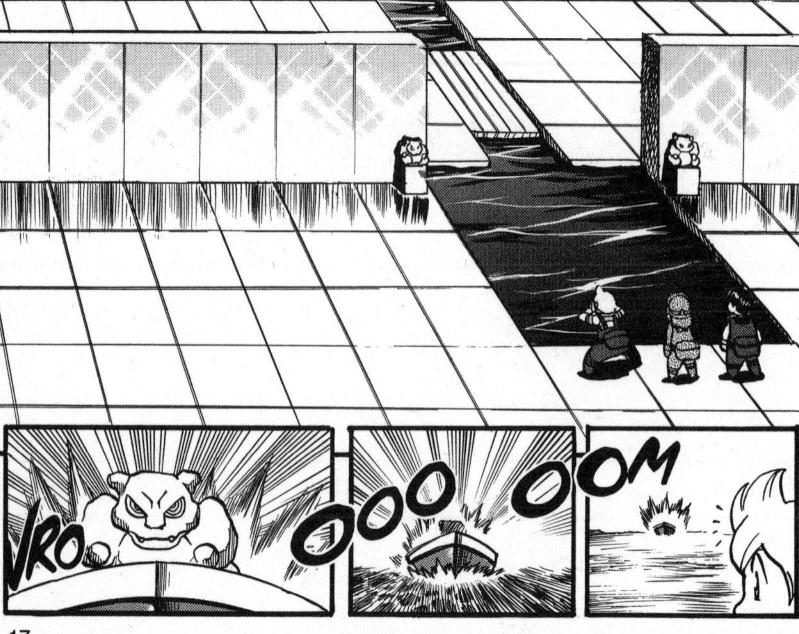
VROOOOOOOM

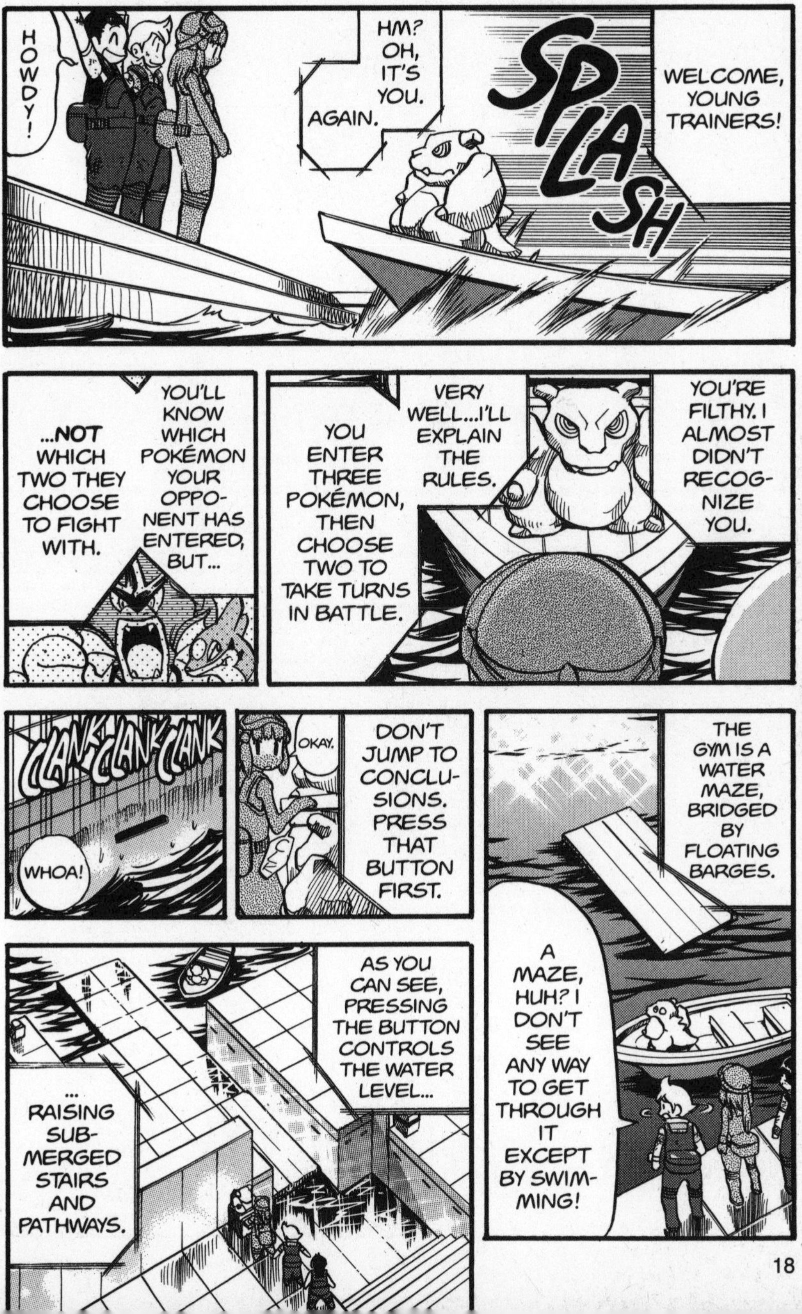
WELCOME, YOUNG TRAINERS!
SPLASH
HM? OH, IT'S YOU. AGAIN.
HOWDY!
YOU'RE FILTHY. I ALMOST DIDN'T RECOGNIZE YOU.
VERY WELL...I'LL EXPLAIN THE RULES.
YOU ENTER THREE POKÉMON, THEN CHOOSE TWO TO TAKE TURNS IN BATTLE.
YOU'LL KNOW WHICH POKÉMON YOUR OPPONENT HAS ENTERED, BUT...
...**NOT** WHICH TWO THEY CHOOSE TO FIGHT WITH.
THE GYM IS A WATER MAZE, BRIDGED BY FLOATING BARGES.
A MAZE, HUH? I DON'T SEE ANY WAY TO GET THROUGH IT EXCEPT BY SWIMMING!
DON'T JUMP TO CONCLUSIONS. PRESS THAT BUTTON FIRST.
OKAY.
CLANK CLANK CLANK
WHOA!
AS YOU CAN SEE, PRESSING THE BUTTON CONTROLS THE WATER LEVEL...
...RAISING SUBMERGED STAIRS AND PATHWAYS.

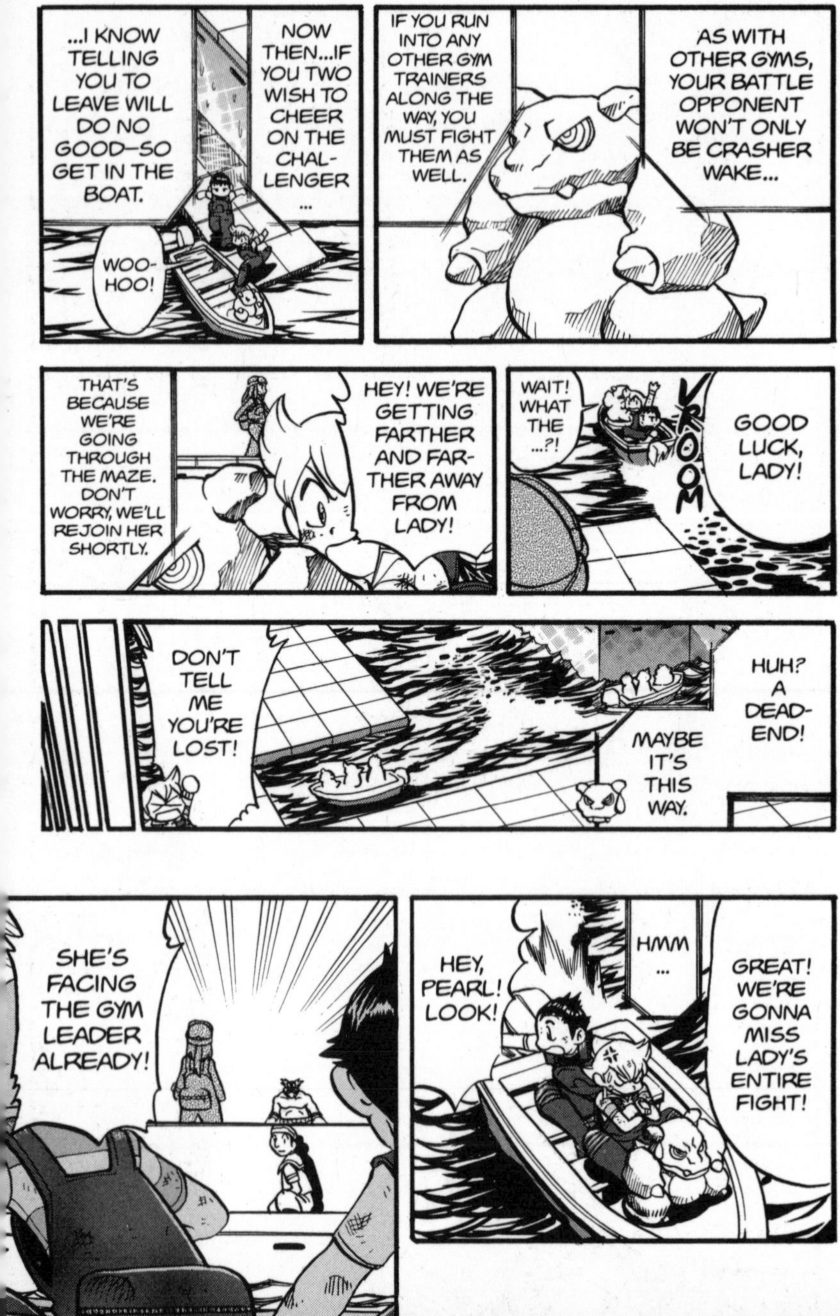
AS WITH OTHER GYMS, YOUR BATTLE OPPONENT WON'T ONLY BE CRASHER WAKE...
IF YOU RUN INTO ANY OTHER GYM TRAINERS ALONG THE WAY, YOU MUST FIGHT THEM AS WELL.
NOW THEN...IF YOU TWO WISH TO CHEER ON THE CHAL-LENGER...
...I KNOW TELLING YOU TO LEAVE WILL DO NO GOOD—SO GET IN THE BOAT.
WOO-HOO!
GOOD LUCK, LADY!
VROOOM
WAIT! WHAT THE ...?!
HEY! WE'RE GETTING FARTHER AND FAR-THER AWAY FROM LADY!
THAT'S BECAUSE WE'RE GOING THROUGH THE MAZE. DON'T WORRY, WE'LL REJOIN HER SHORTLY.
HUH? A DEAD-END!
MAYBE IT'S THIS WAY.
DON'T TELL ME YOU'RE LOST!
GREAT! WE'RE GONNA MISS LADY'S ENTIRE FIGHT!
HMM...
HEY, PEARL! LOOK!
SHE'S FACING THE GYM LEADER ALREADY!

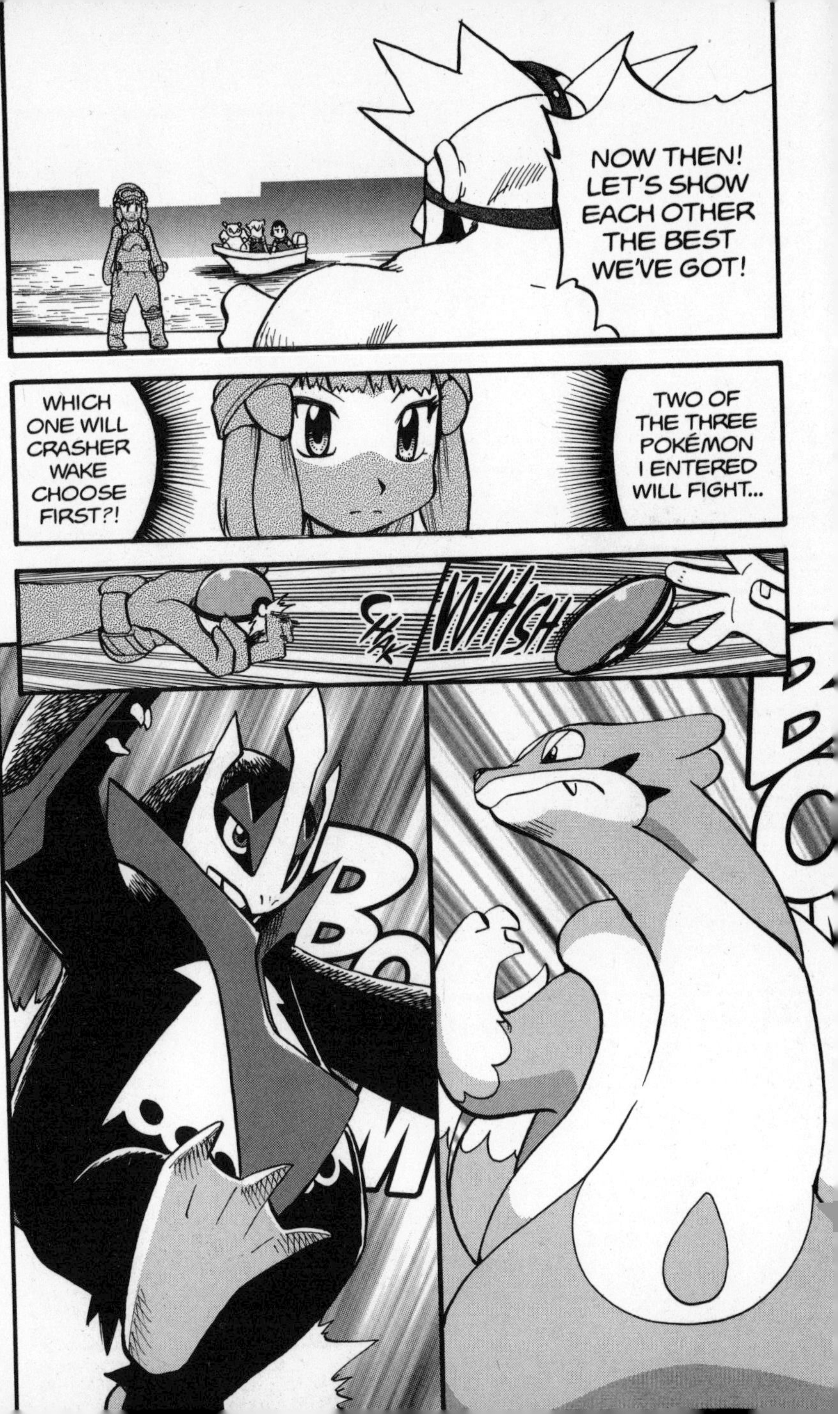
NOW THEN! LET'S SHOW EACH OTHER THE BEST WE'VE GOT!
TWO OF THE THREE POKÉMON I ENTERED WILL FIGHT...
WHICH ONE WILL CRASHER WAKE CHOOSE FIRST?!
WHISH
CHAK
BOOM

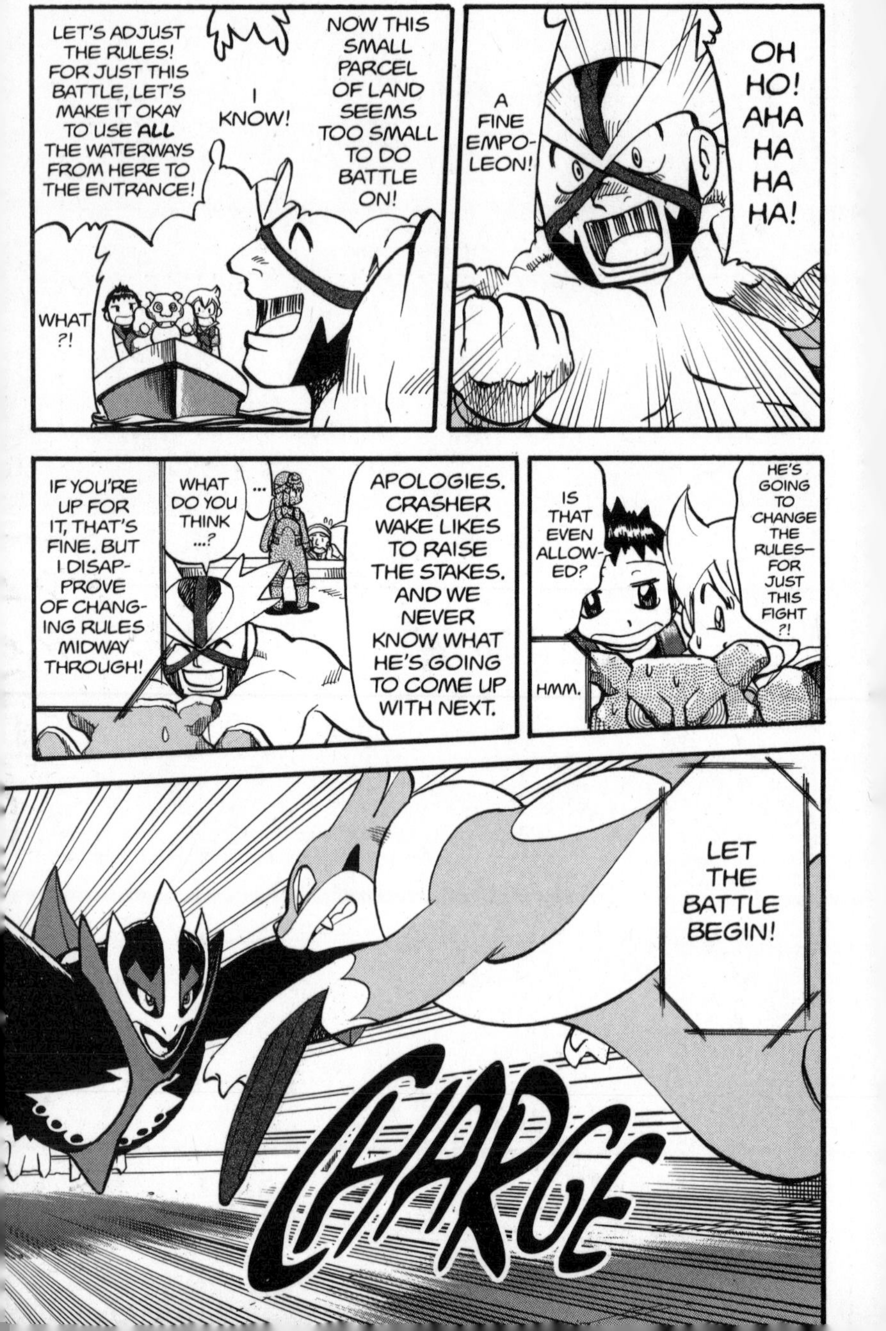
OH HO! AHA HA HA HA!
A FINE EMPOLEON!
NOW THIS SMALL PARCEL OF LAND SEEMS TOO SMALL TO DO BATTLE ON!
I KNOW!
LET'S ADJUST THE RULES! FOR JUST THIS BATTLE, LET'S MAKE IT OKAY TO USE **ALL** THE WATERWAYS FROM HERE TO THE ENTRANCE!
WHAT?!
HE'S GOING TO CHANGE THE RULES—FOR JUST THIS FIGHT?!
IS THAT EVEN ALLOWED?
HMM.
APOLOGIES. CRASHER WAKE LIKES TO RAISE THE STAKES. AND WE NEVER KNOW WHAT HE'S GOING TO COME UP WITH NEXT.
...
WHAT DO YOU THINK...?
IF YOU'RE UP FOR IT, THAT'S FINE. BUT I DISAPPROVE OF CHANGING RULES MIDWAY THROUGH!
LET THE BATTLE BEGIN!
CHARGE

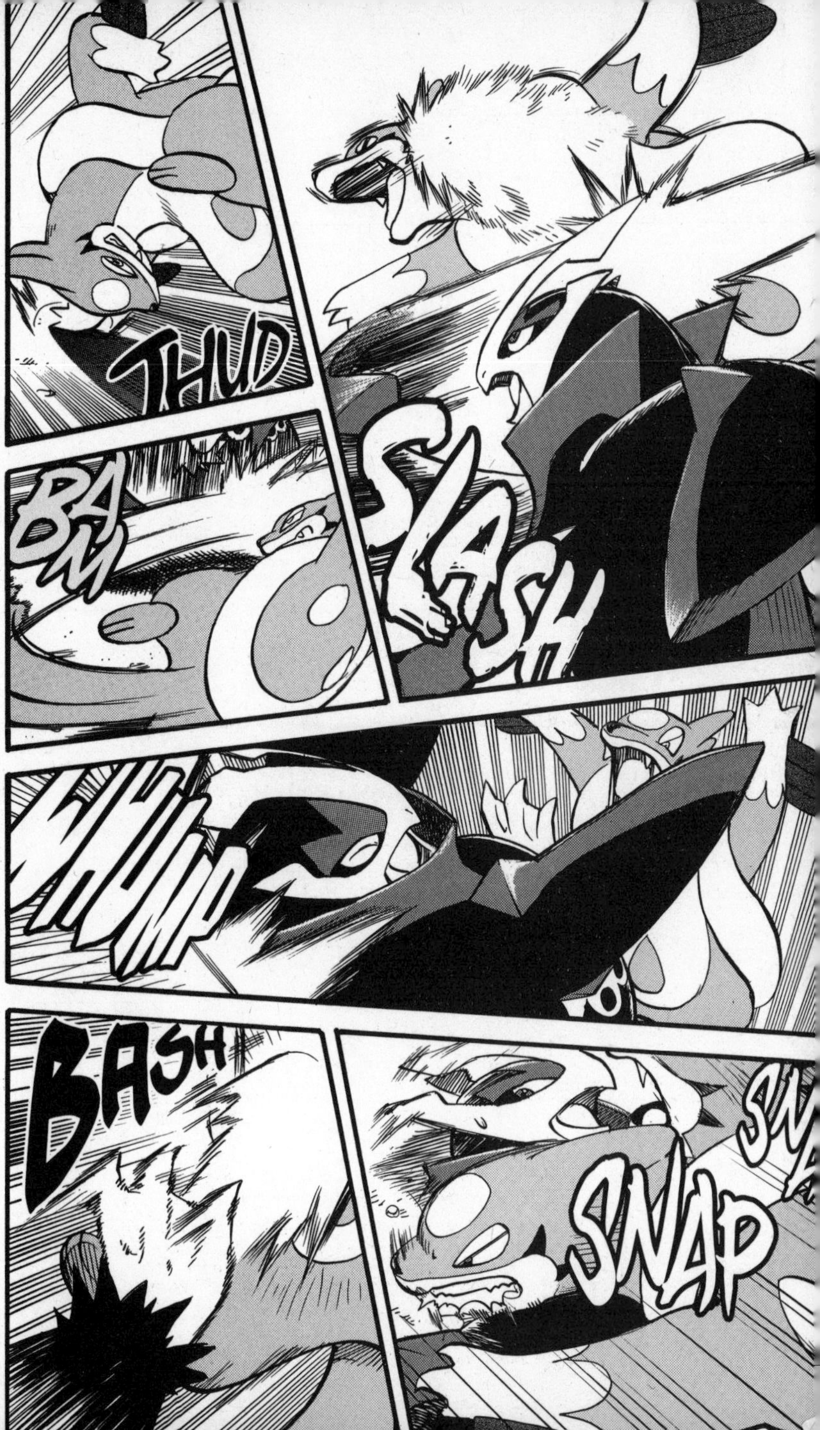
SLASH
THUD
BAM
WHUMP
SNAP
BASH

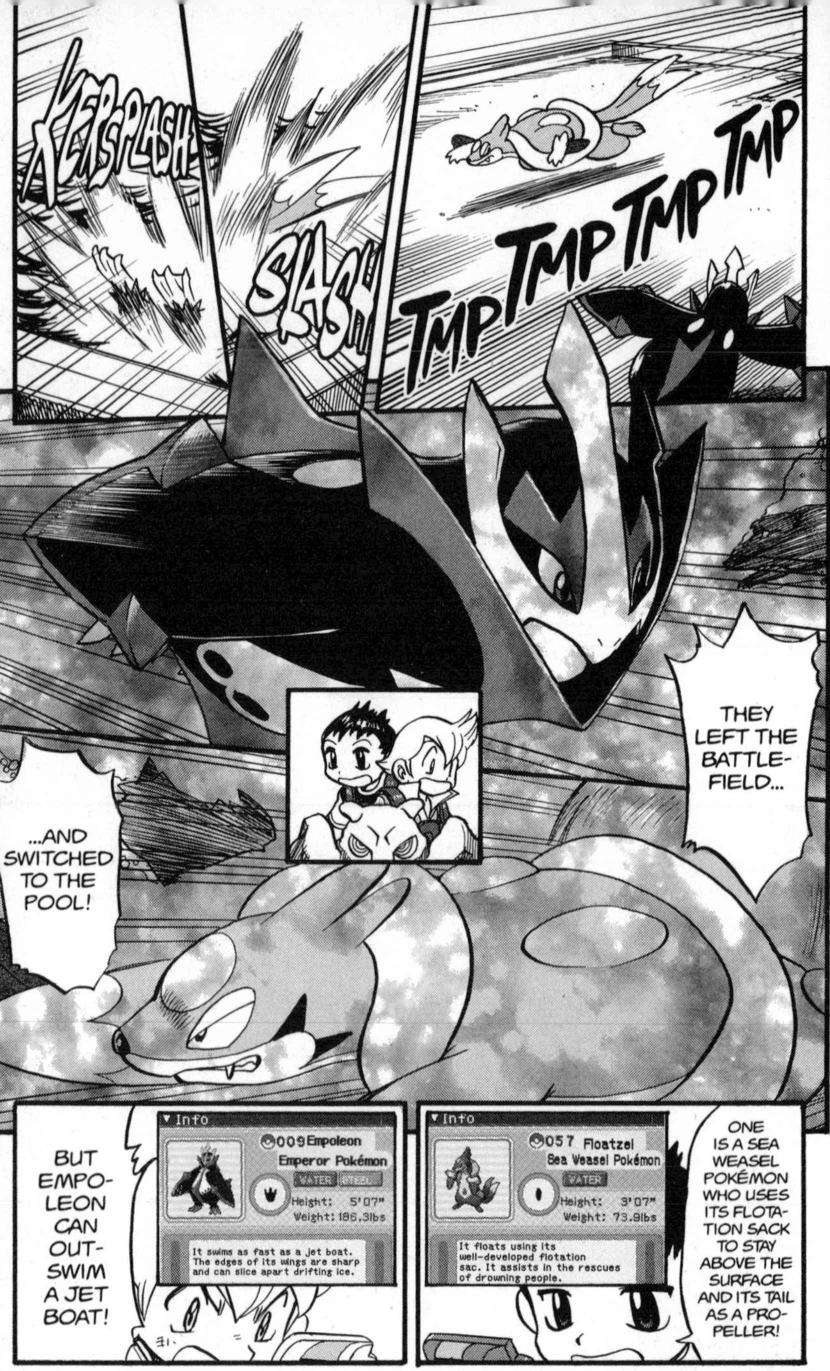
TMP TMP TMP TMP
SLASH
KERSPLASH
THEY LEFT THE BATTLE-FIELD...
...AND SWITCHED TO THE POOL!
ONE IS A SEA WEASEL POKÉMON WHO USES ITS FLOTA-TION SACK TO STAY ABOVE THE SURFACE AND ITS TAIL AS A PRO-PELLER!
Info
057 Floatzel
Sea Weasel Pokémon
WATER
Height: 3'07"
Weight: 73.9lbs
It floats using its well-developed flotation sac. It assists in the rescues of drowning people.
BUT EMPO-LEON CAN OUT-SWIM A JET BOAT!
Info
009 Empoleon
Emperor Pokémon
WATER STEEL
Height: 5'07"
Weight: 186.3lbs
It swims as fast as a jet boat. The edges of its wings are sharp and can slice apart drifting ice.

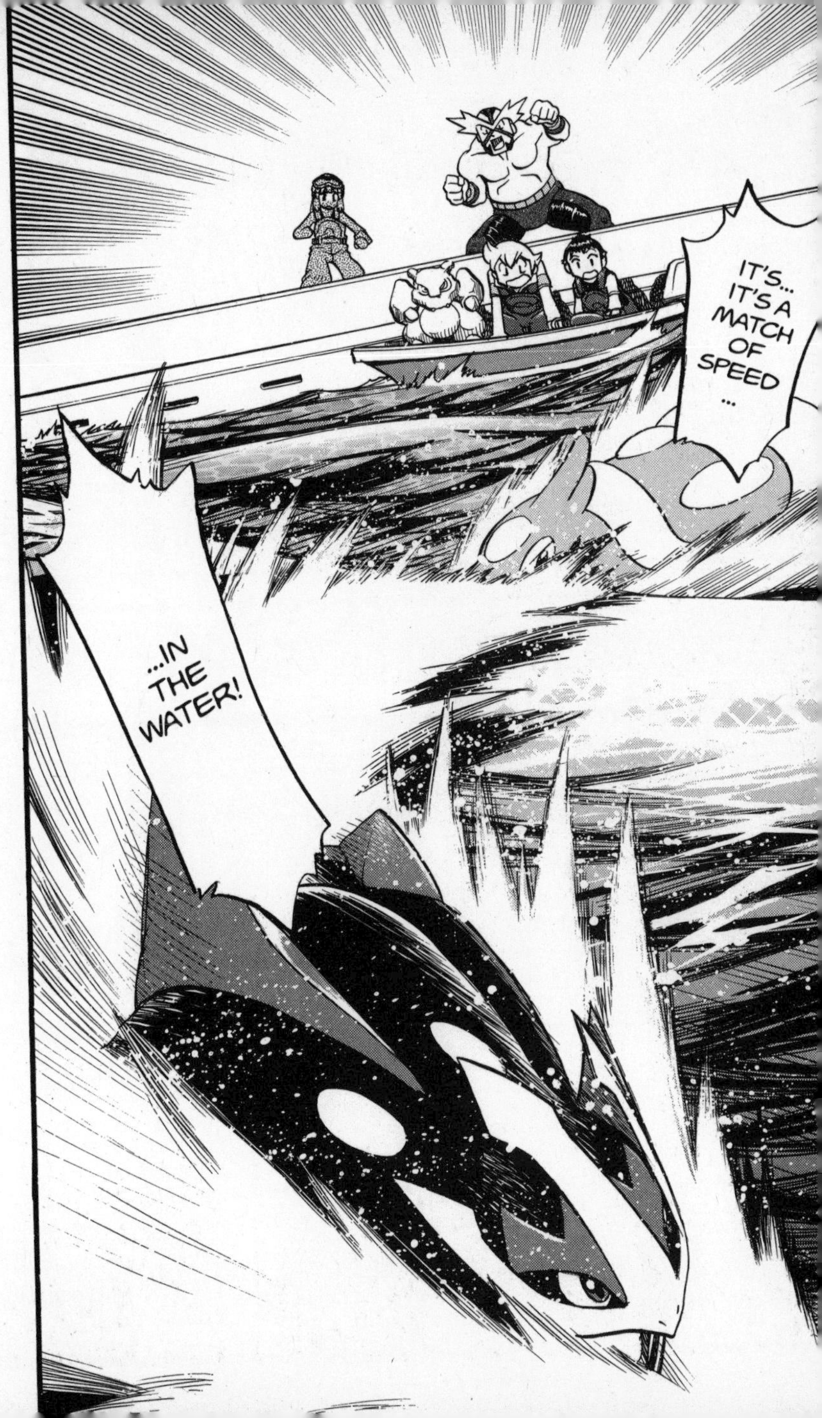
IT'S... IT'S A MATCH OF SPEED ...
...IN THE WATER!

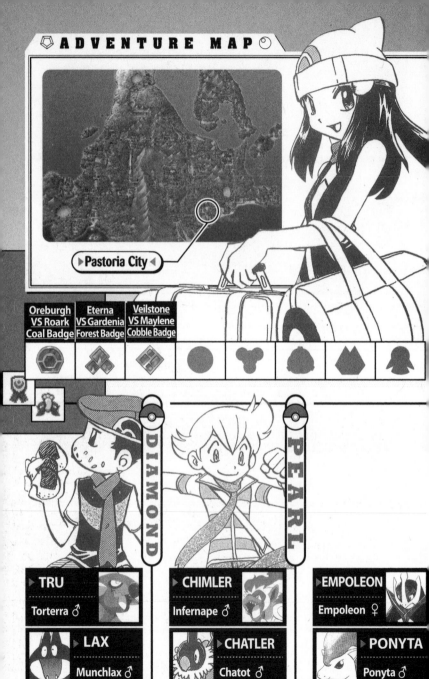

ADVENTURE MAP

▶Pastoria City◀

Oreburgh VS Roark Coal Badge	Eterna VS Gardenia Forest Badge	Veilstone VS Maylene Cobble Badge					

DIAMOND

PEARL

▶TRU
Torterra ♂

▶LAX
Munchlax ♂

▶CHIMLER
Infernape ♂

▶CHATLER
Chatot ♂

▶EMPOLEON
Empoleon ♀

▶PONYTA
Ponyta ♂

29

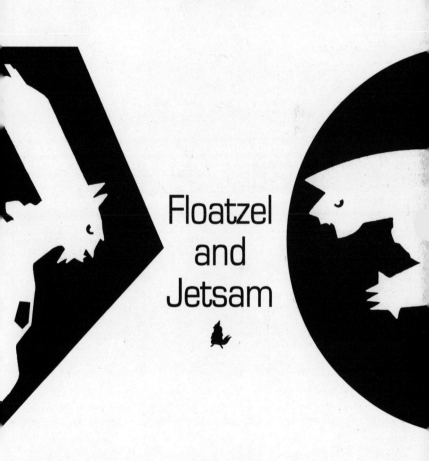

Floatzel
and
Jetsam

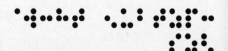

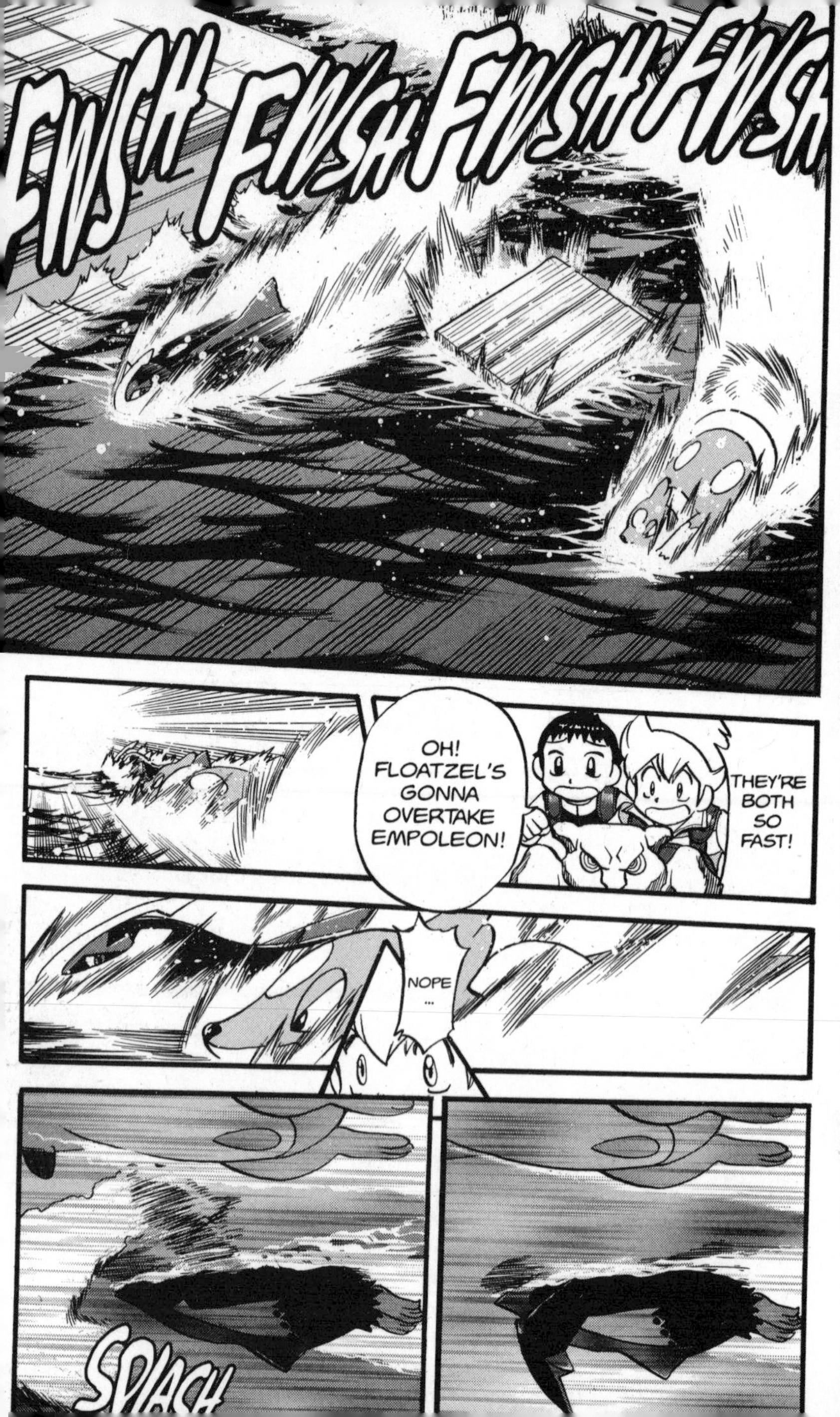
FWSH FWSH FWSH FWSH
OH! FLOATZEL'S GONNA OVERTAKE EMPOLEON!
THEY'RE BOTH SO FAST!
NOPE ...
SPLASH

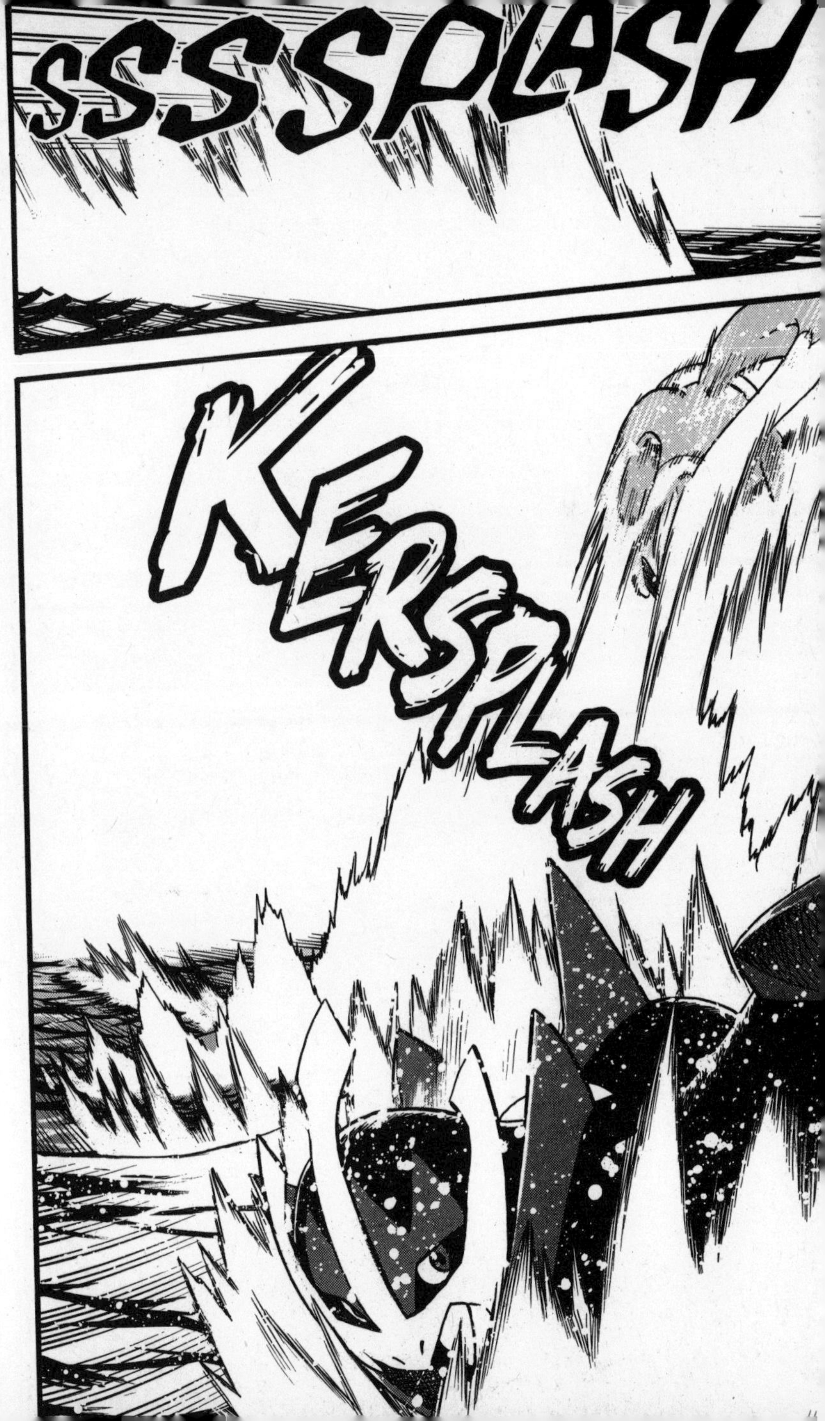
SSSPLASH
KERSPLASH

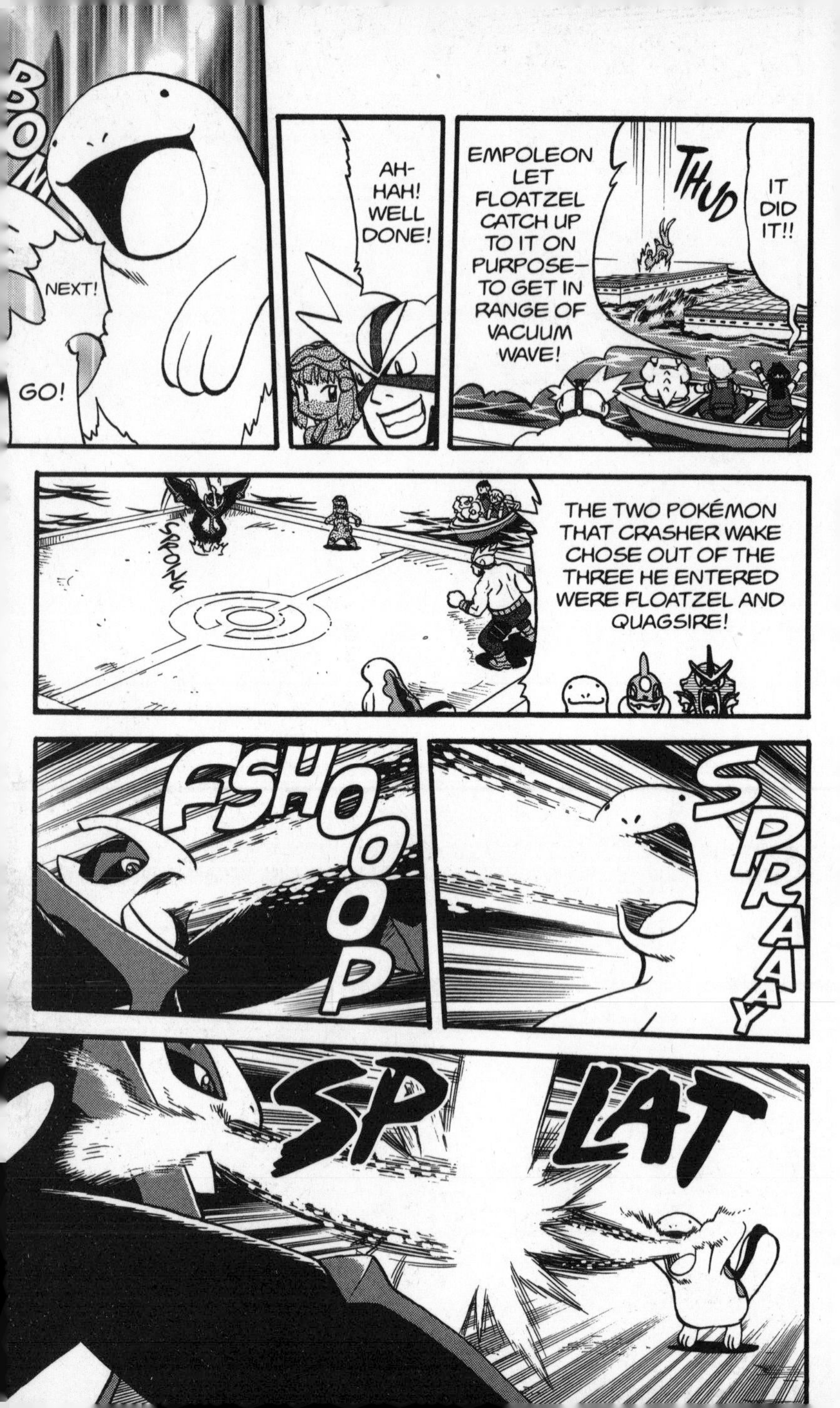
THUD
IT DID IT!!
EMPOLEON LET FLOATZEL CATCH UP TO IT ON PURPOSE—TO GET IN RANGE OF VACUUM WAVE!
AH-HAH! WELL DONE!
NEXT!
GO!
THE TWO POKÉMON THAT CRASHER WAKE CHOSE OUT OF THE THREE HE ENTERED WERE FLOATZEL AND QUAGSIRE!
SPRAAAY
FSHOOOOP
SPLAT

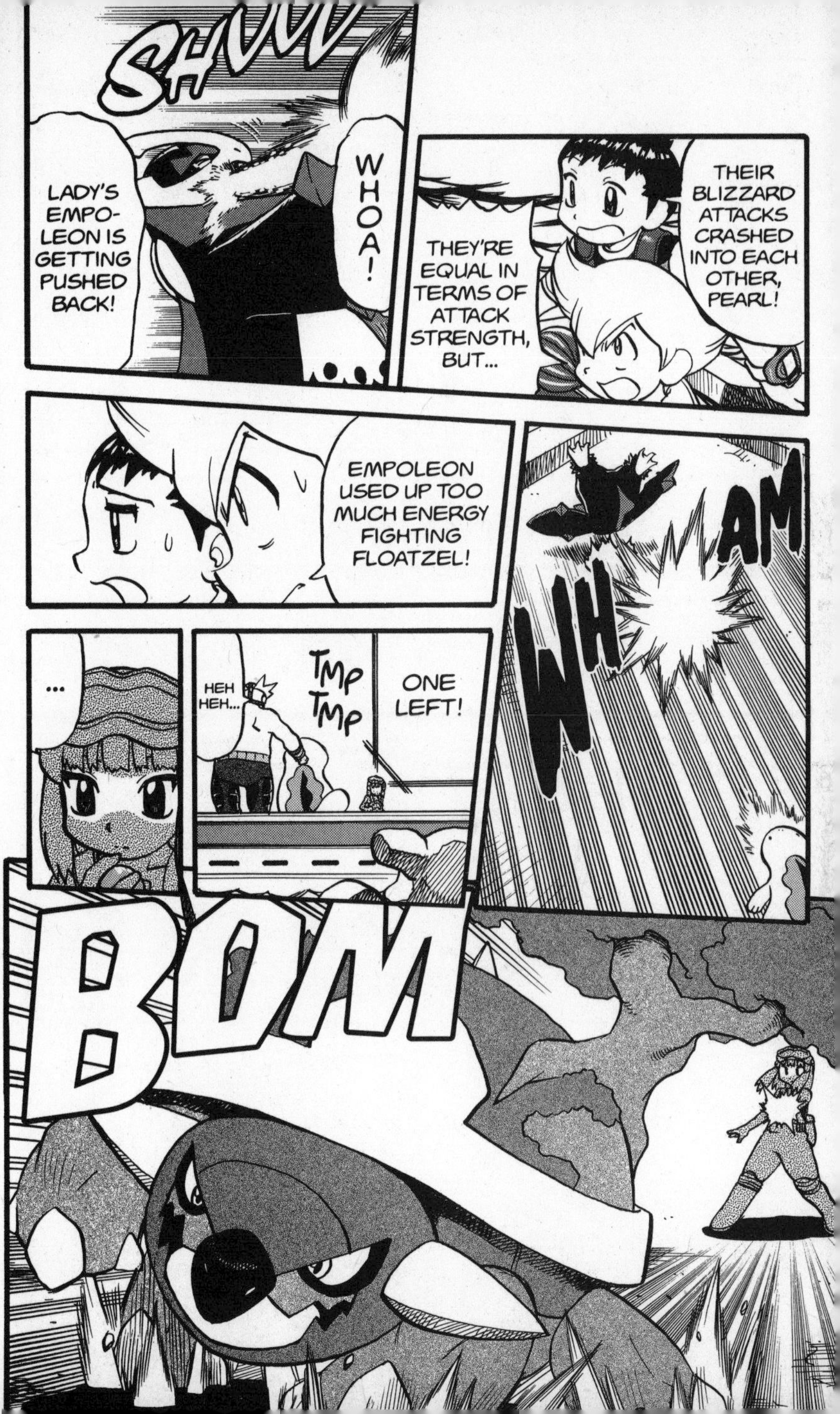
THEIR BLIZZARD ATTACKS CRASHED INTO EACH OTHER, PEARL!
THEY'RE EQUAL IN TERMS OF ATTACK STRENGTH, BUT...
SHVVV
WHOA!
LADY'S EMPO-LEON IS GETTING PUSHED BACK!
WHAM
EMPOLEON USED UP TOO MUCH ENERGY FIGHTING FLOATZEL!
ONE LEFT!
TMP TMP
HEH HEH...
...
BOM

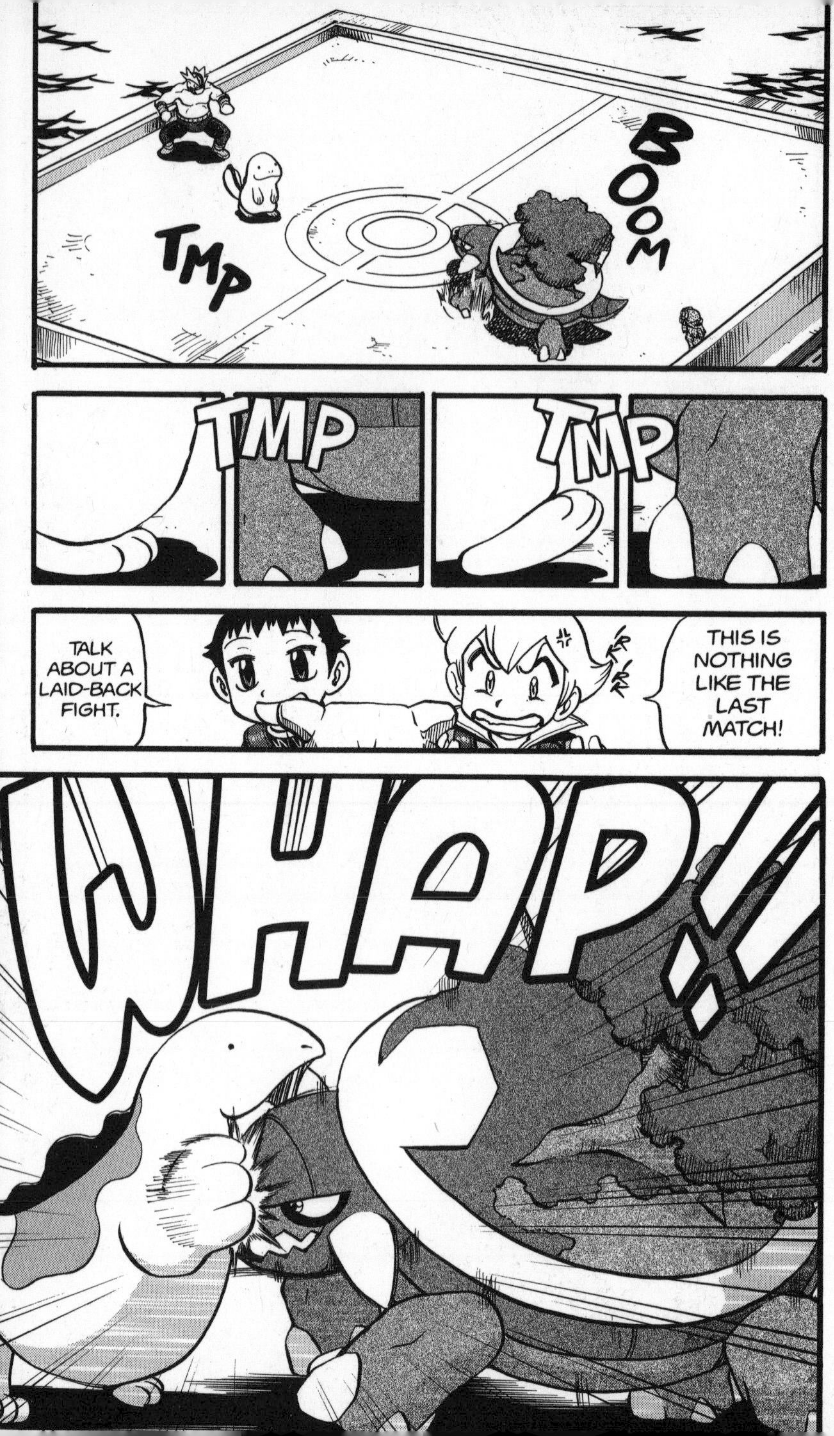
BOOM
TMP
TMP
TMP
THIS IS NOTHING LIKE THE LAST MATCH!
TALK ABOUT A LAID-BACK FIGHT.
WHAP!!

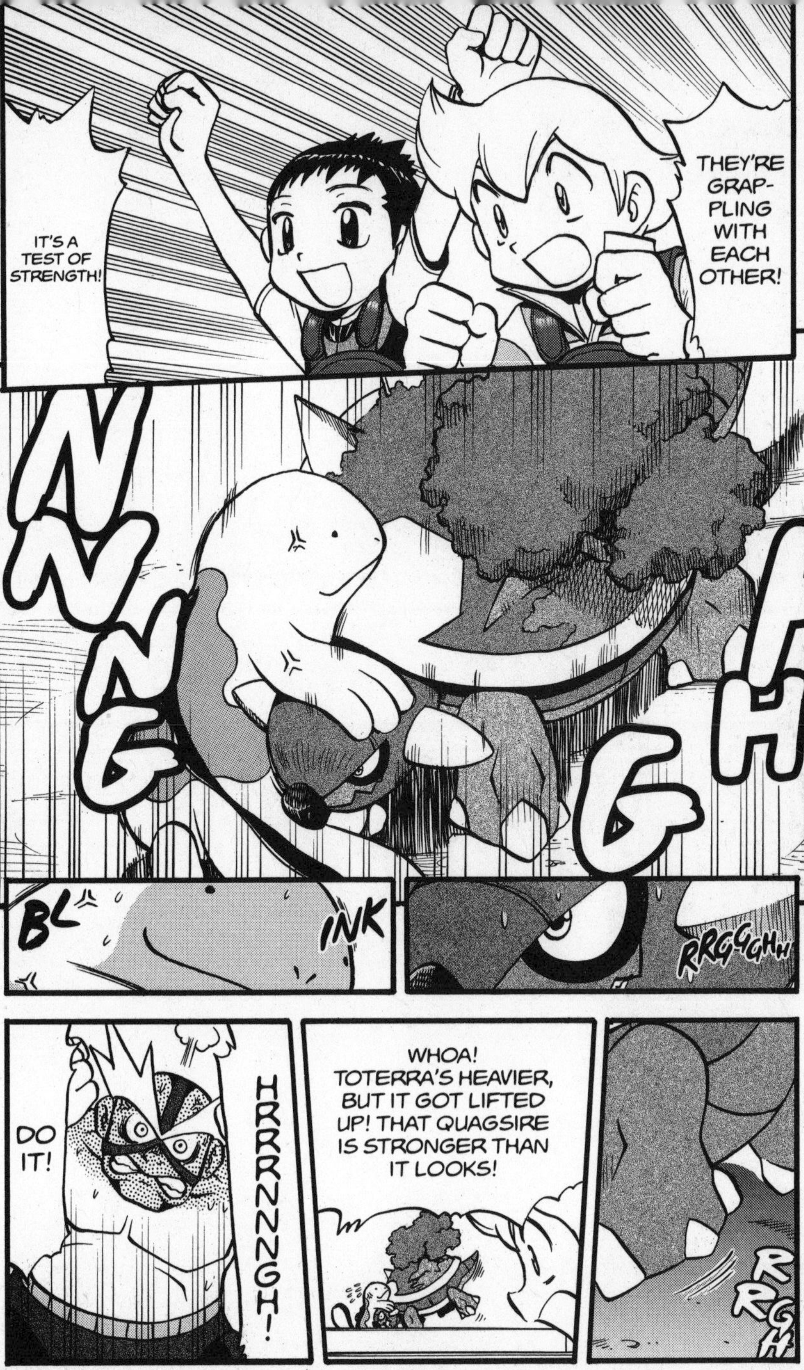

THEY'RE GRAPPLING WITH EACH OTHER!
IT'S A TEST OF STRENGTH!
NNNGGHH
RRGGGHH
BLINK
RRGH
WHOA! TOTERRA'S HEAVIER, BUT IT GOT LIFTED UP! THAT QUAGSIRE IS STRONGER THAN IT LOOKS!
HRRRNNNGH!
DO IT!

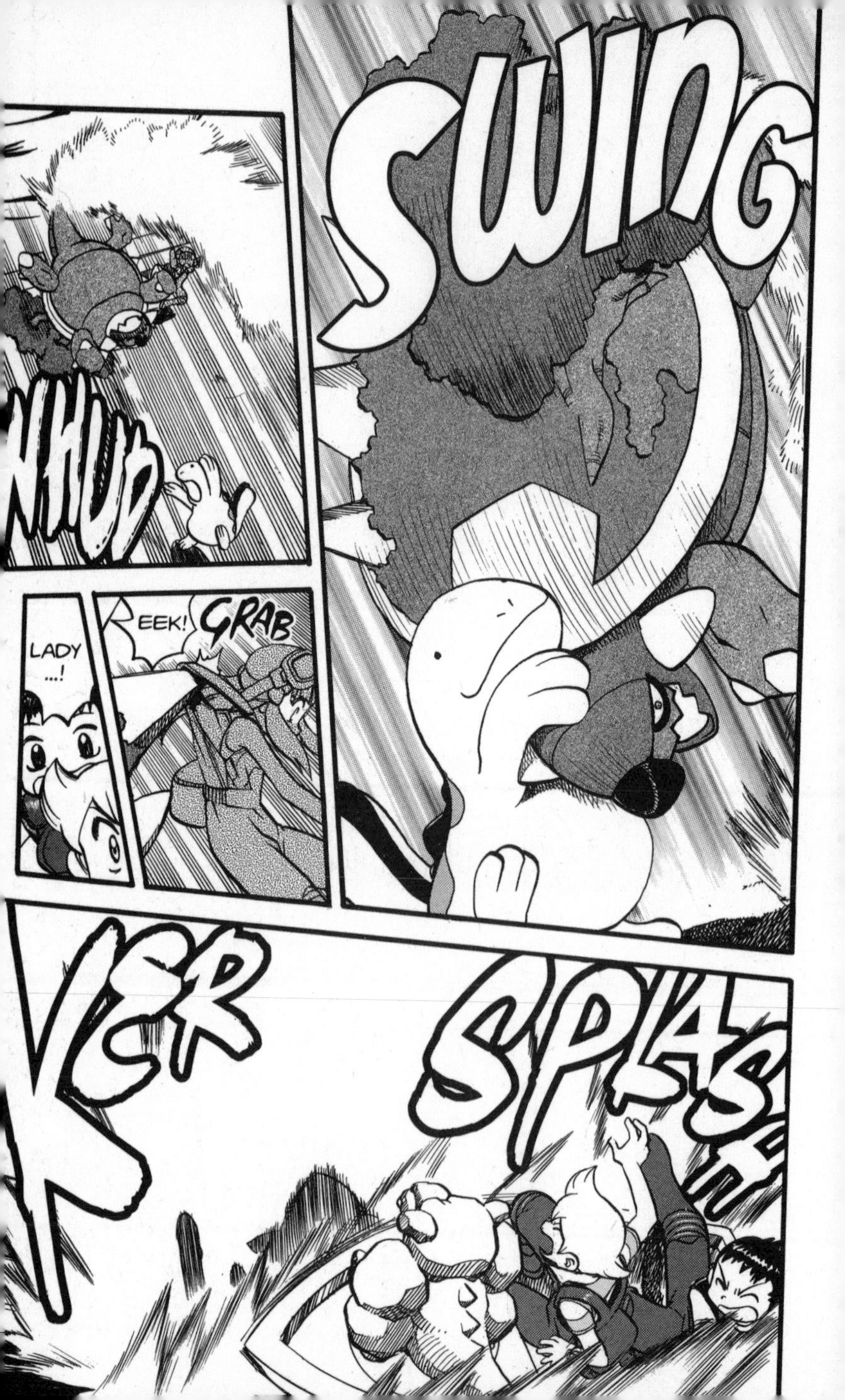
SWING
EEK!
GRAB
LADY ...!
SPLAS
ER

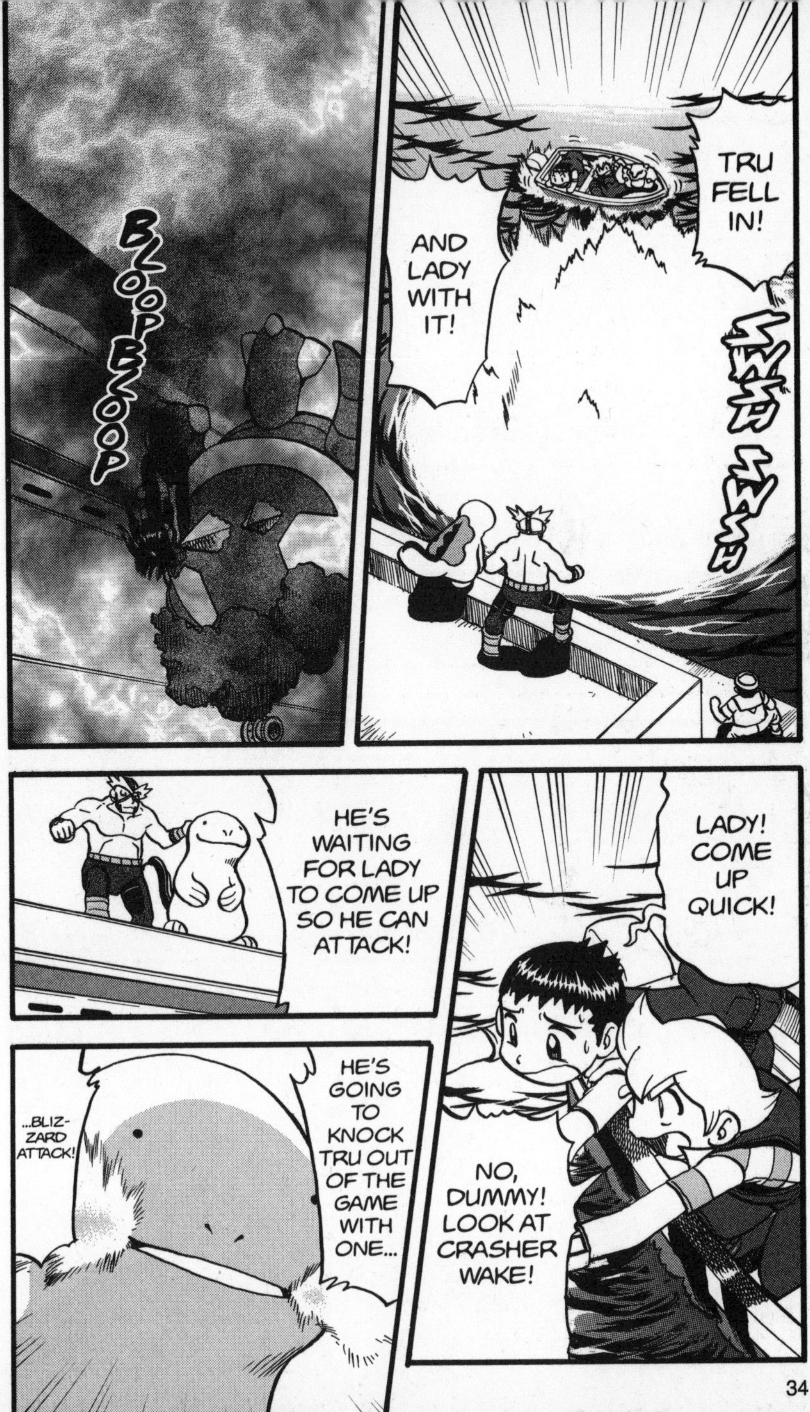
TRU FELL IN!
AND LADY WITH IT!
SWSH SWSH
BLOOPBZOOP
LADY! COME UP QUICK!
NO, DUMMY! LOOK AT CRASHER WAKE!
HE'S WAITING FOR LADY TO COME UP SO HE CAN ATTACK!
HE'S GOING TO KNOCK TRU OUT OF THE GAME WITH ONE...
...BLIZ-ZARD ATTACK!

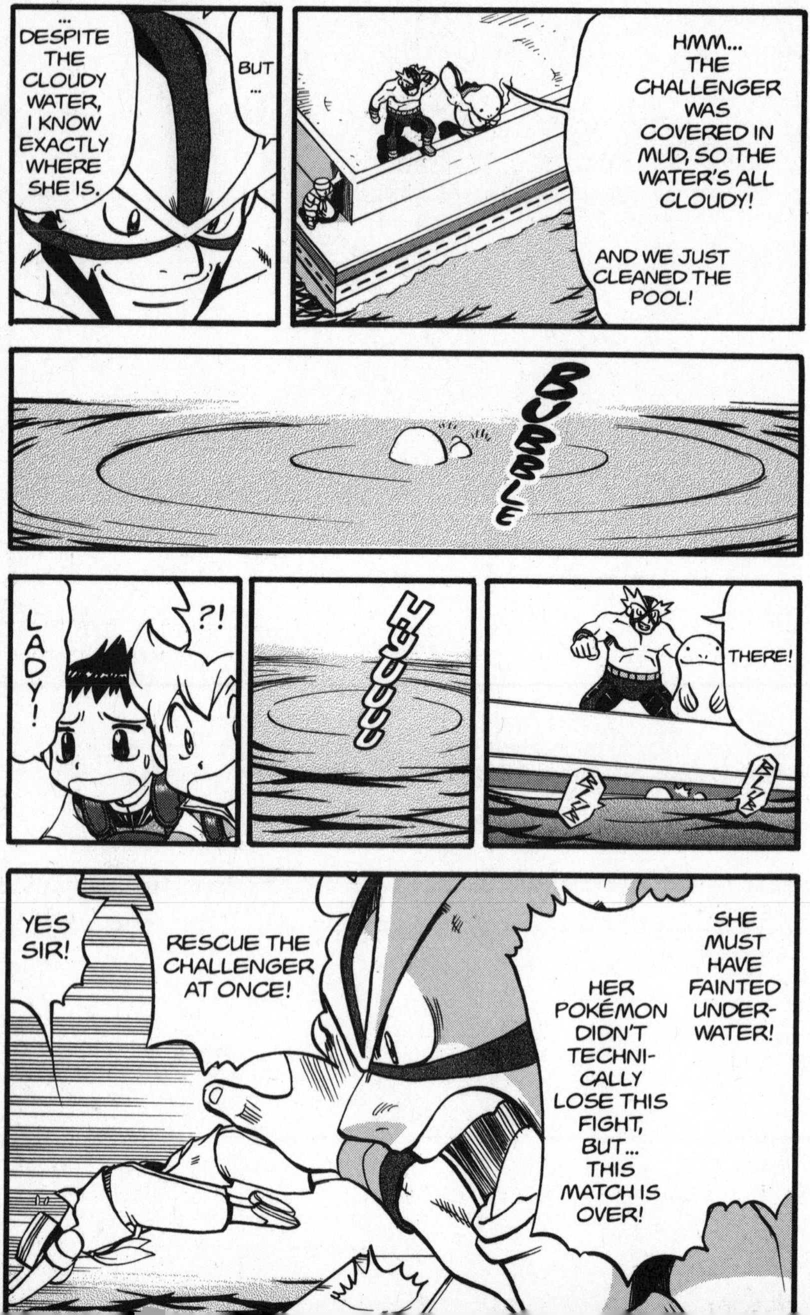
HMM... THE CHALLENGER WAS COVERED IN MUD, SO THE WATER'S ALL CLOUDY!
AND WE JUST CLEANED THE POOL!
BUT ...
... DESPITE THE CLOUDY WATER, I KNOW EXACTLY WHERE SHE IS.
BUBBLE
THERE!
HYUUUU
?!
LADY!
SHE MUST HAVE FAINTED UNDER-WATER!
HER POKÉMON DIDN'T TECHNI-CALLY LOSE THIS FIGHT, BUT... THIS MATCH IS OVER!
RESCUE THE CHALLENGER AT ONCE!
YES SIR!

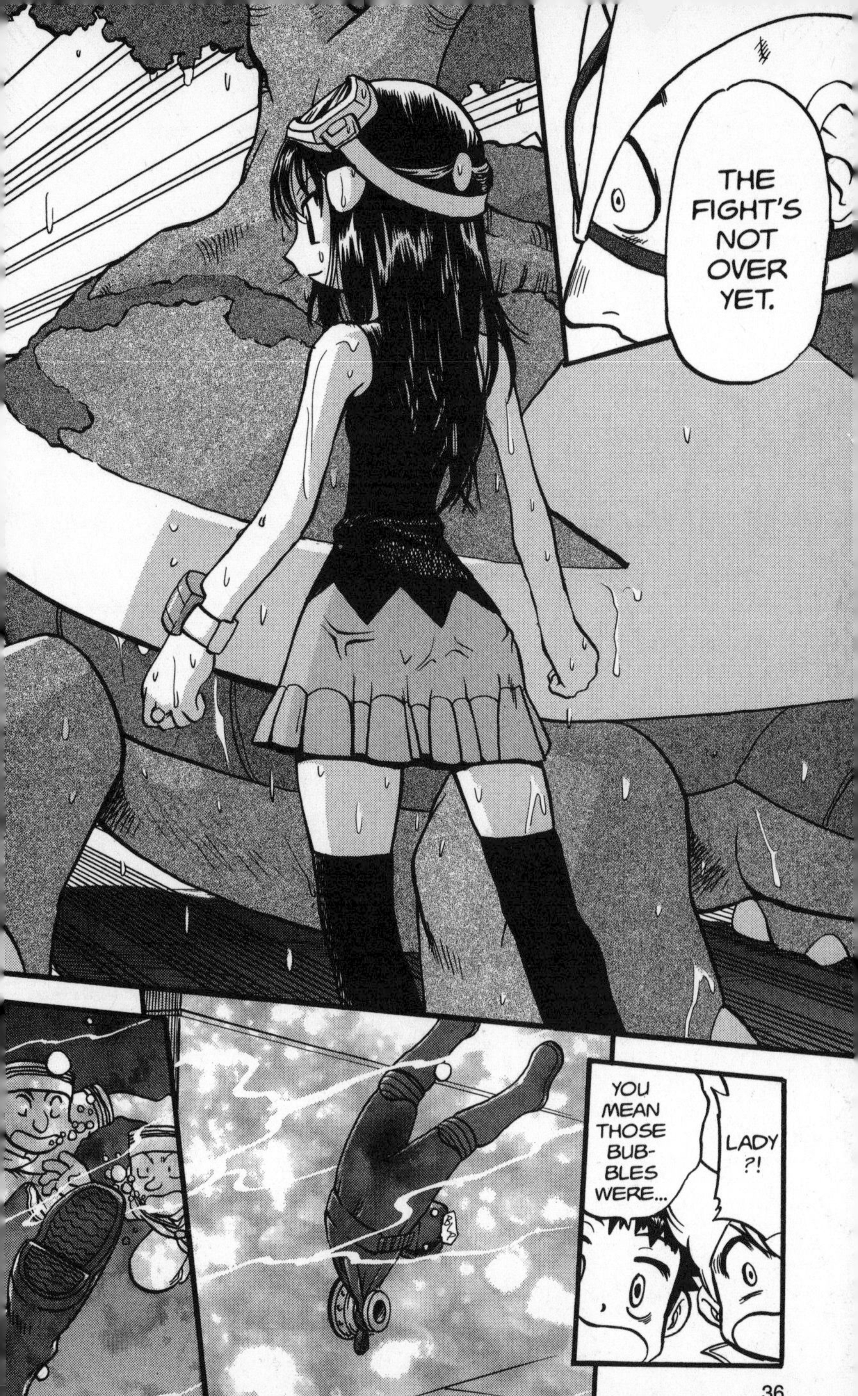
THE FIGHT'S NOT OVER YET.
LADY ?!
YOU MEAN THOSE BUB-BLES WERE...

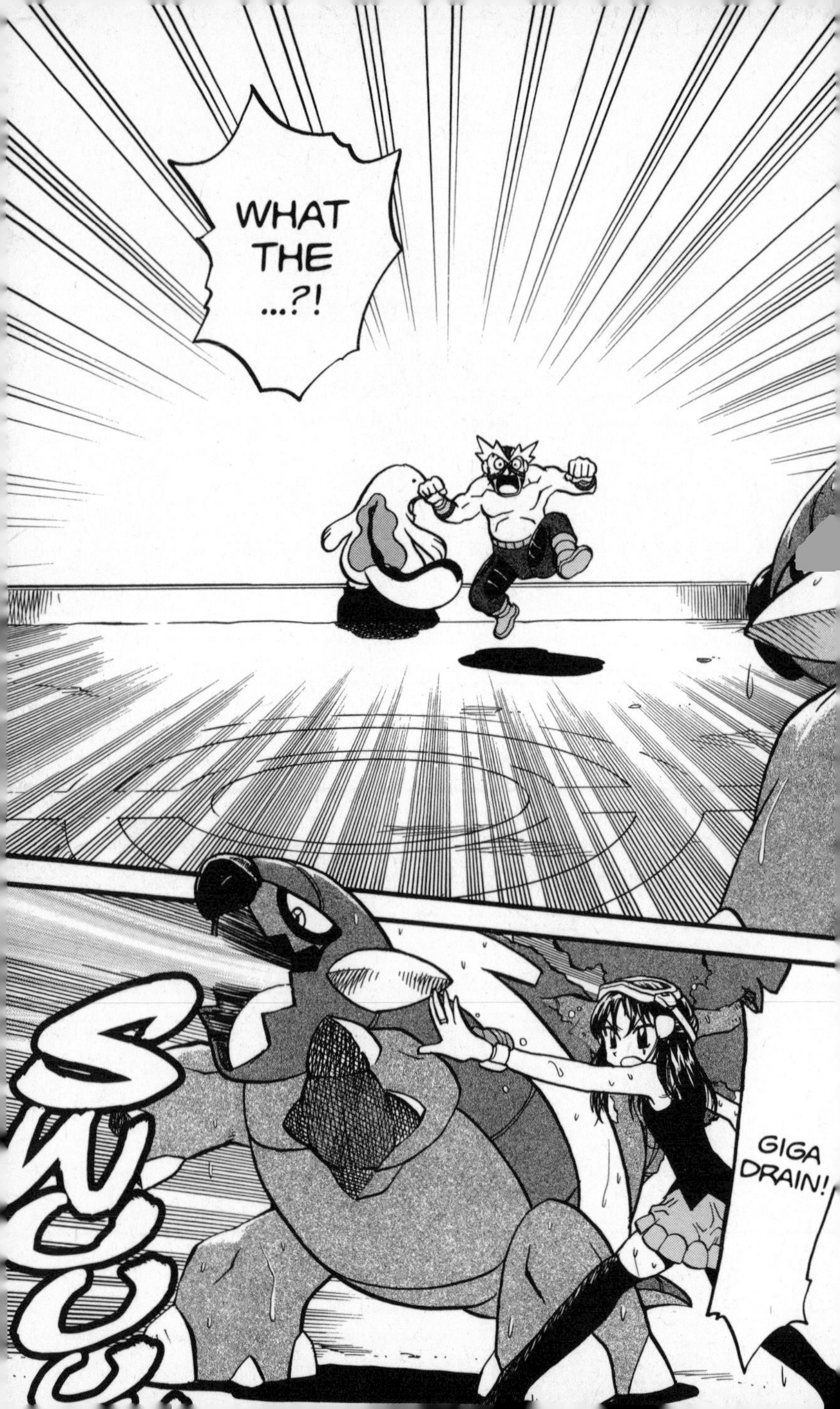
WHAT THE ...?!
GIGA DRAIN!

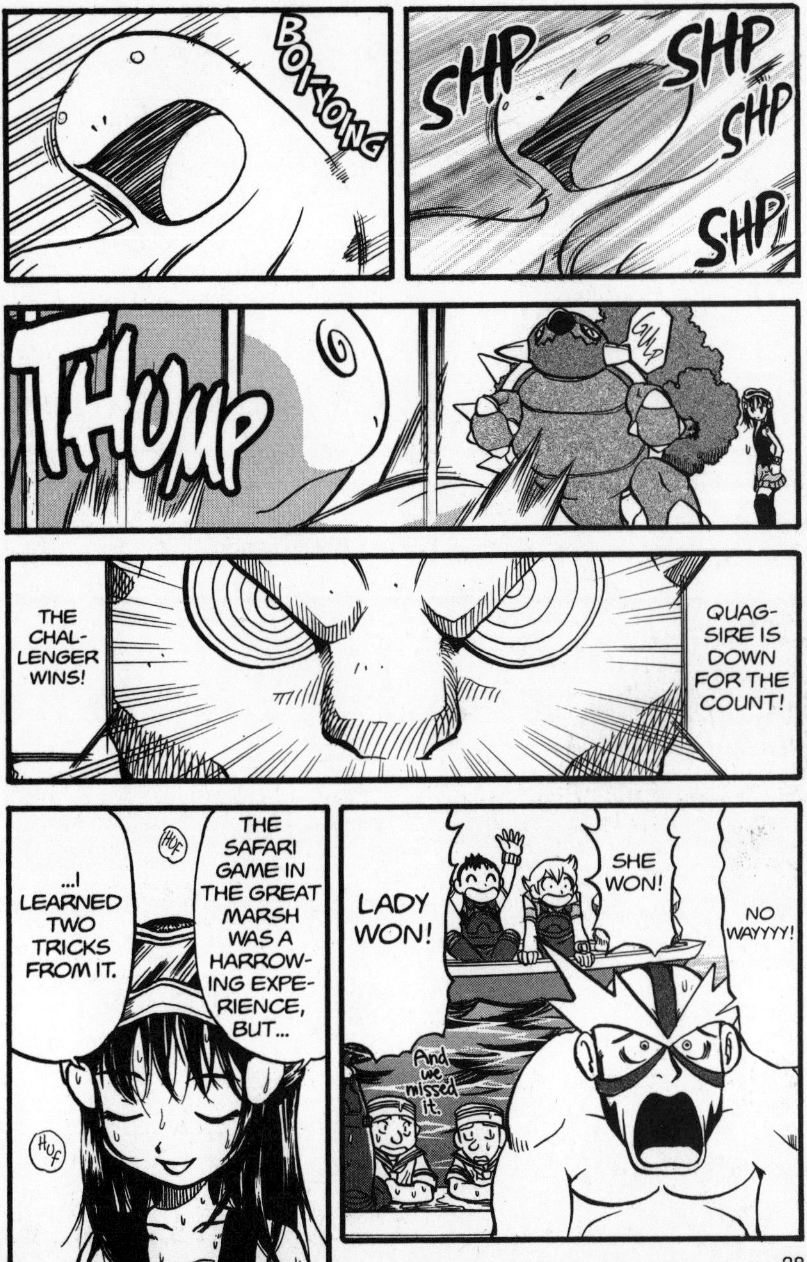
SHP SHP SHP SHP
BOI-YOING
GULP
THUMP
QUAG-SIRE IS DOWN FOR THE COUNT!
THE CHAL-LENGER WINS!
NO WAYYYY!
SHE WON!
LADY WON!
And we missed it.
THE SAFARI GAME IN THE GREAT MARSH WAS A HARROW-ING EXPE-RIENCE, BUT...
HUF
...I LEARNED TWO TRICKS FROM IT.
HUF

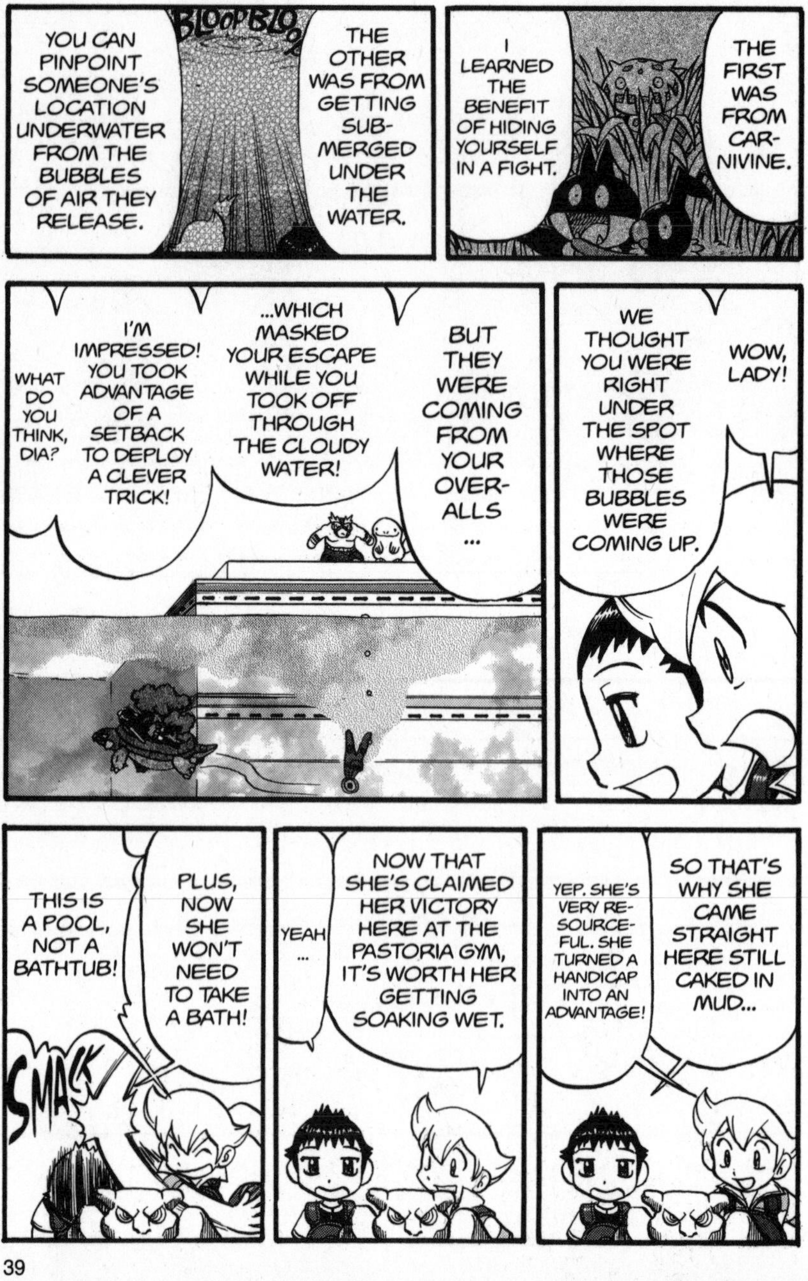
THE FIRST WAS FROM CARNIVINE.
I LEARNED THE BENEFIT OF HIDING YOURSELF IN A FIGHT.
THE OTHER WAS FROM GETTING SUBMERGED UNDER THE WATER.
BLOOP BLOOP
YOU CAN PINPOINT SOMEONE'S LOCATION UNDERWATER FROM THE BUBBLES OF AIR THEY RELEASE.
WOW, LADY!
WE THOUGHT YOU WERE RIGHT UNDER THE SPOT WHERE THOSE BUBBLES WERE COMING UP.
BUT THEY WERE COMING FROM YOUR OVERALLS...
...WHICH MASKED YOUR ESCAPE WHILE YOU TOOK OFF THROUGH THE CLOUDY WATER!
I'M IMPRESSED! YOU TOOK ADVANTAGE OF A SETBACK TO DEPLOY A CLEVER TRICK!
WHAT DO YOU THINK, DIA?
SO THAT'S WHY SHE CAME STRAIGHT HERE STILL CAKED IN MUD...
YEP. SHE'S VERY RESOURCEFUL. SHE TURNED A HANDICAP INTO AN ADVANTAGE!
NOW THAT SHE'S CLAIMED HER VICTORY HERE AT THE PASTORIA GYM, IT'S WORTH HER GETTING SOAKING WET.
YEAH...
PLUS, NOW SHE WON'T NEED TO TAKE A BATH!
THIS IS A POOL, NOT A BATHTUB!
SMACK

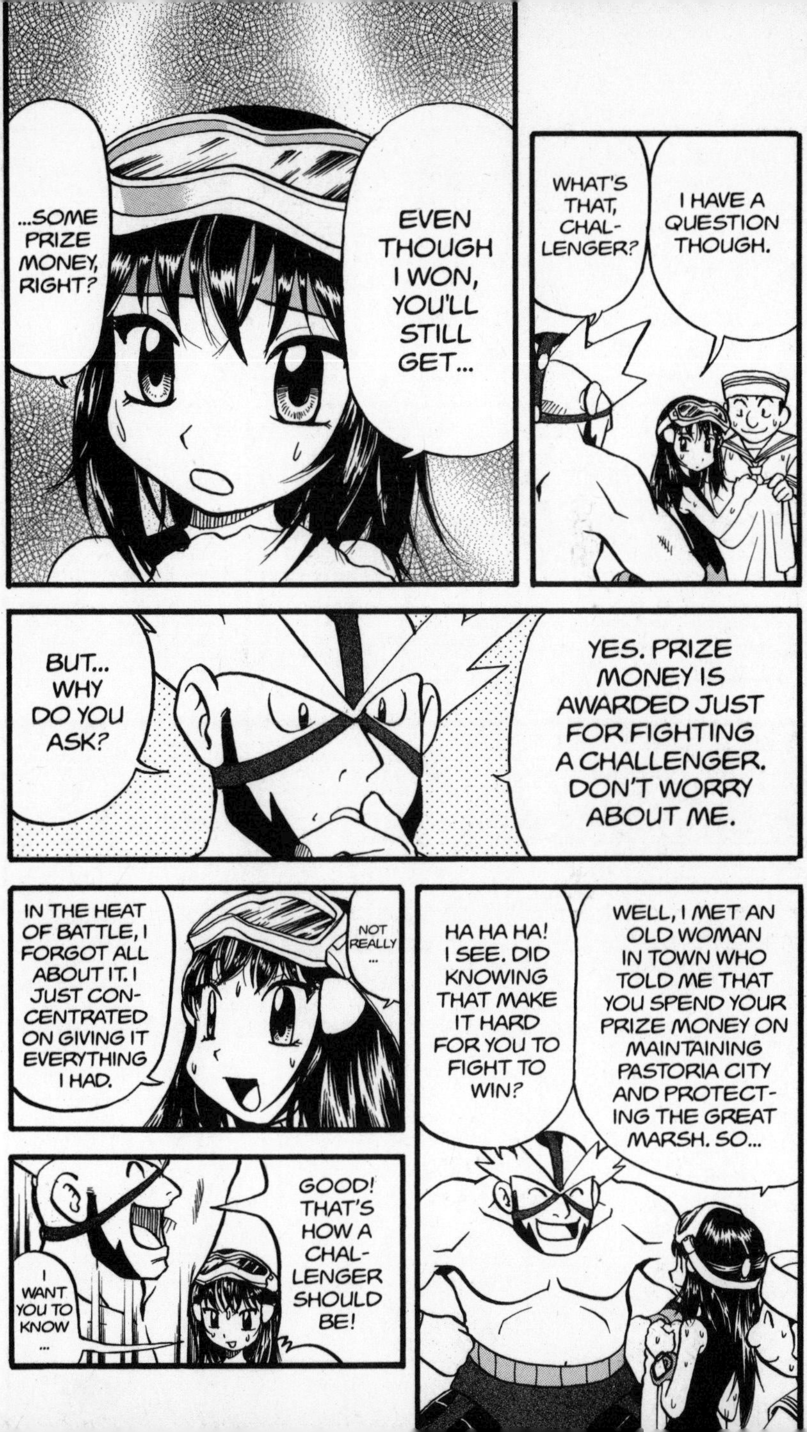

I HAVE A QUESTION THOUGH.
WHAT'S THAT, CHAL-LENGER?
EVEN THOUGH I WON, YOU'LL STILL GET...
...SOME PRIZE MONEY, RIGHT?
YES. PRIZE MONEY IS AWARDED JUST FOR FIGHTING A CHALLENGER. DON'T WORRY ABOUT ME.
BUT... WHY DO YOU ASK?
WELL, I MET AN OLD WOMAN IN TOWN WHO TOLD ME THAT YOU SPEND YOUR PRIZE MONEY ON MAINTAINING PASTORIA CITY AND PROTECT-ING THE GREAT MARSH. SO...
HA HA HA! I SEE. DID KNOWING THAT MAKE IT HARD FOR YOU TO FIGHT TO WIN?
NOT REALLY...
IN THE HEAT OF BATTLE, I FORGOT ALL ABOUT IT. I JUST CON-CENTRATED ON GIVING IT EVERYTHING I HAD.
GOOD! THAT'S HOW A CHAL-LENGER SHOULD BE!
I WANT YOU TO KNOW...

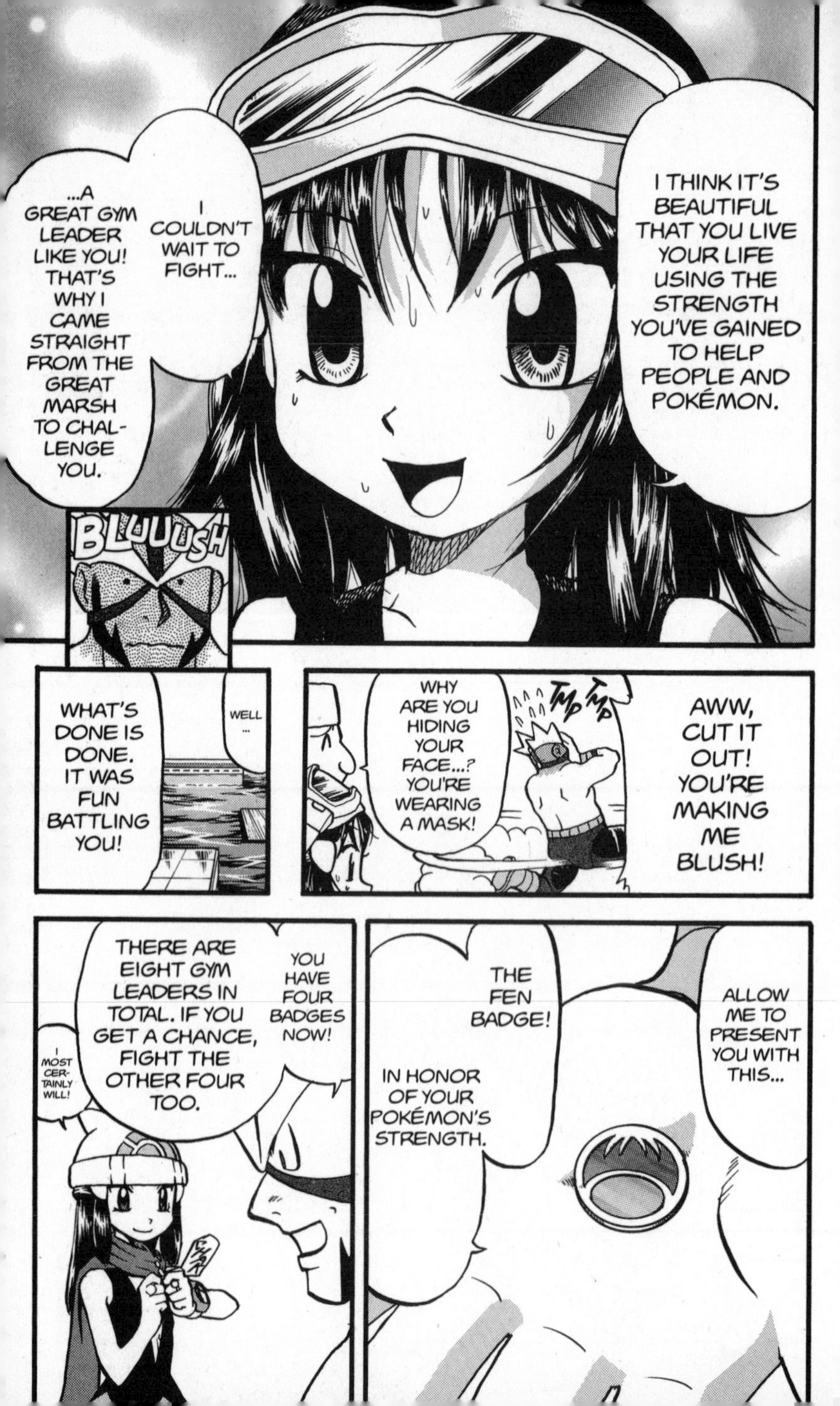
I THINK IT'S BEAUTIFUL THAT YOU LIVE YOUR LIFE USING THE STRENGTH YOU'VE GAINED TO HELP PEOPLE AND POKÉMON.
I COULDN'T WAIT TO FIGHT...
...A GREAT GYM LEADER LIKE YOU! THAT'S WHY I CAME STRAIGHT FROM THE GREAT MARSH TO CHAL-LENGE YOU.
BLUUUSH
AWW, CUT IT OUT! YOU'RE MAKING ME BLUSH!
TMP TMP
WHY ARE YOU HIDING YOUR FACE...? YOU'RE WEARING A MASK!
WELL ...
WHAT'S DONE IS DONE. IT WAS FUN BATTLING YOU!
ALLOW ME TO PRESENT YOU WITH THIS...
THE FEN BADGE!
IN HONOR OF YOUR POKÉMON'S STRENGTH.
YOU HAVE FOUR BADGES NOW!
THERE ARE EIGHT GYM LEADERS IN TOTAL. IF YOU GET A CHANCE, FIGHT THE OTHER FOUR TOO.
I MOST CER-TAINLY WILL!

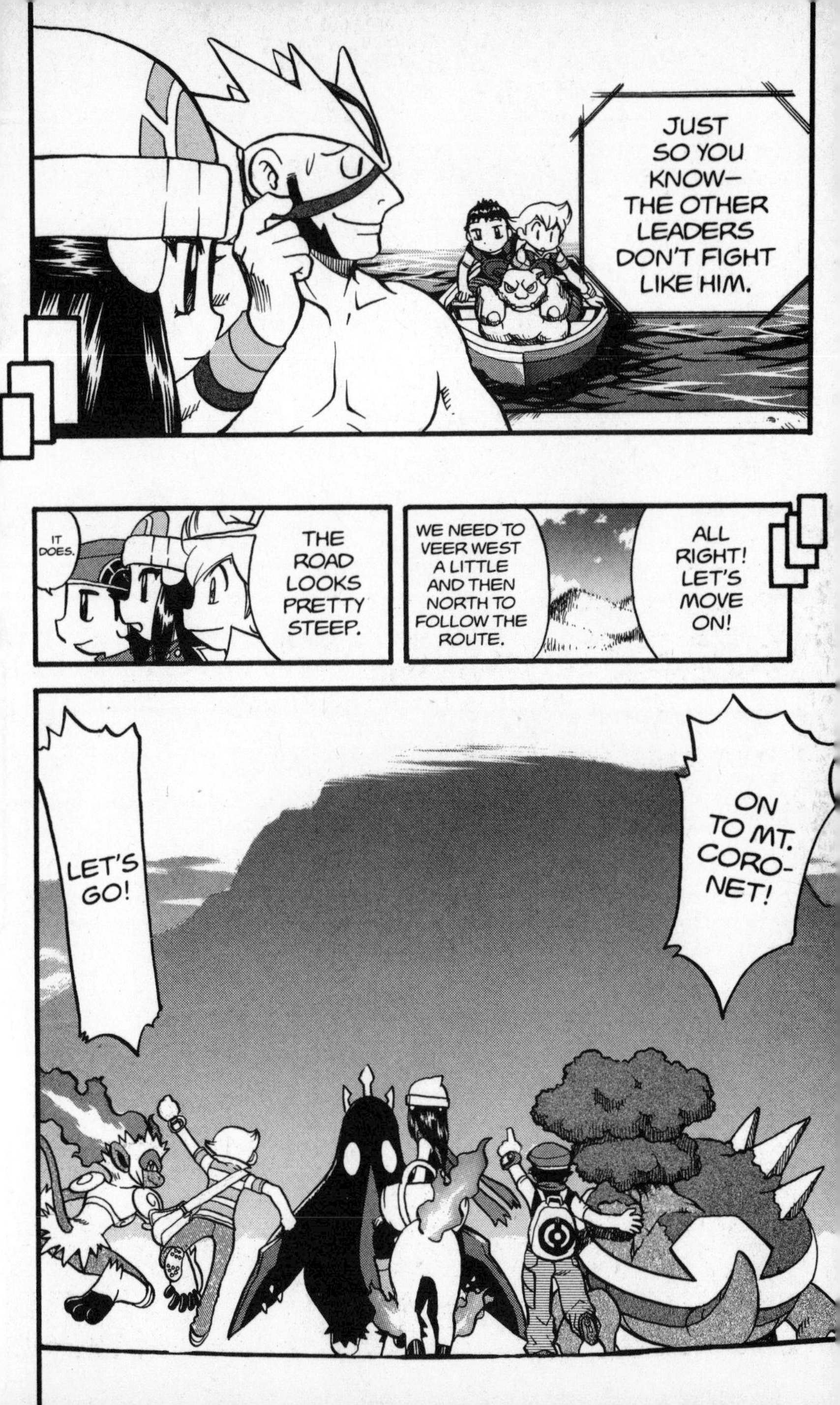
JUST SO YOU KNOW— THE OTHER LEADERS DON'T FIGHT LIKE HIM.
ALL RIGHT! LET'S MOVE ON!
WE NEED TO VEER WEST A LITTLE AND THEN NORTH TO FOLLOW THE ROUTE.
THE ROAD LOOKS PRETTY STEEP.
IT DOES.
ON TO MT. CORO-NET!
LET'S GO!

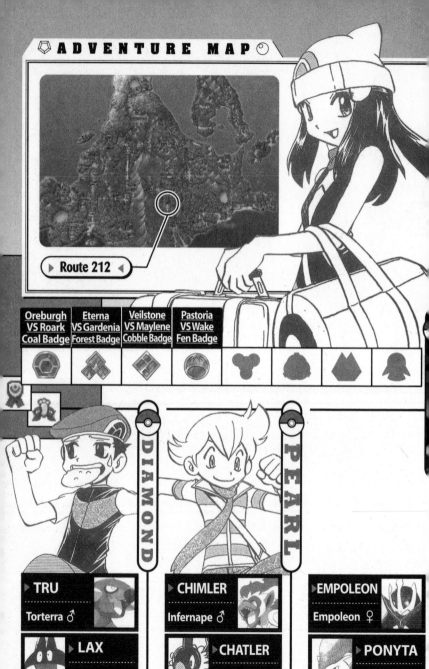

ADVENTURE MAP

▶ Route 212 ◀

Oreburgh VS Roark Coal Badge	Eterna VS Gardenia Forest Badge	Veilstone VS Maylene Cobble Badge	Pastoria VS Wake Fen Badge				

DIAMOND

▶ TRU
Torterra ♂

▶ LAX
Munchlax ♂

PEARL

▶ CHIMLER
Infernape ♂

▶ CHATLER
Chatot ♂

▶ EMPOLEON
Empoleon ♀

▶ PONYTA
Ponyta ♂

30

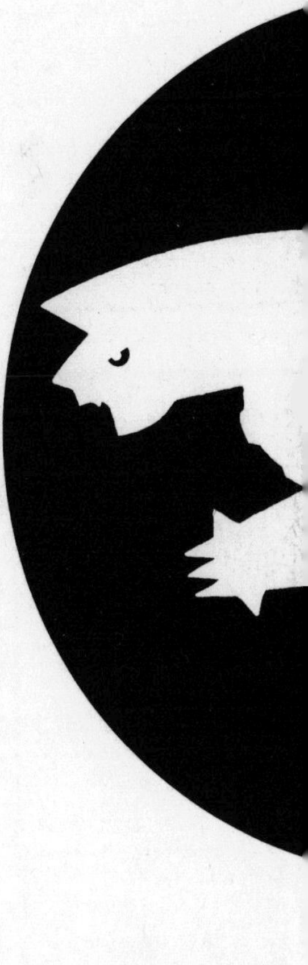

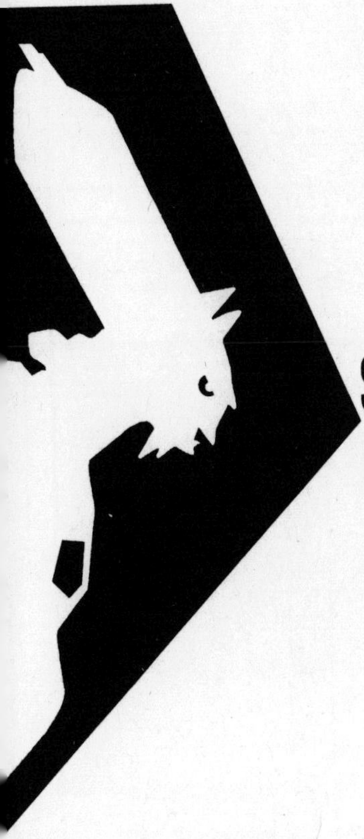

Suffering Psyduck!

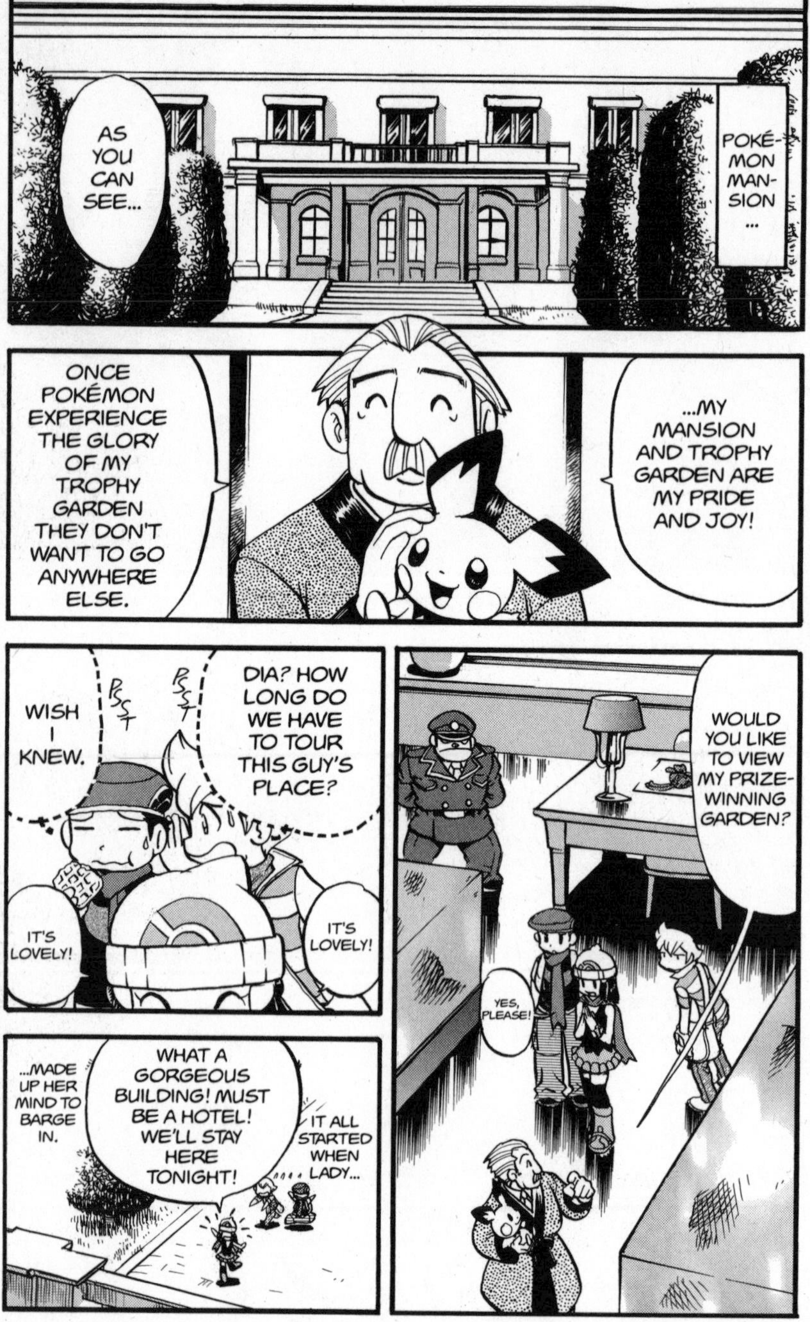
POKÉ-MON MAN-SION ...
AS YOU CAN SEE...
...MY MANSION AND TROPHY GARDEN ARE MY PRIDE AND JOY!
ONCE POKÉMON EXPERIENCE THE GLORY OF MY TROPHY GARDEN THEY DON'T WANT TO GO ANYWHERE ELSE.
WOULD YOU LIKE TO VIEW MY PRIZE-WINNING GARDEN?
YES, PLEASE!
DIA? HOW LONG DO WE HAVE TO TOUR THIS GUY'S PLACE?
PSST
PSST
WISH I KNEW.
IT'S LOVELY!
IT'S LOVELY!
IT ALL STARTED WHEN LADY...
WHAT A GORGEOUS BUILDING! MUST BE A HOTEL! WE'LL STAY HERE TONIGHT!
...MADE UP HER MIND TO BARGE IN.

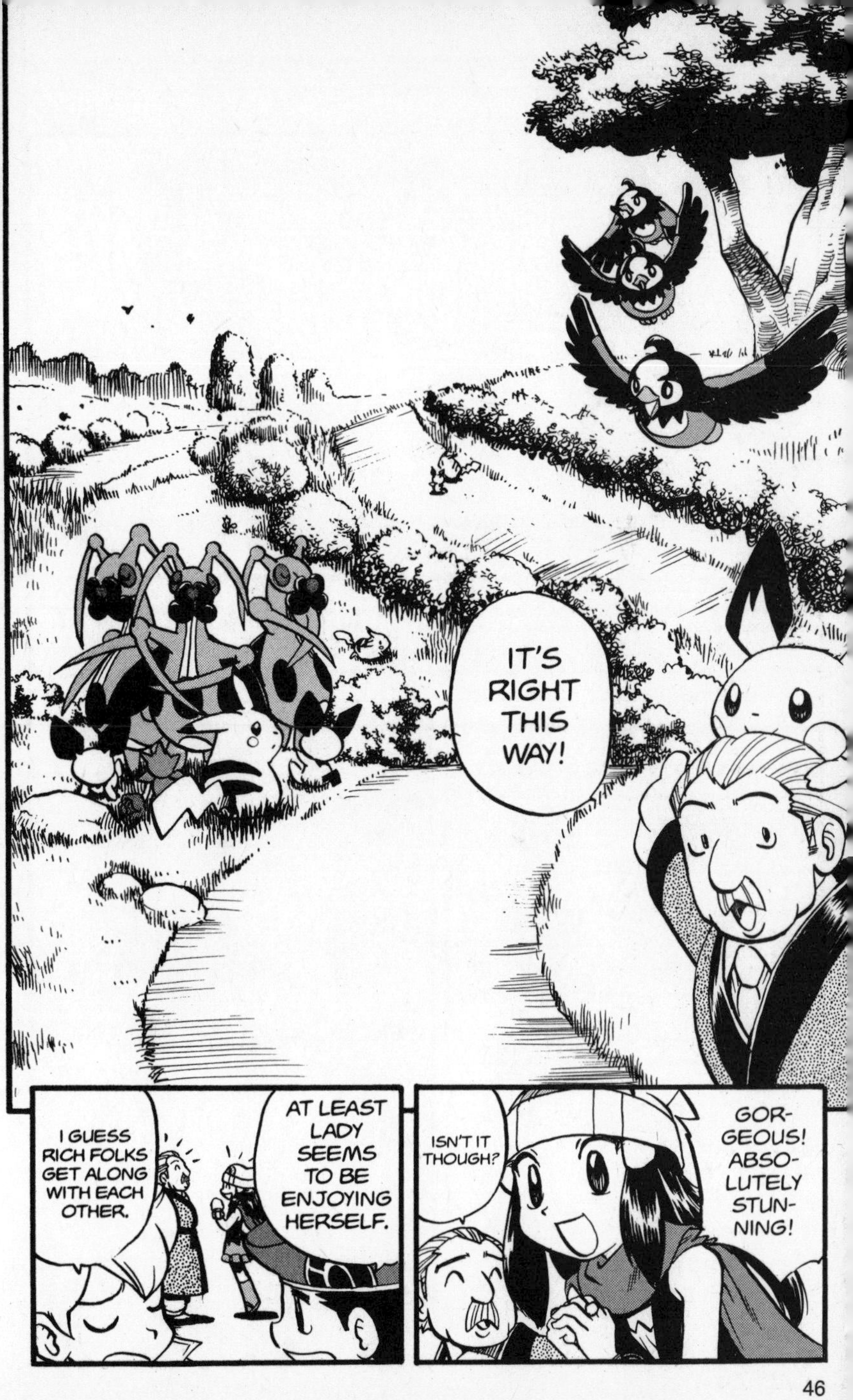
IT'S RIGHT THIS WAY!
GOR-GEOUS! ABSO-LUTELY STUN-NING!
ISN'T IT THOUGH?
AT LEAST LADY SEEMS TO BE ENJOYING HERSELF.
I GUESS RICH FOLKS GET ALONG WITH EACH OTHER.

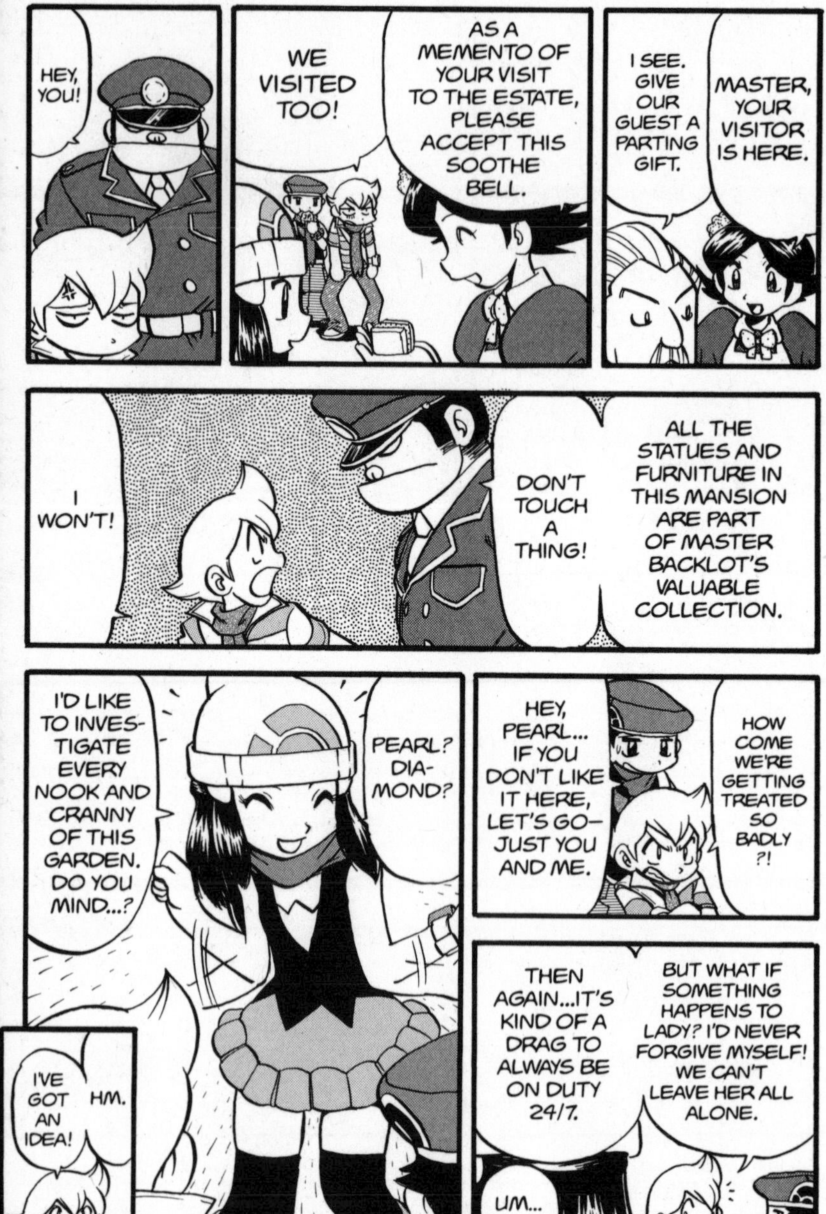
MASTER, YOUR VISITOR IS HERE.
I SEE. GIVE OUR GUEST A PARTING GIFT.
AS A MEMENTO OF YOUR VISIT TO THE ESTATE, PLEASE ACCEPT THIS SOOTHE BELL.
WE VISITED TOO!
HEY, YOU!
ALL THE STATUES AND FURNITURE IN THIS MANSION ARE PART OF MASTER BACKLOT'S VALUABLE COLLECTION.
DON'T TOUCH A THING!
I WON'T!
HOW COME WE'RE GETTING TREATED SO BADLY?!
HEY, PEARL... IF YOU DON'T LIKE IT HERE, LET'S GO—JUST YOU AND ME.
BUT WHAT IF SOMETHING HAPPENS TO LADY? I'D NEVER FORGIVE MYSELF! WE CAN'T LEAVE HER ALL ALONE.
THEN AGAIN...IT'S KIND OF A DRAG TO ALWAYS BE ON DUTY 24/7.
UM...
PEARL? DIA-MOND?
I'D LIKE TO INVES-TIGATE EVERY NOOK AND CRANNY OF THIS GARDEN. DO YOU MIND...?
HM.
I'VE GOT AN IDEA!

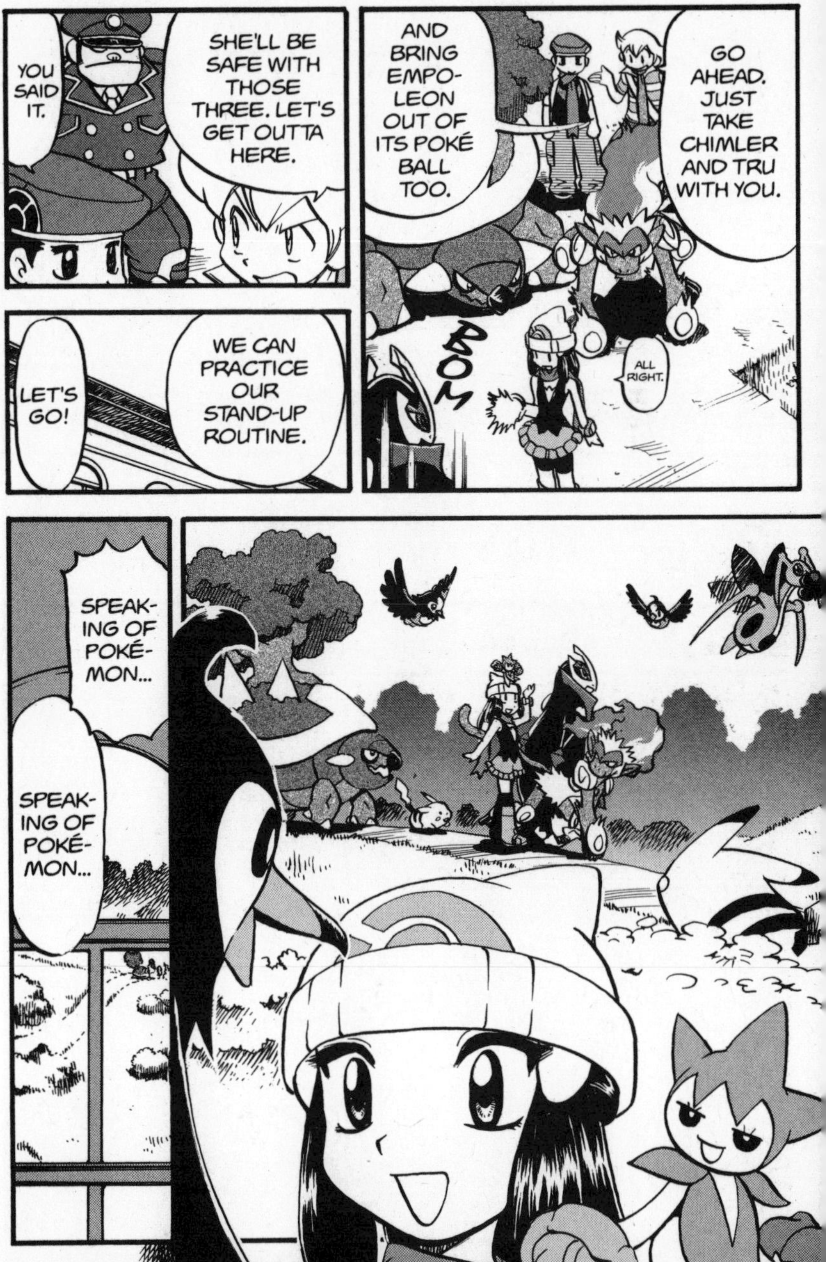
GO AHEAD. JUST TAKE CHIMLER AND TRU WITH YOU.
AND BRING EMPOLEON OUT OF ITS POKÉ BALL TOO.
BOM
ALL RIGHT.
SHE'LL BE SAFE WITH THOSE THREE. LET'S GET OUTTA HERE.
YOU SAID IT.
WE CAN PRACTICE OUR STAND-UP ROUTINE.
LET'S GO!
SPEAKING OF POKÉMON...
SPEAKING OF POKÉMON...

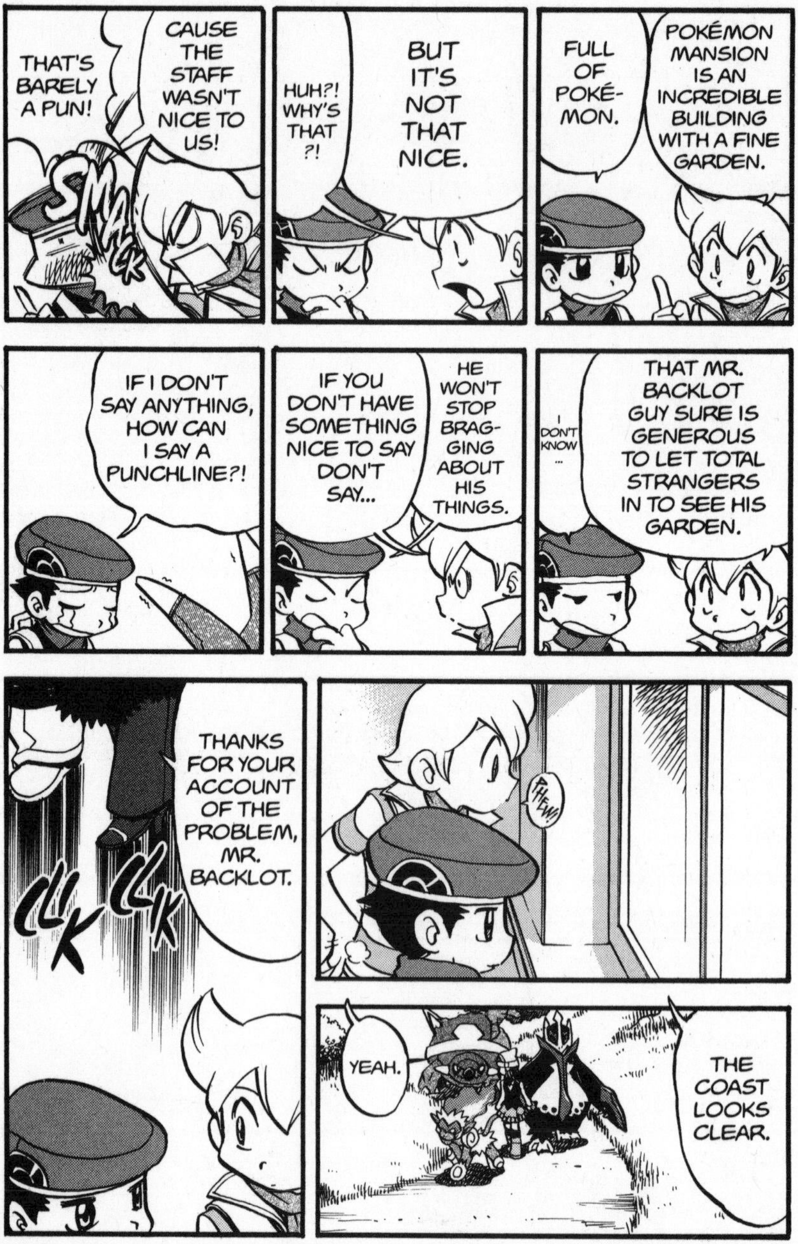
POKÉMON MANSION IS AN INCREDIBLE BUILDING WITH A FINE GARDEN.
FULL OF POKÉ-MON.
BUT IT'S NOT THAT NICE.
HUH?! WHY'S THAT ?!
CAUSE THE STAFF WASN'T NICE TO US!
THAT'S BARELY A PUN!
SMACK
THAT MR. BACKLOT GUY SURE IS GENEROUS TO LET TOTAL STRANGERS IN TO SEE HIS GARDEN.
I DON'T KNOW ...
HE WON'T STOP BRAG-GING ABOUT HIS THINGS.
IF YOU DON'T HAVE SOMETHING NICE TO SAY DON'T SAY...
IF I DON'T SAY ANYTHING, HOW CAN I SAY A PUNCHLINE?!
PHEW!
THE COAST LOOKS CLEAR.
YEAH.
THANKS FOR YOUR ACCOUNT OF THE PROBLEM, MR. BACKLOT.
CLIK
CLIK

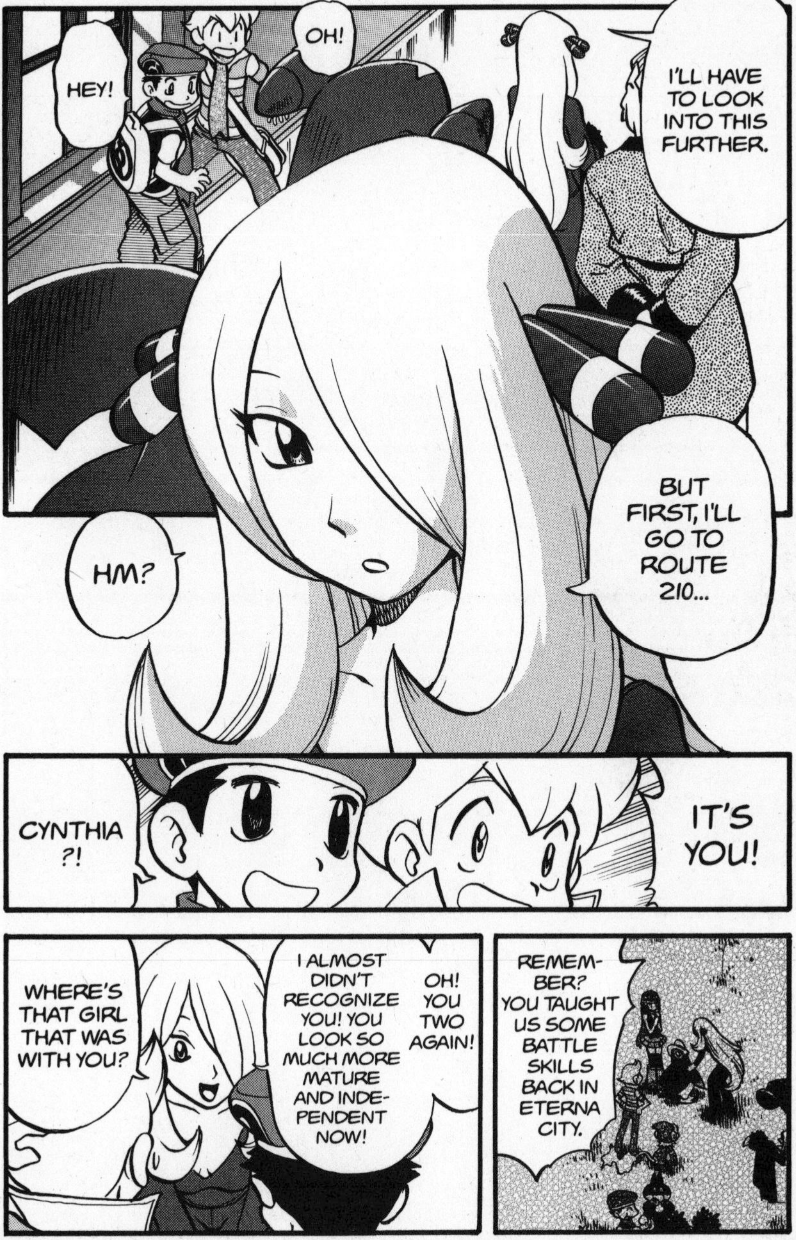
I'LL HAVE TO LOOK INTO THIS FURTHER.
BUT FIRST, I'LL GO TO ROUTE 210...
OH!
HEY!
HM?
IT'S YOU!
CYNTHIA ?!
REMEM-BER? YOU TAUGHT US SOME BATTLE SKILLS BACK IN ETERNA CITY.
OH! YOU TWO AGAIN!
I ALMOST DIDN'T RECOGNIZE YOU! YOU LOOK SO MUCH MORE MATURE AND INDE-PENDENT NOW!
WHERE'S THAT GIRL THAT WAS WITH YOU?

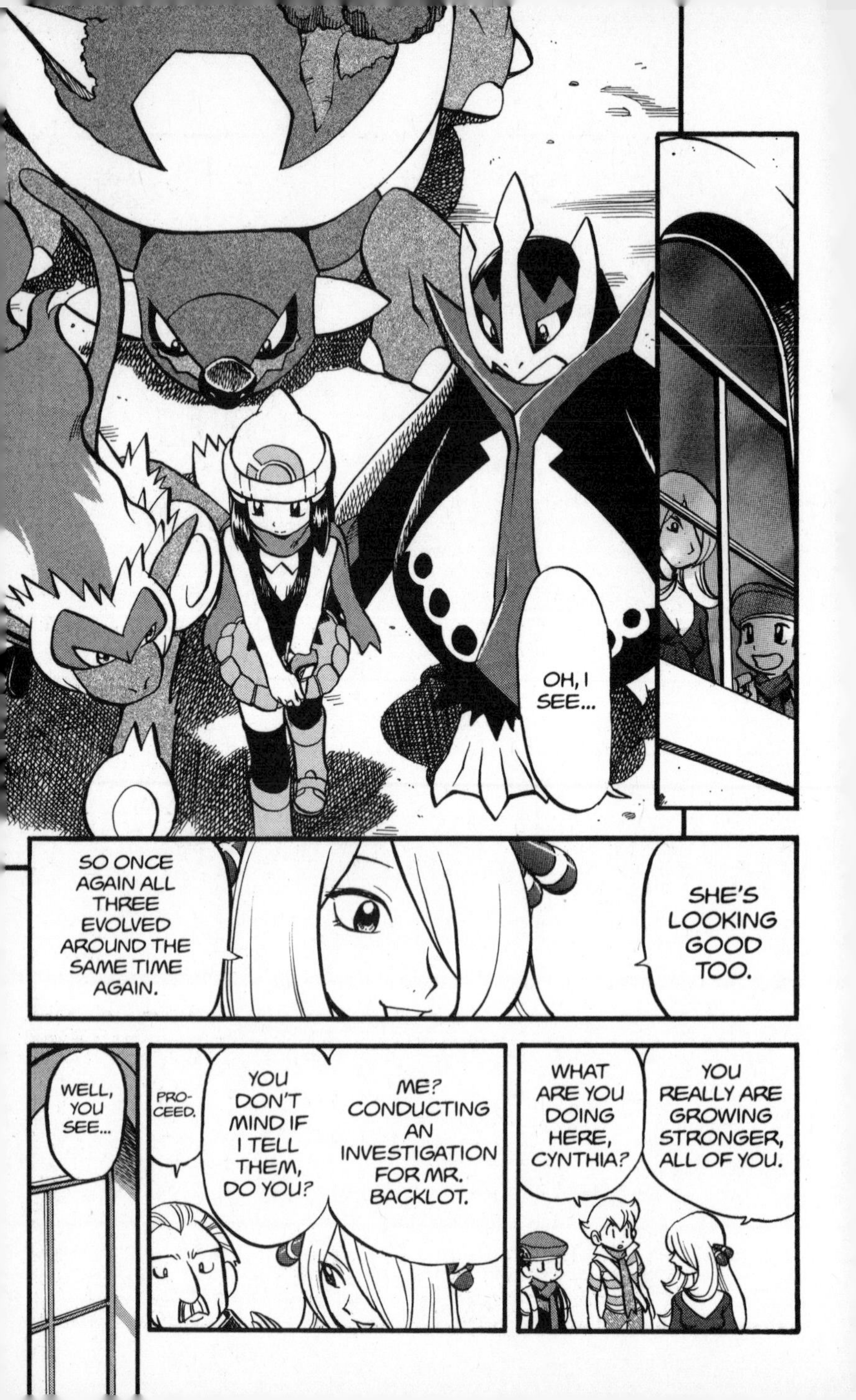
OH, I SEE...
SHE'S LOOKING GOOD TOO.
SO ONCE AGAIN ALL THREE EVOLVED AROUND THE SAME TIME AGAIN.
YOU REALLY ARE GROWING STRONGER, ALL OF YOU.
WHAT ARE YOU DOING HERE, CYNTHIA?
ME? CONDUCTING AN INVESTIGATION FOR MR. BACKLOT.
YOU DON'T MIND IF I TELL THEM, DO YOU?
PRO-CEED.
WELL, YOU SEE...

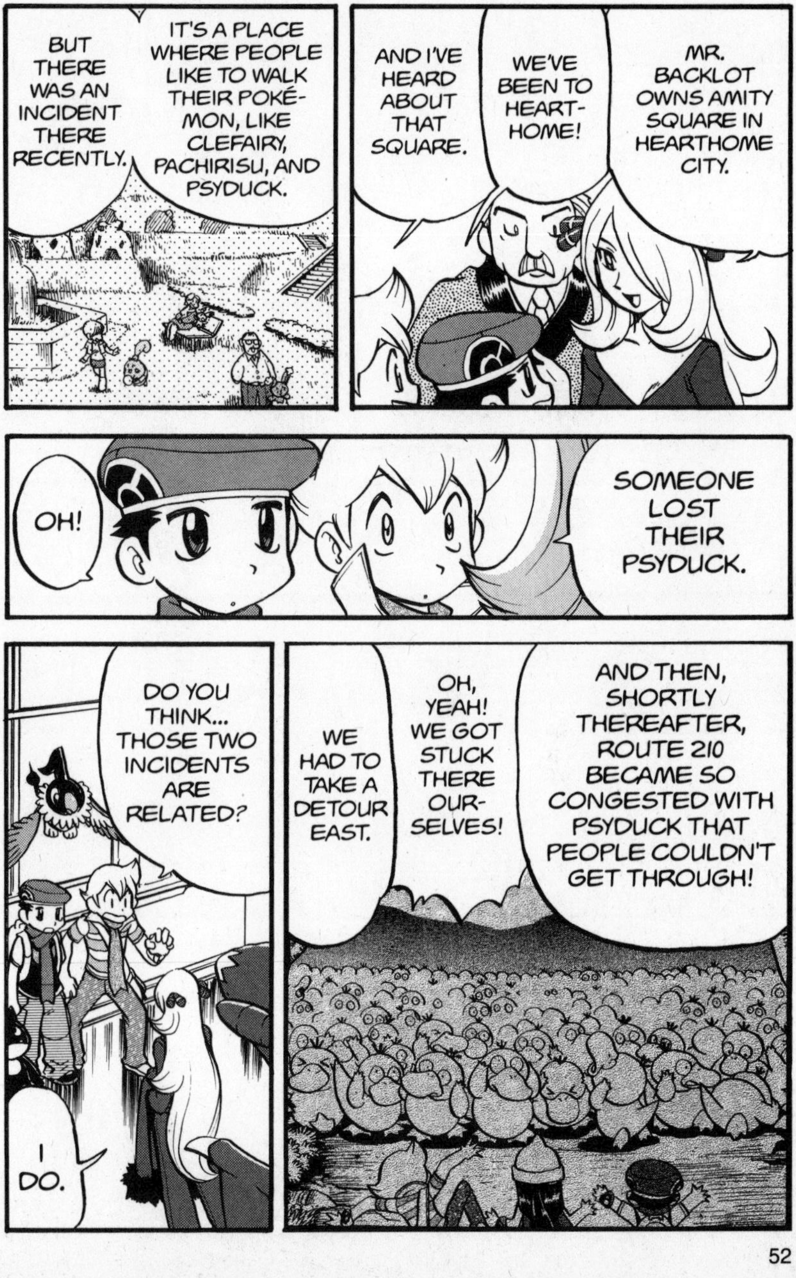
MR. BACKLOT OWNS AMITY SQUARE IN HEARTHOME CITY.
WE'VE BEEN TO HEART-HOME!
AND I'VE HEARD ABOUT THAT SQUARE.
IT'S A PLACE WHERE PEOPLE LIKE TO WALK THEIR POKÉ-MON, LIKE CLEFAIRY, PACHIRISU, AND PSYDUCK.
BUT THERE WAS AN INCIDENT THERE RECENTLY.
SOMEONE LOST THEIR PSYDUCK.
OH!
AND THEN, SHORTLY THEREAFTER, ROUTE 210 BECAME SO CONGESTED WITH PSYDUCK THAT PEOPLE COULDN'T GET THROUGH!
OH, YEAH! WE GOT STUCK THERE OUR-SELVES!
WE HAD TO TAKE A DETOUR EAST.
DO YOU THINK... THOSE TWO INCIDENTS ARE RELATED?
I DO.

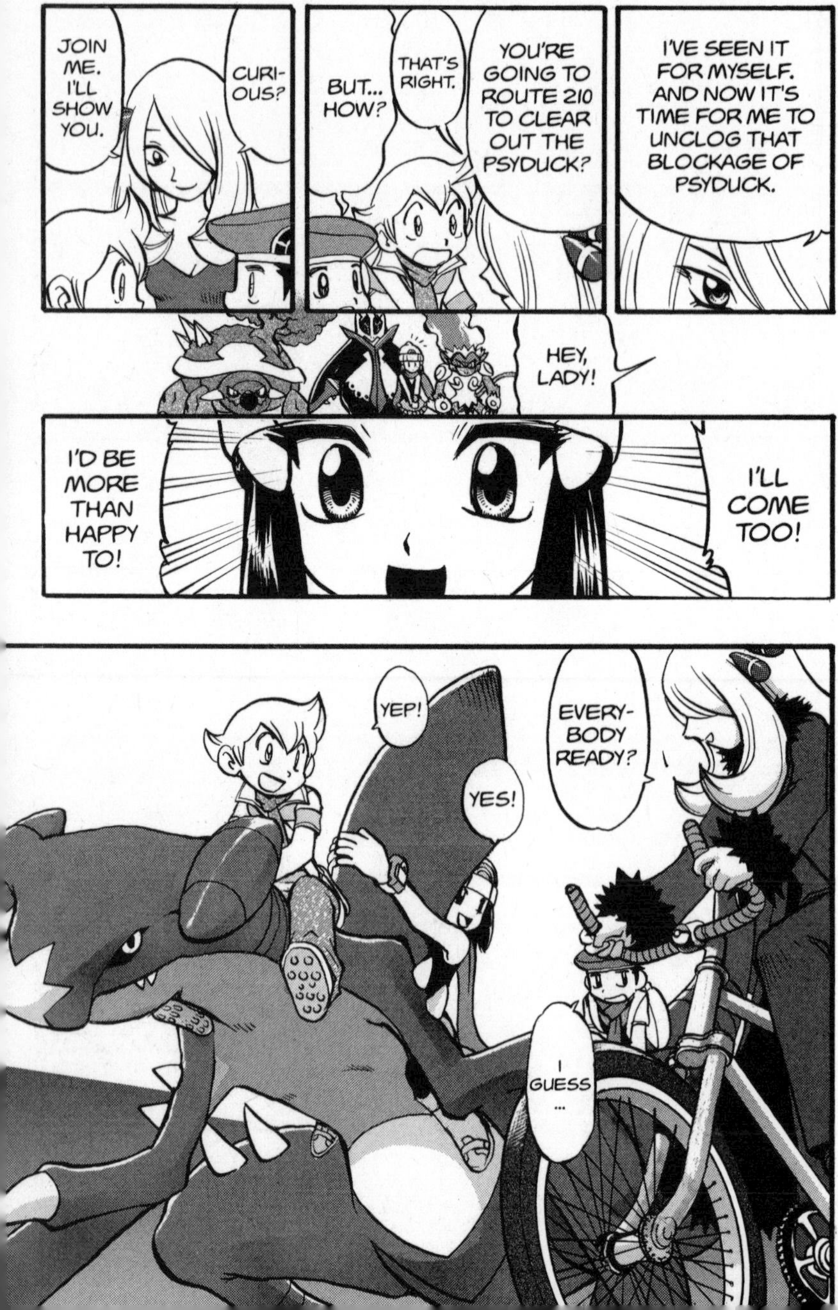
I'VE SEEN IT FOR MYSELF. AND NOW IT'S TIME FOR ME TO UNCLOG THAT BLOCKAGE OF PSYDUCK.
YOU'RE GOING TO ROUTE 210 TO CLEAR OUT THE PSYDUCK?
THAT'S RIGHT.
BUT... HOW?
CURIOUS?
JOIN ME. I'LL SHOW YOU.
HEY, LADY!
I'LL COME TOO!
I'D BE MORE THAN HAPPY TO!
EVERYBODY READY?
YEP!
YES!
I GUESS ...

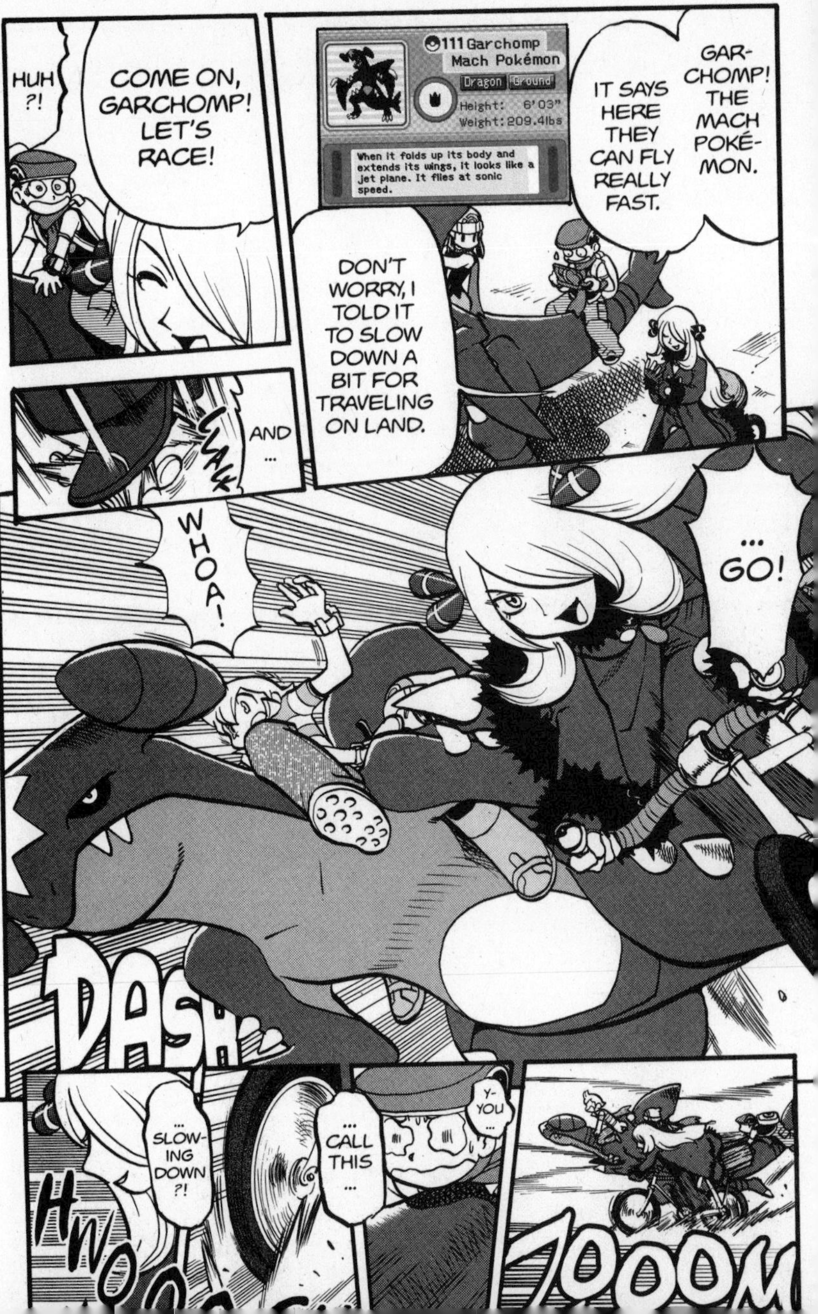
111 Garchomp
Mach Pokémon
Dragon Ground
Height: 6'03"
Weight: 209.4lbs
When it folds up its body and extends its wings, it looks like a jet plane. It flies at sonic speed.
GAR-CHOMP! THE MACH POKÉ-MON.
IT SAYS HERE THEY CAN FLY REALLY FAST.
DON'T WORRY, I TOLD IT TO SLOW DOWN A BIT FOR TRAVELING ON LAND.
COME ON, GARCHOMP! LET'S RACE!
HUH?!
AND ...
CLAK
...GO!
WHOA!
DASH
ZOOOM
Y-YOU ...
... CALL THIS ...
... SLOW-ING DOWN?!
HWOOO

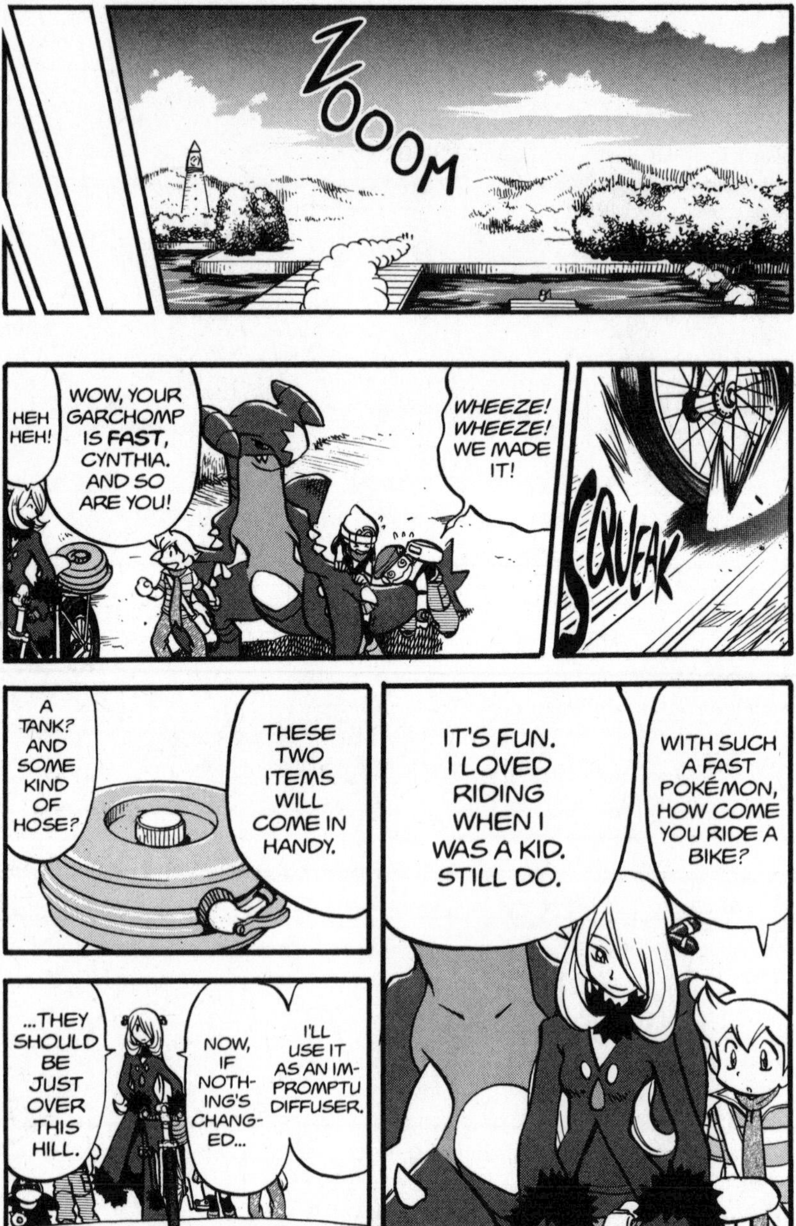
ZOOOM
SQUEAK
WHEEZE! WHEEZE! WE MADE IT!
WOW, YOUR GARCHOMP IS **FAST**, CYNTHIA. AND SO ARE YOU!
HEH HEH!
WITH SUCH A FAST POKÉMON, HOW COME YOU RIDE A BIKE?
IT'S FUN. I LOVED RIDING WHEN I WAS A KID. STILL DO.
THESE TWO ITEMS WILL COME IN HANDY.
A TANK? AND SOME KIND OF HOSE?
I'LL USE IT AS AN IMPROMPTU DIFFUSER.
NOW, IF NOTHING'S CHANGED...
...THEY SHOULD BE JUST OVER THIS HILL.

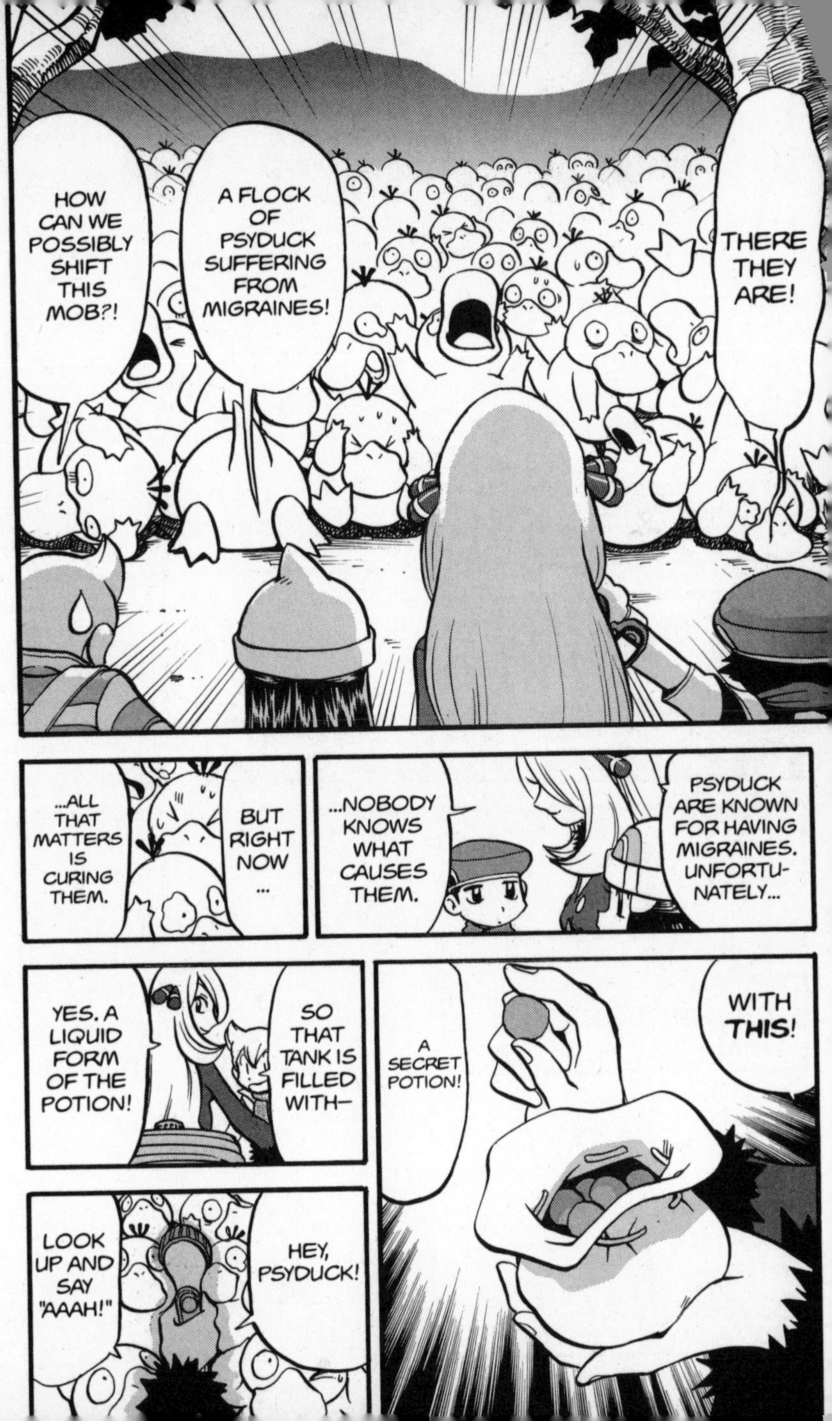

THERE THEY ARE!
A FLOCK OF PSYDUCK SUFFERING FROM MIGRAINES!
HOW CAN WE POSSIBLY SHIFT THIS MOB?!
PSYDUCK ARE KNOWN FOR HAVING MIGRAINES. UNFORTU-NATELY...
...NOBODY KNOWS WHAT CAUSES THEM.
BUT RIGHT NOW...
...ALL THAT MATTERS IS CURING THEM.
WITH **THIS**!
A SECRET POTION!
SO THAT TANK IS FILLED WITH—
YES. A LIQUID FORM OF THE POTION!
HEY, PSYDUCK!
LOOK UP AND SAY "AAAH!"

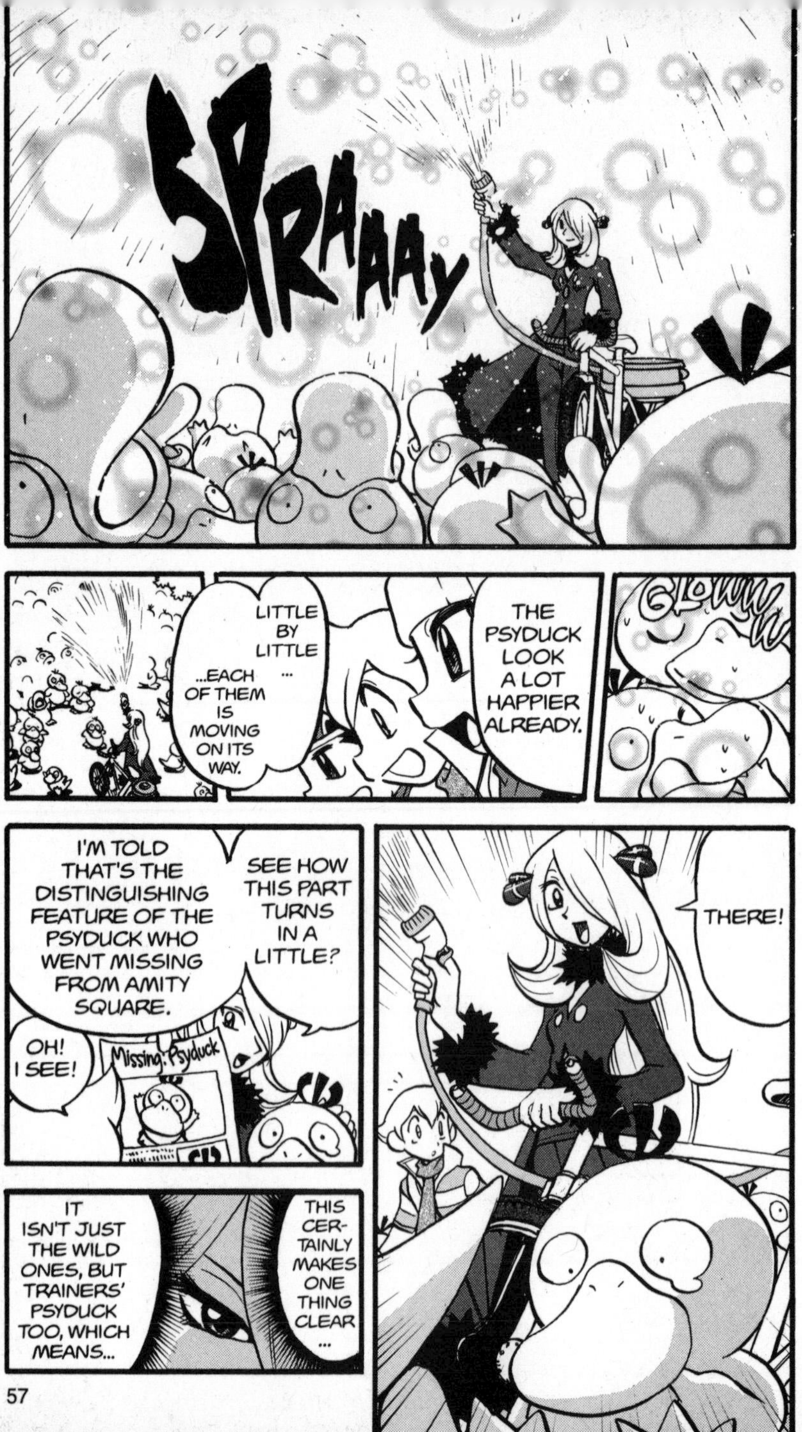
SPRAAAY
THE PSYDUCK LOOK A LOT HAPPIER ALREADY.
LITTLE BY LITTLE ...
...EACH OF THEM IS MOVING ON ITS WAY.
THERE!
SEE HOW THIS PART TURNS IN A LITTLE?
I'M TOLD THAT'S THE DISTINGUISHING FEATURE OF THE PSYDUCK WHO WENT MISSING FROM AMITY SQUARE.
Missing: Psyduck
OH! I SEE!
THIS CER-TAINLY MAKES ONE THING CLEAR ...
IT ISN'T JUST THE WILD ONES, BUT TRAINERS' PSYDUCK TOO, WHICH MEANS...

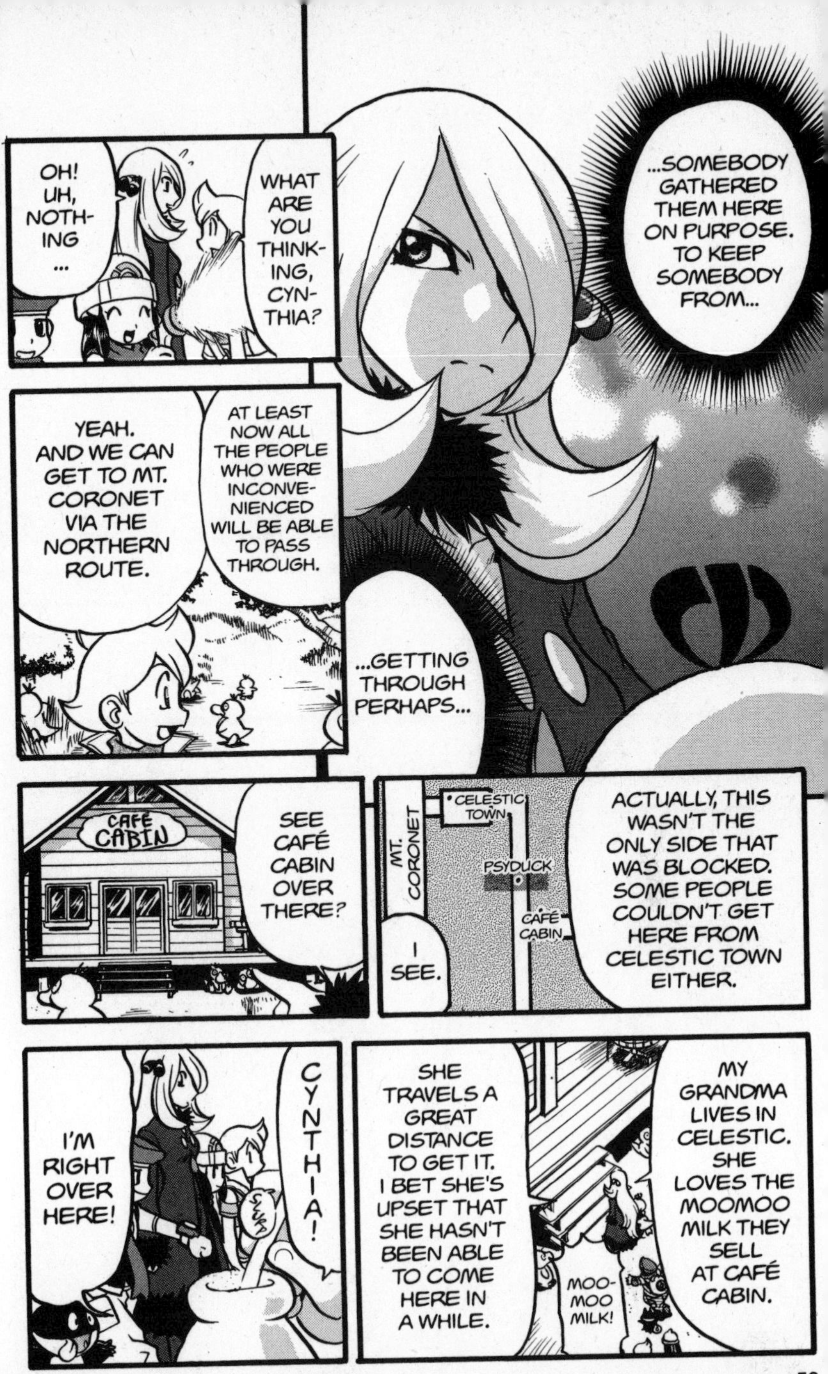
...SOMEBODY GATHERED THEM HERE ON PURPOSE. TO KEEP SOMEBODY FROM...
...GETTING THROUGH PERHAPS...
WHAT ARE YOU THINKING, CYNTHIA?
OH! UH, NOTHING...
AT LEAST NOW ALL THE PEOPLE WHO WERE INCONVENIENCED WILL BE ABLE TO PASS THROUGH.
YEAH. AND WE CAN GET TO MT. CORONET VIA THE NORTHERN ROUTE.
ACTUALLY, THIS WASN'T THE ONLY SIDE THAT WAS BLOCKED. SOME PEOPLE COULDN'T GET HERE FROM CELESTIC TOWN EITHER.
CELESTIC TOWN
MT. CORONET
PSYDUCK
CAFÉ CABIN
I SEE.
SEE CAFÉ CABIN OVER THERE?
CAFÉ CABIN
MY GRANDMA LIVES IN CELESTIC. SHE LOVES THE MOOMOO MILK THEY SELL AT CAFÉ CABIN.
SHE TRAVELS A GREAT DISTANCE TO GET IT. I BET SHE'S UPSET THAT SHE HASN'T BEEN ABLE TO COME HERE IN A WHILE.
MOO-MOO MILK!
CYNTHIA!
I'M RIGHT OVER HERE!

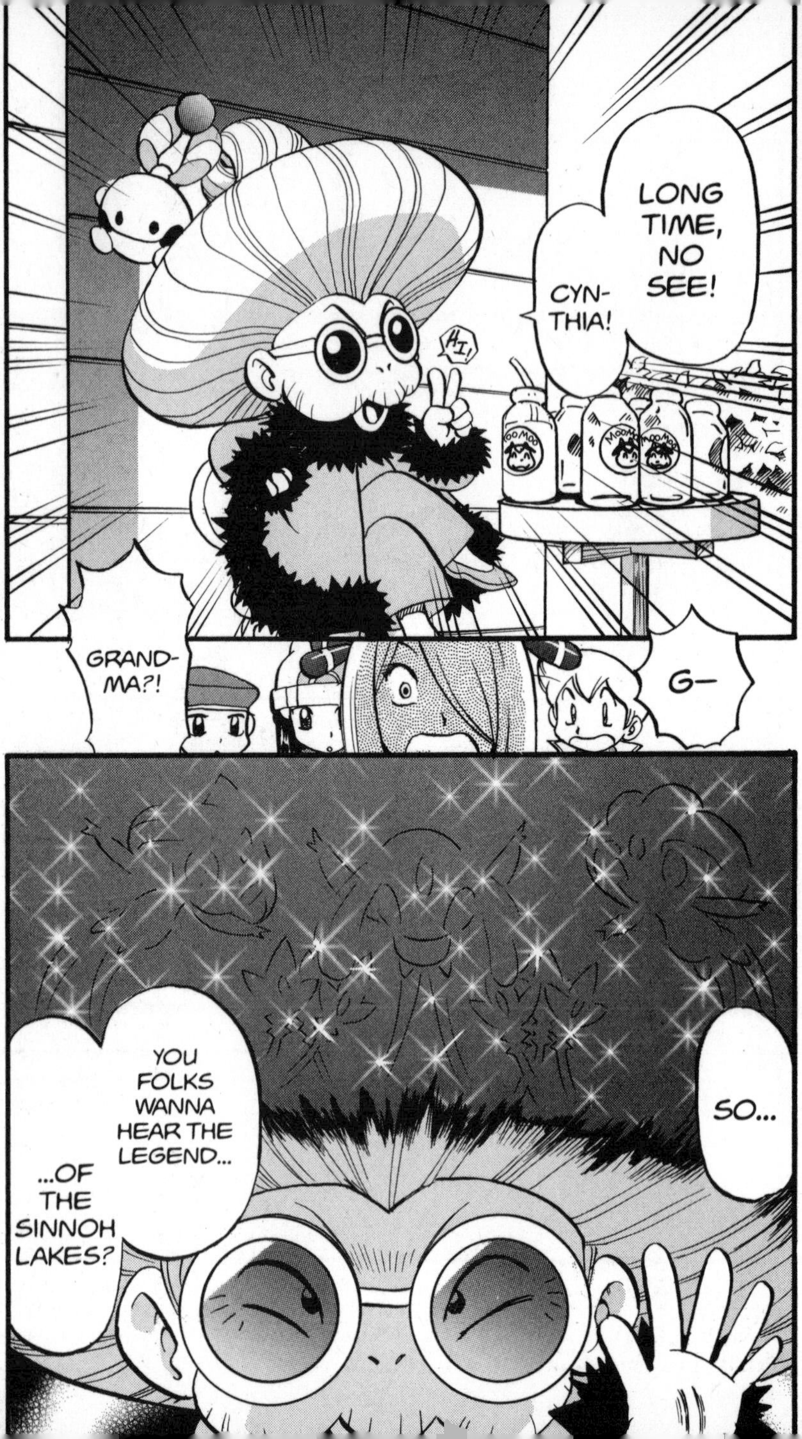
LONG TIME, NO SEE!
CYN-THIA!
HI!
G—
GRAND-MA?!
SO...
YOU FOLKS WANNA HEAR THE LEGEND...
...OF THE SINNOH LAKES?

31

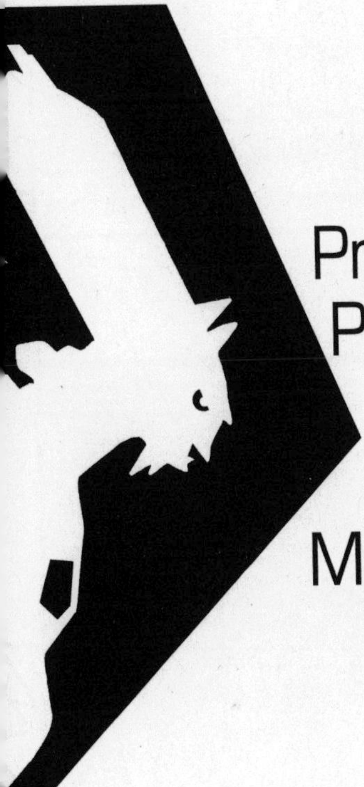

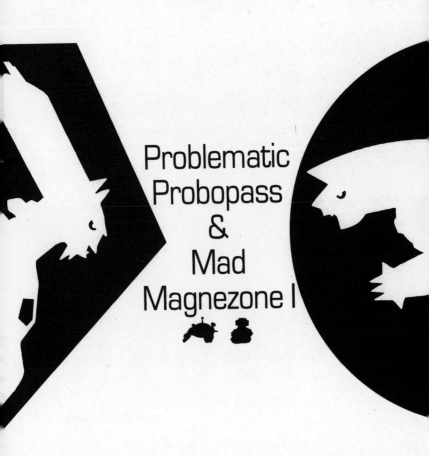

Problematic Probopass & Mad Magnezone I

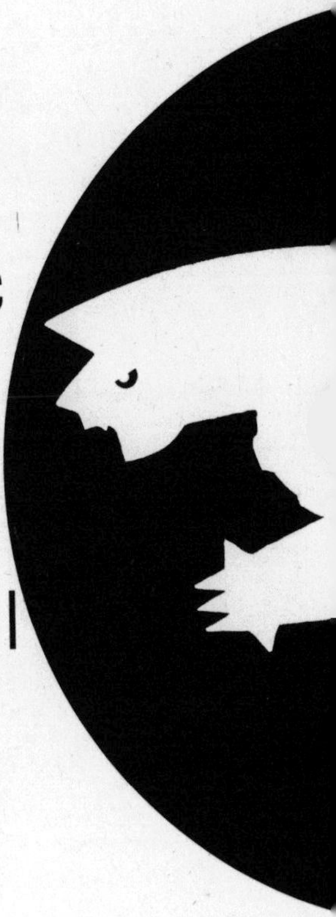

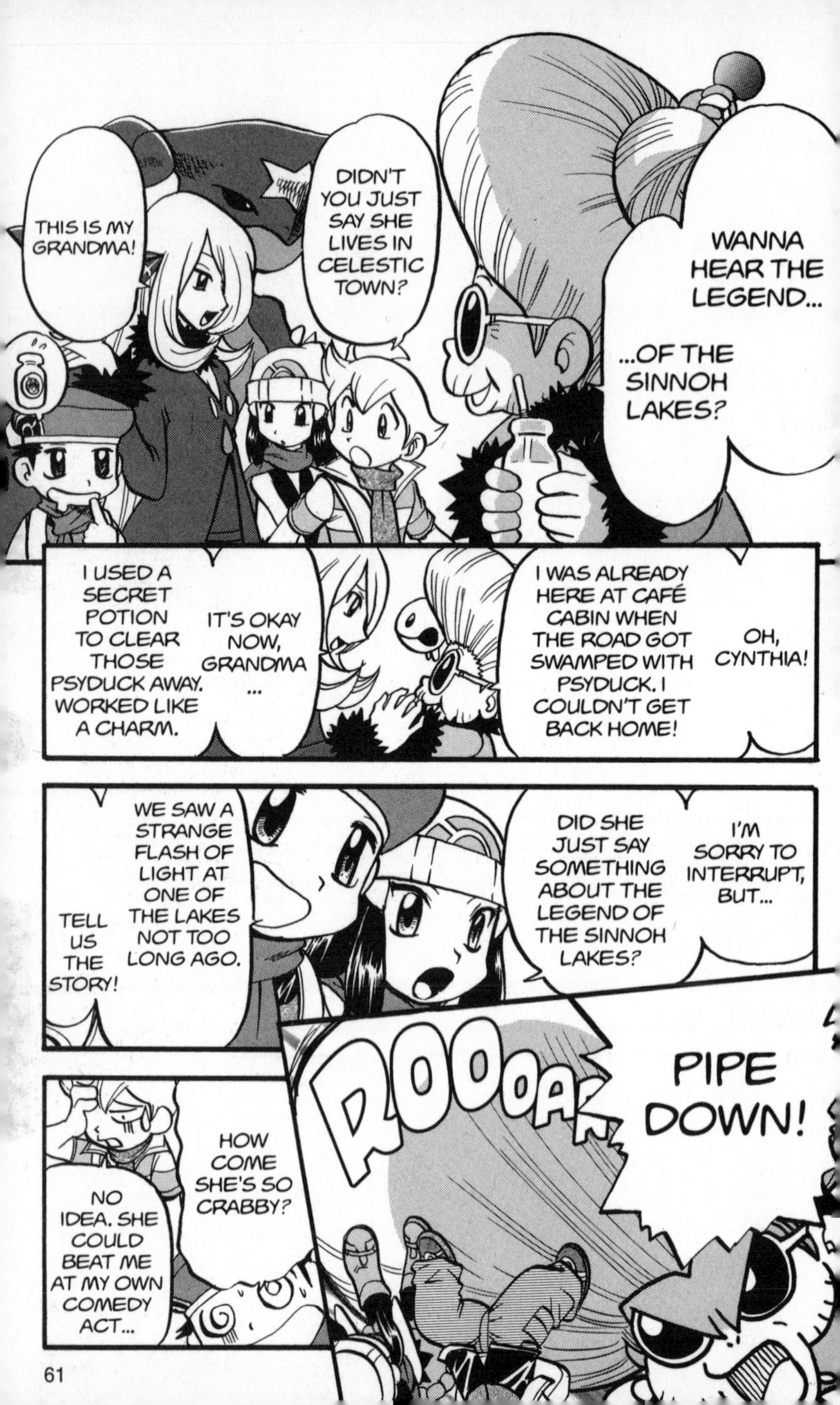
WANNA HEAR THE LEGEND...
...OF THE SINNOH LAKES?
DIDN'T YOU JUST SAY SHE LIVES IN CELESTIC TOWN?
THIS IS MY GRANDMA!
OH, CYNTHIA!
I WAS ALREADY HERE AT CAFÉ CABIN WHEN THE ROAD GOT SWAMPED WITH PSYDUCK. I COULDN'T GET BACK HOME!
IT'S OKAY NOW, GRANDMA...
I USED A SECRET POTION TO CLEAR THOSE PSYDUCK AWAY. WORKED LIKE A CHARM.
I'M SORRY TO INTERRUPT, BUT...
DID SHE JUST SAY SOMETHING ABOUT THE LEGEND OF THE SINNOH LAKES?
WE SAW A STRANGE FLASH OF LIGHT AT ONE OF THE LAKES NOT TOO LONG AGO.
TELL US THE STORY!
ROOOAR
PIPE DOWN!
HOW COME SHE'S SO CRABBY?
NO IDEA. SHE COULD BEAT ME AT MY OWN COMEDY ACT...

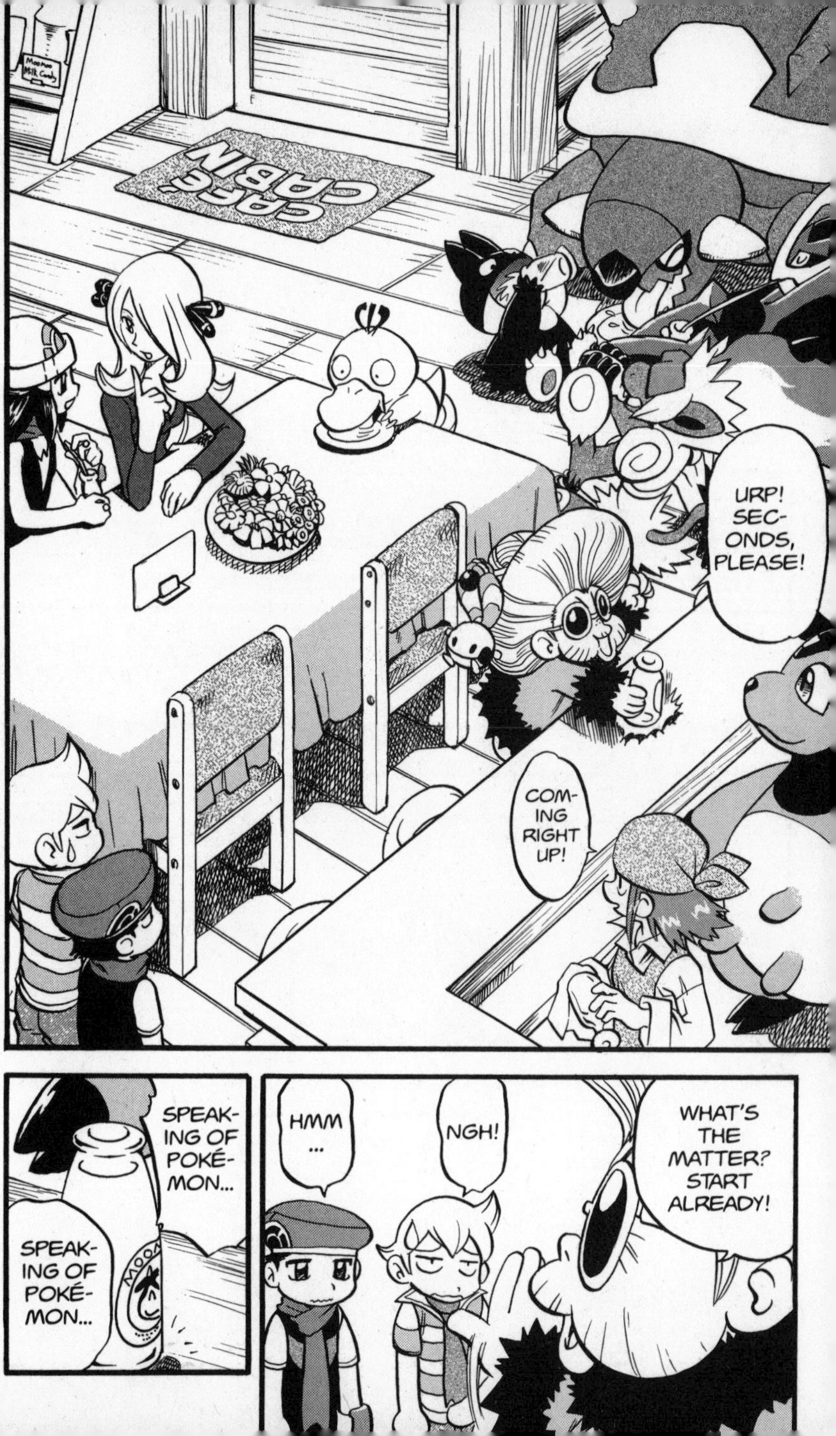
Moomoo Milk Candy
CAFÉ CABIN
URP! SEC-ONDS, PLEASE!
COM-ING RIGHT UP!
WHAT'S THE MATTER? START ALREADY!
NGH!
HMM ...
SPEAK-ING OF POKÉ-MON...
SPEAK-ING OF POKÉ-MON...

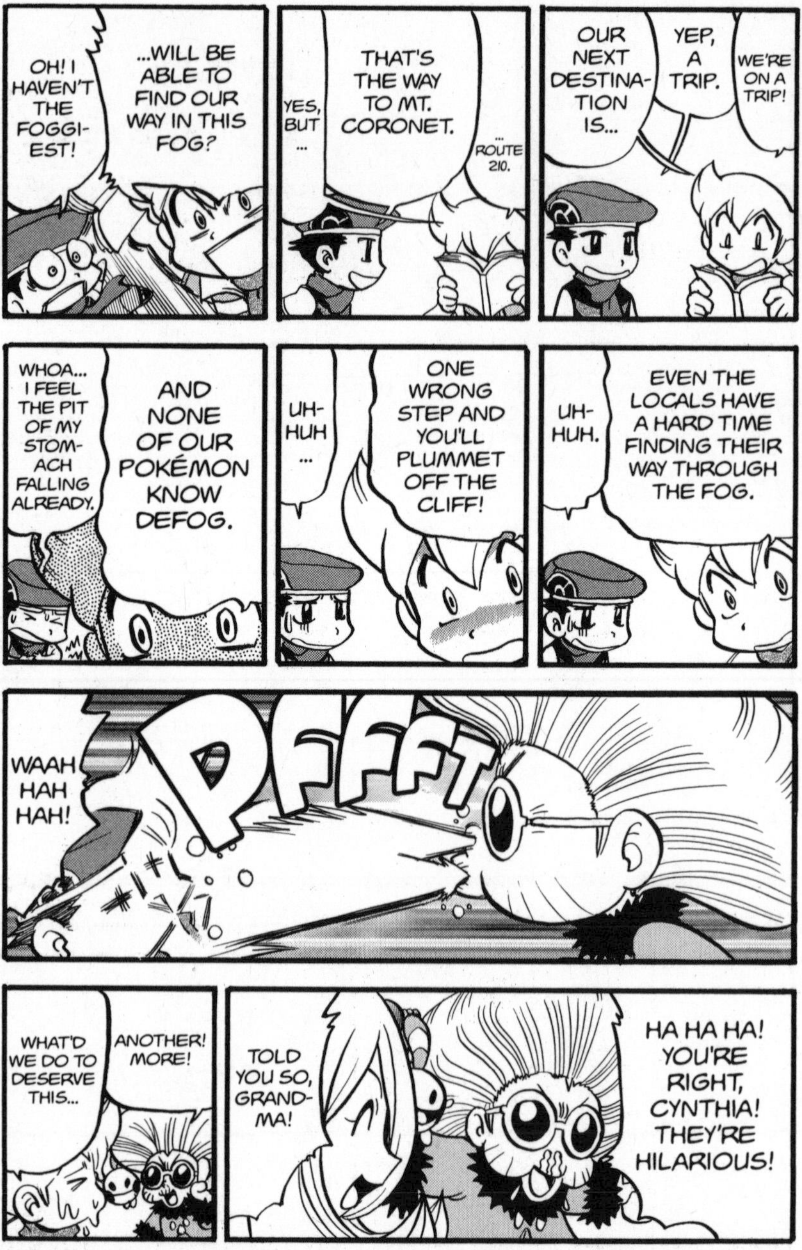
WE'RE ON A TRIP!
YEP, A TRIP.
OUR NEXT DESTINATION IS...
... ROUTE 210.
THAT'S THE WAY TO MT. CORONET.
YES, BUT ...
...WILL BE ABLE TO FIND OUR WAY IN THIS FOG?
OH! I HAVEN'T THE FOGGIEST!
EVEN THE LOCALS HAVE A HARD TIME FINDING THEIR WAY THROUGH THE FOG.
UH-HUH.
ONE WRONG STEP AND YOU'LL PLUMMET OFF THE CLIFF!
UH-HUH ...
AND NONE OF OUR POKÉMON KNOW DEFOG.
WHOA... I FEEL THE PIT OF MY STOMACH FALLING ALREADY.
PFFFT
WAAH HAH HAH!
HA HA HA! YOU'RE RIGHT, CYNTHIA! THEY'RE HILARIOUS!
TOLD YOU SO, GRANDMA!
ANOTHER! MORE!
WHAT'D WE DO TO DESERVE THIS...

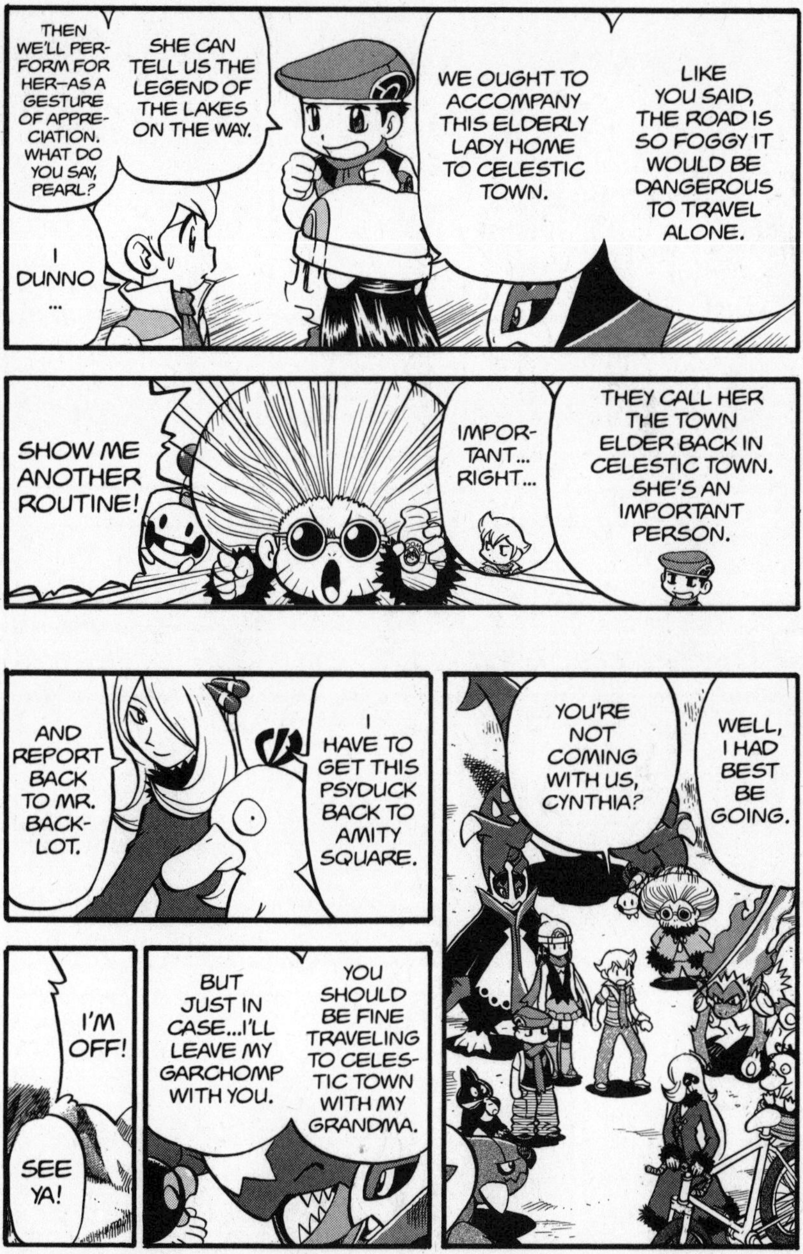
LIKE YOU SAID, THE ROAD IS SO FOGGY IT WOULD BE DANGEROUS TO TRAVEL ALONE.
WE OUGHT TO ACCOMPANY THIS ELDERLY LADY HOME TO CELESTIC TOWN.
SHE CAN TELL US THE LEGEND OF THE LAKES ON THE WAY.
THEN WE'LL PERFORM FOR HER—AS A GESTURE OF APPRECIATION. WHAT DO YOU SAY, PEARL?
I DUNNO ...
THEY CALL HER THE TOWN ELDER BACK IN CELESTIC TOWN. SHE'S AN IMPORTANT PERSON.
IMPORTANT... RIGHT...
SHOW ME ANOTHER ROUTINE!
WELL, I HAD BEST BE GOING.
YOU'RE NOT COMING WITH US, CYNTHIA?
I HAVE TO GET THIS PSYDUCK BACK TO AMITY SQUARE.
AND REPORT BACK TO MR. BACKLOT.
YOU SHOULD BE FINE TRAVELING TO CELESTIC TOWN WITH MY GRANDMA.
BUT JUST IN CASE...I'LL LEAVE MY GARCHOMP WITH YOU.
I'M OFF!
SEE YA!

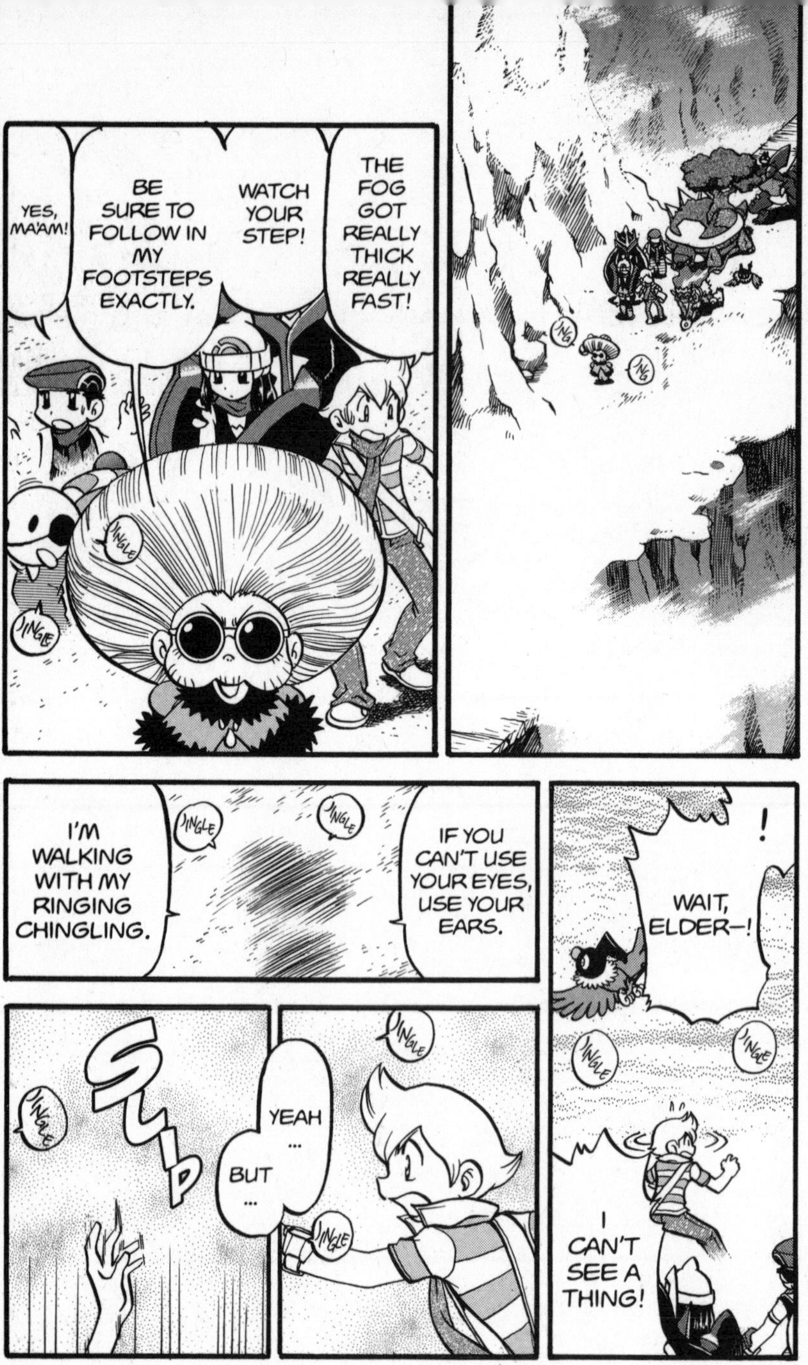
JING
JING
THE FOG GOT REALLY THICK REALLY FAST!
WATCH YOUR STEP!
BE SURE TO FOLLOW IN MY FOOTSTEPS EXACTLY.
YES, MA'AM!
JINGLE
JINGLE
!
WAIT, ELDER—!
JINGLE
JINGLE
I CAN'T SEE A THING!
IF YOU CAN'T USE YOUR EYES, USE YOUR EARS.
JINGLE
JINGLE
I'M WALKING WITH MY RINGING CHINGLING.
JINGLE
YEAH... BUT...
JINGLE
SLIP
JINGLE

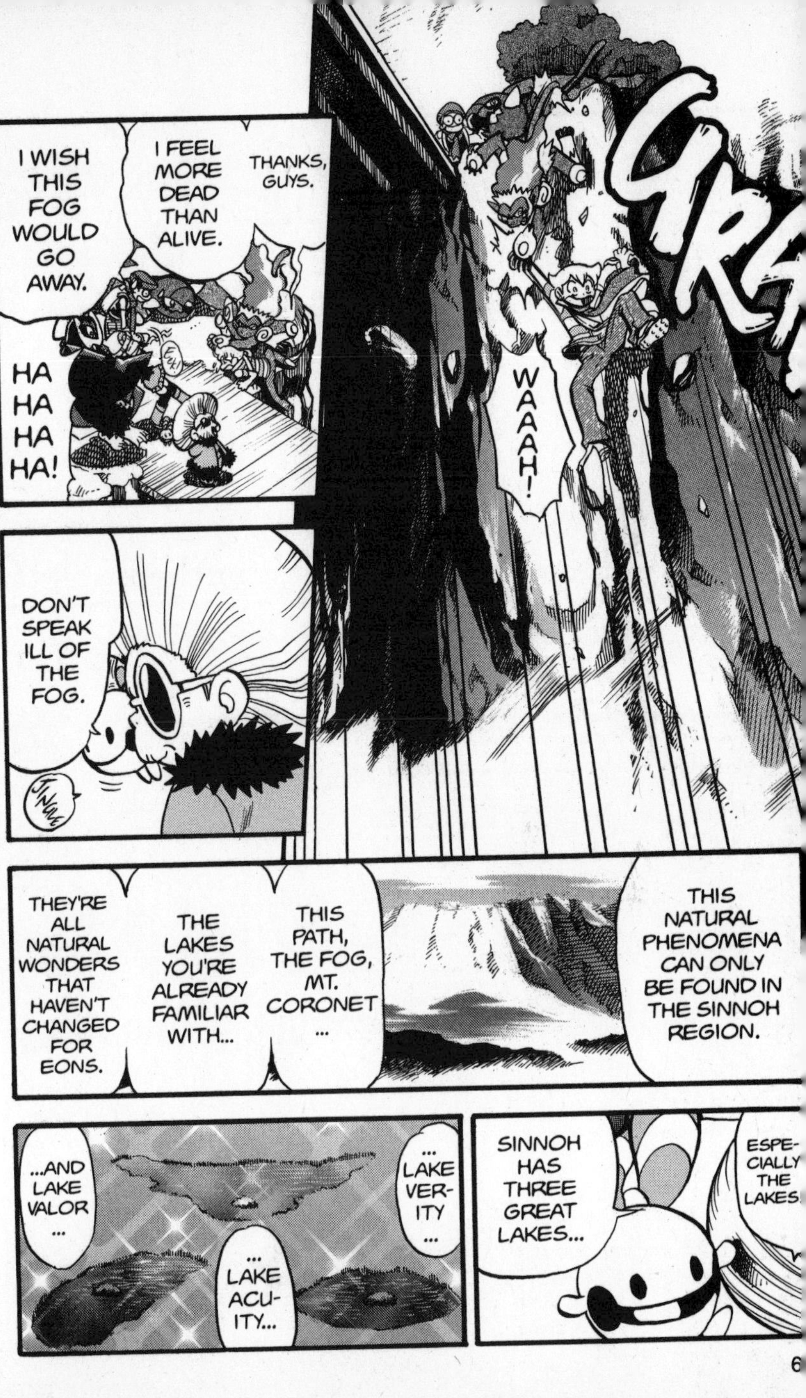
WAAAH!
THANKS, GUYS.
I FEEL MORE DEAD THAN ALIVE.
I WISH THIS FOG WOULD GO AWAY.
HA HA HA HA HA!
DON'T SPEAK ILL OF THE FOG.
THIS NATURAL PHENOMENA CAN ONLY BE FOUND IN THE SINNOH REGION.
THIS PATH, THE FOG, MT. CORONET...
THE LAKES YOU'RE ALREADY FAMILIAR WITH...
THEY'RE ALL NATURAL WONDERS THAT HAVEN'T CHANGED FOR EONS.
ESPE-CIALLY THE LAKES.
SINNOH HAS THREE GREAT LAKES...
...LAKE VER-ITY...
...LAKE ACU-ITY...
...AND LAKE VALOR...

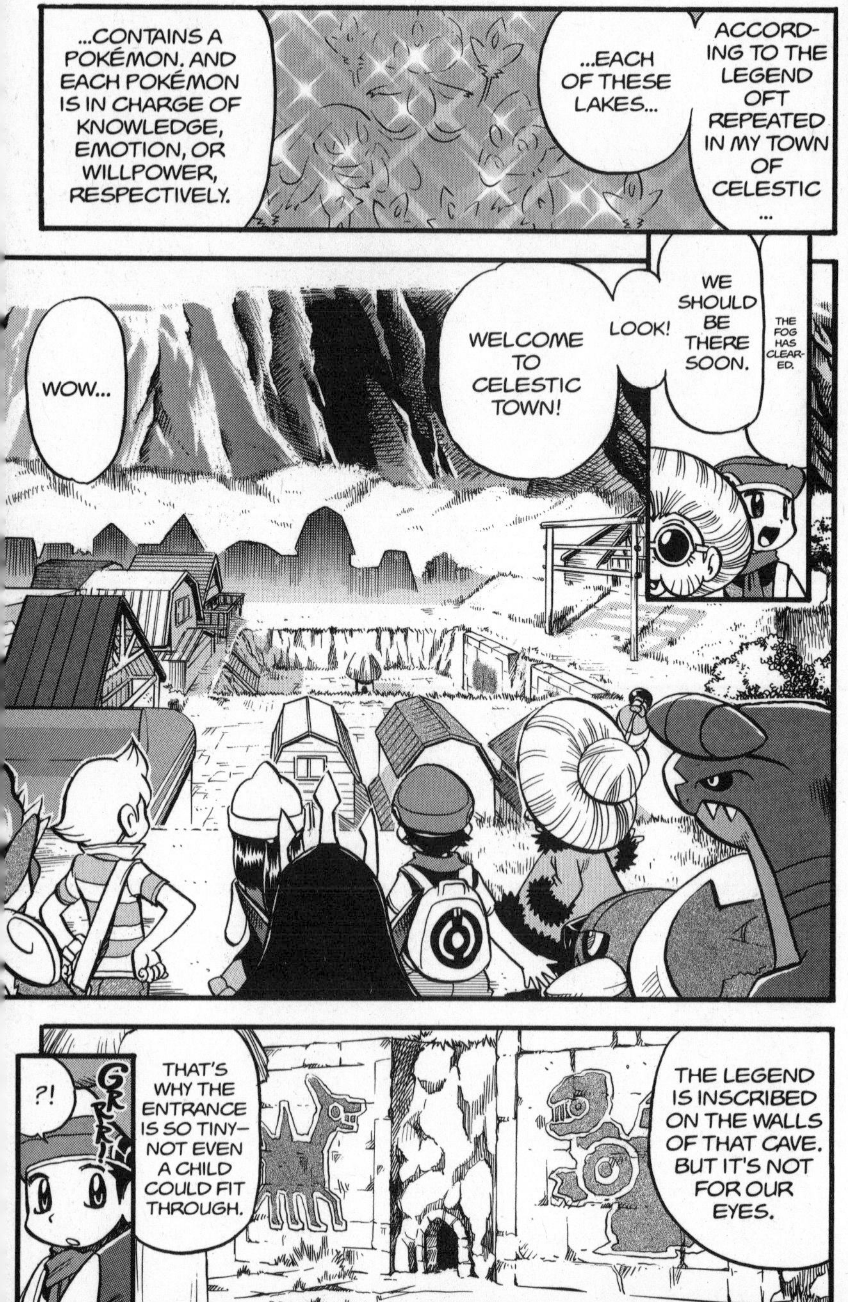

ACCORDING TO THE LEGEND OFT REPEATED IN MY TOWN OF CELESTIC...
...EACH OF THESE LAKES...
...CONTAINS A POKÉMON. AND EACH POKÉMON IS IN CHARGE OF KNOWLEDGE, EMOTION, OR WILLPOWER, RESPECTIVELY.
THE FOG HAS CLEARED.
WE SHOULD BE THERE SOON.
LOOK!
WELCOME TO CELESTIC TOWN!
WOW...
THE LEGEND IS INSCRIBED ON THE WALLS OF THAT CAVE. BUT IT'S NOT FOR OUR EYES.
THAT'S WHY THE ENTRANCE IS SO TINY—NOT EVEN A CHILD COULD FIT THROUGH.
GRRR!!
?!

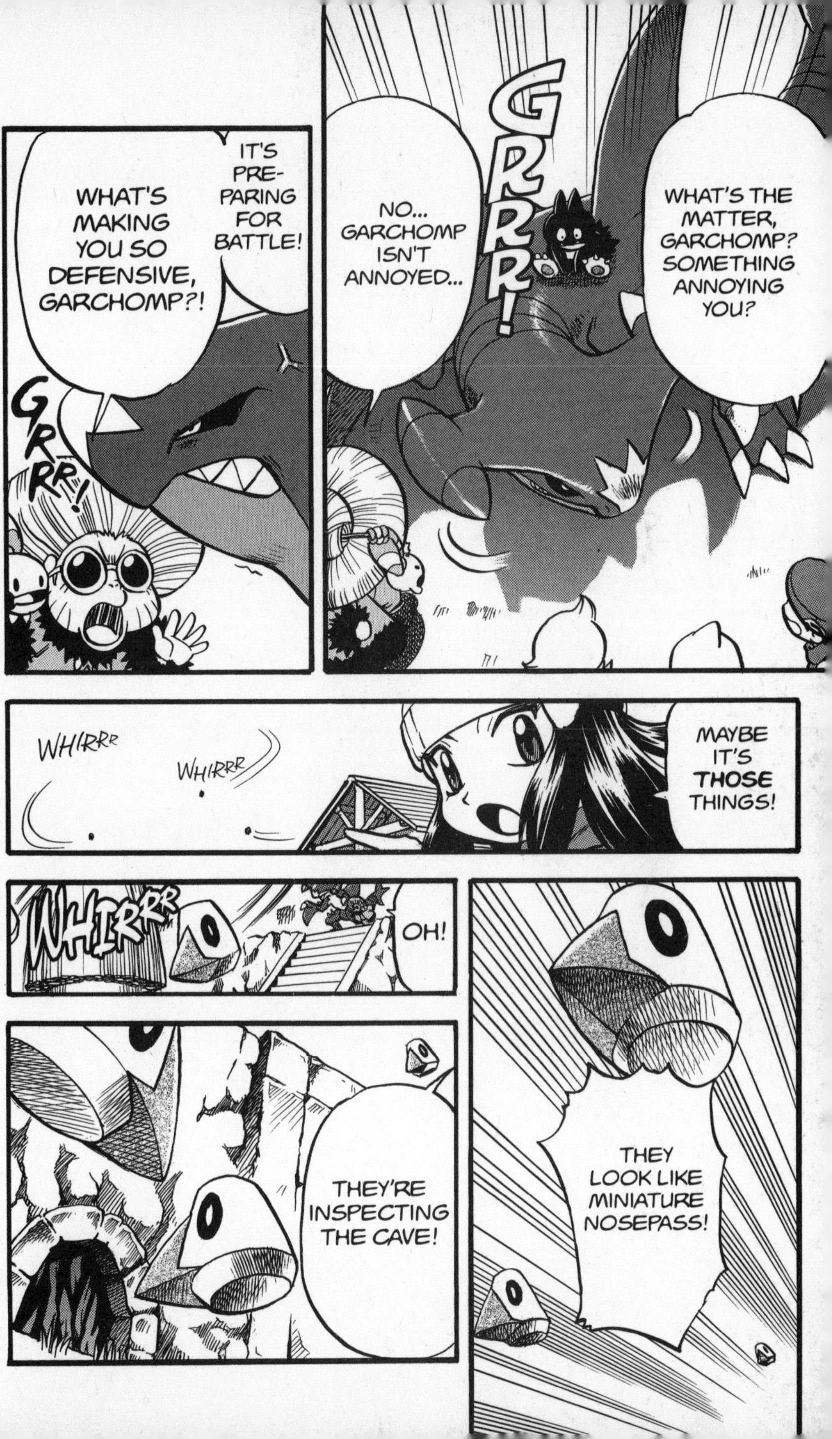
GRRR!
WHAT'S THE MATTER, GARCHOMP? SOMETHING ANNOYING YOU?
NO... GARCHOMP ISN'T ANNOYED...
IT'S PRE-PARING FOR BATTLE!
WHAT'S MAKING YOU SO DEFENSIVE, GARCHOMP?!
GRRR!
MAYBE IT'S **THOSE** THINGS!
WHIRRR
WHIRRR
THEY LOOK LIKE MINIATURE NOSEPASS!
OH!
WHIRRR
THEY'RE INSPECTING THE CAVE!

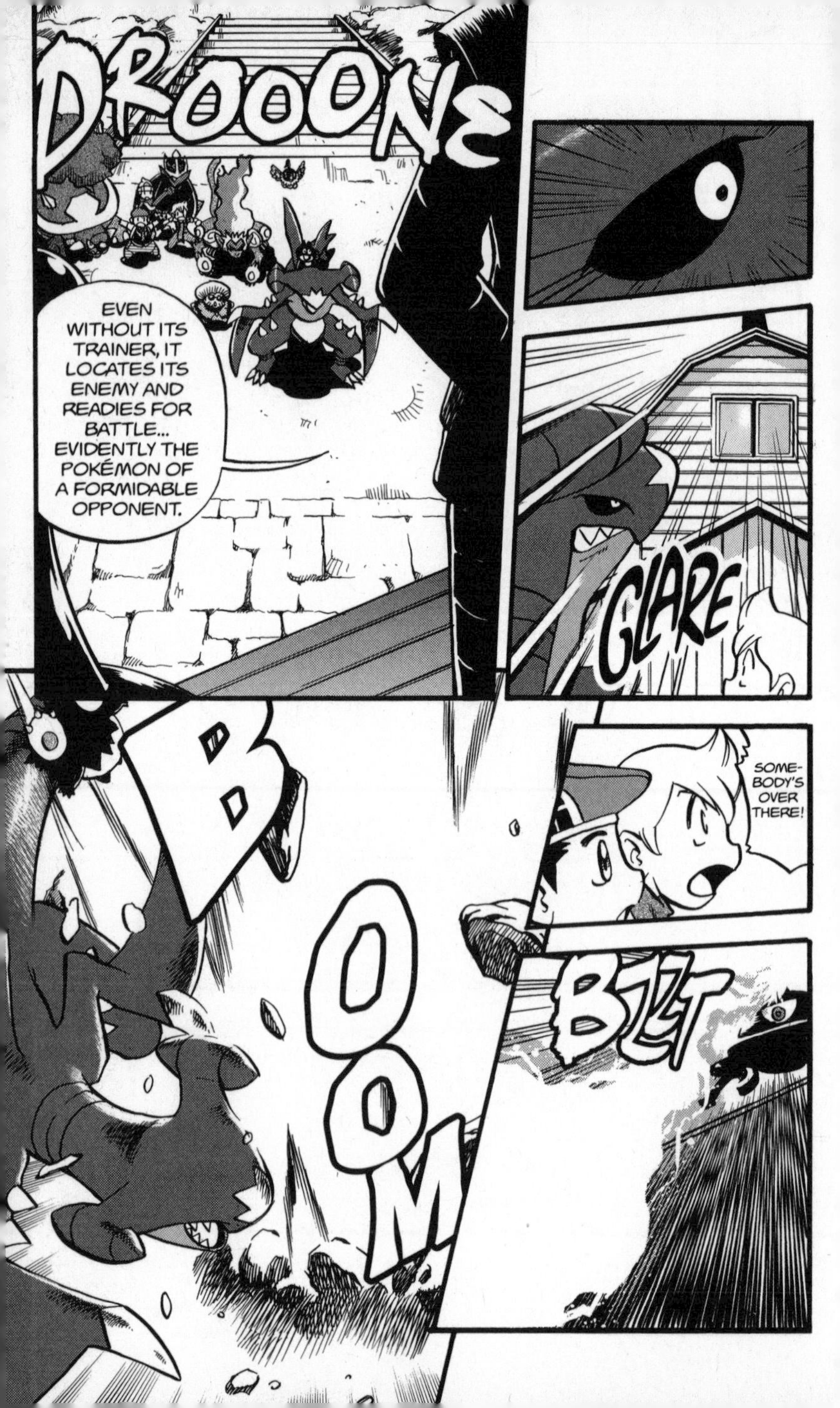
GLARE
DROOONE
EVEN WITHOUT ITS TRAINER, IT LOCATES ITS ENEMY AND READIES FOR BATTLE... EVIDENTLY THE POKÉMON OF A FORMIDABLE OPPONENT.
SOME-BODY'S OVER THERE!
BZZT
BOOOM

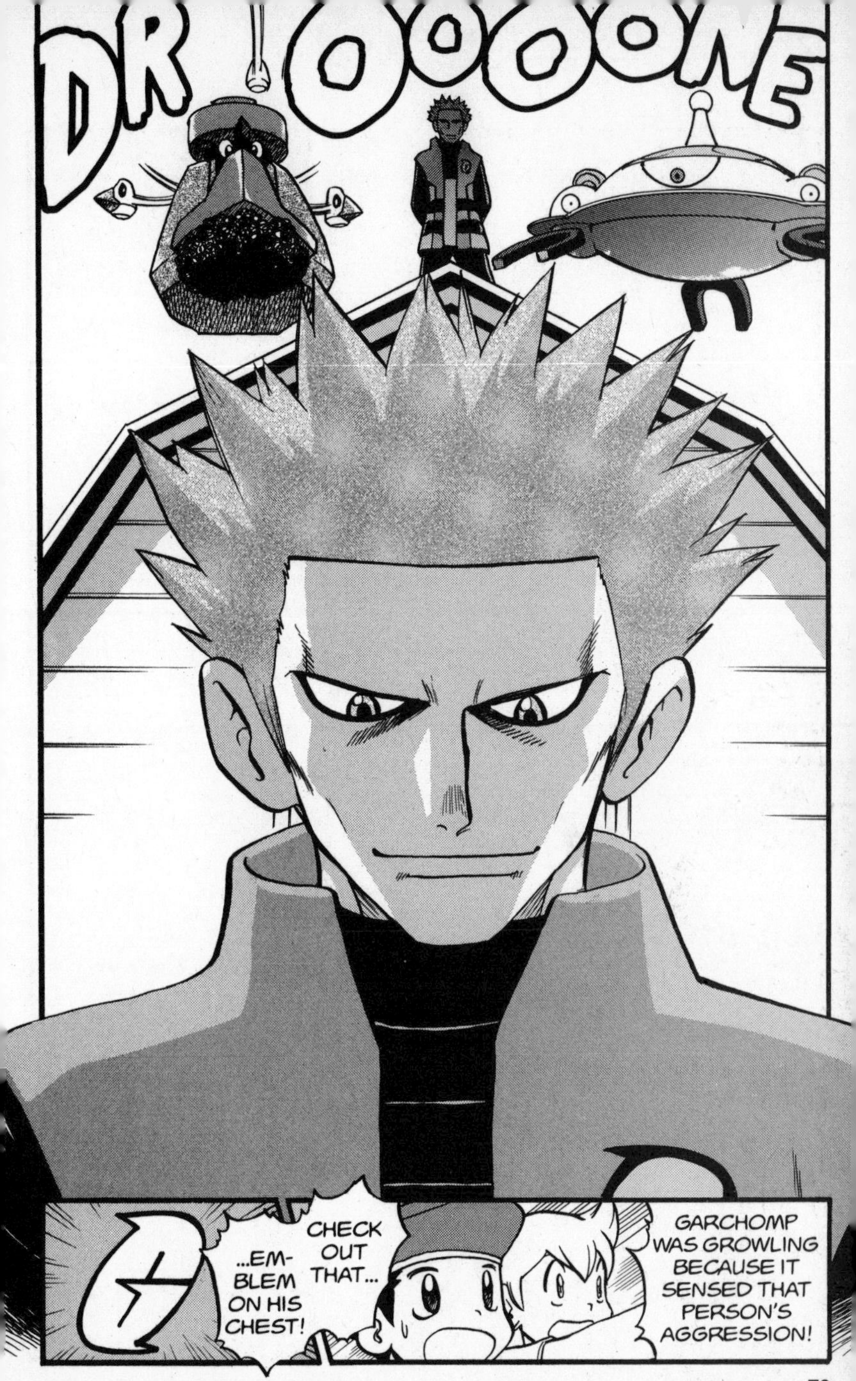
DROOOONE
GARCHOMP WAS GROWLING BECAUSE IT SENSED THAT PERSON'S AGGRESSION!
CHECK OUT THAT...
...EM-BLEM ON HIS CHEST!

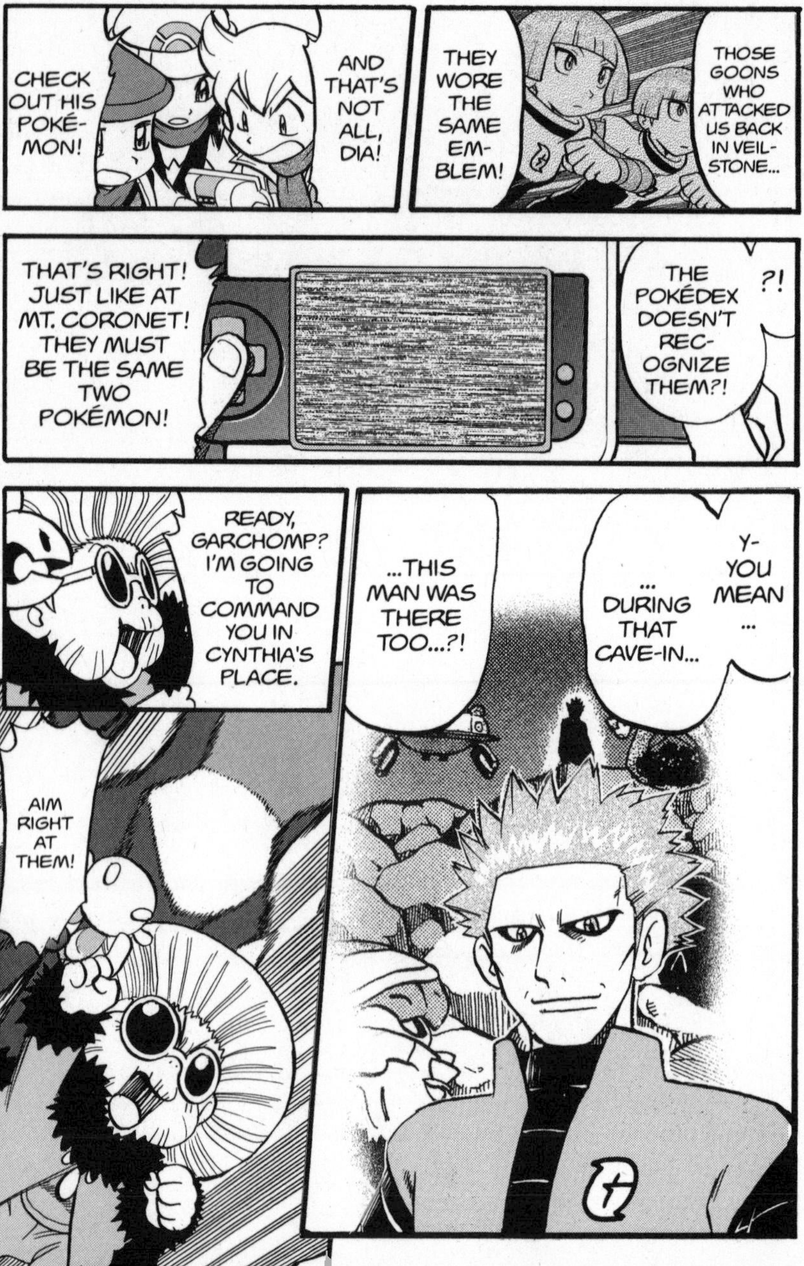
THOSE GOONS WHO ATTACKED US BACK IN VEILSTONE...
THEY WORE THE SAME EMBLEM!
AND THAT'S NOT ALL, DIA!
CHECK OUT HIS POKÉMON!
?!
THE POKÉDEX DOESN'T RECOGNIZE THEM?!
THAT'S RIGHT! JUST LIKE AT MT. CORONET! THEY MUST BE THE SAME TWO POKÉMON!
Y-YOU MEAN...
...DURING THAT CAVE-IN...
...THIS MAN WAS THERE TOO...?!
READY, GARCHOMP? I'M GOING TO COMMAND YOU IN CYNTHIA'S PLACE.
AIM RIGHT AT THEM!

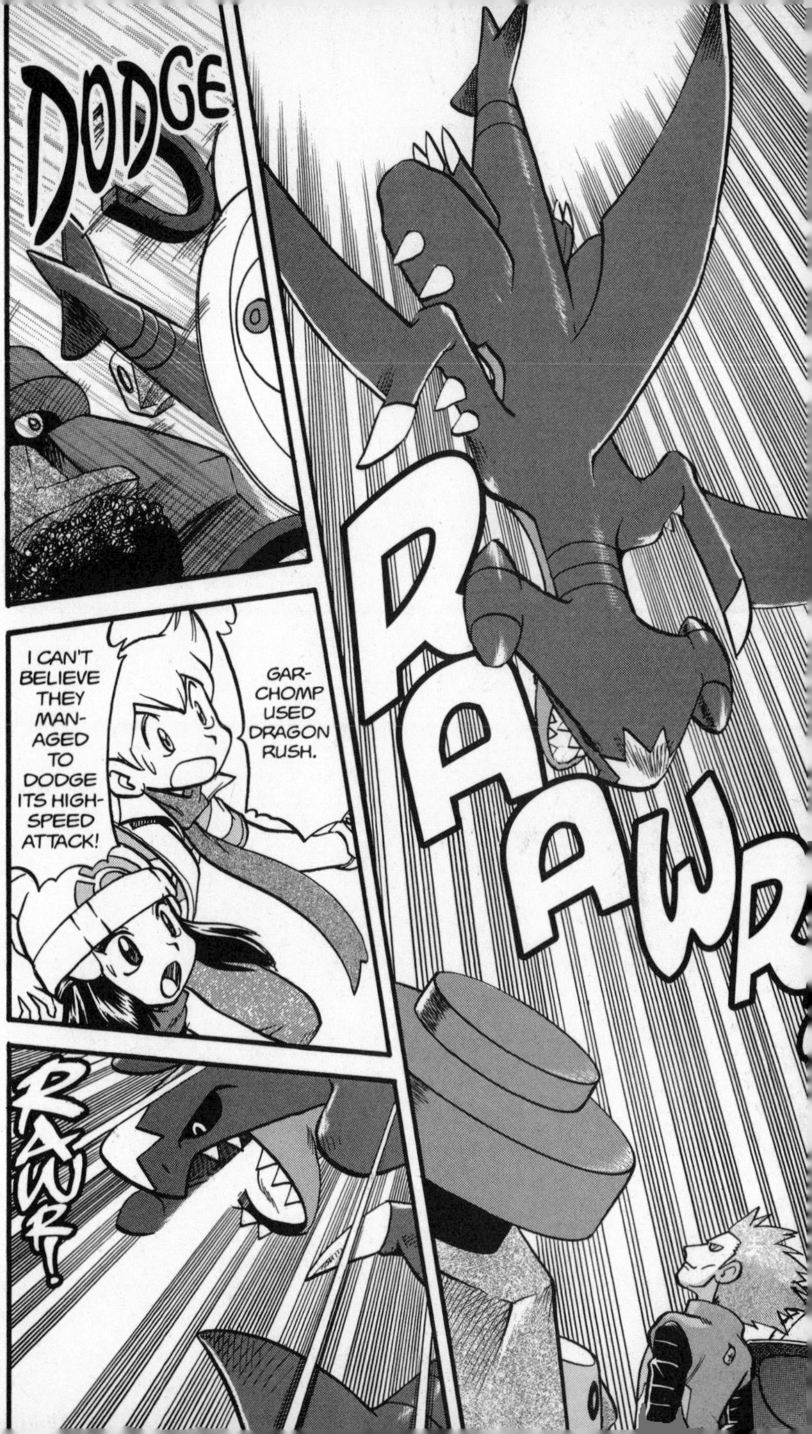
RAAWR
DODGE
GARCHOMP USED DRAGON RUSH.
I CAN'T BELIEVE THEY MANAGED TO DODGE ITS HIGH-SPEED ATTACK!
RAWR!

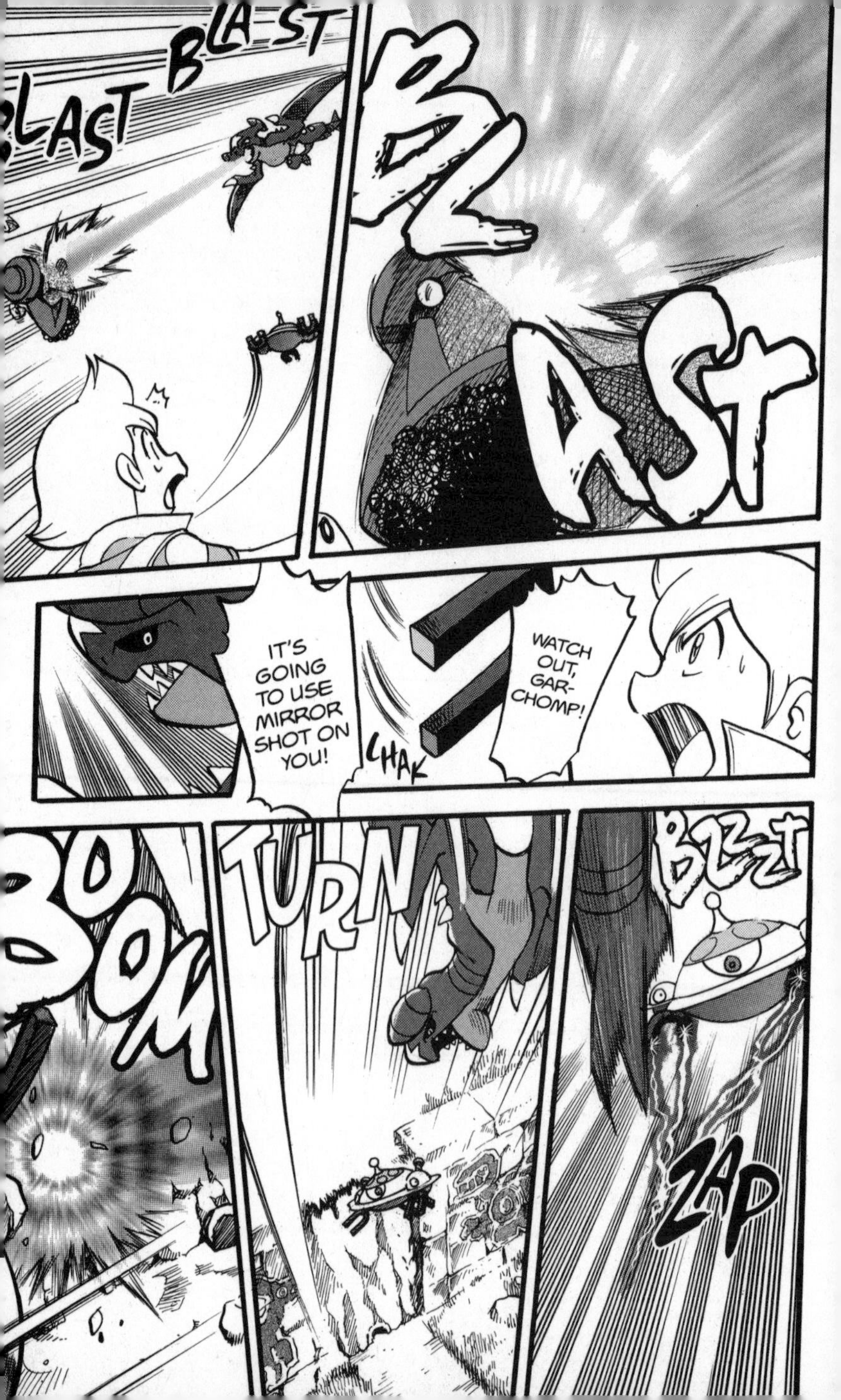
BLAST
BLAST BLAST
WATCH OUT, GAR-CHOMP!
CHAK
IT'S GOING TO USE MIRROR SHOT ON YOU!
BZZT
ZAP
TURN
BOOM

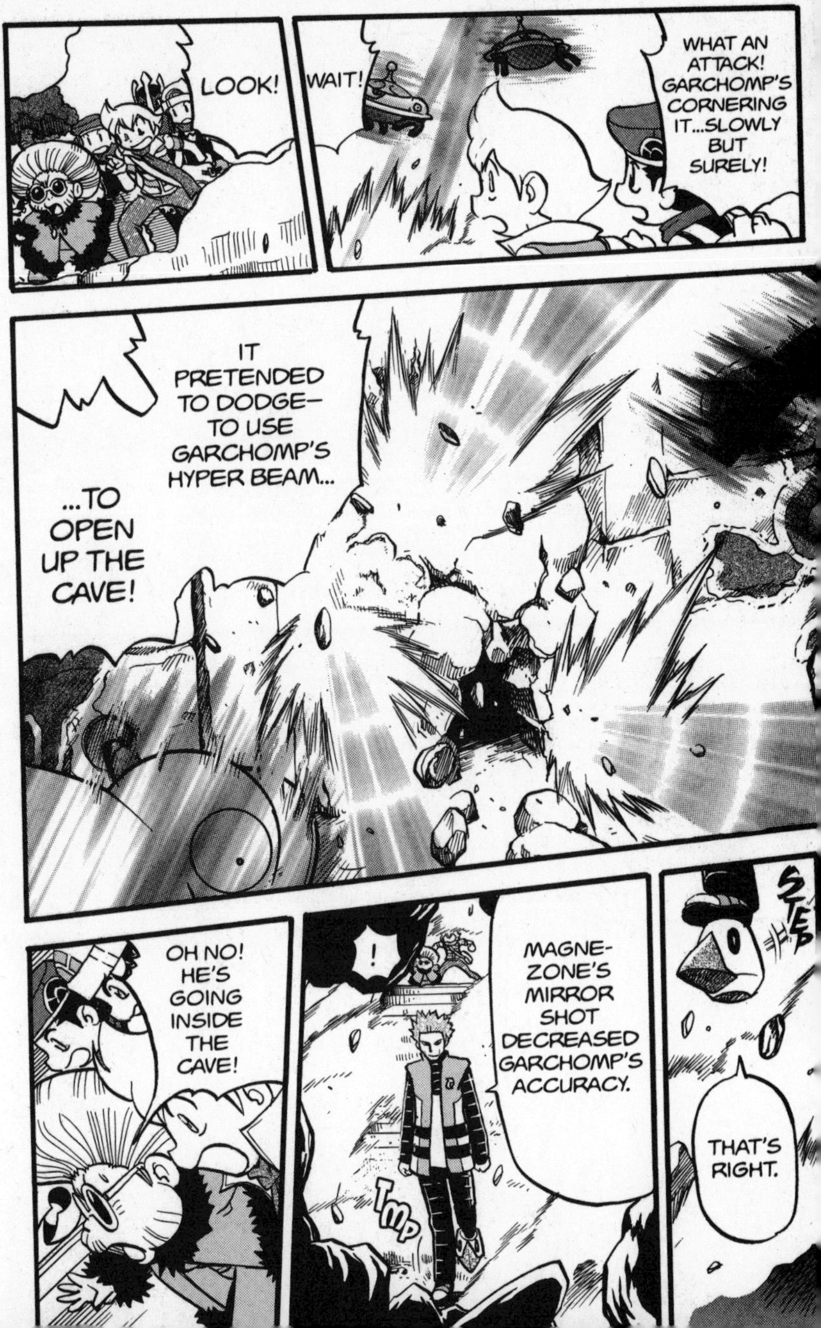
WHAT AN ATTACK! GARCHOMP'S CORNERING IT...SLOWLY BUT SURELY!
WAIT!
LOOK!
IT PRETENDED TO DODGE— TO USE GARCHOMP'S HYPER BEAM...
...TO OPEN UP THE CAVE!
STEP
THAT'S RIGHT.
MAGNE-ZONE'S MIRROR SHOT DECREASED GARCHOMP'S ACCURACY.
!
TMP
OH NO! HE'S GOING INSIDE THE CAVE!

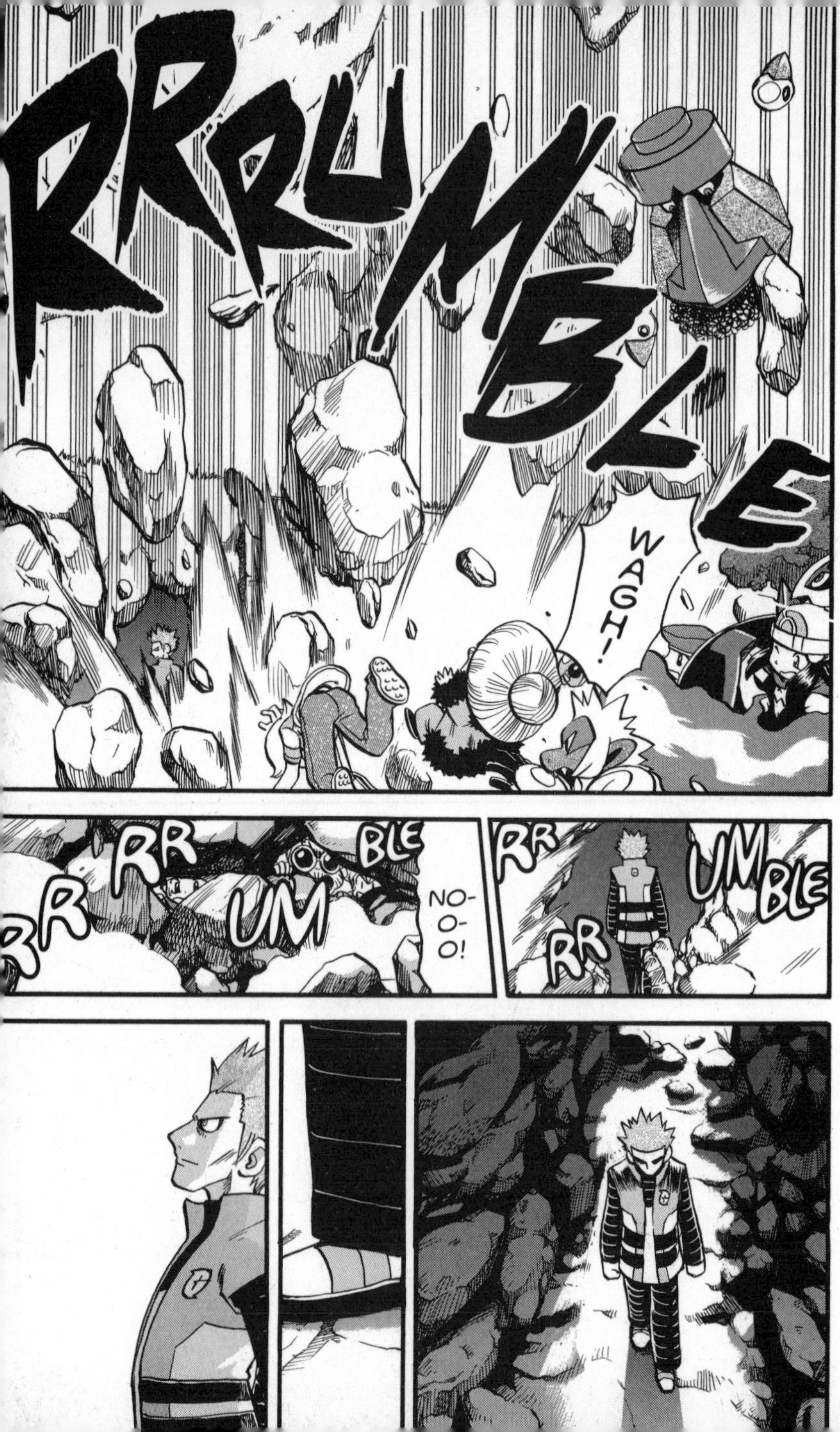
RRRUMBLE
WAGH!
RR UMBLE RR
RR RR UM BLE
NO-O-O!

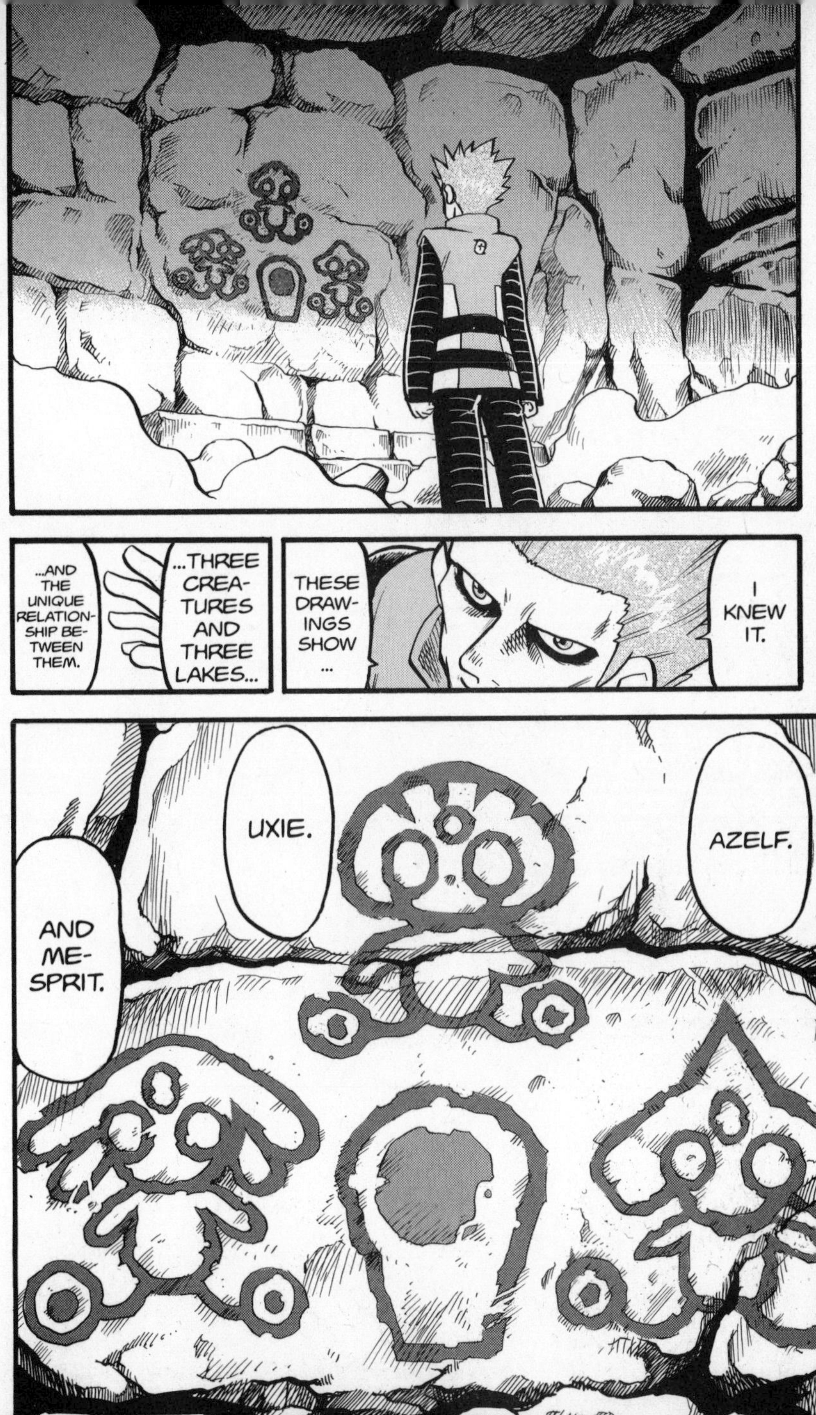

I KNEW IT.
THESE DRAWINGS SHOW...
...THREE CREATURES AND THREE LAKES...
...AND THE UNIQUE RELATIONSHIP BETWEEN THEM.
AZELF.
UXIE.
AND MESPRIT.

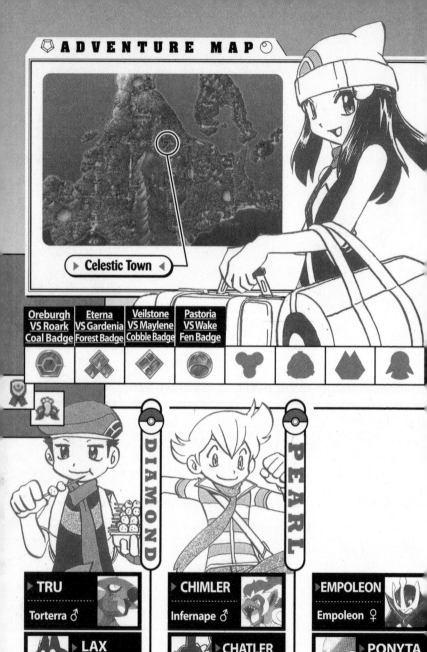

◇ ADVENTURE MAP ○

▶ Celestic Town ◀

Oreburgh VS Roark Coal Badge	Eterna VS Gardenia Forest Badge	Veilstone VS Maylene Cobble Badge	Pastoria VS Wake Fen Badge				

DIAMOND

PEARL

▶ TRU
Torterra ♂

LAX ◀
Munchlax ♂

▶ CHIMLER
Infernape ♂

CHATLER ◀
Chatot ♂

▶ EMPOLEON
Empoleon ♀

PONYTA ◀
Ponyta ♂

32

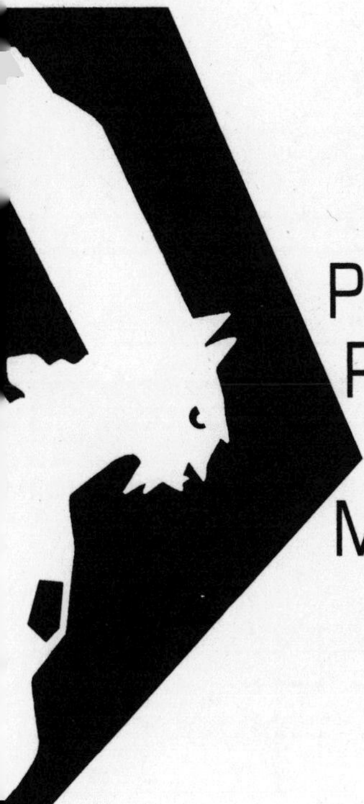

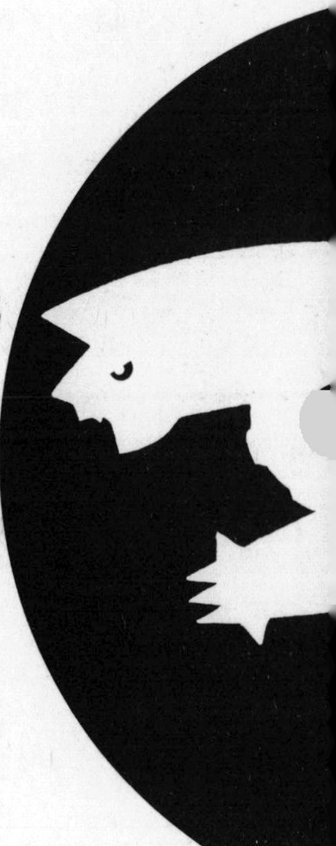

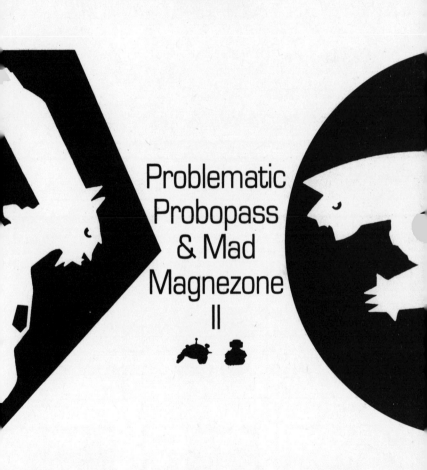

Problematic Probopass & Mad Magnezone II

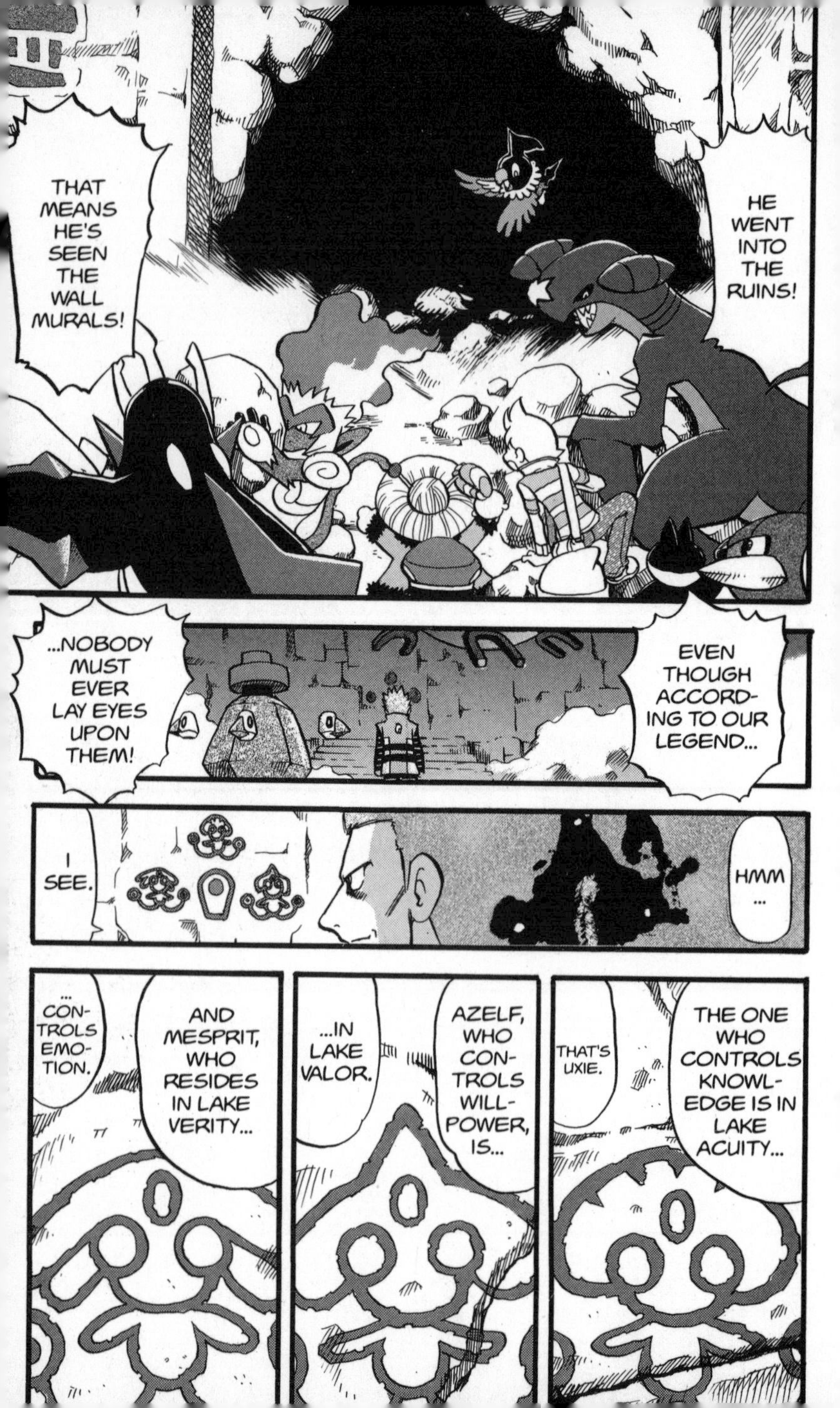
HE WENT INTO THE RUINS!
THAT MEANS HE'S SEEN THE WALL MURALS!
EVEN THOUGH ACCORDING TO OUR LEGEND...
...NOBODY MUST EVER LAY EYES UPON THEM!
HMM...
I SEE.
THE ONE WHO CONTROLS KNOWLEDGE IS IN LAKE ACUITY...
THAT'S UXIE.
AZELF, WHO CONTROLS WILLPOWER, IS...
...IN LAKE VALOR.
AND MESPRIT, WHO RESIDES IN LAKE VERITY...
...CONTROLS EMOTION.

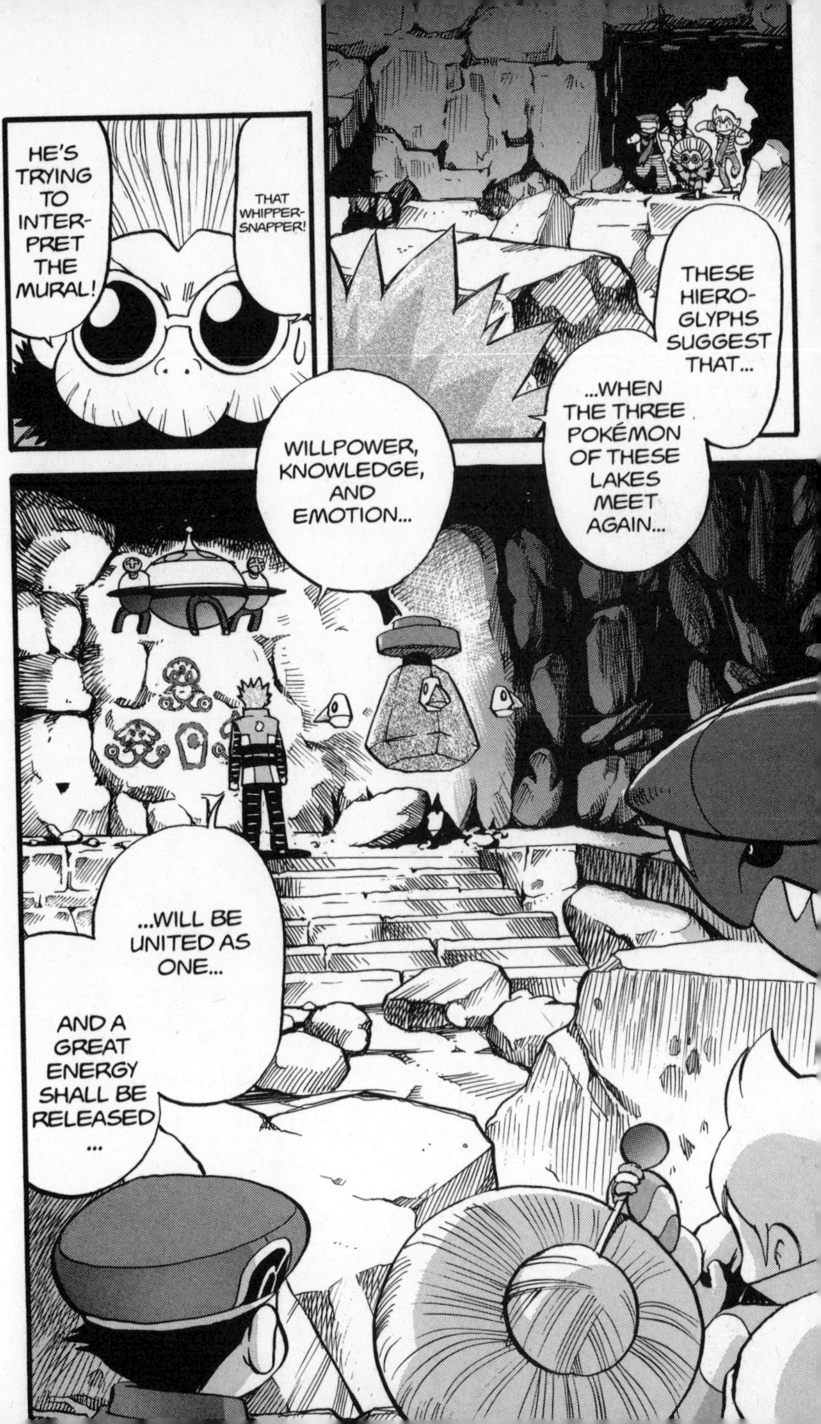
THESE HIEROGLYPHS SUGGEST THAT...
...WHEN THE THREE POKéMON OF THESE LAKES MEET AGAIN...
HE'S TRYING TO INTERPRET THE MURAL!
THAT WHIPPER-SNAPPER!
WILLPOWER, KNOWLEDGE, AND EMOTION...
...WILL BE UNITED AS ONE...
AND A GREAT ENERGY SHALL BE RELEASED ...

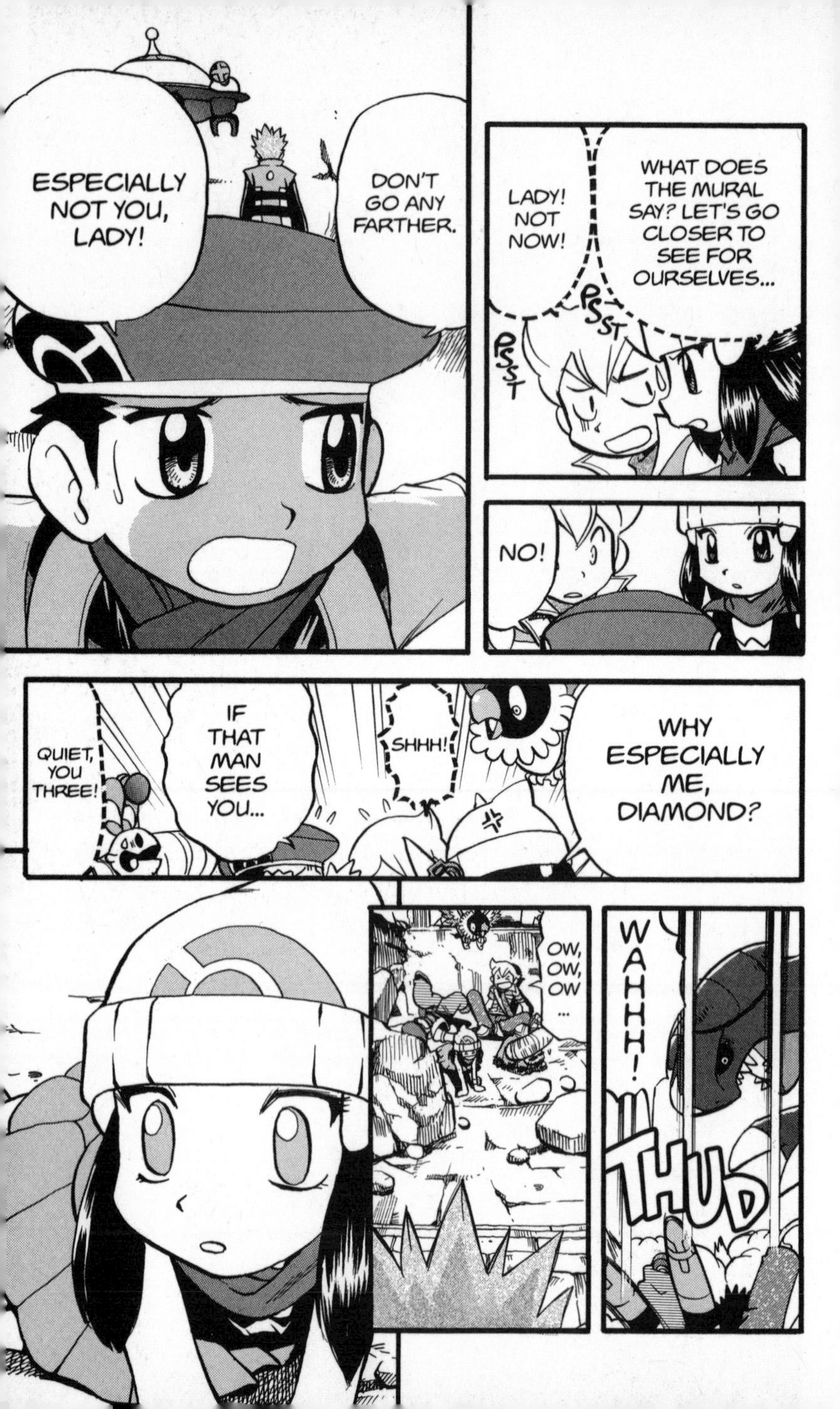
WHAT DOES THE MURAL SAY? LET'S GO CLOSER TO SEE FOR OURSELVES...
LADY! NOT NOW!
PSSST
PSSST
NO!
DON'T GO ANY FARTHER.
ESPECIALLY NOT YOU, LADY!
WHY ESPECIALLY ME, DIAMOND?
SHHH!
IF THAT MAN SEES YOU...
QUIET, YOU THREE!
WAHHH!
THUD
OW, OW, OW ...

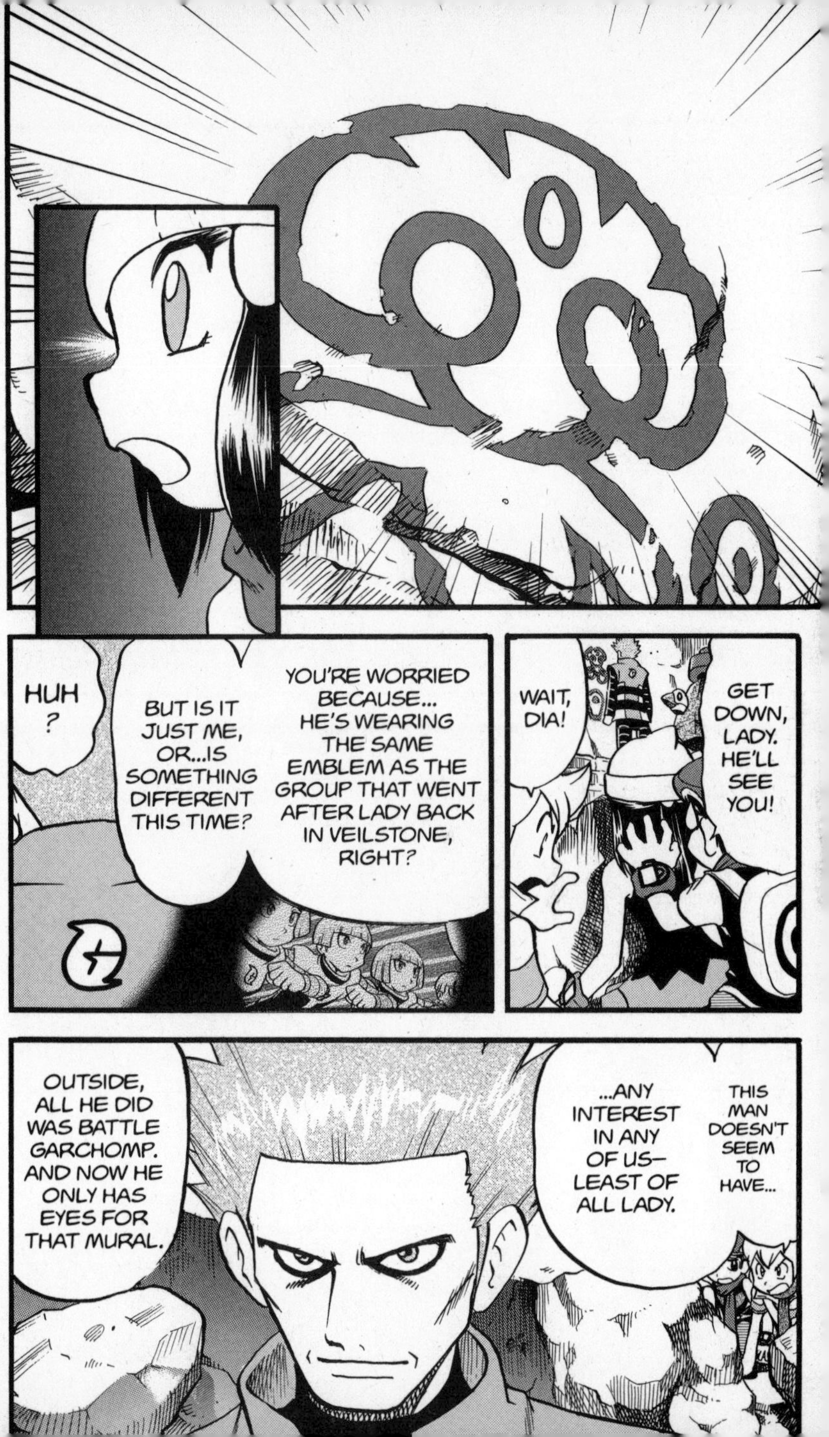
GET DOWN, LADY. HE'LL SEE YOU!
WAIT, DIA!
YOU'RE WORRIED BECAUSE... HE'S WEARING THE SAME EMBLEM AS THE GROUP THAT WENT AFTER LADY BACK IN VEILSTONE, RIGHT?
BUT IS IT JUST ME, OR...IS SOMETHING DIFFERENT THIS TIME?
HUH ?
THIS MAN DOESN'T SEEM TO HAVE...
...ANY INTEREST IN ANY OF US— LEAST OF ALL LADY.
OUTSIDE, ALL HE DID WAS BATTLE GARCHOMP. AND NOW HE ONLY HAS EYES FOR THAT MURAL.

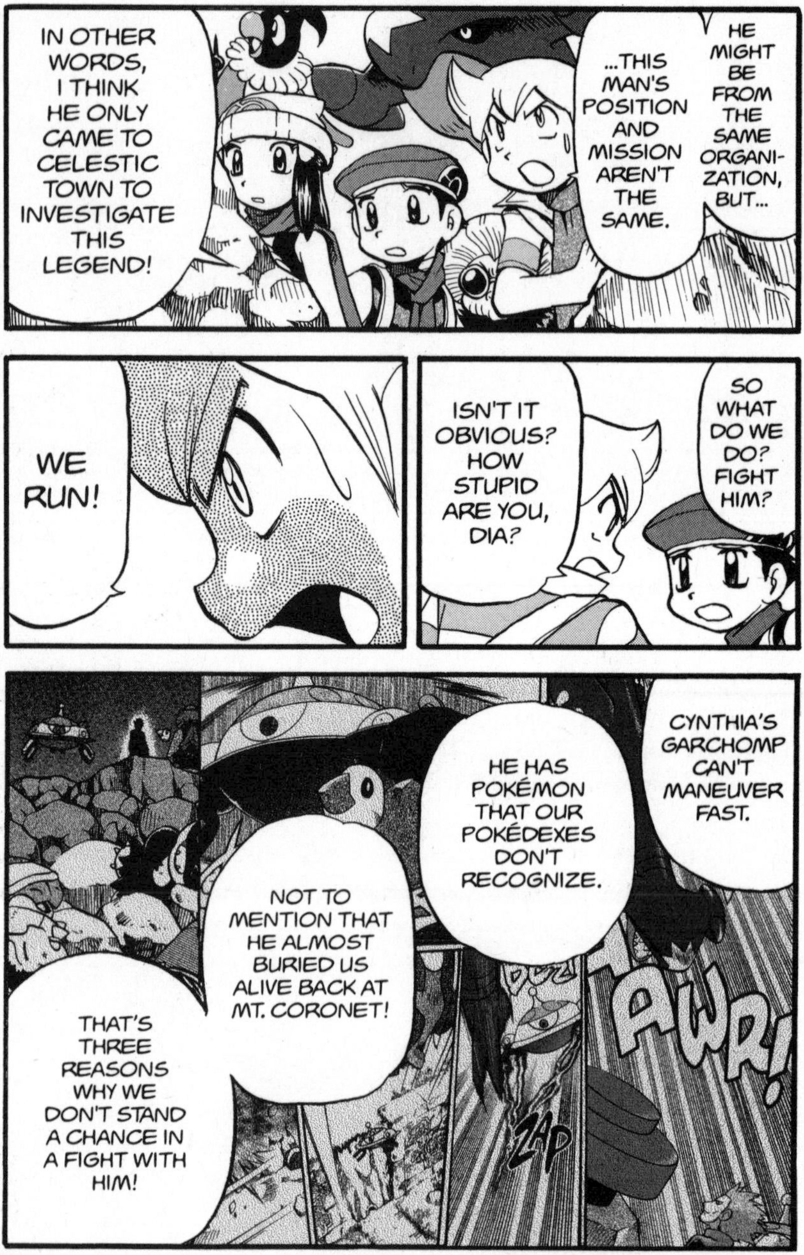
HE MIGHT BE FROM THE SAME ORGANIZATION, BUT...
...THIS MAN'S POSITION AND MISSION AREN'T THE SAME.
IN OTHER WORDS, I THINK HE ONLY CAME TO CELESTIC TOWN TO INVESTIGATE THIS LEGEND!
SO WHAT DO WE DO? FIGHT HIM?
ISN'T IT OBVIOUS? HOW STUPID ARE YOU, DIA?
WE RUN!
CYNTHIA'S GARCHOMP CAN'T MANEUVER FAST.
HE HAS POKÉMON THAT OUR POKÉDEXES DON'T RECOGNIZE.
NOT TO MENTION THAT HE ALMOST BURIED US ALIVE BACK AT MT. CORONET!
THAT'S THREE REASONS WHY WE DON'T STAND A CHANCE IN A FIGHT WITH HIM!
AWR!
ZAP

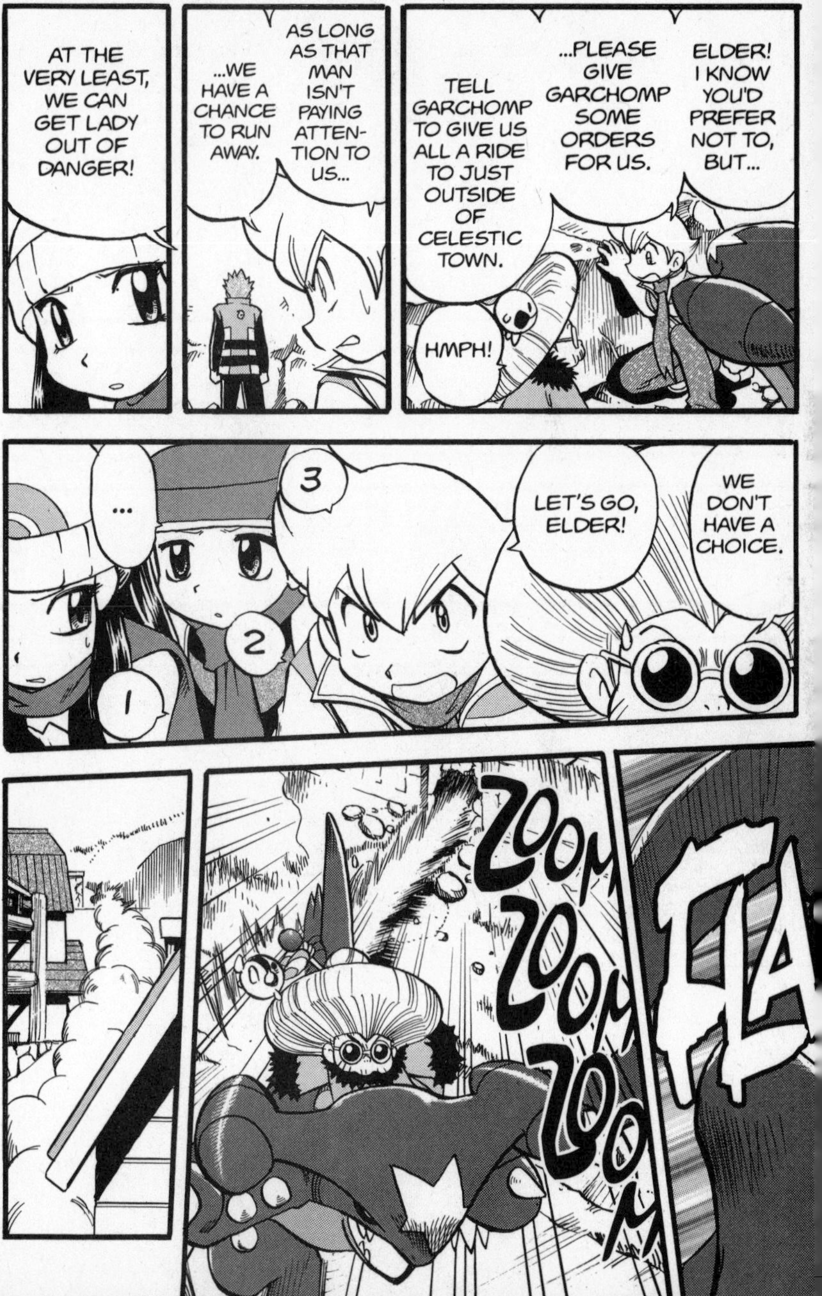
ELDER! I KNOW YOU'D PREFER NOT TO, BUT...
...PLEASE GIVE GARCHOMP SOME ORDERS FOR US.
TELL GARCHOMP TO GIVE US ALL A RIDE TO JUST OUTSIDE OF CELESTIC TOWN.
HMPH!
AS LONG AS THAT MAN ISN'T PAYING ATTENTION TO US...
...WE HAVE A CHANCE TO RUN AWAY.
AT THE VERY LEAST, WE CAN GET LADY OUT OF DANGER!
WE DON'T HAVE A CHOICE.
LET'S GO, ELDER!
3
...
2
1
FLA
ZOOM
ZOOM
ZOOM
ZOOM

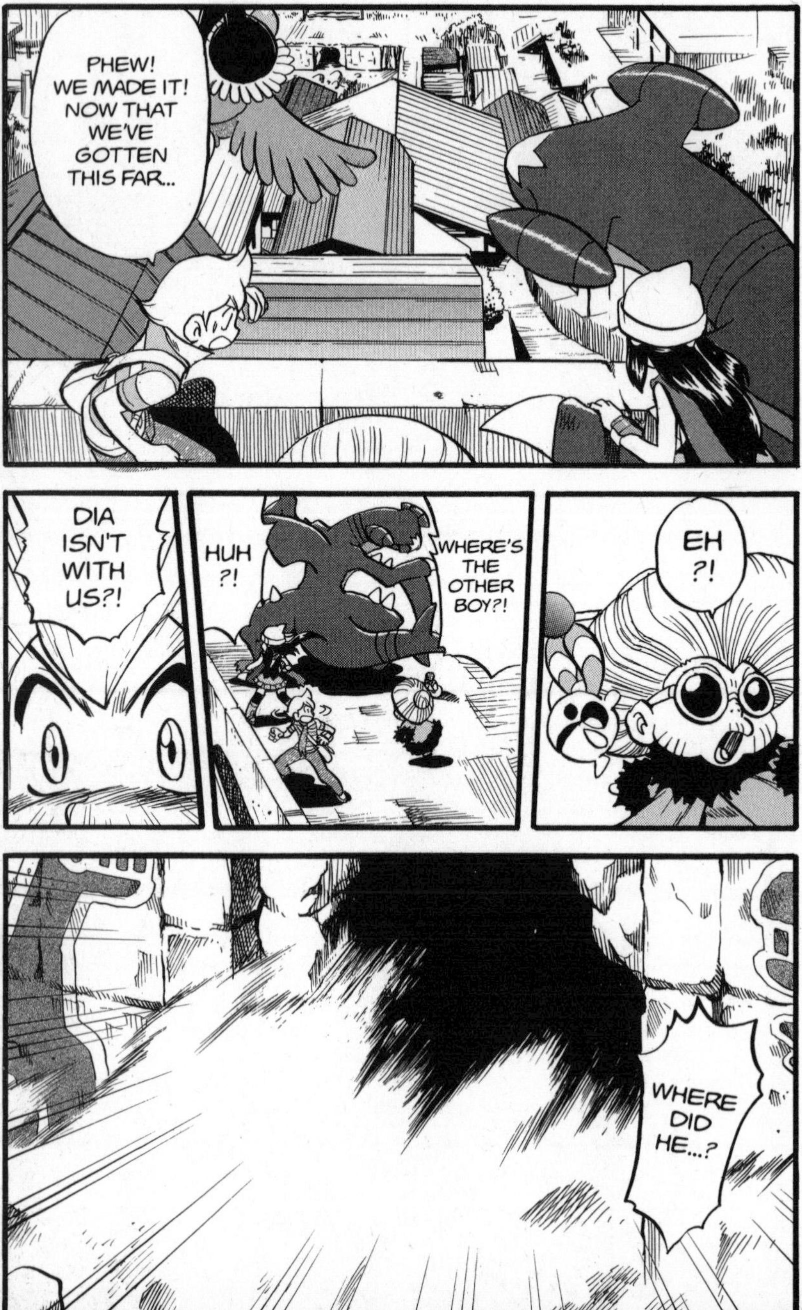
PHEW! WE MADE IT! NOW THAT WE'VE GOTTEN THIS FAR...
EH ?!
WHERE'S THE OTHER BOY?!
HUH ?!
DIA ISN'T WITH US?!
WHERE DID HE...?

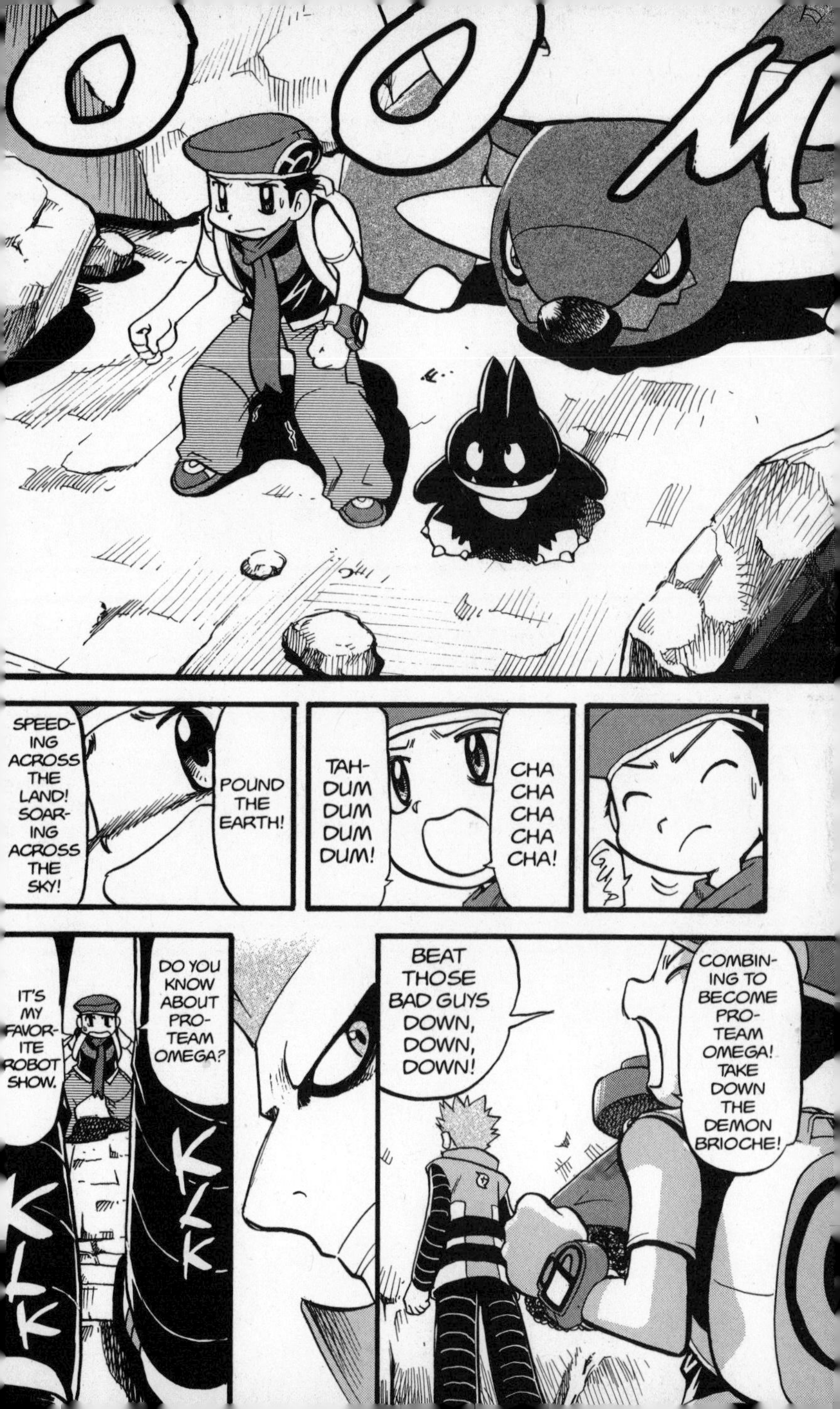
OOM
SPEED-ING ACROSS THE LAND! SOAR-ING ACROSS THE SKY!
POUND THE EARTH!
TAH-DUM DUM DUM DUM!
CHA CHA CHA CHA CHA!
GULP
IT'S MY FAVOR-ITE ROBOT SHOW.
DO YOU KNOW ABOUT PRO-TEAM OMEGA?
BEAT THOSE BAD GUYS DOWN, DOWN, DOWN!
COMBIN-ING TO BECOME PRO-TEAM OMEGA! TAKE DOWN THE DEMON BRIOCHE!
K K K
K K K

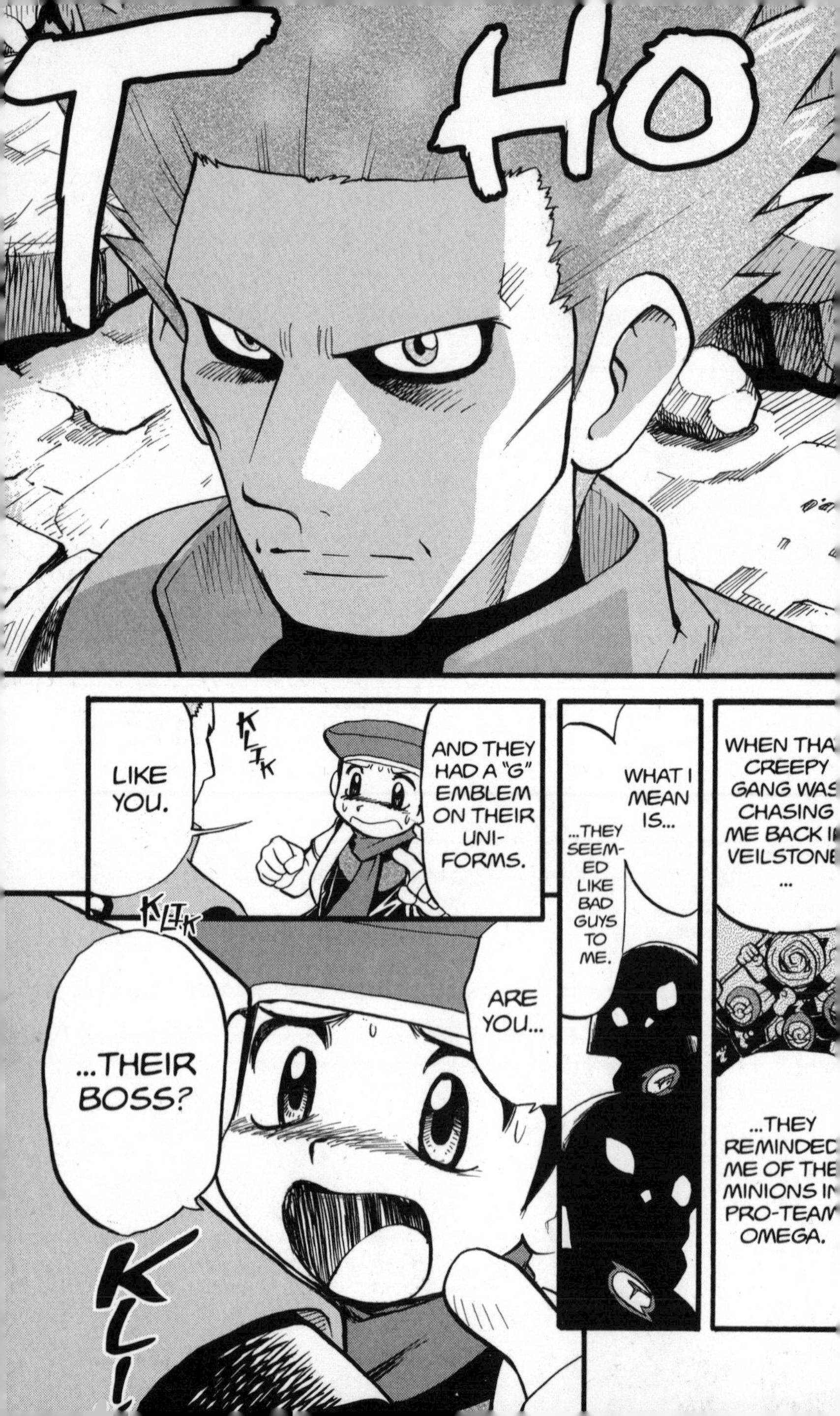
THO
WHEN THA CREEPY GANG WAS CHASING ME BACK I VEILSTONE ...
...THEY REMINDED ME OF THE MINIONS I PRO-TEAM OMEGA.
WHAT I MEAN IS...
...THEY SEEM-ED LIKE BAD GUYS TO ME.
AND THEY HAD A "G" EMBLEM ON THEIR UNI-FORMS.
KLIK
LIKE YOU.
KLIK
ARE YOU...
...THEIR BOSS?
KLI

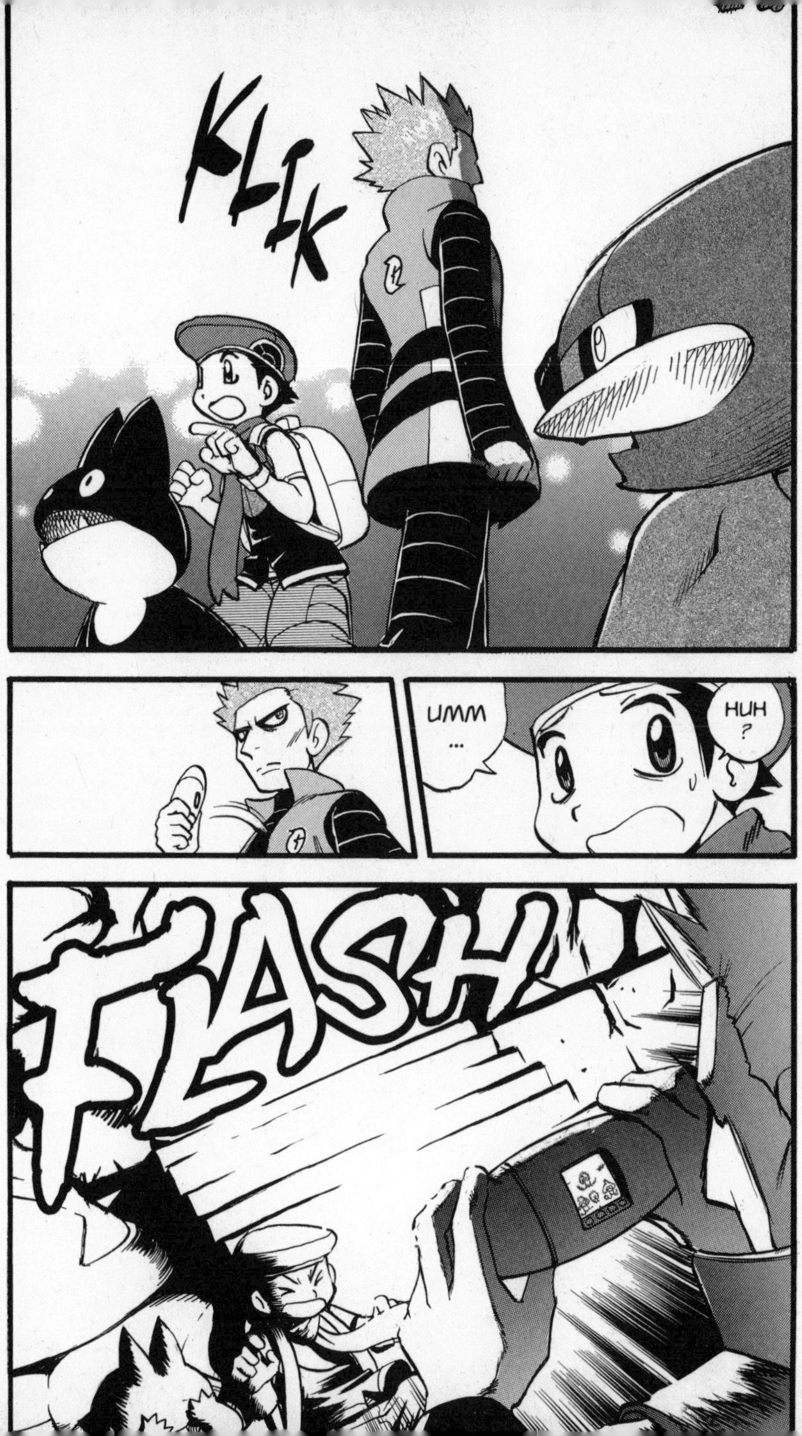
KLIK
HUH ?
UMM ...
FLASH

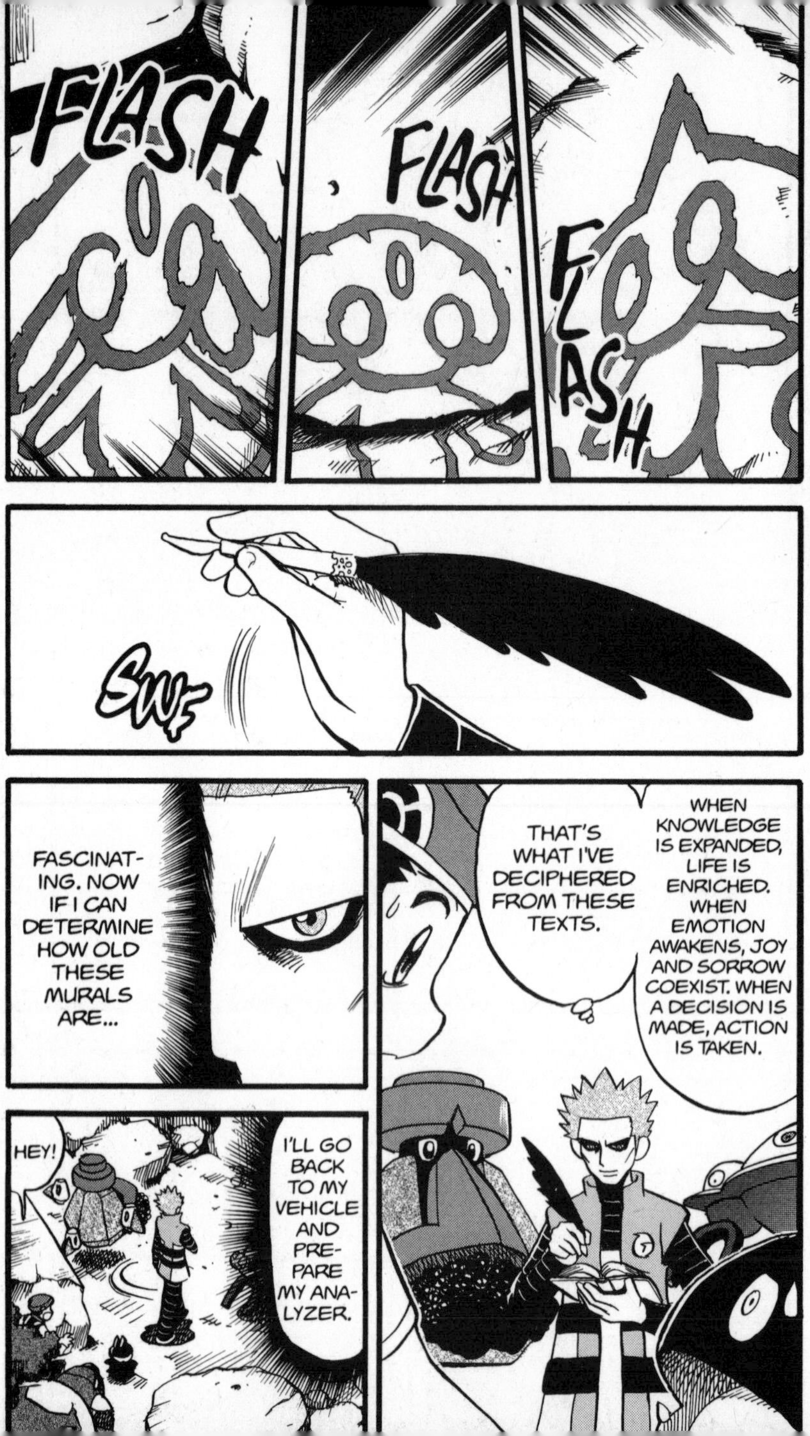
FLASH
FLASH
FLASH
SWF
WHEN KNOWLEDGE IS EXPANDED, LIFE IS ENRICHED. WHEN EMOTION AWAKENS, JOY AND SORROW COEXIST. WHEN A DECISION IS MADE, ACTION IS TAKEN.
THAT'S WHAT I'VE DECIPHERED FROM THESE TEXTS.
FASCINAT-ING. NOW IF I CAN DETERMINE HOW OLD THESE MURALS ARE...
I'LL GO BACK TO MY VEHICLE AND PRE-PARE MY ANA-LYZER.
HEY!

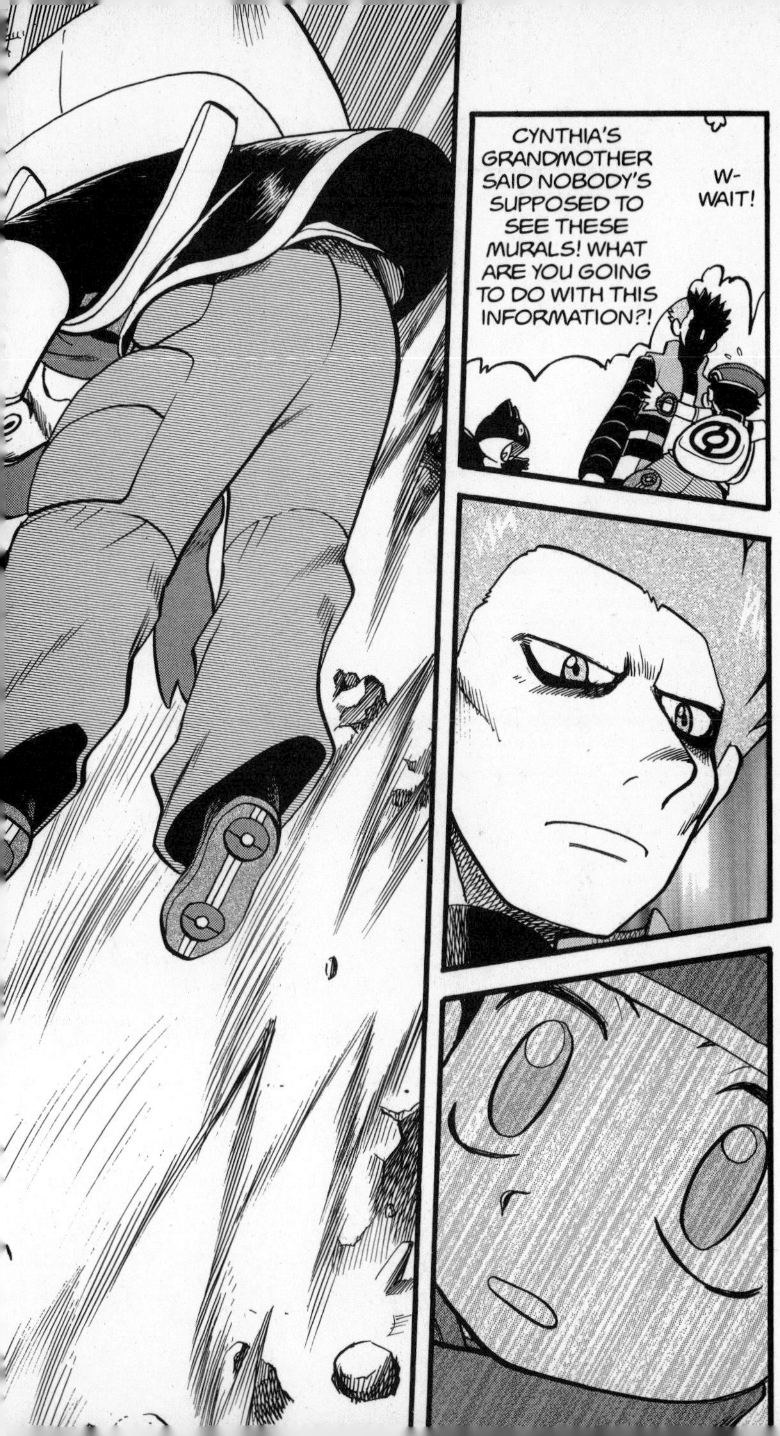
W-
WAIT!
CYNTHIA'S GRANDMOTHER SAID NOBODY'S SUPPOSED TO SEE THESE MURALS! WHAT ARE YOU GOING TO DO WITH THIS INFORMATION?!

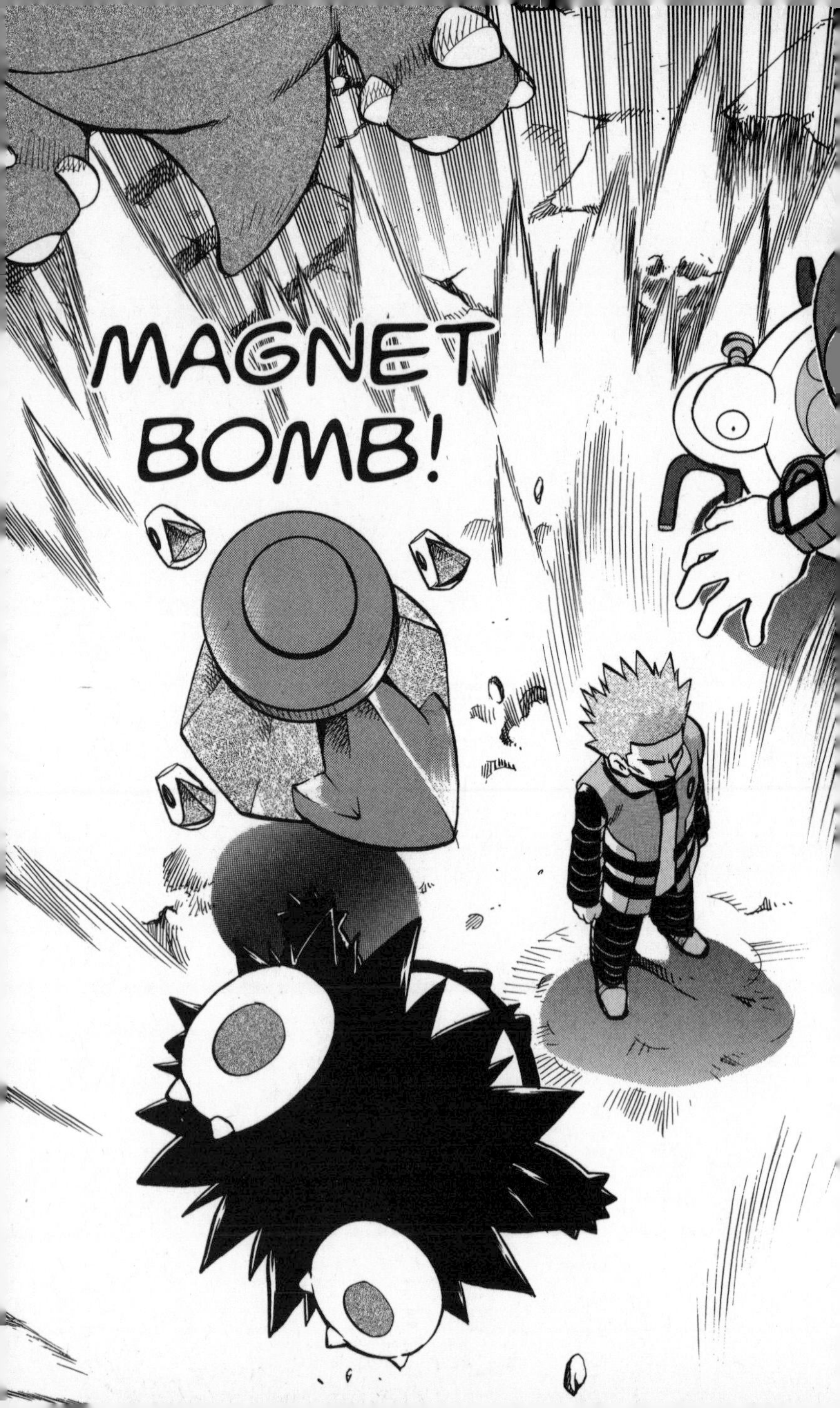
MAGNET BOMB!

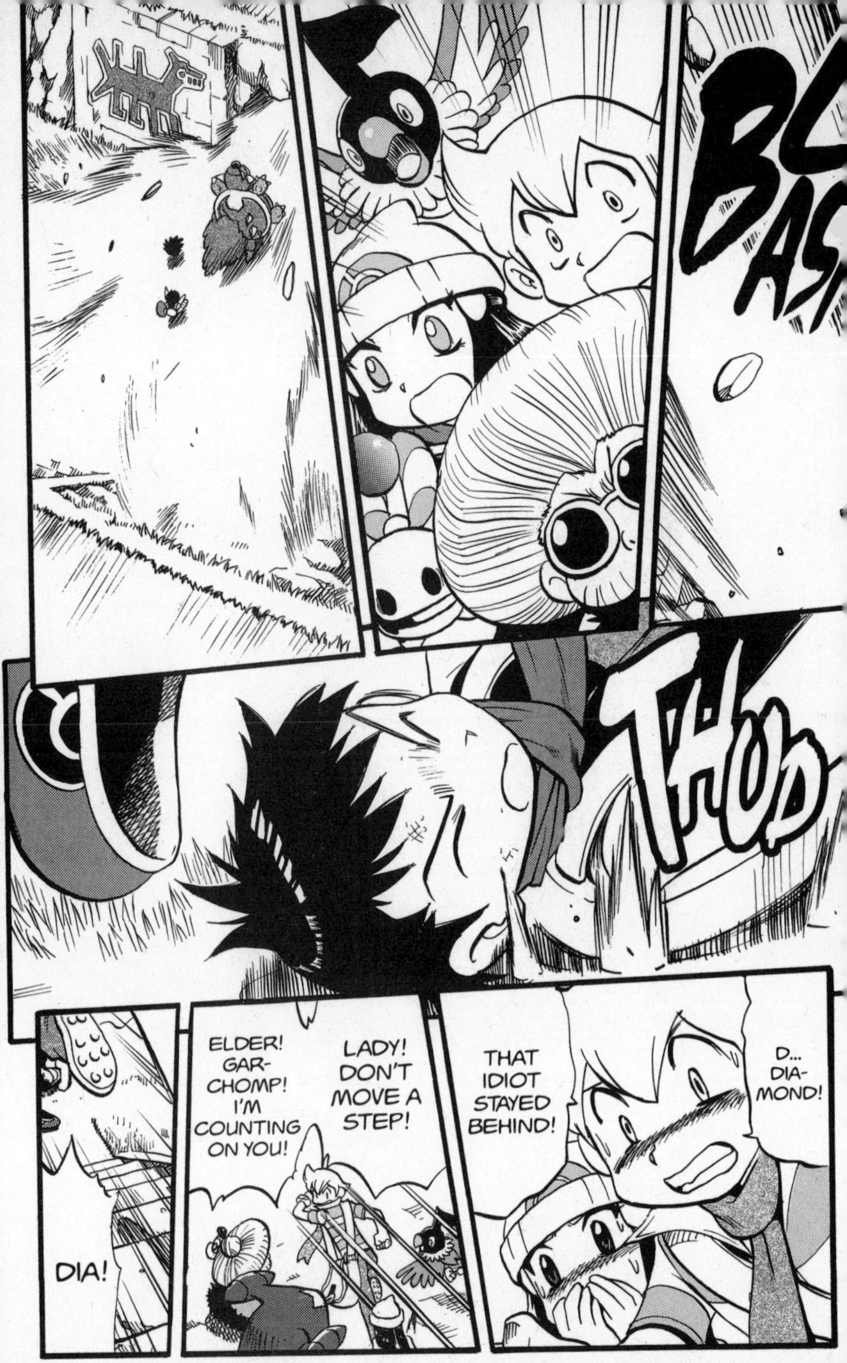
THUD
D... DIA-MOND!
THAT IDIOT STAYED BEHIND!
LADY! DON'T MOVE A STEP!
ELDER! GAR-CHOMP! I'M COUNTING ON YOU!
DIA!

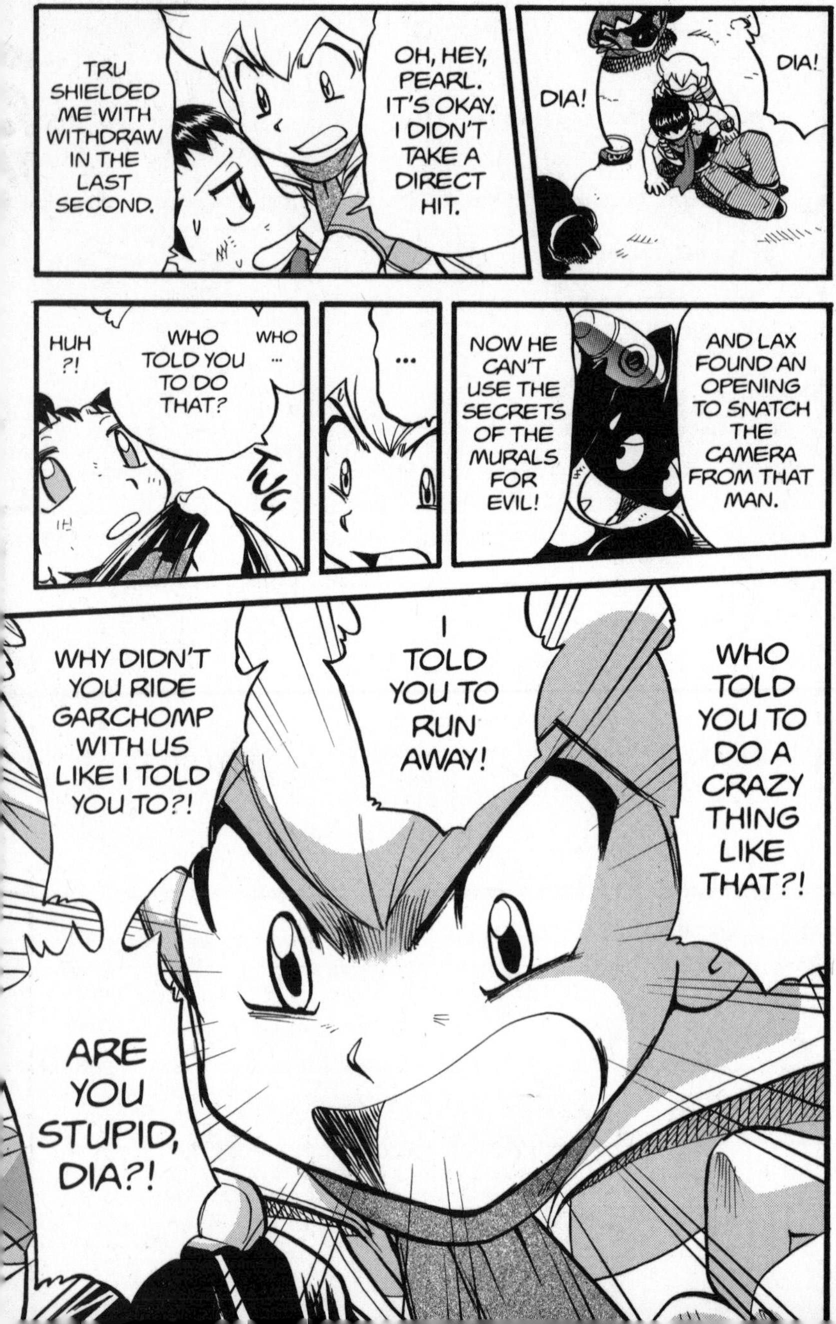
DIA!
DIA!
OH, HEY, PEARL. IT'S OKAY. I DIDN'T TAKE A DIRECT HIT.
TRU SHIELDED ME WITH WITHDRAW IN THE LAST SECOND.
AND LAX FOUND AN OPENING TO SNATCH THE CAMERA FROM THAT MAN.
NOW HE CAN'T USE THE SECRETS OF THE MURALS FOR EVIL!
...
WHO ...
WHO TOLD YOU TO DO THAT?
HUH ?!
TUG
WHO TOLD YOU TO DO A CRAZY THING LIKE THAT?!
I TOLD YOU TO RUN AWAY!
WHY DIDN'T YOU RIDE GARCHOMP WITH US LIKE I TOLD YOU TO?!
ARE YOU STUPID, DIA?!

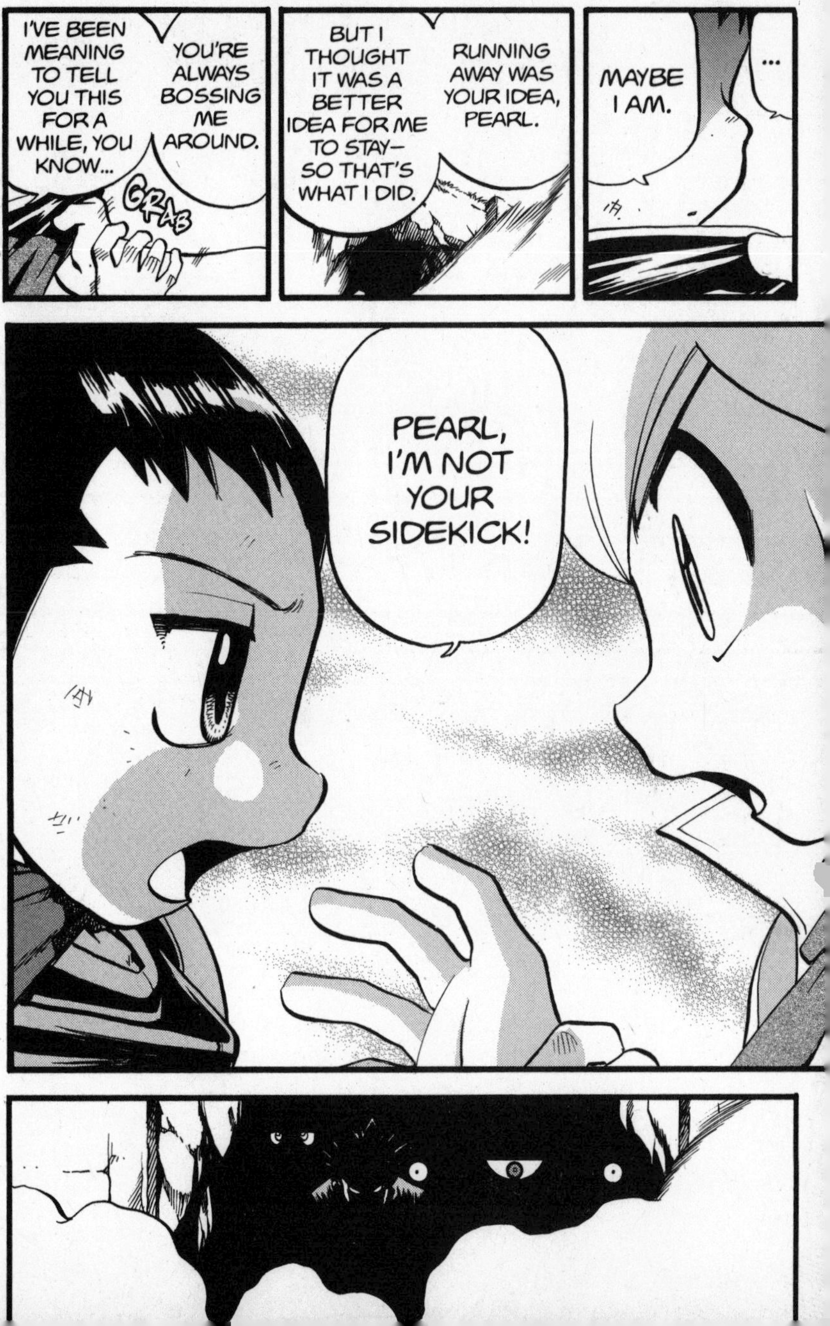
...
MAYBE I AM.
RUNNING AWAY WAS YOUR IDEA, PEARL.
BUT I THOUGHT IT WAS A BETTER IDEA FOR ME TO STAY— SO THAT'S WHAT I DID.
YOU'RE ALWAYS BOSSING ME AROUND.
I'VE BEEN MEANING TO TELL YOU THIS FOR A WHILE, YOU KNOW...
GRAB
PEARL, I'M NOT YOUR SIDEKICK!

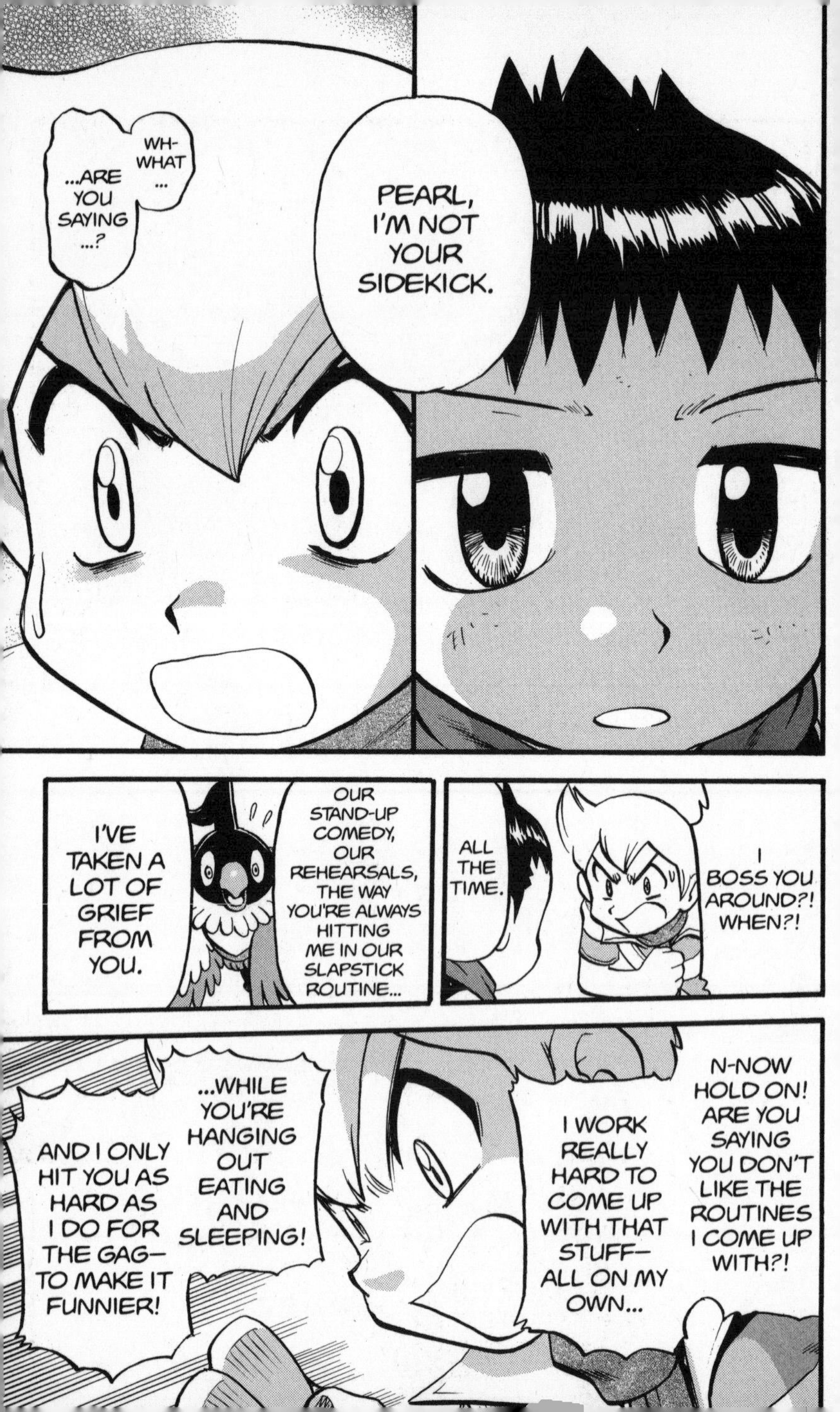
PEARL, I'M NOT YOUR SIDEKICK.
WH-WHAT ... ...ARE YOU SAYING ...?
I BOSS YOU AROUND?! WHEN?!
ALL THE TIME.
OUR STAND-UP COMEDY, OUR REHEARSALS, THE WAY YOU'RE ALWAYS HITTING ME IN OUR SLAPSTICK ROUTINE...
I'VE TAKEN A LOT OF GRIEF FROM YOU.
N-NOW HOLD ON! ARE YOU SAYING YOU DON'T LIKE THE ROUTINES I COME UP WITH?!
I WORK REALLY HARD TO COME UP WITH THAT STUFF— ALL ON MY OWN...
...WHILE YOU'RE HANGING OUT EATING AND SLEEPING!
AND I ONLY HIT YOU AS HARD AS I DO FOR THE GAG— TO MAKE IT FUNNIER!

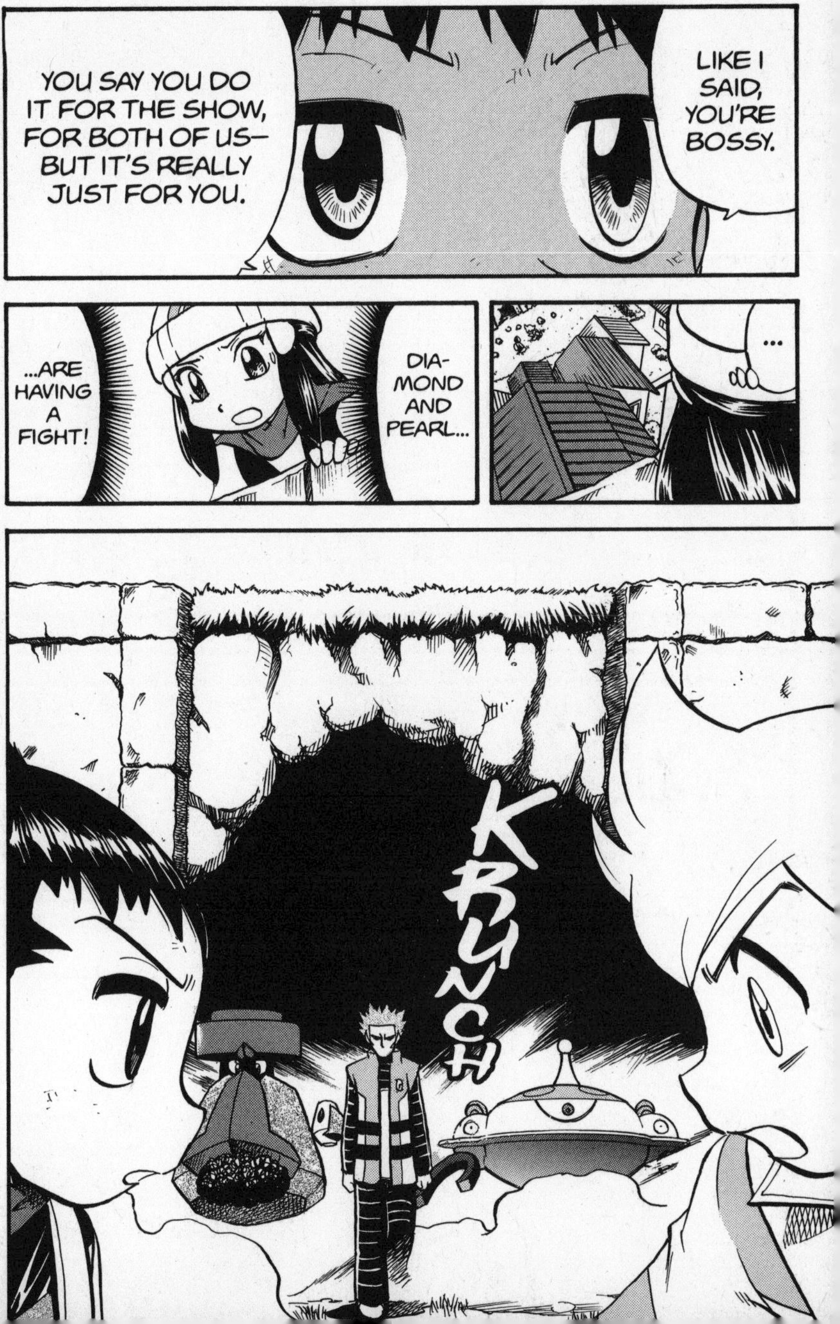
LIKE I SAID, YOU'RE BOSSY.
YOU SAY YOU DO IT FOR THE SHOW, FOR BOTH OF US— BUT IT'S REALLY JUST FOR YOU.
...
DIA-MOND AND PEARL...
...ARE HAVING A FIGHT!
KRUNCH

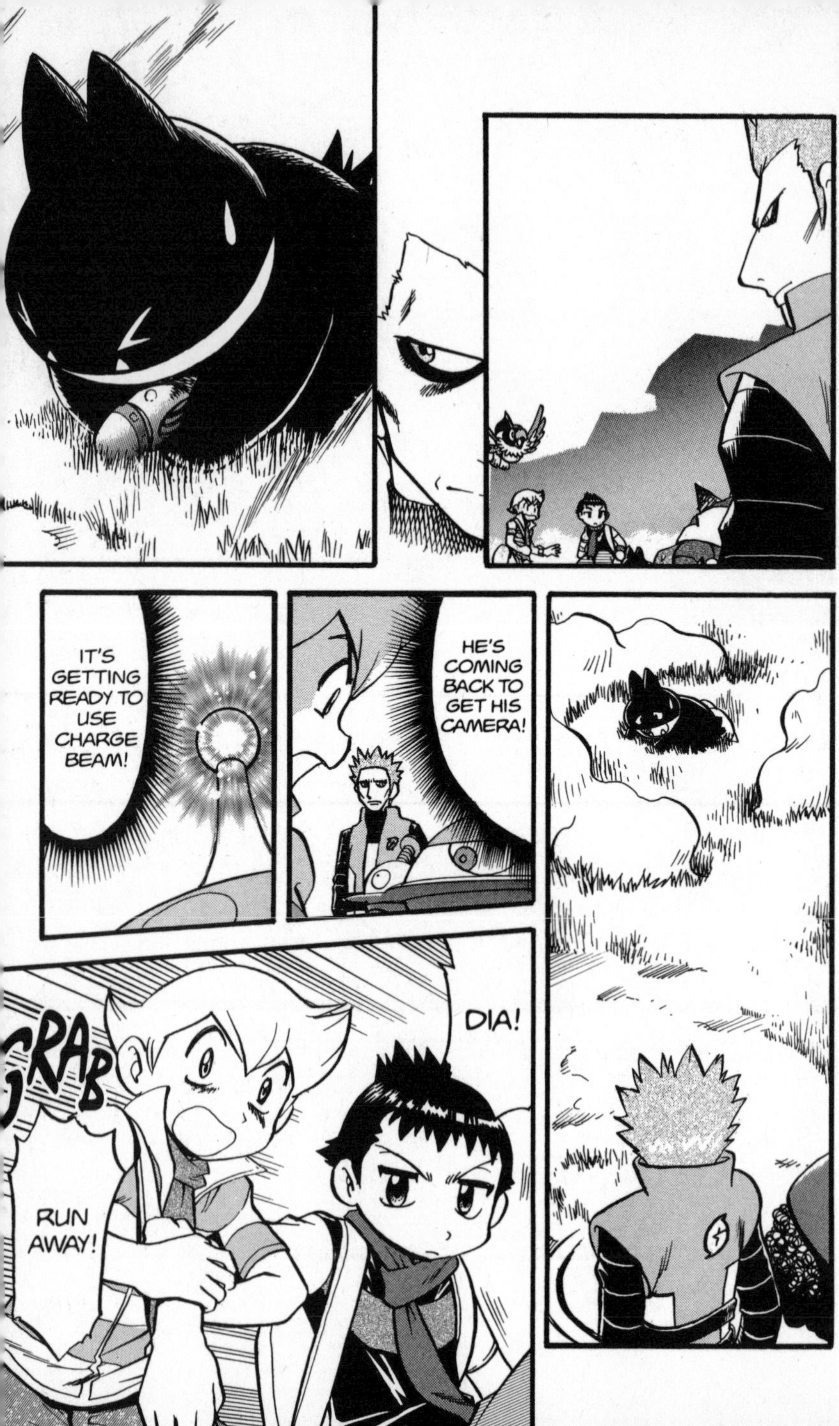
HE'S COMING BACK TO GET HIS CAMERA!
IT'S GETTING READY TO USE CHARGE BEAM!
DIA!
GRAB
RUN AWAY!

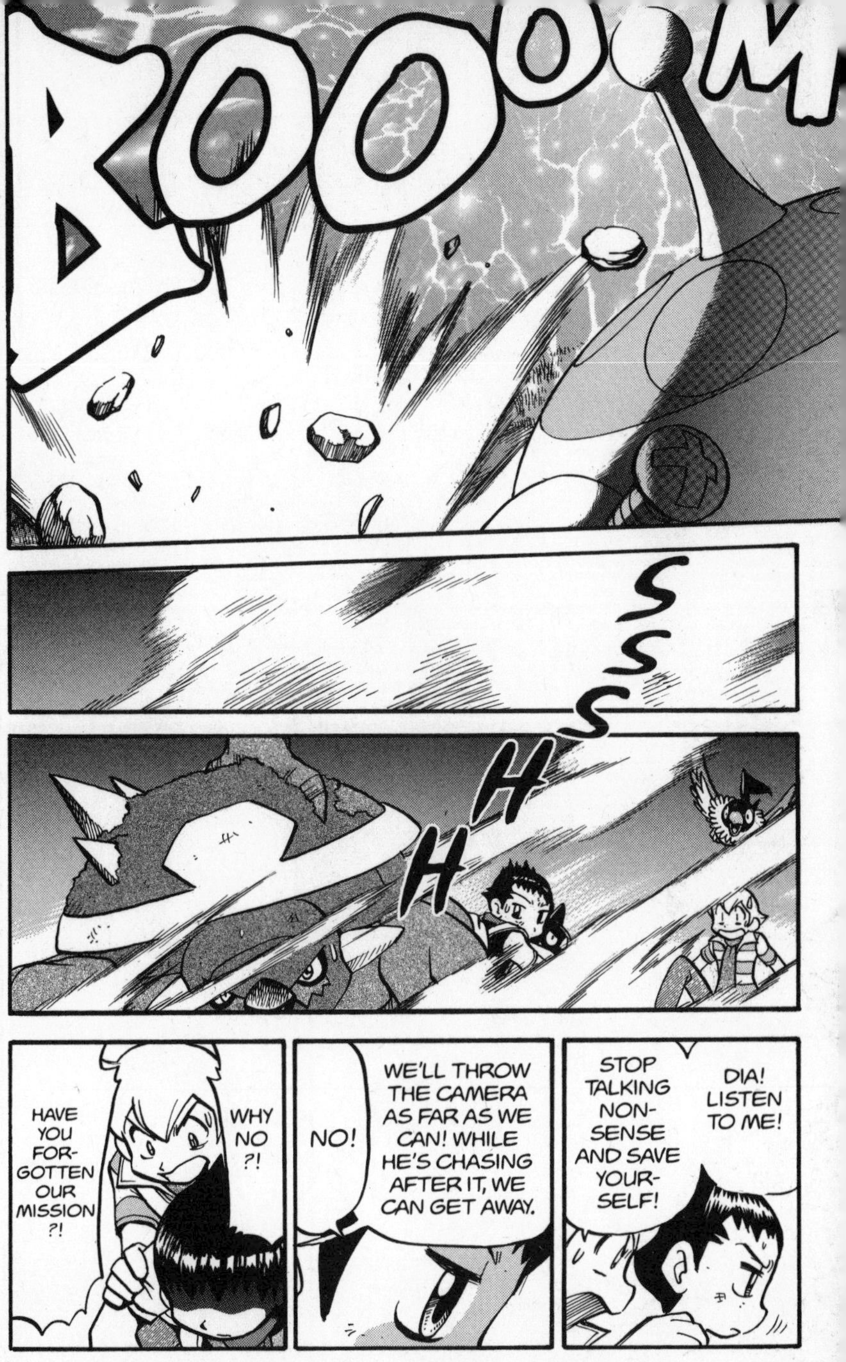

BOOOOM
SSSHH
DIA! LISTEN TO ME!
STOP TALKING NON-SENSE AND SAVE YOUR-SELF!
WE'LL THROW THE CAMERA AS FAR AS WE CAN! WHILE HE'S CHASING AFTER IT, WE CAN GET AWAY.
NO!
WHY NO?!
HAVE YOU FOR-GOTTEN OUR MISSION?!

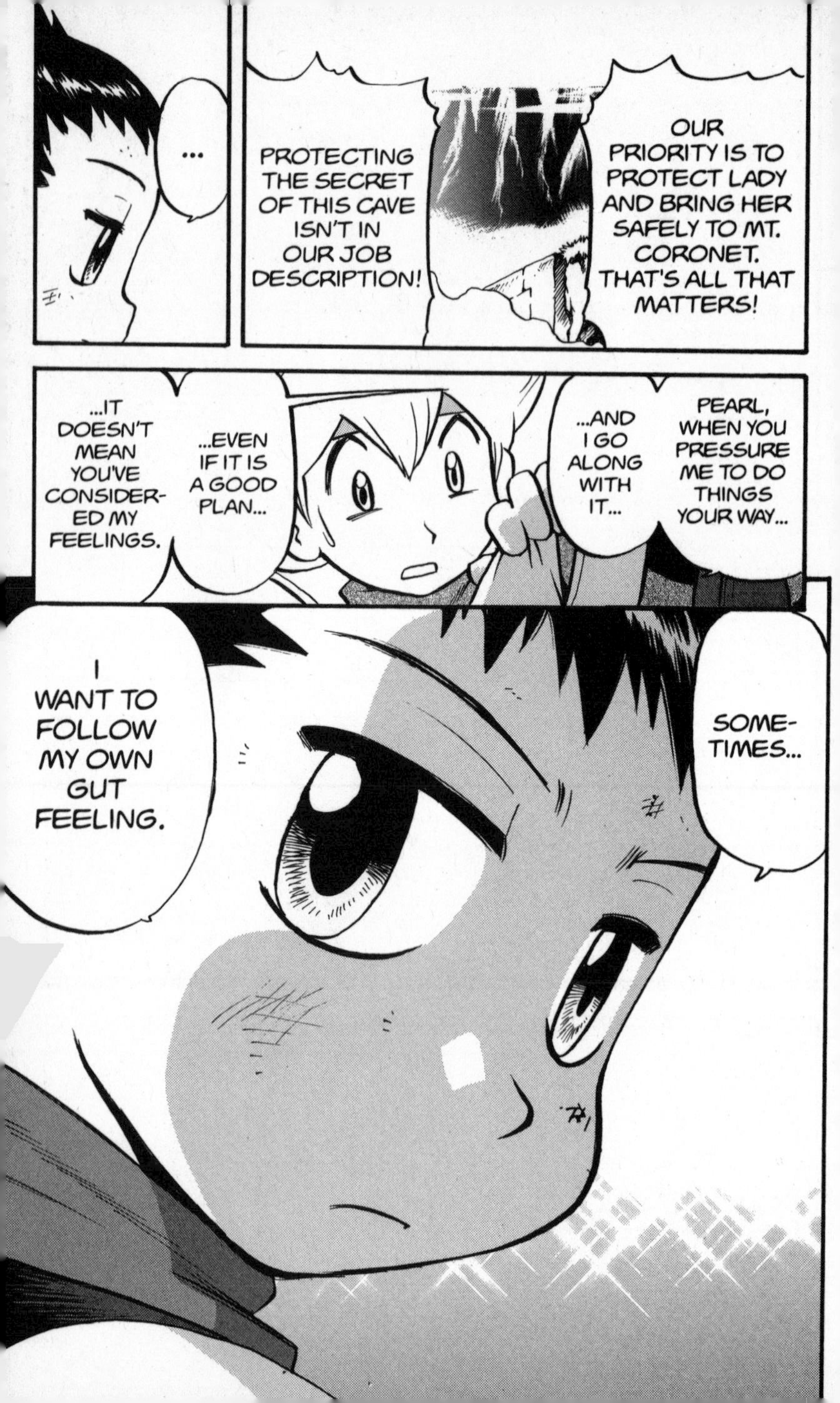
OUR PRIORITY IS TO PROTECT LADY AND BRING HER SAFELY TO MT. CORONET. THAT'S ALL THAT MATTERS!
PROTECTING THE SECRET OF THIS CAVE ISN'T IN OUR JOB DESCRIPTION!
...
PEARL, WHEN YOU PRESSURE ME TO DO THINGS YOUR WAY...
...AND I GO ALONG WITH IT...
...EVEN IF IT IS A GOOD PLAN...
...IT DOESN'T MEAN YOU'VE CONSIDERED MY FEELINGS.
SOMETIMES...
I WANT TO FOLLOW MY OWN GUT FEELING.

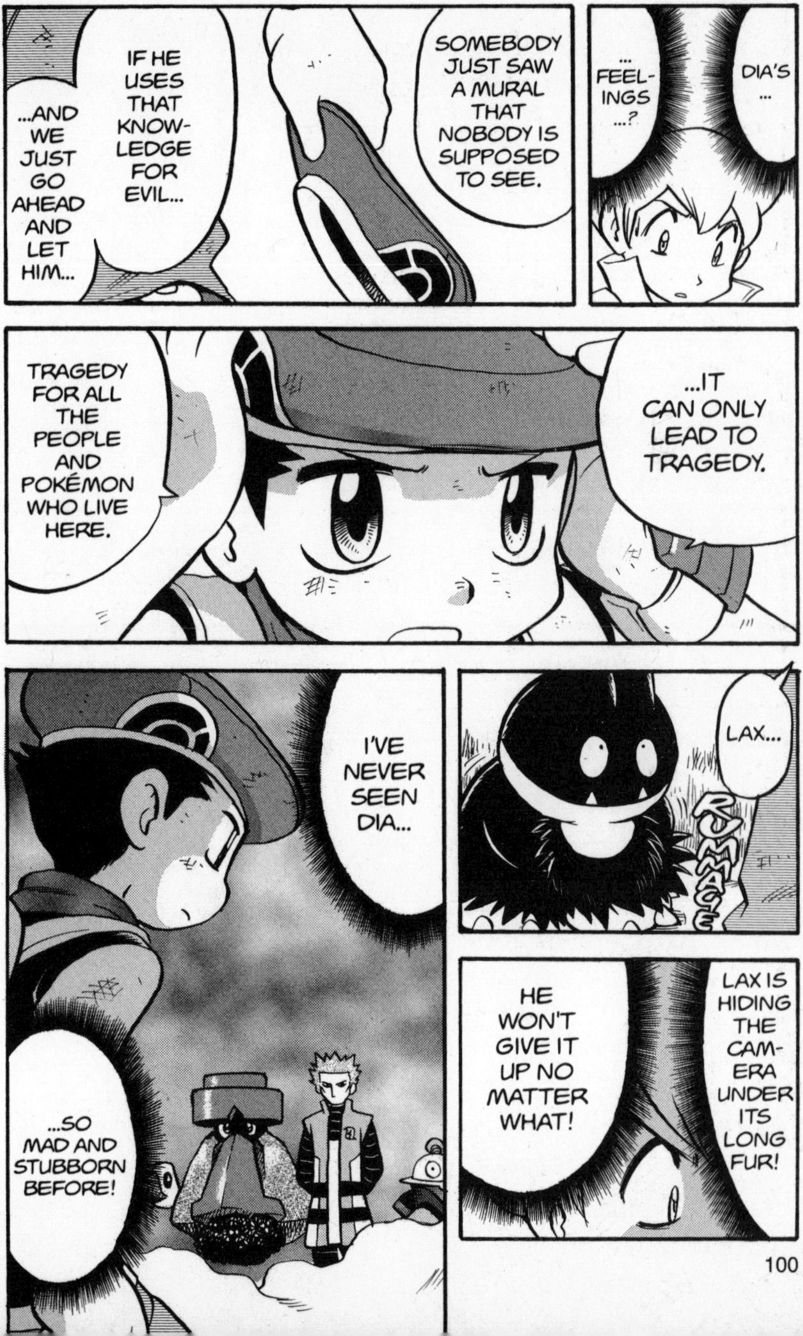
DIA'S ...
... FEEL-INGS ...?
SOMEBODY JUST SAW A MURAL THAT NOBODY IS SUPPOSED TO SEE.
IF HE USES THAT KNOW-LEDGE FOR EVIL...
...AND WE JUST GO AHEAD AND LET HIM...
...IT CAN ONLY LEAD TO TRAGEDY.
TRAGEDY FOR ALL THE PEOPLE AND POKÉMON WHO LIVE HERE.
LAX...
RUMMAGE
LAX IS HIDING THE CAM-ERA UNDER ITS LONG FUR!
HE WON'T GIVE IT UP NO MATTER WHAT!
I'VE NEVER SEEN DIA...
...SO MAD AND STUBBORN BEFORE!

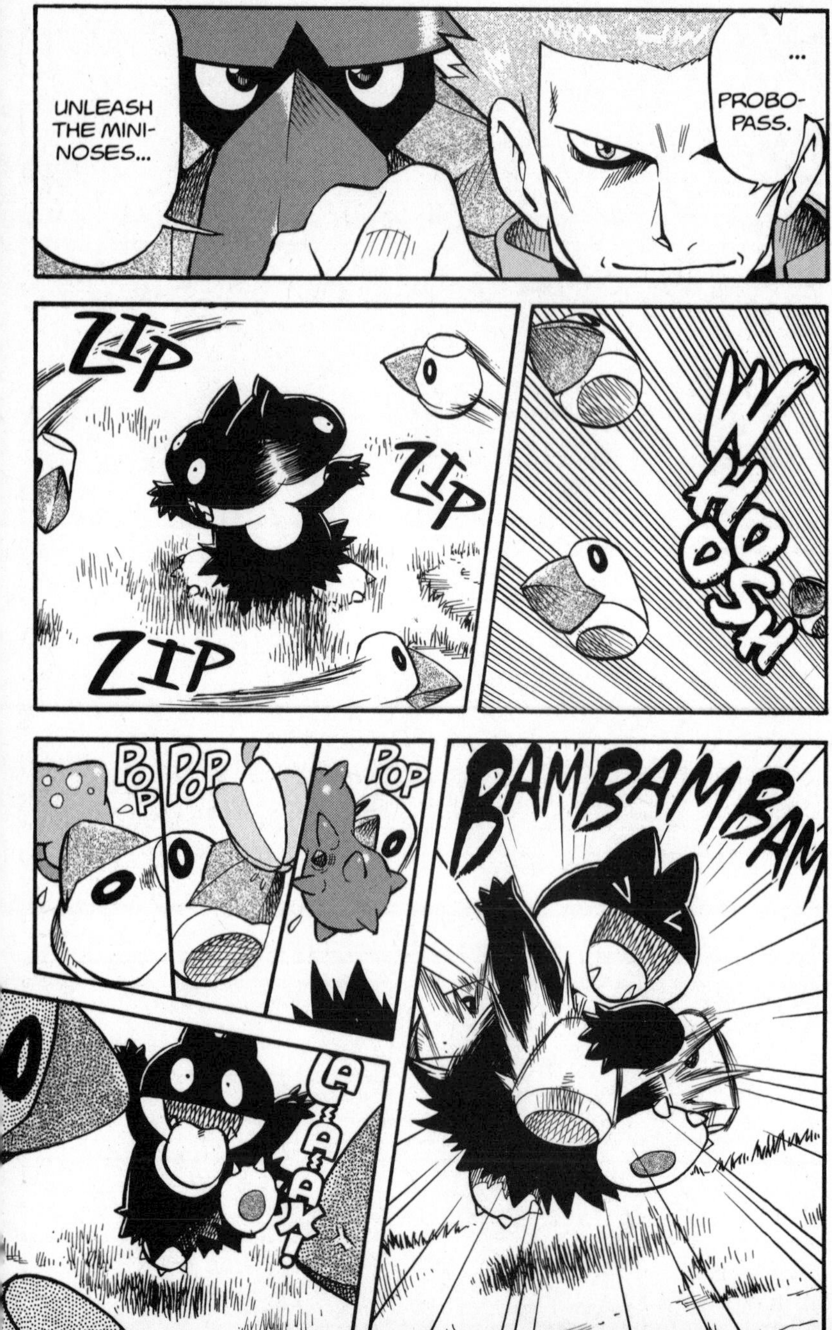
...
PROBO-PASS.
UNLEASH THE MINI-NOSES...
WHOOSH
ZIP
ZIP
ZIP
BAMBAMBAM
POP
POP
POP
LA-A-A-AX!

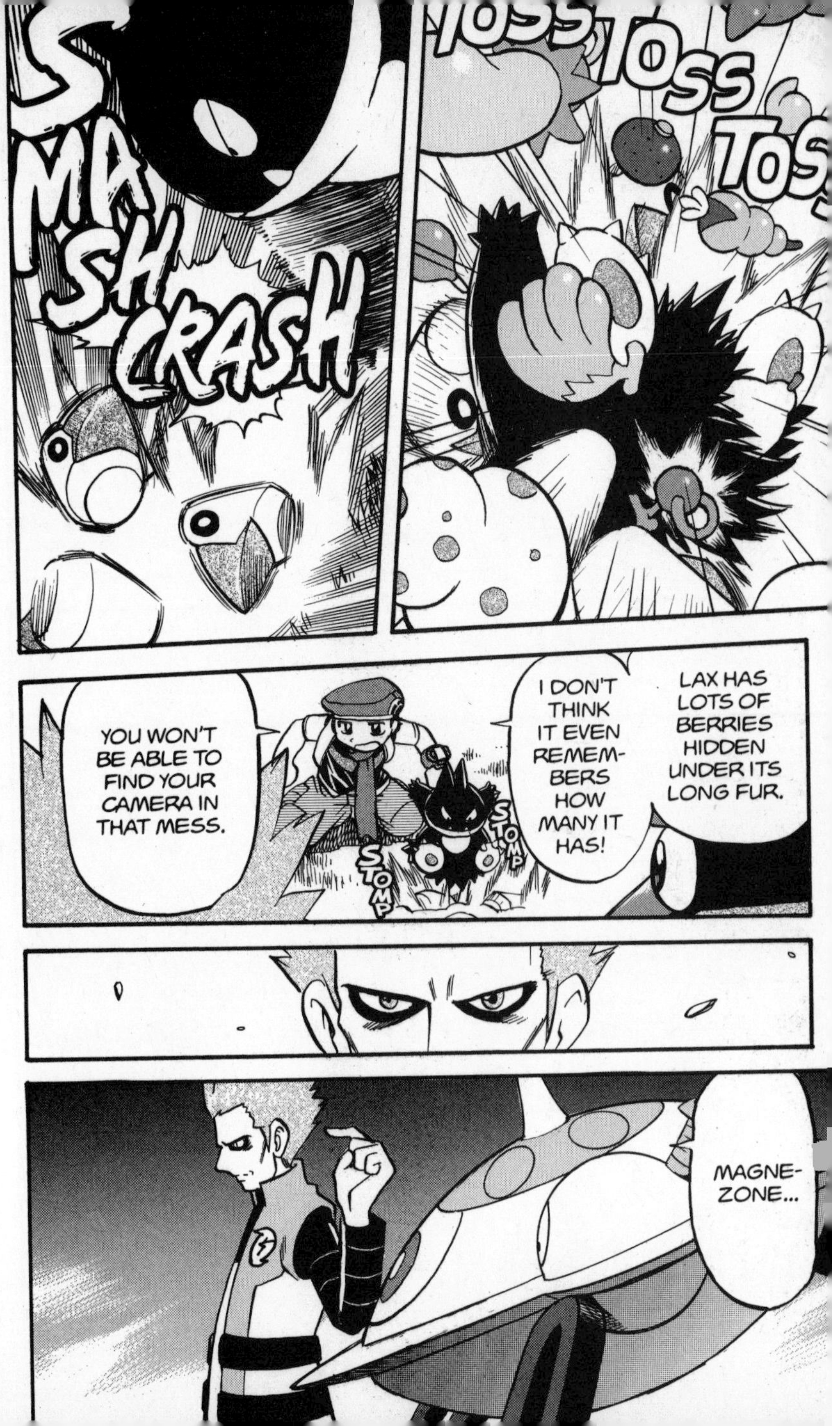
TOSS TOSS TOS
SMASH
CRASH
LAX HAS LOTS OF BERRIES HIDDEN UNDER ITS LONG FUR.
I DON'T THINK IT EVEN REMEM-BERS HOW MANY IT HAS!
STOMP
STOMP
YOU WON'T BE ABLE TO FIND YOUR CAMERA IN THAT MESS.
MAGNE-ZONE...

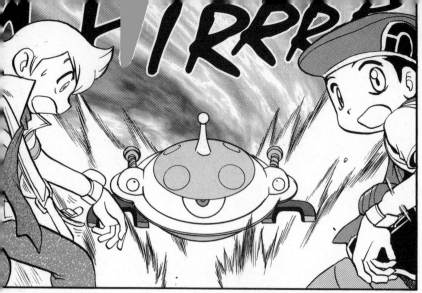

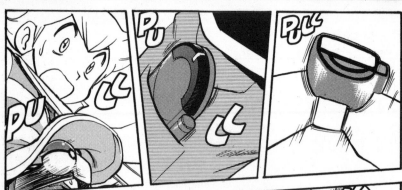

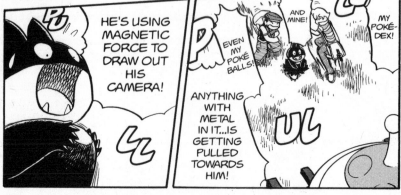

IRRR
PULL
PU
LL
PU
LL
MY POKÉ-DEX!
AND MINE!
EVEN MY POKÉ BALLS!
LL
P
UL
ANYTHING WITH METAL IN IT...IS GETTING PULLED TOWARDS HIM!
PU
HE'S USING MAGNETIC FORCE TO DRAW OUT HIS CAMERA!
LL

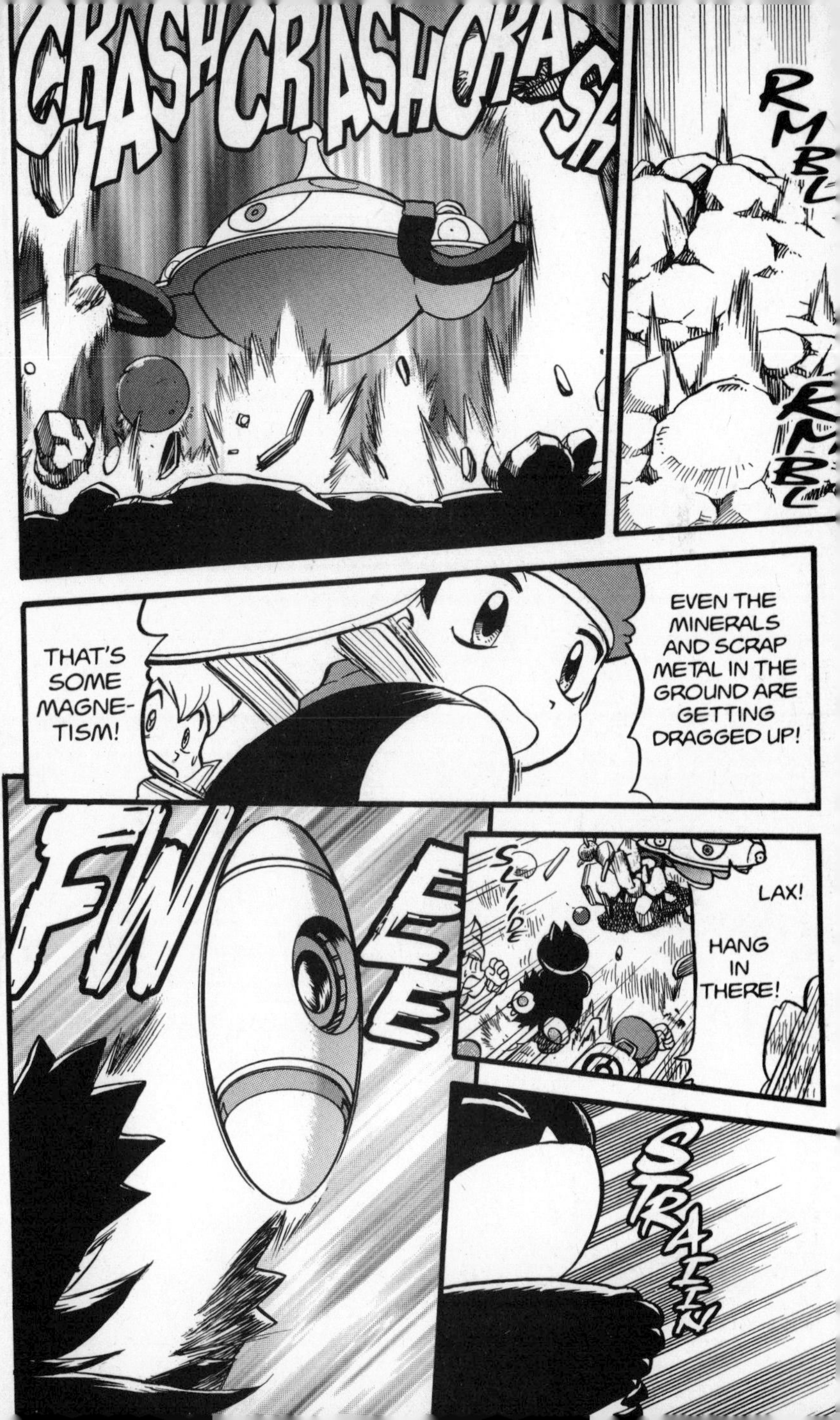
RMBL
RMBL
CRASH CRASH CRASH
EVEN THE MINERALS AND SCRAP METAL IN THE GROUND ARE GETTING DRAGGED UP!
THAT'S SOME MAGNETISM!
LAX!
HANG IN THERE!
SLIDE
STRAIN
FWEE

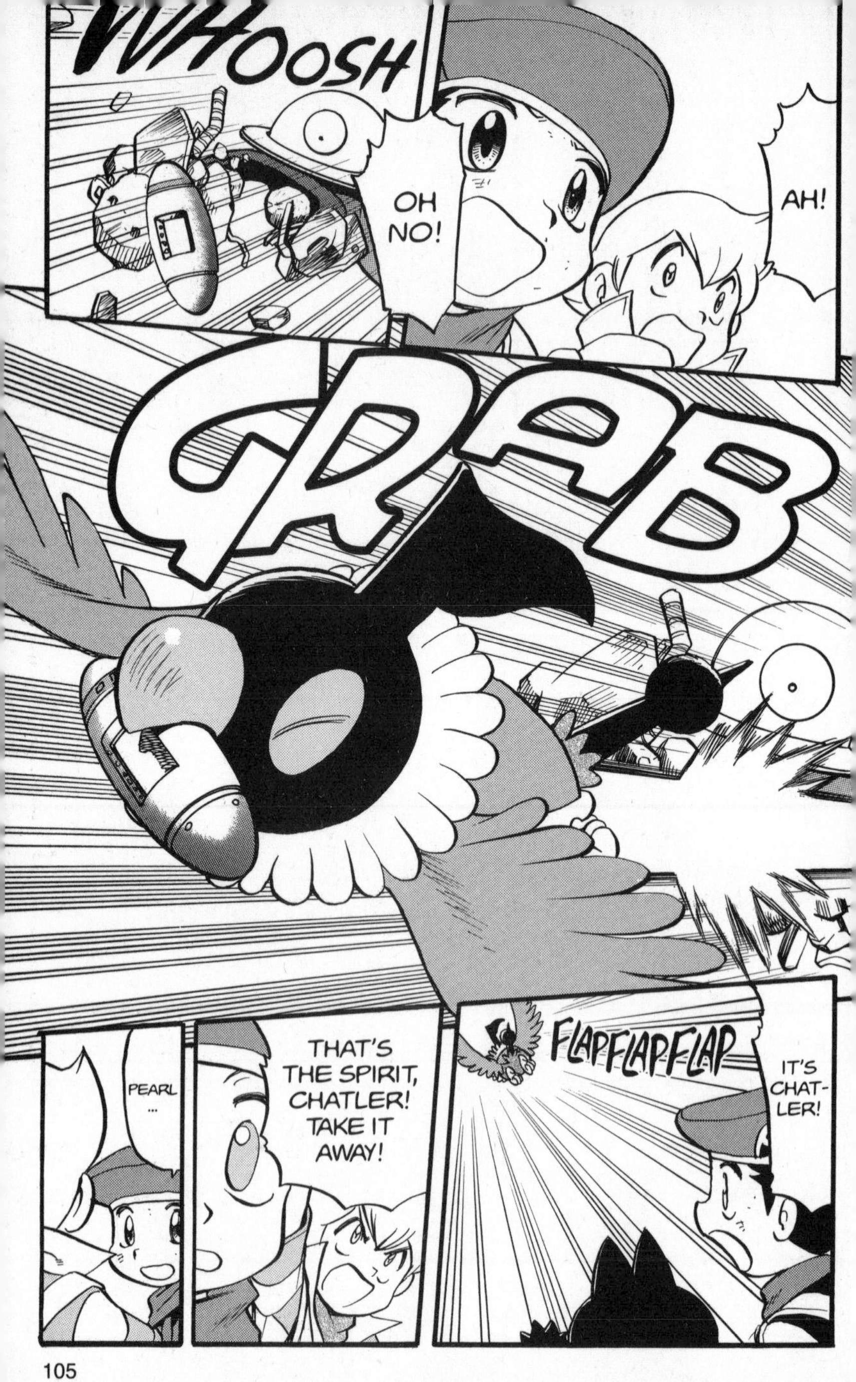
VVHOOSH
AH!
OH NO!
GRAB
FLAPFLAPFLAP
IT'S CHAT-LER!
THAT'S THE SPIRIT, CHATLER! TAKE IT AWAY!
PEARL...

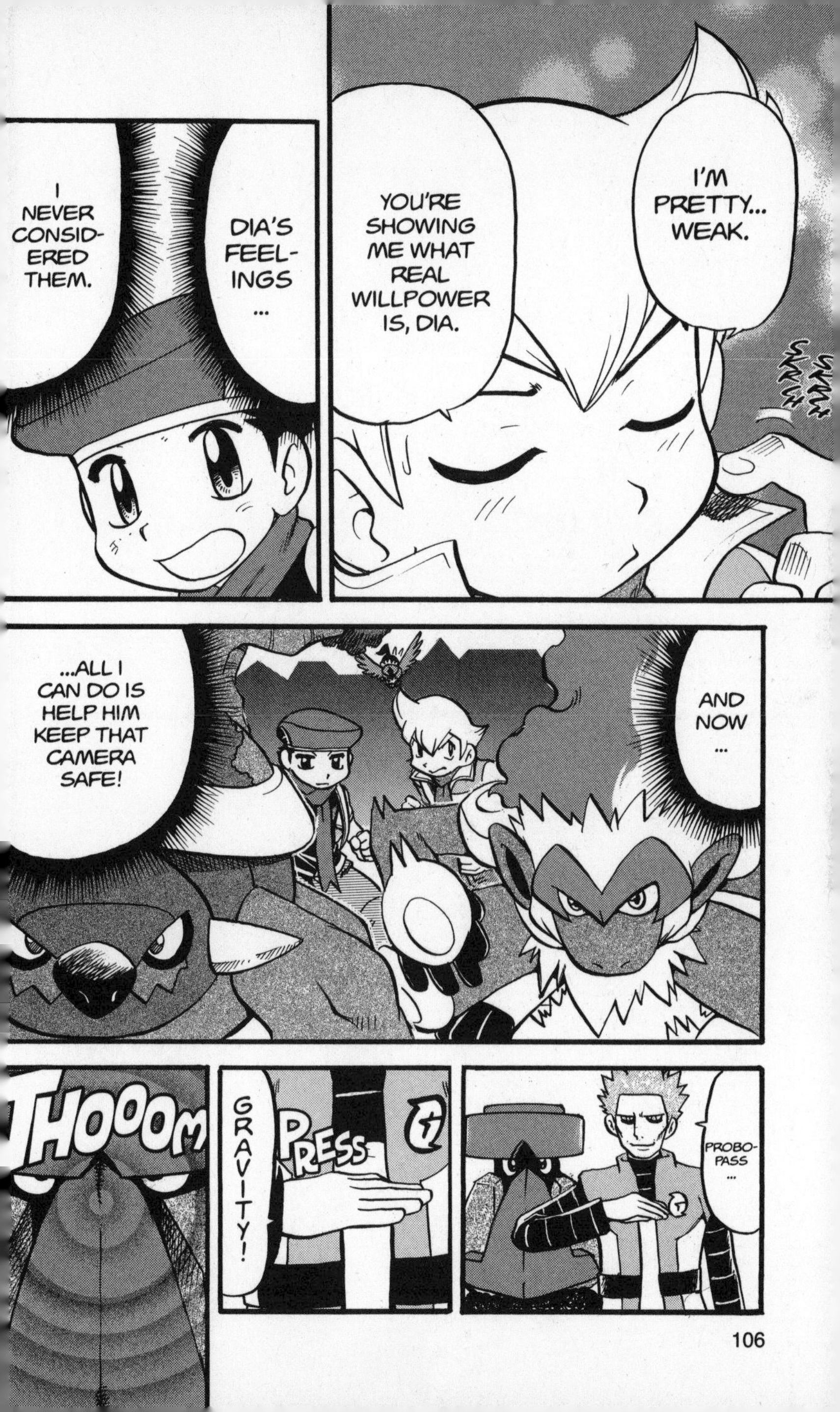
I'M PRETTY... WEAK.
YOU'RE SHOWING ME WHAT REAL WILLPOWER IS, DIA.
DIA'S FEEL-INGS ...
I NEVER CONSID-ERED THEM.
AND NOW ...
...ALL I CAN DO IS HELP HIM KEEP THAT CAMERA SAFE!
PROBO-PASS ...
GRAVITY!
PRESS
THOOOM

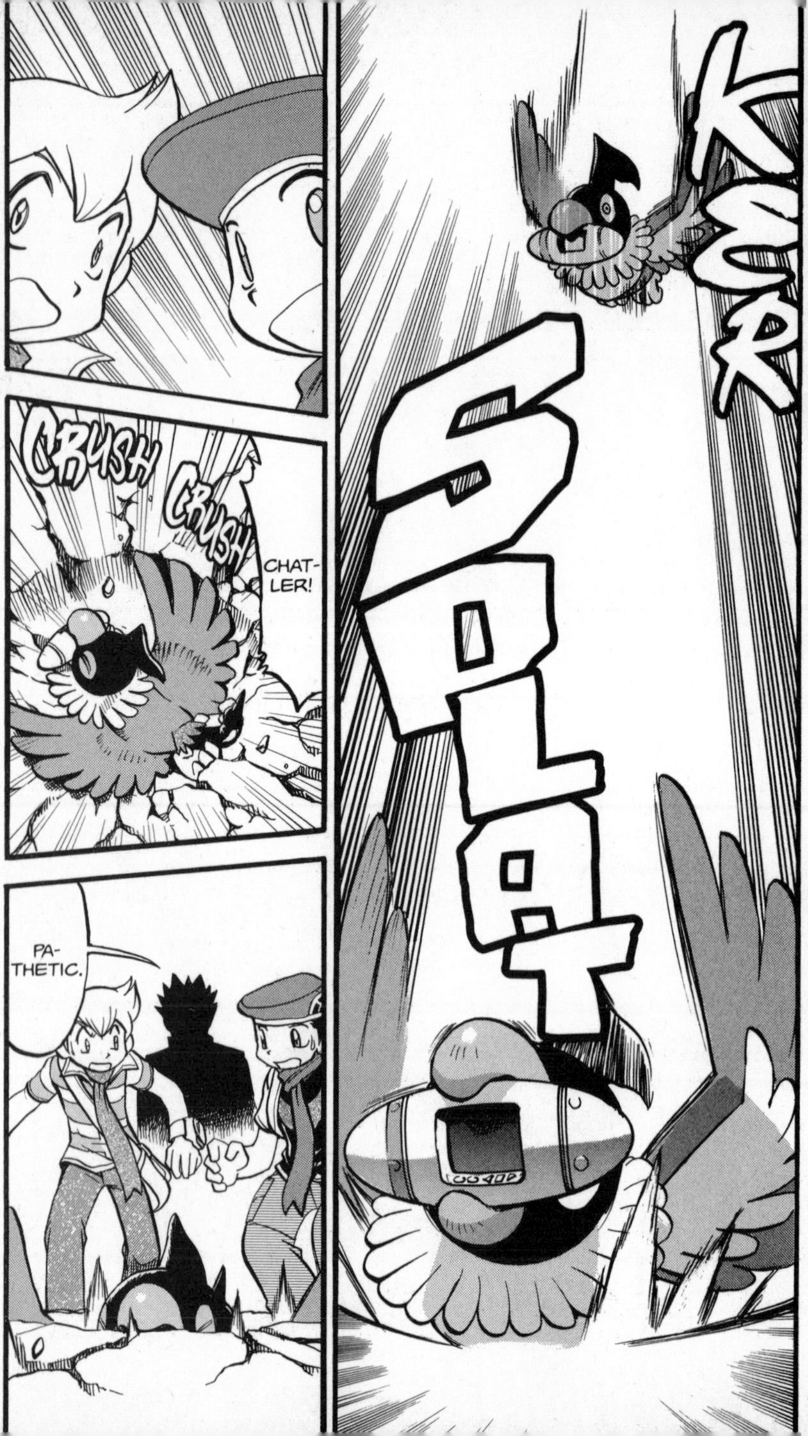
KWUR
SPLAT
CRUSH
CRUSH
CHAT-
LER!
PA-
THETIC.

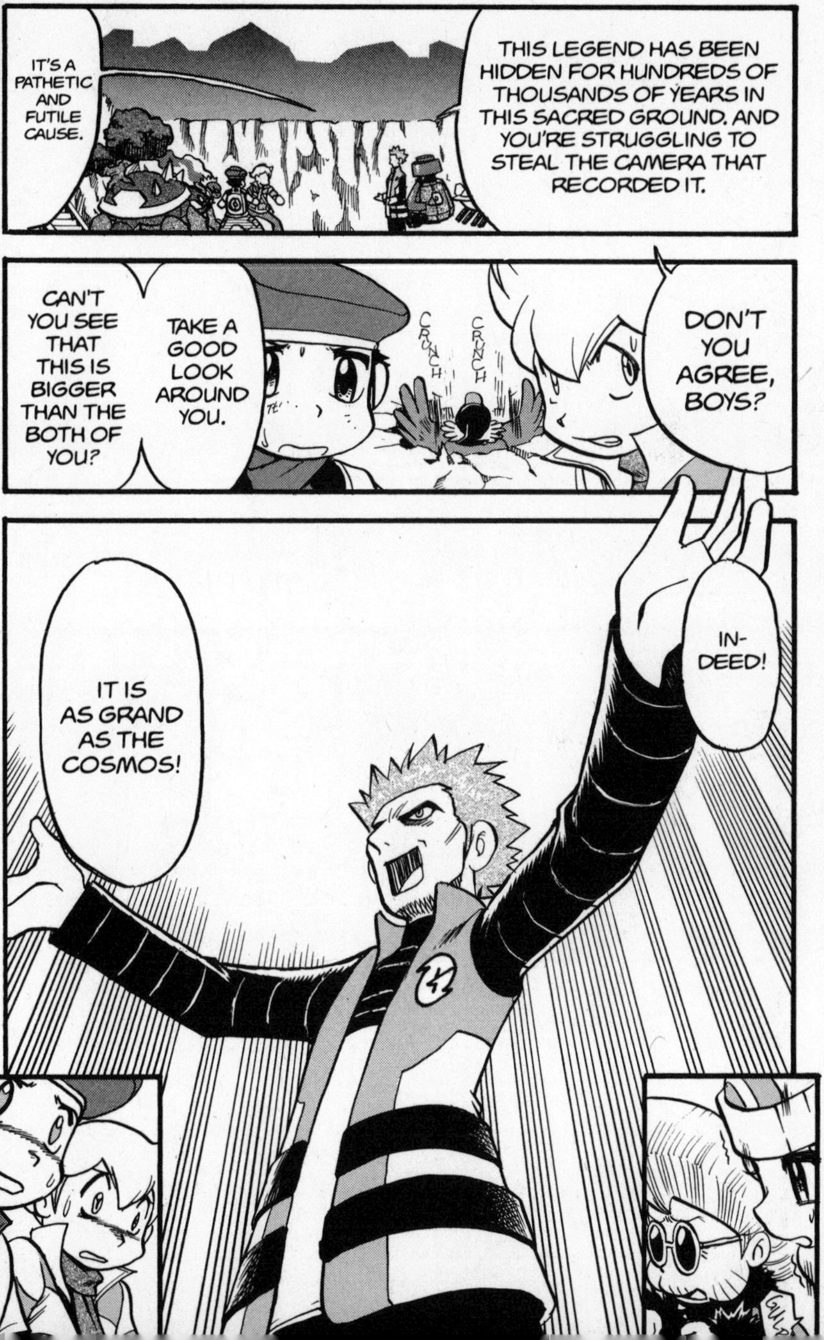
THIS LEGEND HAS BEEN HIDDEN FOR HUNDREDS OF THOUSANDS OF YEARS IN THIS SACRED GROUND. AND YOU'RE STRUGGLING TO STEAL THE CAMERA THAT RECORDED IT.
IT'S A PATHETIC AND FUTILE CAUSE.
DON'T YOU AGREE, BOYS?
CRUNCH
CRUNCH
TAKE A GOOD LOOK AROUND YOU.
CAN'T YOU SEE THAT THIS IS BIGGER THAN THE BOTH OF YOU?
IN-DEED!
IT IS AS GRAND AS THE COSMOS!
GULP

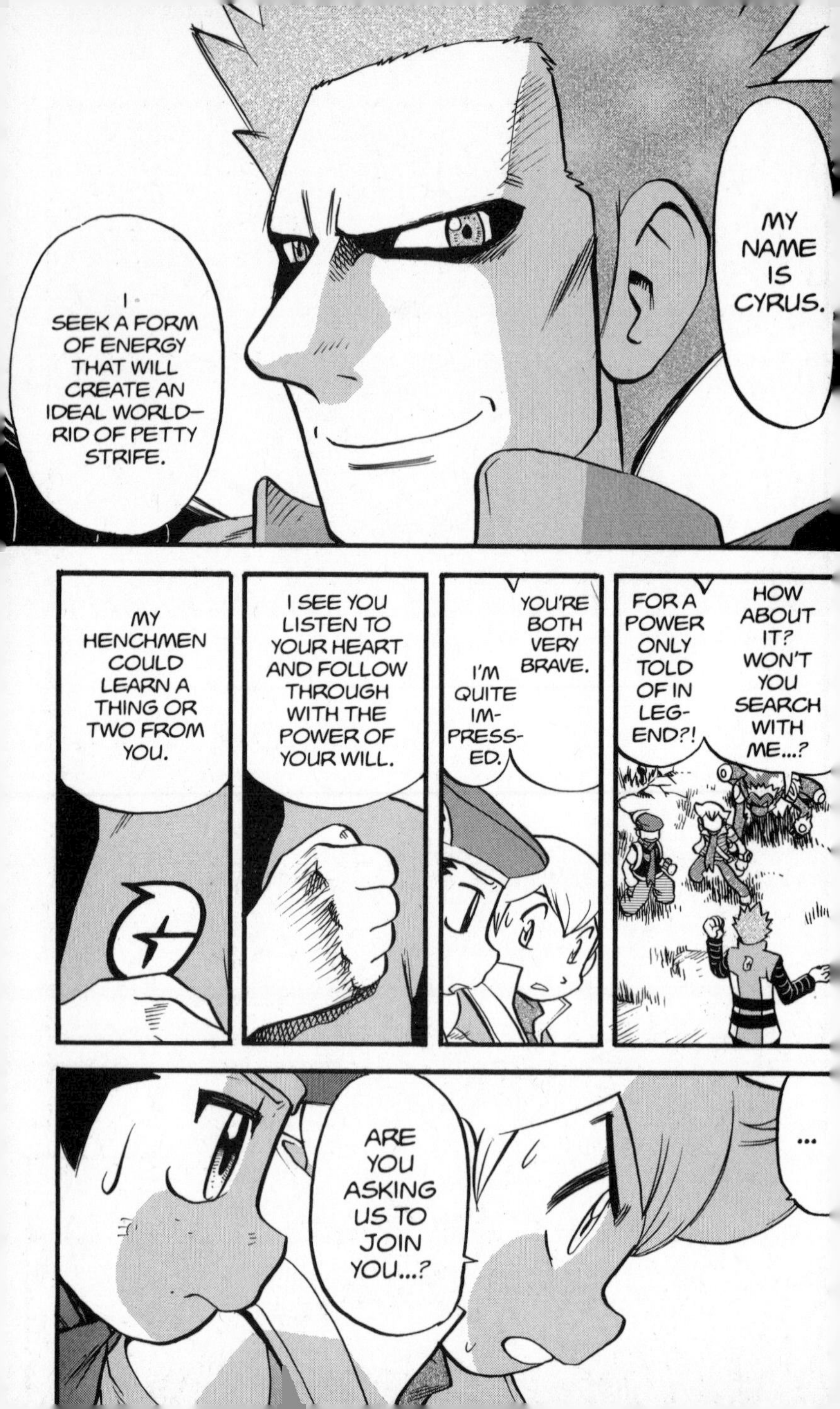
MY NAME IS CYRUS.
I SEEK A FORM OF ENERGY THAT WILL CREATE AN IDEAL WORLD—RID OF PETTY STRIFE.
HOW ABOUT IT? WON'T YOU SEARCH WITH ME...?
FOR A POWER ONLY TOLD OF IN LEG-END?!
YOU'RE BOTH VERY BRAVE.
I'M QUITE IM-PRESS-ED.
I SEE YOU LISTEN TO YOUR HEART AND FOLLOW THROUGH WITH THE POWER OF YOUR WILL.
MY HENCHMEN COULD LEARN A THING OR TWO FROM YOU.
...
ARE YOU ASKING US TO JOIN YOU...?

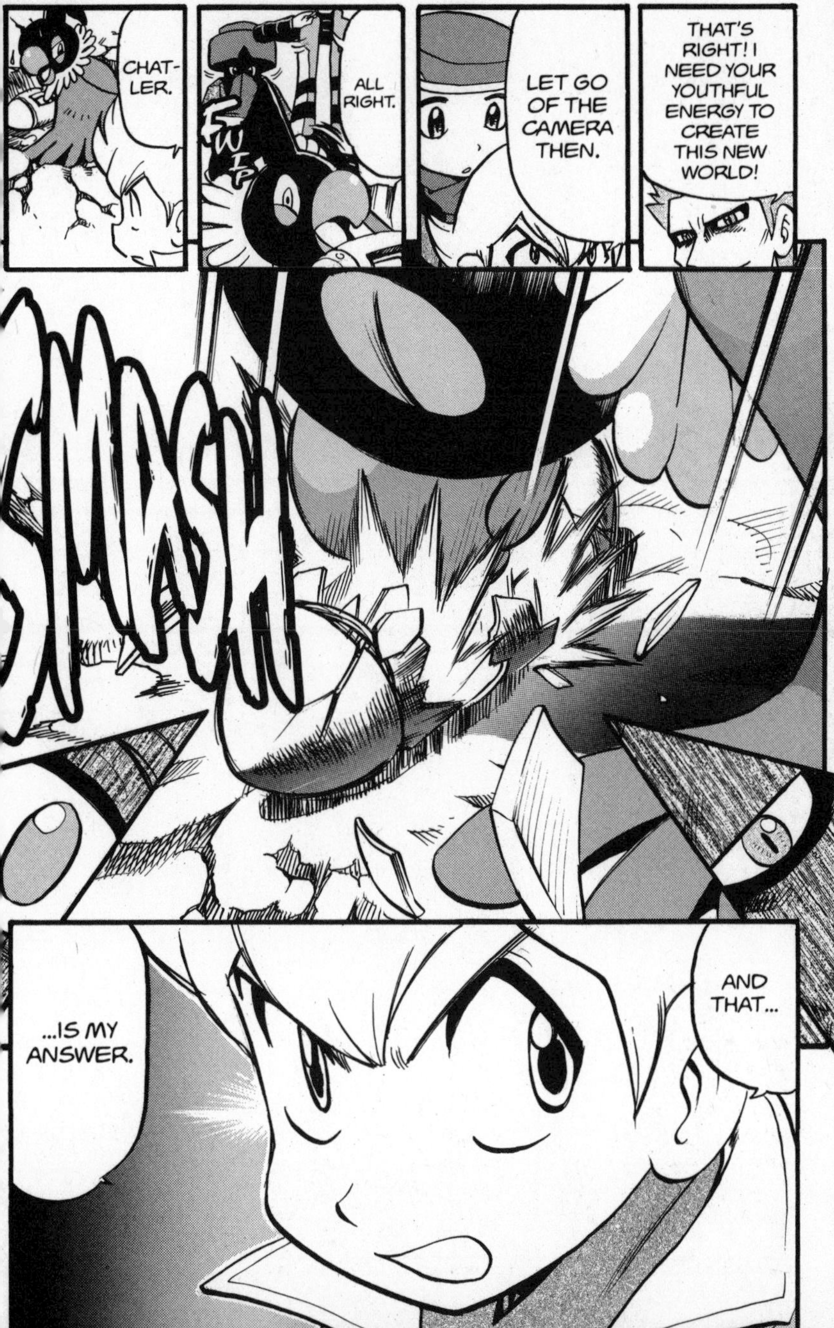
THAT'S RIGHT! I NEED YOUR YOUTHFUL ENERGY TO CREATE THIS NEW WORLD!
LET GO OF THE CAMERA THEN.
ALL RIGHT.
FWIP
CHAT-LER.
SMASH
AND THAT...
...IS MY ANSWER.

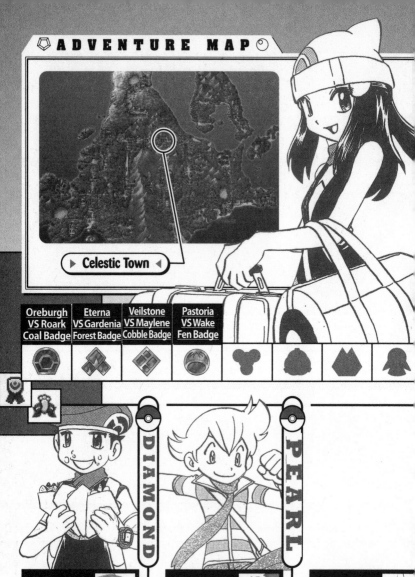

▶ Celestic Town ◀

Oreburgh VS Roark Coal Badge	Eterna VS Gardenia Forest Badge	Veilstone VS Maylene Cobble Badge	Pastoria VS Wake Fen Badge				

DIAMOND

PEARL

▶ TRU
Torterra ♂

LAX ◀
Munchlax ♂

▶ CHIMLER
Infernape ♂

▶ CHATLER
Chatot ♂

▶ EMPOLEON
Empoleon ♀

▶ PONYTA
Ponyta ♂

33

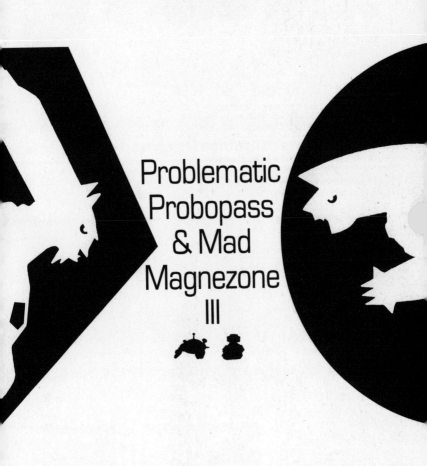

Problematic
Probopass
& Mad
Magnezone
III

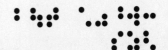

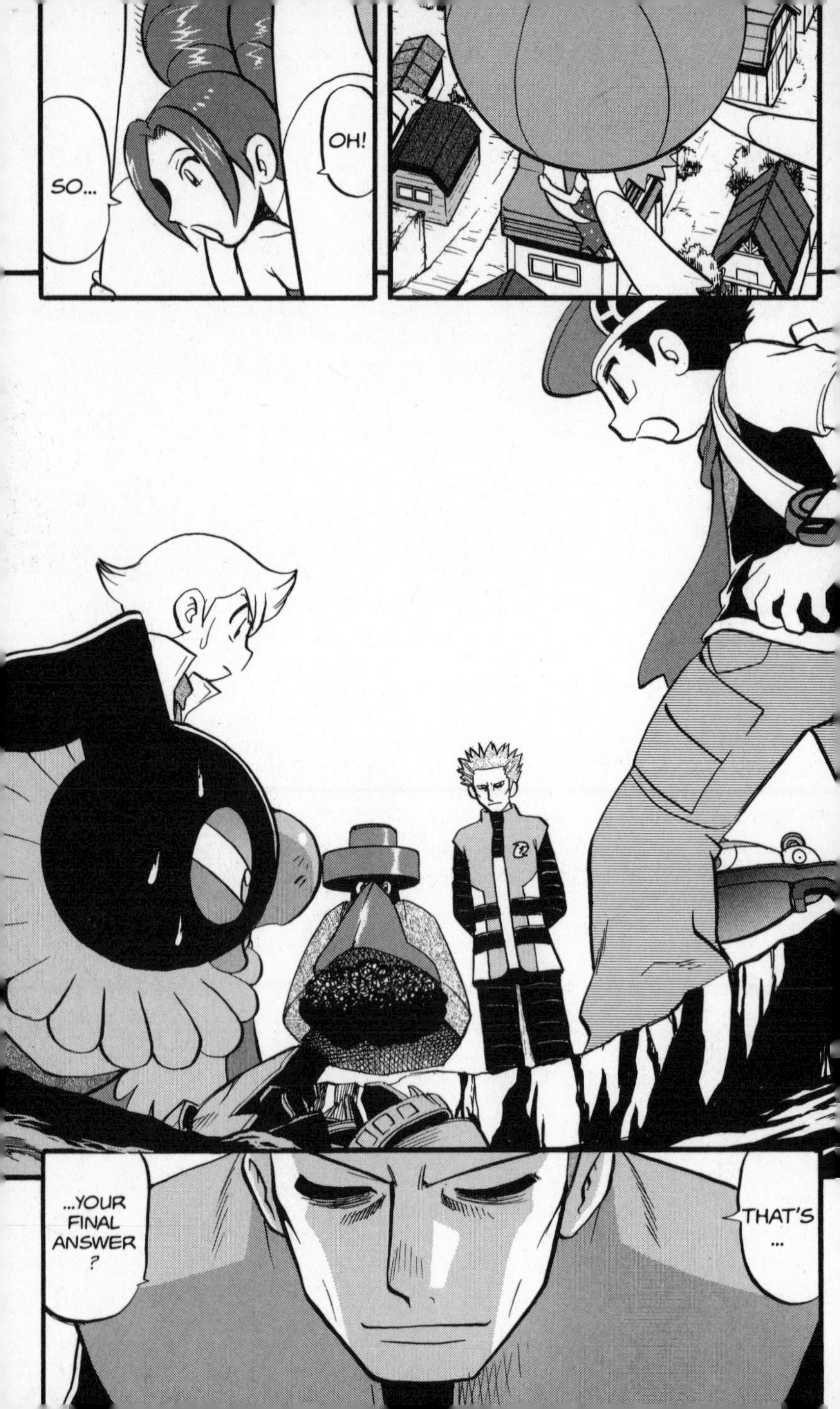
OH!
SO...
THAT'S ...
...YOUR FINAL ANSWER ?

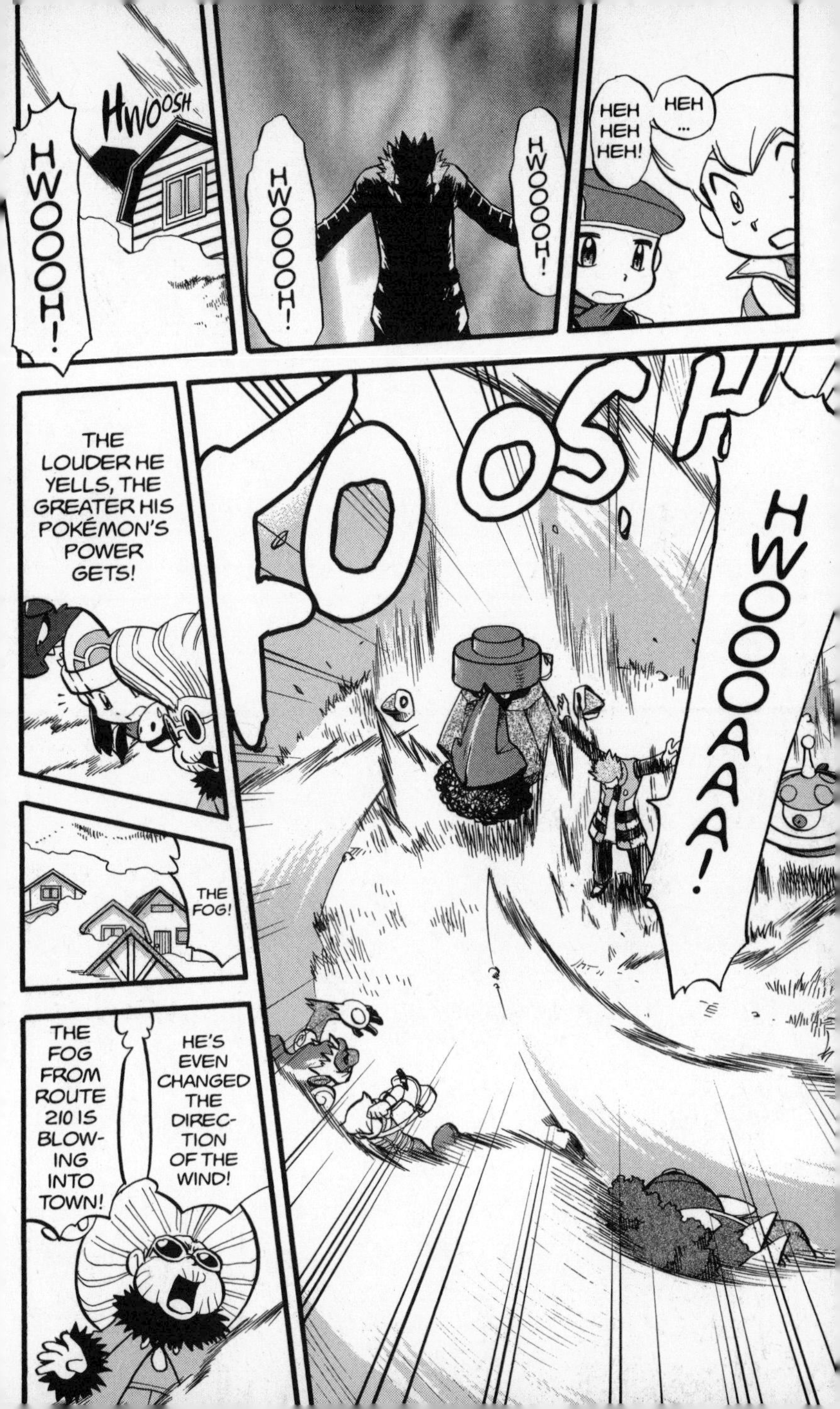
HEH ...
HEH HEH HEH!
HWOOOOH!
HWOOOOH!
HWOOSH
HWOOOH!
OOSH
HWOOOOAAA!
THE LOUDER HE YELLS, THE GREATER HIS POKÉMON'S POWER GETS!
THE FOG!
HE'S EVEN CHANGED THE DIREC-TION OF THE WIND!
THE FOG FROM ROUTE 210 IS BLOW-ING INTO TOWN!

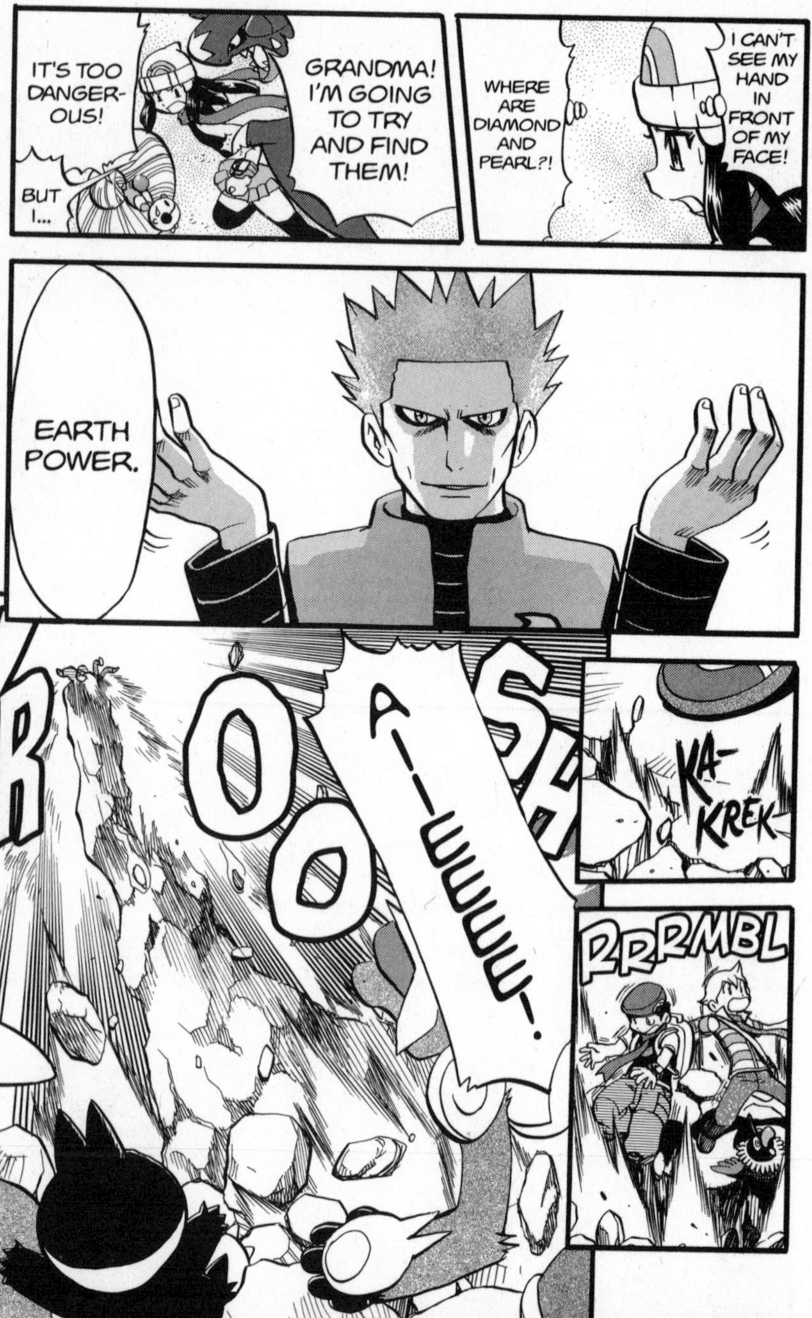
I CAN'T SEE MY HAND IN FRONT OF MY FACE!
WHERE ARE DIAMOND AND PEARL?!
GRANDMA! I'M GOING TO TRY AND FIND THEM!
IT'S TOO DANGEROUS!
BUT I...
EARTH POWER.
KA-KREK
RRRMBL
ROOSH
AIEEEE!

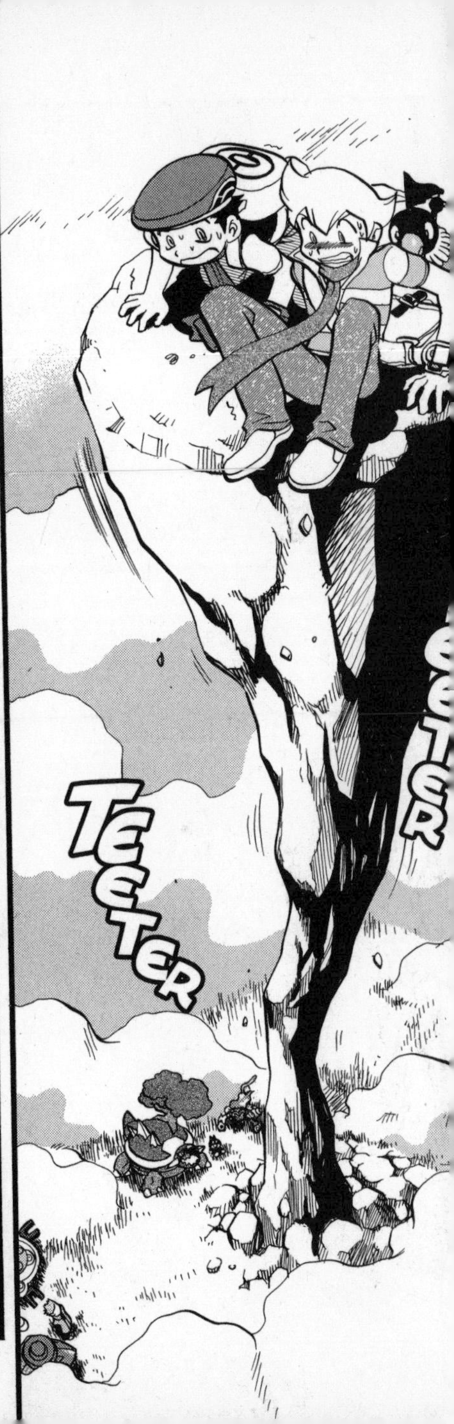
TEETER

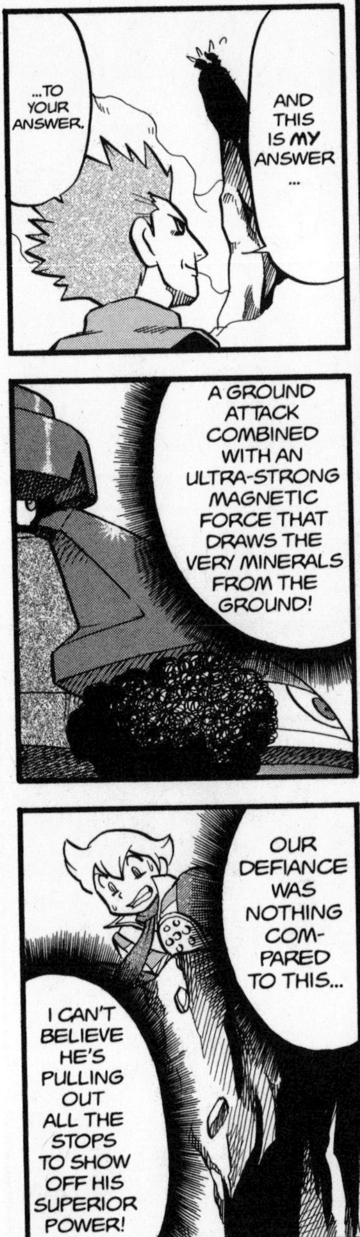
AND THIS IS MY ANSWER ...
...TO YOUR ANSWER.
A GROUND ATTACK COMBINED WITH AN ULTRA-STRONG MAGNETIC FORCE THAT DRAWS THE VERY MINERALS FROM THE GROUND!
OUR DEFIANCE WAS NOTHING COMPARED TO THIS...
I CAN'T BELIEVE HE'S PULLING OUT ALL THE STOPS TO SHOW OFF HIS SUPERIOR POWER!

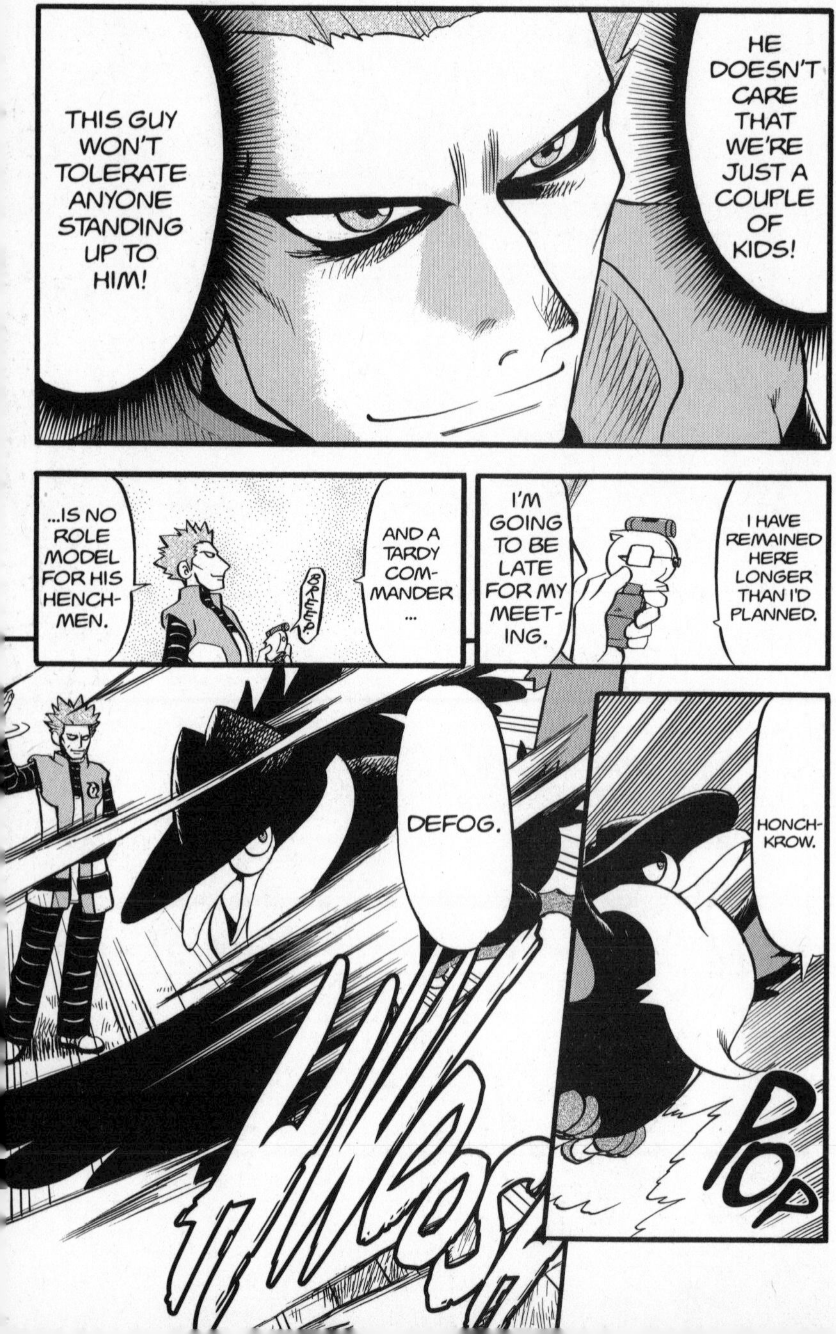
HE DOESN'T CARE THAT WE'RE JUST A COUPLE OF KIDS!
THIS GUY WON'T TOLERATE ANYONE STANDING UP TO HIM!
I HAVE REMAINED HERE LONGER THAN I'D PLANNED.
I'M GOING TO BE LATE FOR MY MEET-ING.
AND A TARDY COM-MANDER ...
BREEP.
...IS NO ROLE MODEL FOR HIS HENCH-MEN.
HONCH-KROW.
POP
DEFOG.

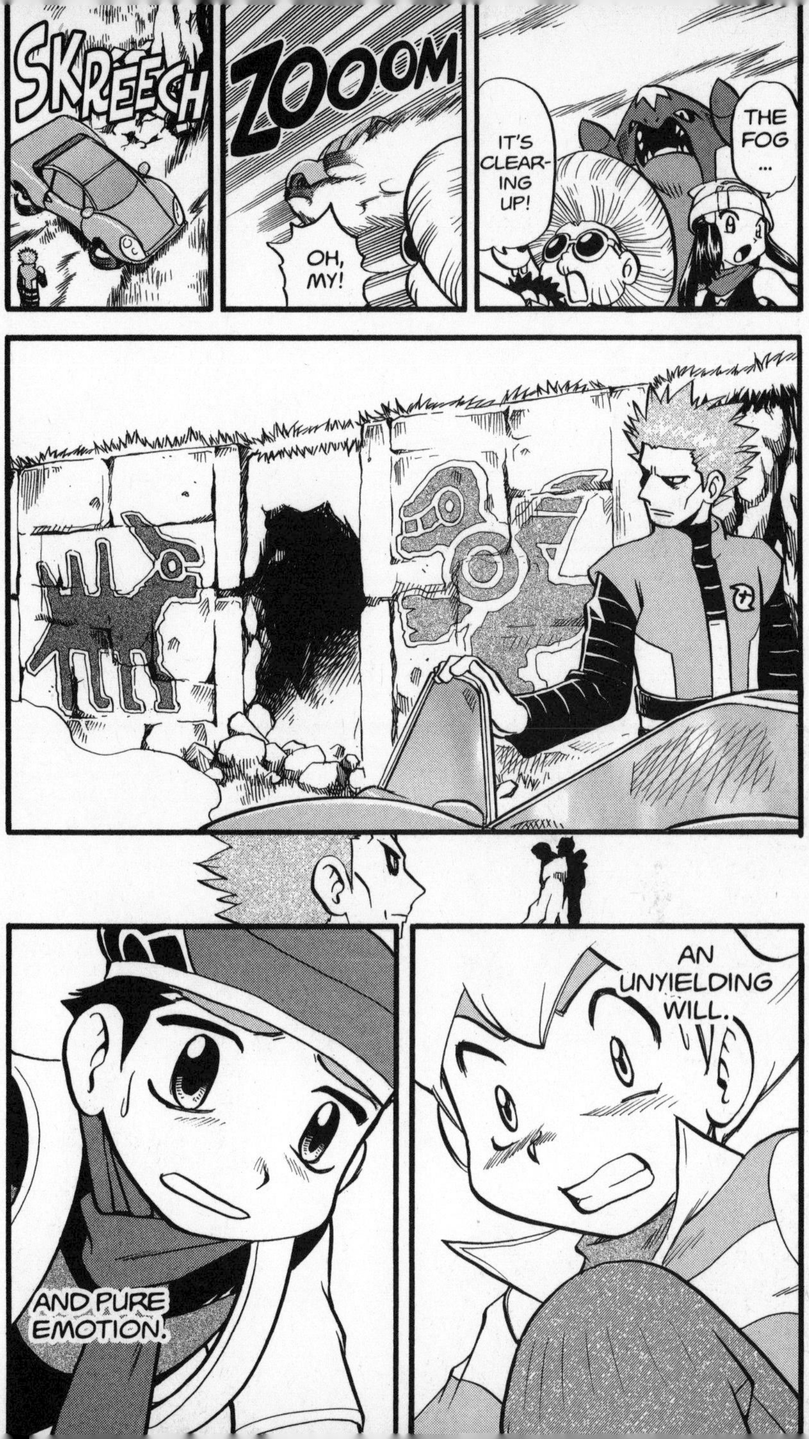
THE FOG ...
IT'S CLEARING UP!
ZOOOM
OH, MY!
SKREECH
AN UNYIELDING WILL.
AND PURE EMOTION.

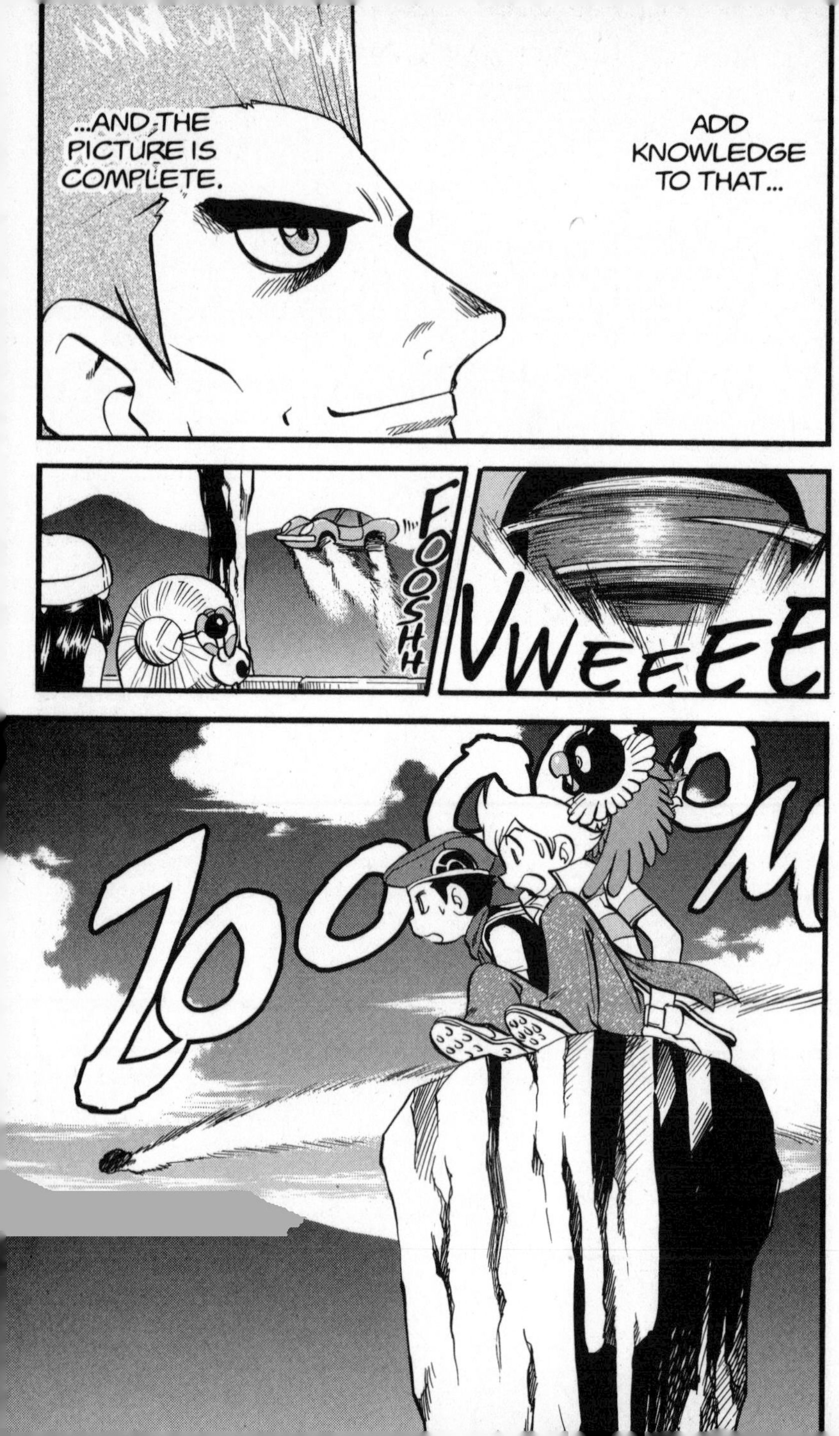
ADD KNOWLEDGE TO THAT...
...AND THE PICTURE IS COMPLETE.
VWEEEE
FOOOSHH
ZOOOM

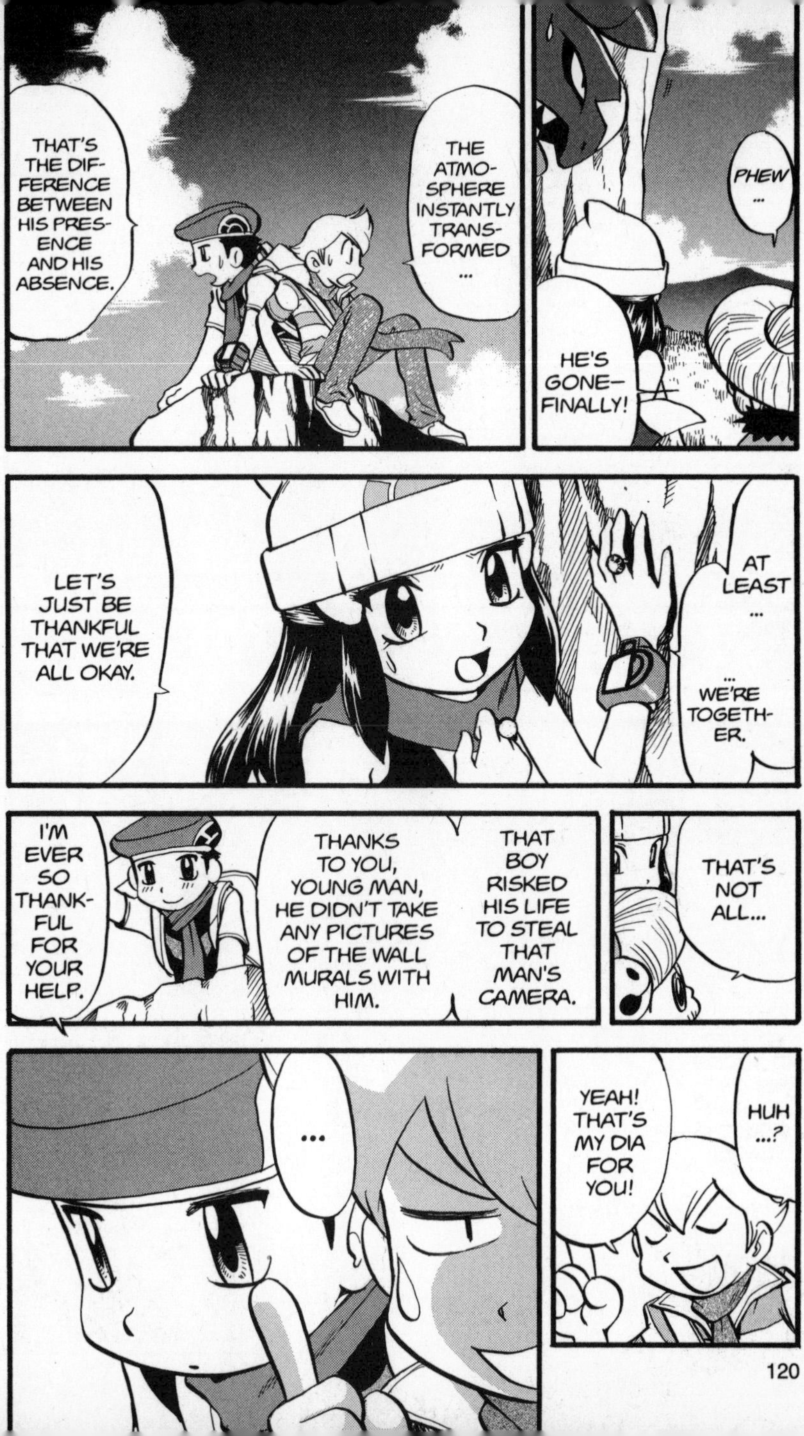
PHEW...
HE'S GONE—FINALLY!
THE ATMOSPHERE INSTANTLY TRANSFORMED...
THAT'S THE DIFFERENCE BETWEEN HIS PRESENCE AND HIS ABSENCE.
AT LEAST...
...WE'RE TOGETHER.
LET'S JUST BE THANKFUL THAT WE'RE ALL OKAY.
THAT'S NOT ALL...
THAT BOY RISKED HIS LIFE TO STEAL THAT MAN'S CAMERA.
THANKS TO YOU, YOUNG MAN, HE DIDN'T TAKE ANY PICTURES OF THE WALL MURALS WITH HIM.
I'M EVER SO THANKFUL FOR YOUR HELP.
HUH...?
YEAH! THAT'S MY DIA FOR YOU!
...

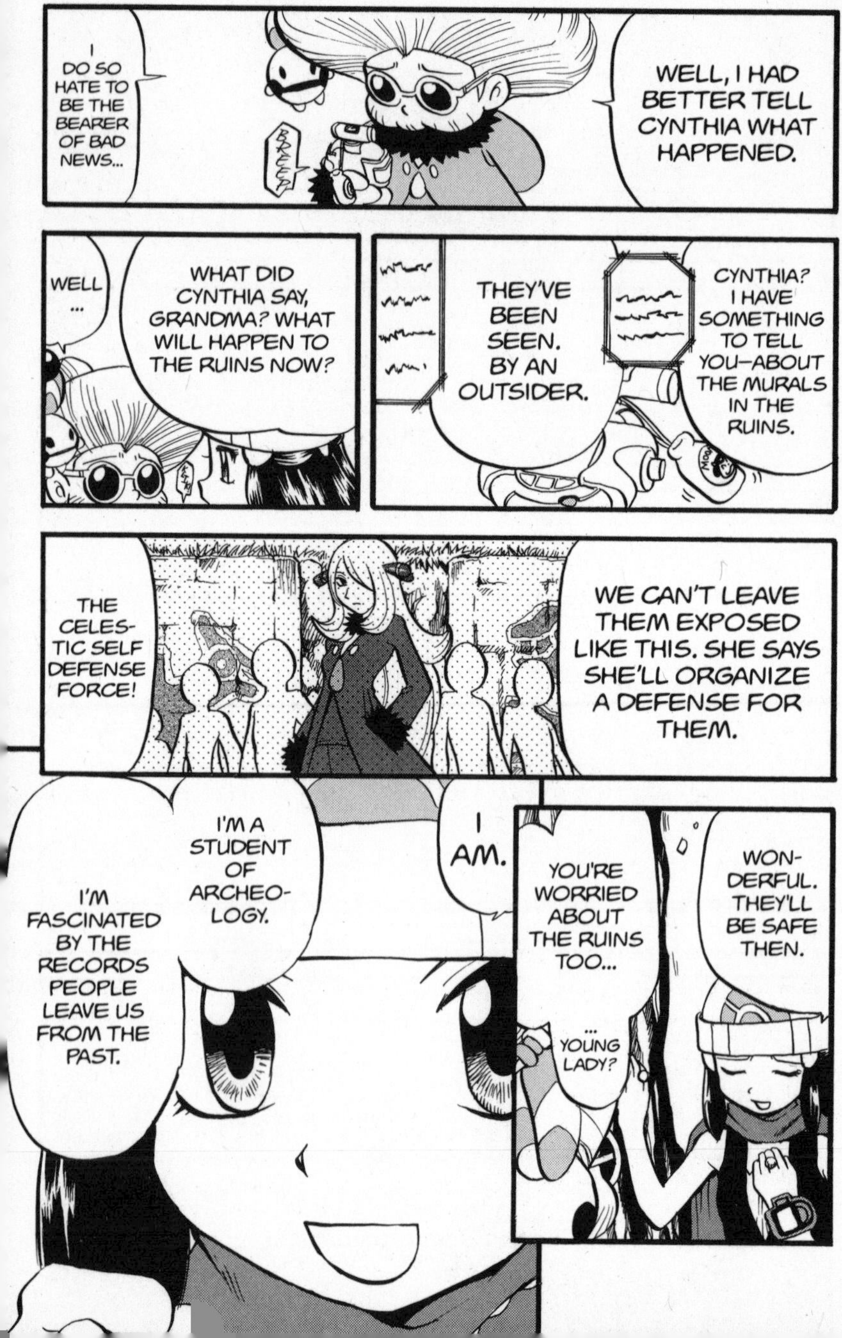
WELL, I HAD BETTER TELL CYNTHIA WHAT HAPPENED.
BREEEP!
I DO SO HATE TO BE THE BEARER OF BAD NEWS...
CYNTHIA? I HAVE SOMETHING TO TELL YOU—ABOUT THE MURALS IN THE RUINS.
THEY'VE BEEN SEEN. BY AN OUTSIDER.
WHAT DID CYNTHIA SAY, GRANDMA? WHAT WILL HAPPEN TO THE RUINS NOW?
WELL ...
WE CAN'T LEAVE THEM EXPOSED LIKE THIS. SHE SAYS SHE'LL ORGANIZE A DEFENSE FOR THEM.
THE CELESTIC SELF DEFENSE FORCE!
WONDERFUL. THEY'LL BE SAFE THEN.
YOU'RE WORRIED ABOUT THE RUINS TOO...
... YOUNG LADY?
I AM.
I'M A STUDENT OF ARCHEOLOGY.
I'M FASCINATED BY THE RECORDS PEOPLE LEAVE US FROM THE PAST.

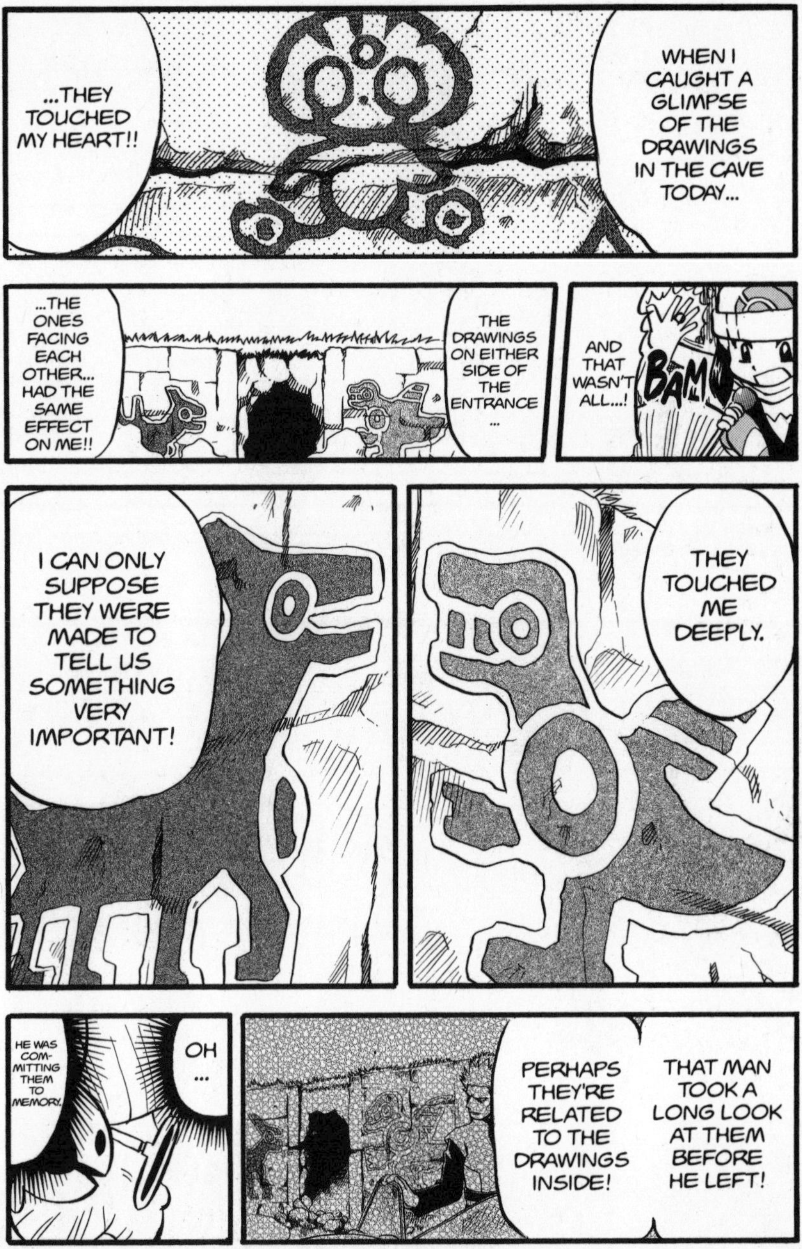
WHEN I CAUGHT A GLIMPSE OF THE DRAWINGS IN THE CAVE TODAY...
...THEY TOUCHED MY HEART!!
AND THAT WASN'T ALL...!
BAM
THE DRAWINGS ON EITHER SIDE OF THE ENTRANCE ...
...THE ONES FACING EACH OTHER... HAD THE SAME EFFECT ON ME!!
THEY TOUCHED ME DEEPLY.
I CAN ONLY SUPPOSE THEY WERE MADE TO TELL US SOMETHING VERY IMPORTANT!
THAT MAN TOOK A LONG LOOK AT THEM BEFORE HE LEFT!
PERHAPS THEY'RE RELATED TO THE DRAWINGS INSIDE!
OH ...
HE WAS COM-MITTING THEM TO MEMORY.

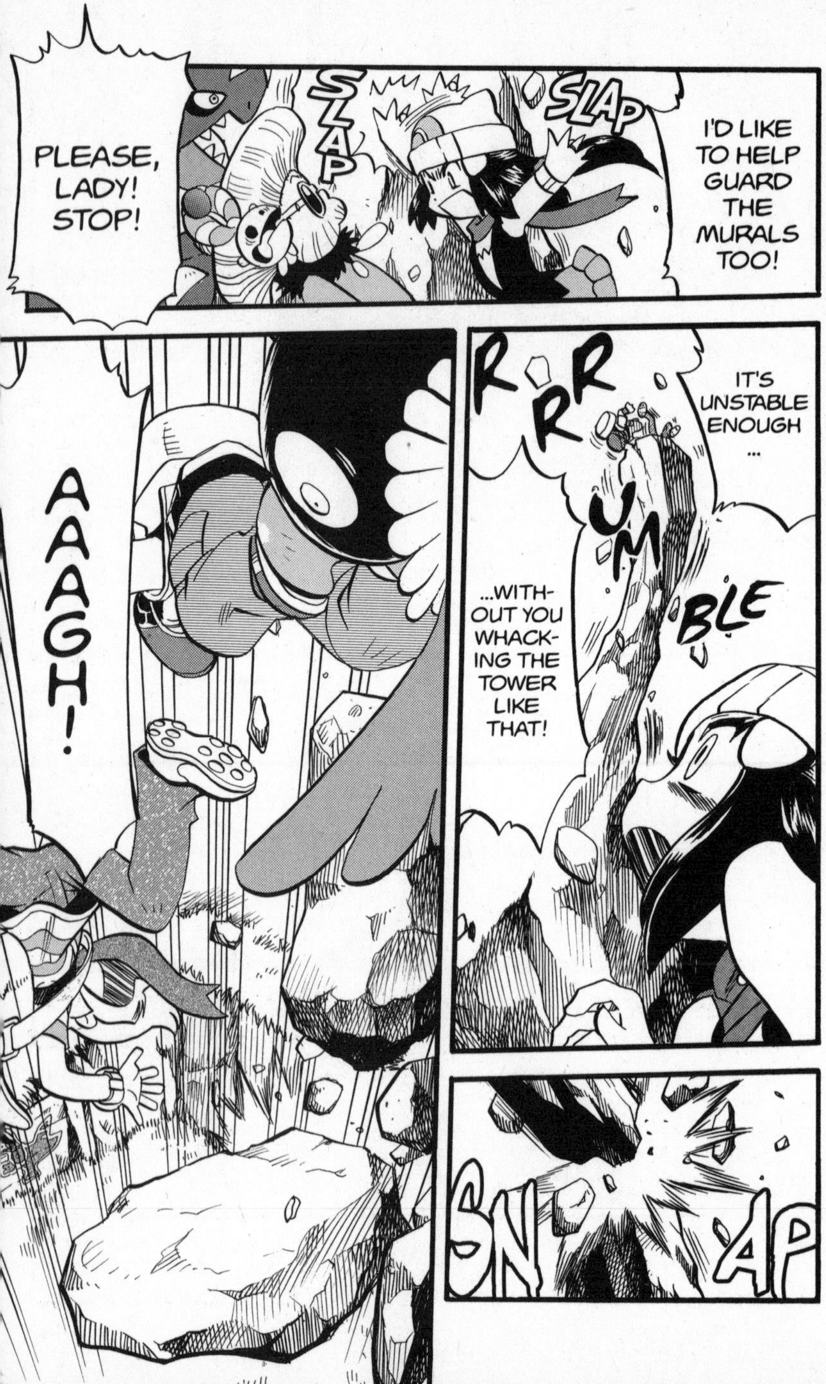
SLAP
I'D LIKE TO HELP GUARD THE MURALS TOO!
SLAP
PLEASE, LADY! STOP!
RRR
IT'S UNSTABLE ENOUGH ...
UMBLE
...WITH-OUT YOU WHACK-ING THE TOWER LIKE THAT!
SNAP
AAAGH!

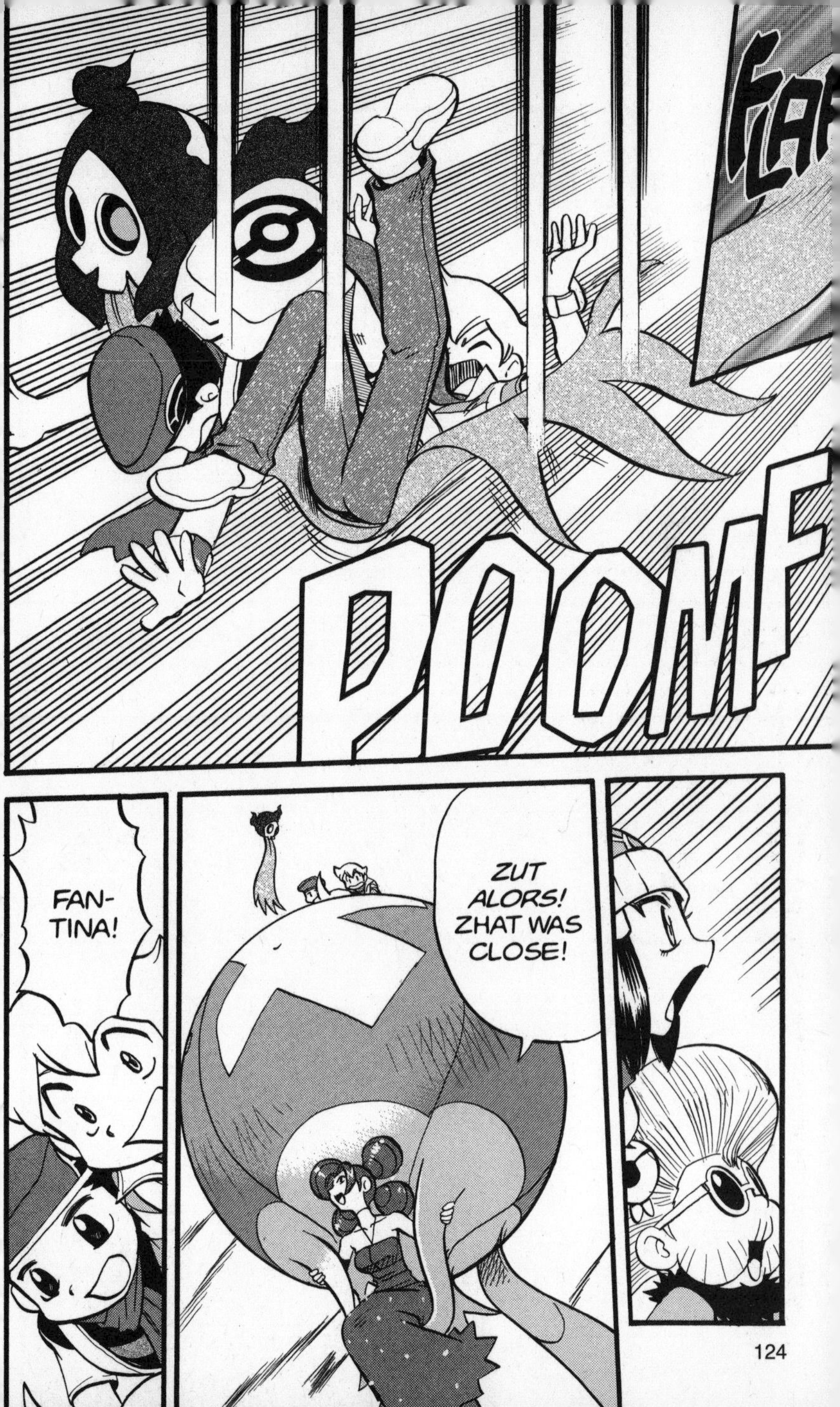
FLA
DOOMF
ZUT ALORS! ZHAT WAS CLOSE!
FAN-TINA!

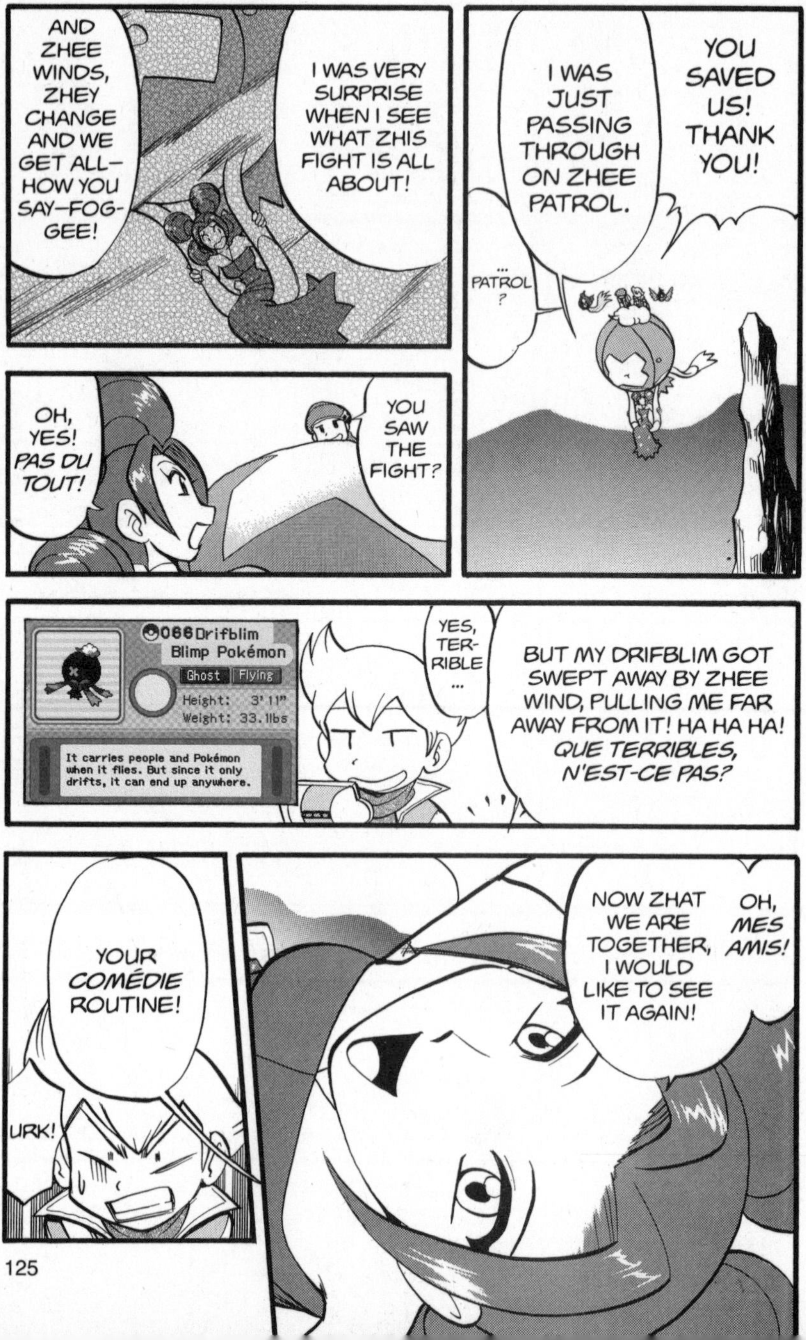
YOU SAVED US! THANK YOU!
I WAS JUST PASSING THROUGH ON ZHEE PATROL.
... PATROL?
I WAS VERY SURPRISE WHEN I SEE WHAT ZHIS FIGHT IS ALL ABOUT!
AND ZHEE WINDS, ZHEY CHANGE AND WE GET ALL—HOW YOU SAY—FOG-GEE!
YOU SAW THE FIGHT?
OH, YES! *PAS DU TOUT!*
BUT MY DRIFBLIM GOT SWEPT AWAY BY ZHEE WIND, PULLING ME FAR AWAY FROM IT! HA HA HA! *QUE TERRIBLES, N'EST-CE PAS?*
YES, TERRIBLE...
066 Drifblim
Blimp Pokémon
Ghost
Flying
Height: 3' 11"
Weight: 33.1lbs
It carries people and Pokémon when it flies. But since it only drifts, it can end up anywhere.
OH, *MES AMIS!*
NOW ZHAT WE ARE TOGETHER, I WOULD LIKE TO SEE IT AGAIN!
YOUR *COMÉDIE* ROUTINE!
URK!

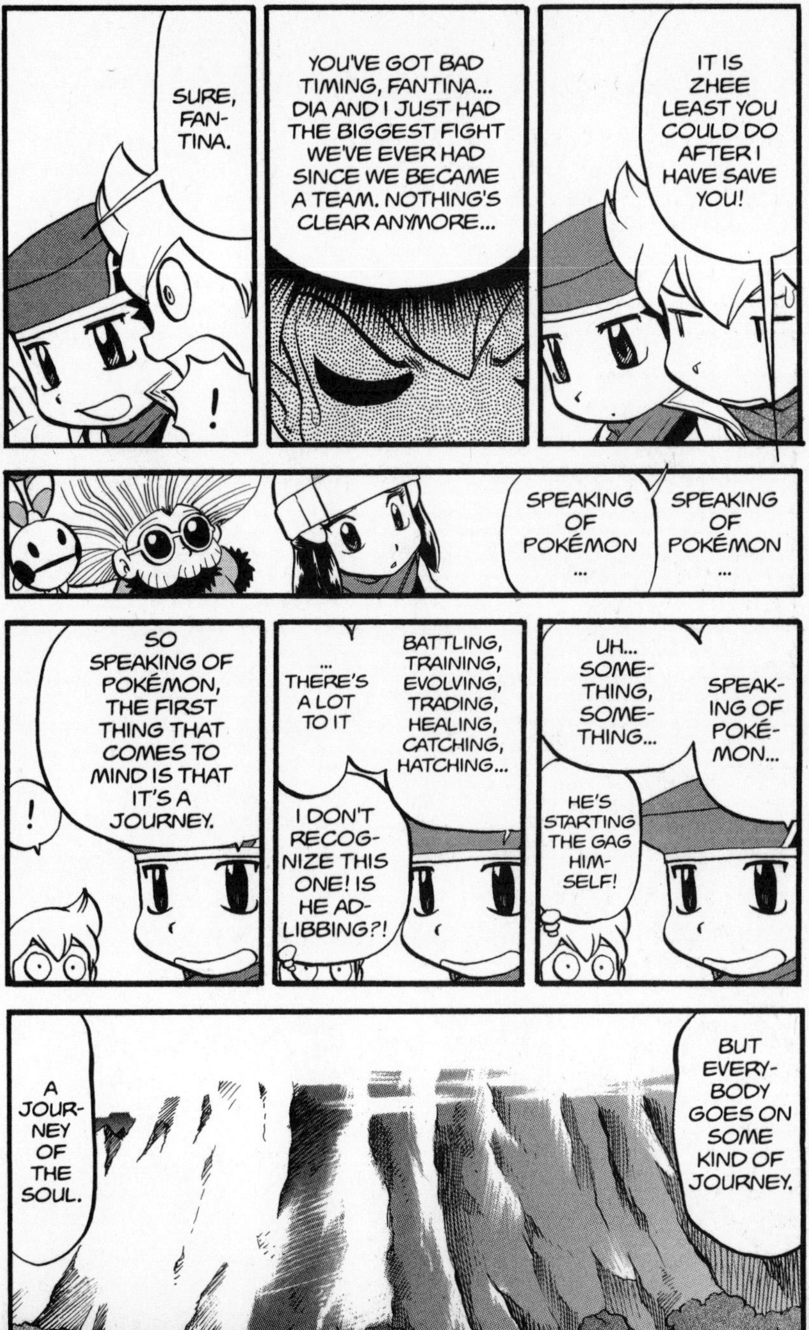

IT IS ZHEE LEAST YOU COULD DO AFTER I HAVE SAVE YOU!
YOU'VE GOT BAD TIMING, FANTINA... DIA AND I JUST HAD THE BIGGEST FIGHT WE'VE EVER HAD SINCE WE BECAME A TEAM. NOTHING'S CLEAR ANYMORE...
SURE, FANTINA.
!
SPEAKING OF POKÉMON ...
SPEAKING OF POKÉMON ...
SPEAKING OF POKÉMON...
UH... SOMETHING, SOMETHING...
HE'S STARTING THE GAG HIMSELF!
BATTLING, TRAINING, EVOLVING, TRADING, HEALING, CATCHING, HATCHING...
... THERE'S A LOT TO IT
I DON'T RECOGNIZE THIS ONE! IS HE AD-LIBBING?!
SO SPEAKING OF POKÉMON, THE FIRST THING THAT COMES TO MIND IS THAT IT'S A JOURNEY.
!
BUT EVERYBODY GOES ON SOME KIND OF JOURNEY.
A JOURNEY OF THE SOUL.

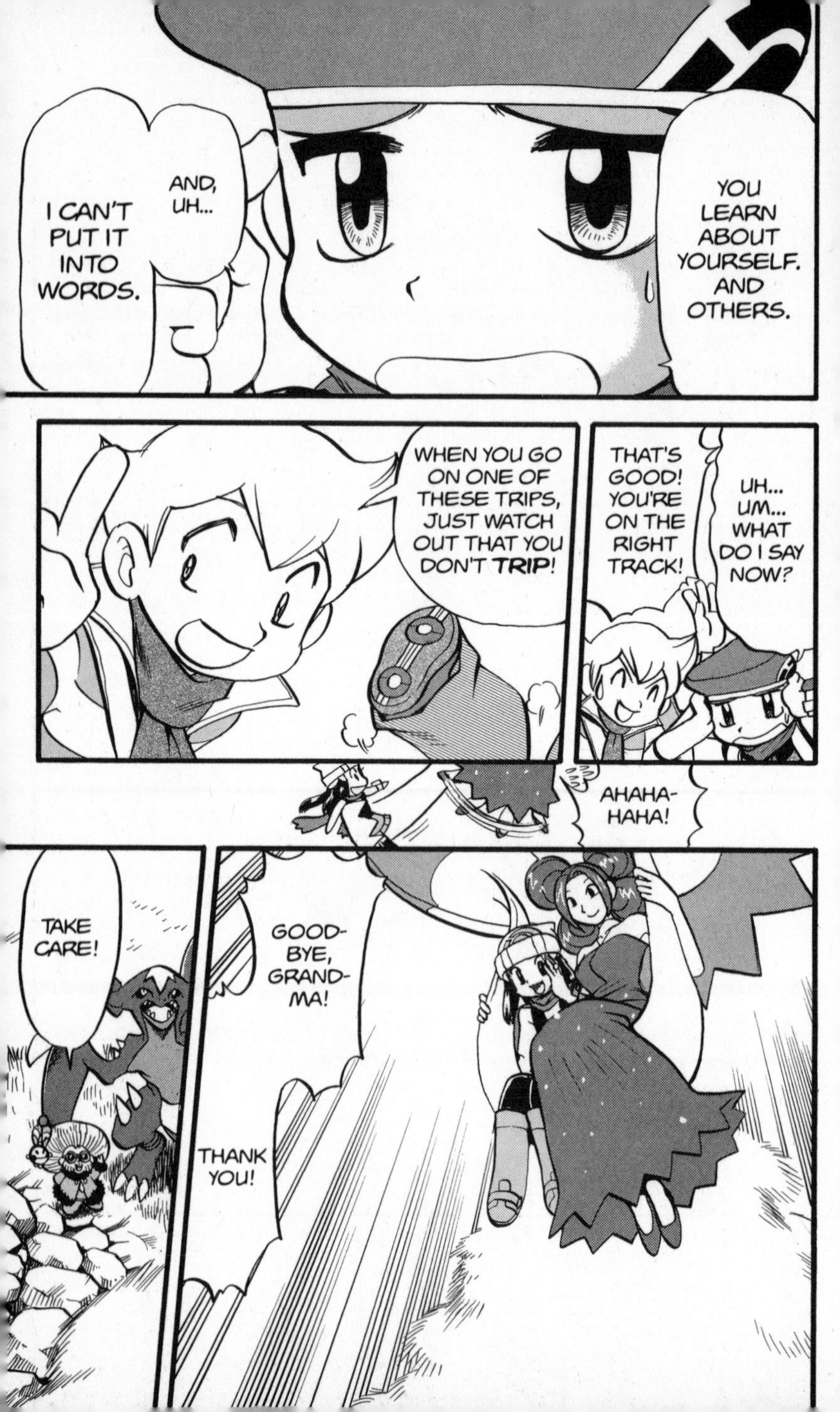
YOU LEARN ABOUT YOURSELF. AND OTHERS.
AND, UH...
I CAN'T PUT IT INTO WORDS.
UH... UM... WHAT DO I SAY NOW?
THAT'S GOOD! YOU'RE ON THE RIGHT TRACK!
WHEN YOU GO ON ONE OF THESE TRIPS, JUST WATCH OUT THAT YOU DON'T **TRIP**!
AHAHA-HAHA!
GOOD-BYE, GRAND-MA!
THANK YOU!
TAKE CARE!

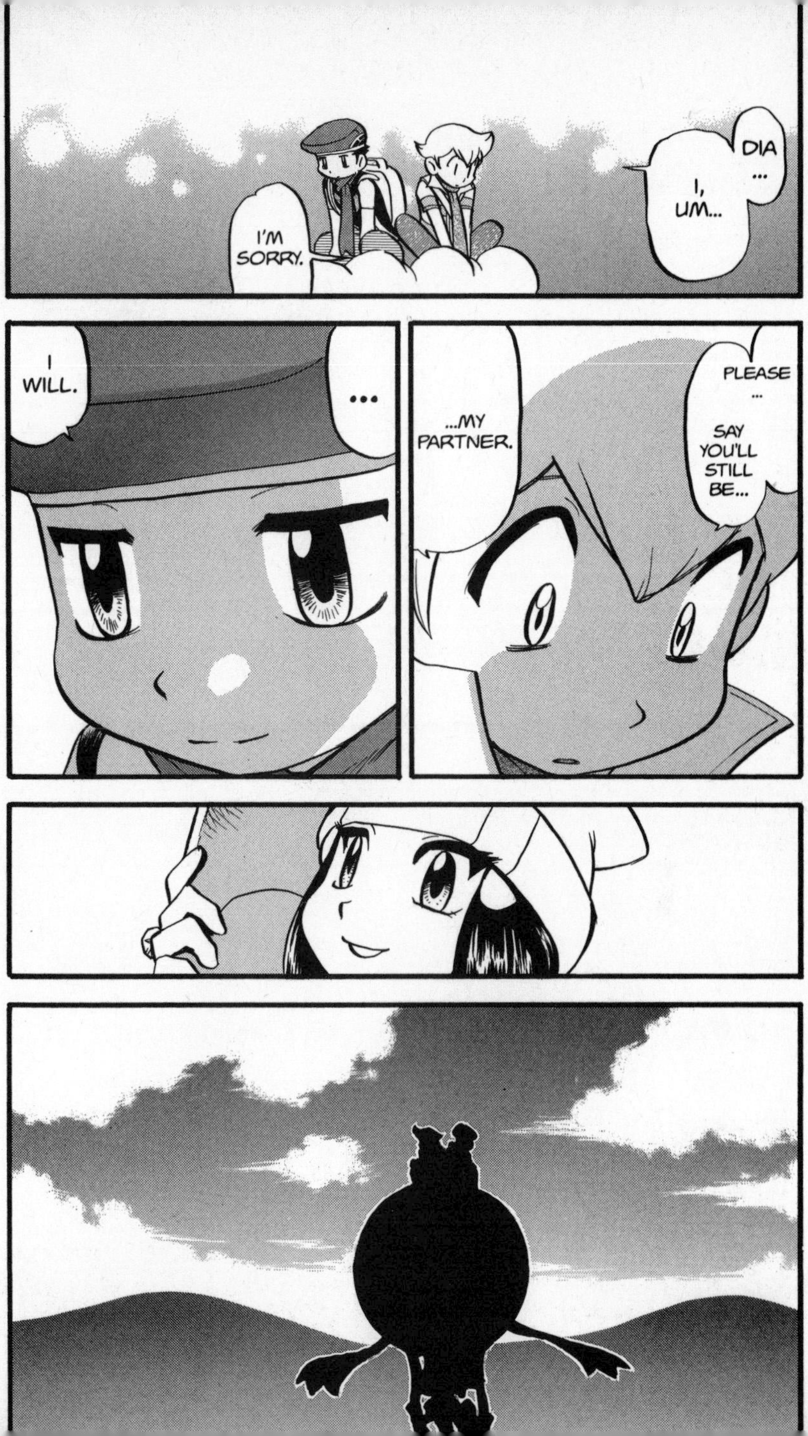
DIA... I, UM...
I'M SORRY.
PLEASE... SAY YOU'LL STILL BE...
...MY PARTNER.
...
I WILL.

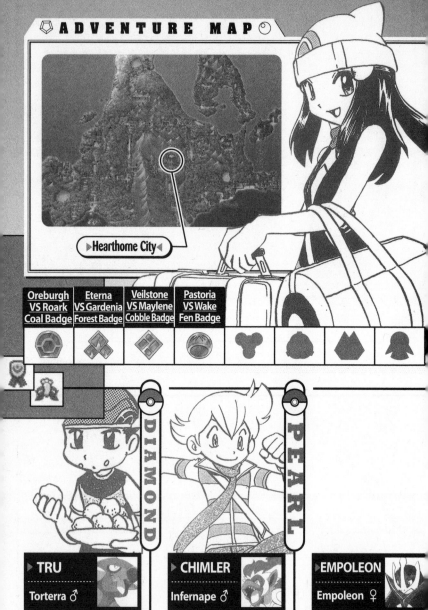

◇ ADVENTURE MAP ◎

▶Hearthome City◀

Oreburgh VS Roark Coal Badge	Eterna VS Gardenia Forest Badge	Veilstone VS Maylene Cobble Badge	Pastoria VS Wake Fen Badge				

DIAMOND

PEARL

▶TRU
Torterra ♂

▶LAX
Munchlax ♂

▶CHIMLER
Infernape ♂

▶CHATLER
Chatot ♂

▶EMPOLEON
Empoleon ♀

▶PONYTA
Ponyta ♂

34

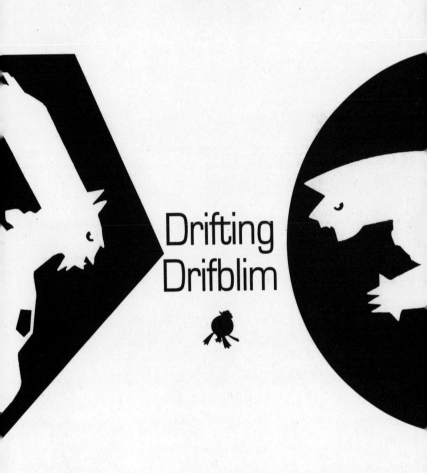

Drifting
Drifblim

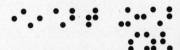

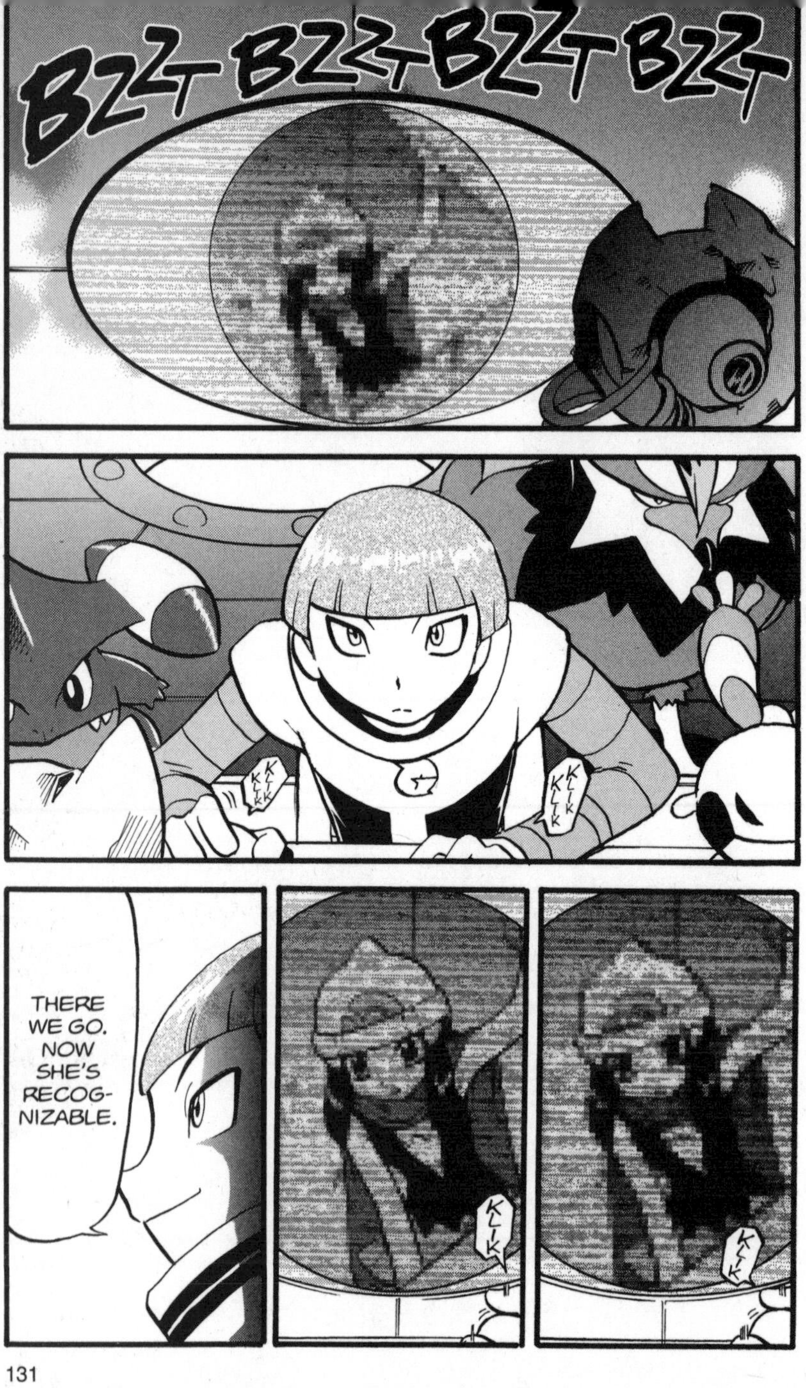
BZZT BZZT BZZT BZZT
KLIK KLIK
KLIK KLIK
KLIK
KLIK
THERE WE GO. NOW SHE'S RECOG-NIZABLE.

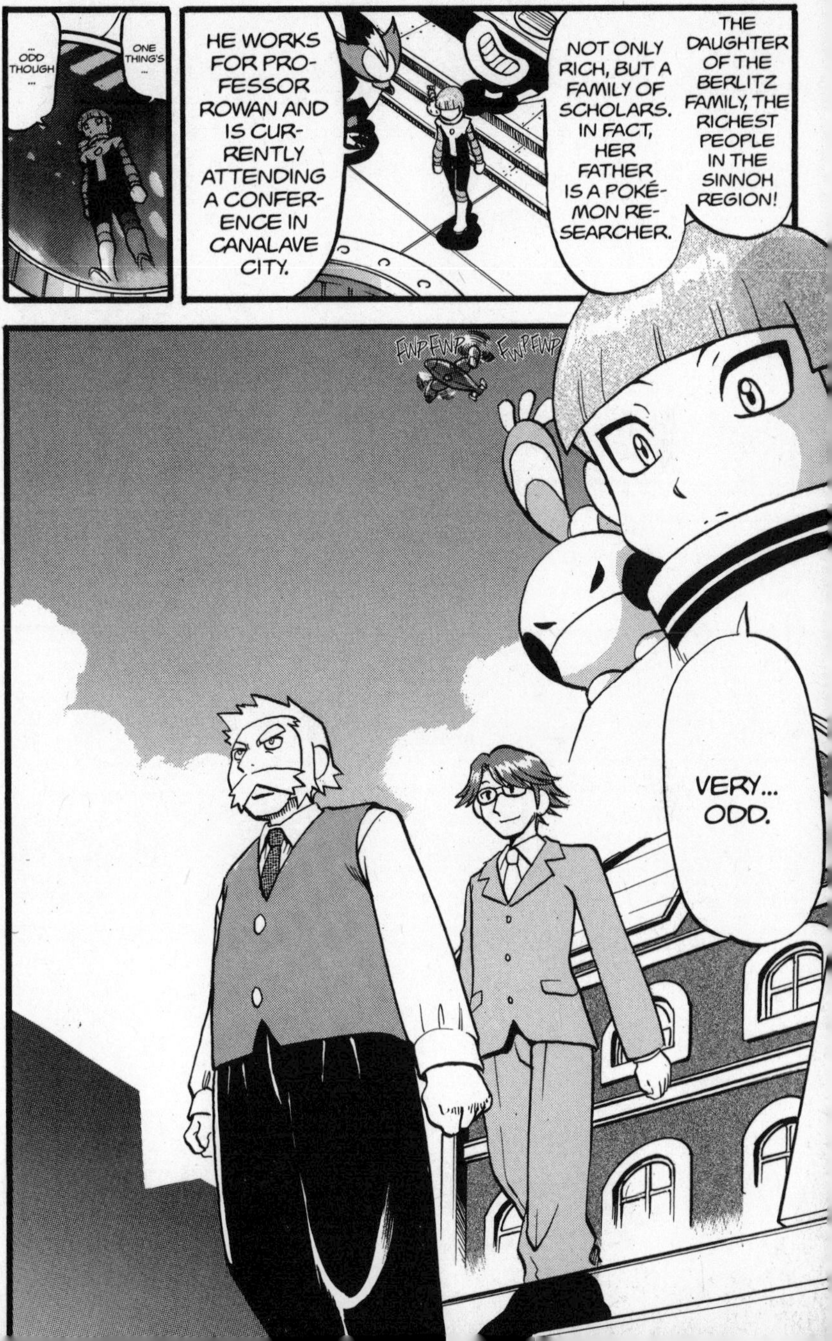
THE DAUGHTER OF THE BERLITZ FAMILY, THE RICHEST PEOPLE IN THE SINNOH REGION!
NOT ONLY RICH, BUT A FAMILY OF SCHOLARS. IN FACT, HER FATHER IS A POKÉMON RESEARCHER.
HE WORKS FOR PROFESSOR ROWAN AND IS CURRENTLY ATTENDING A CONFERENCE IN CANALAVE CITY.
ONE THING'S...
...ODD THOUGH...
FWP FWP
FWP FWP
VERY... ODD.

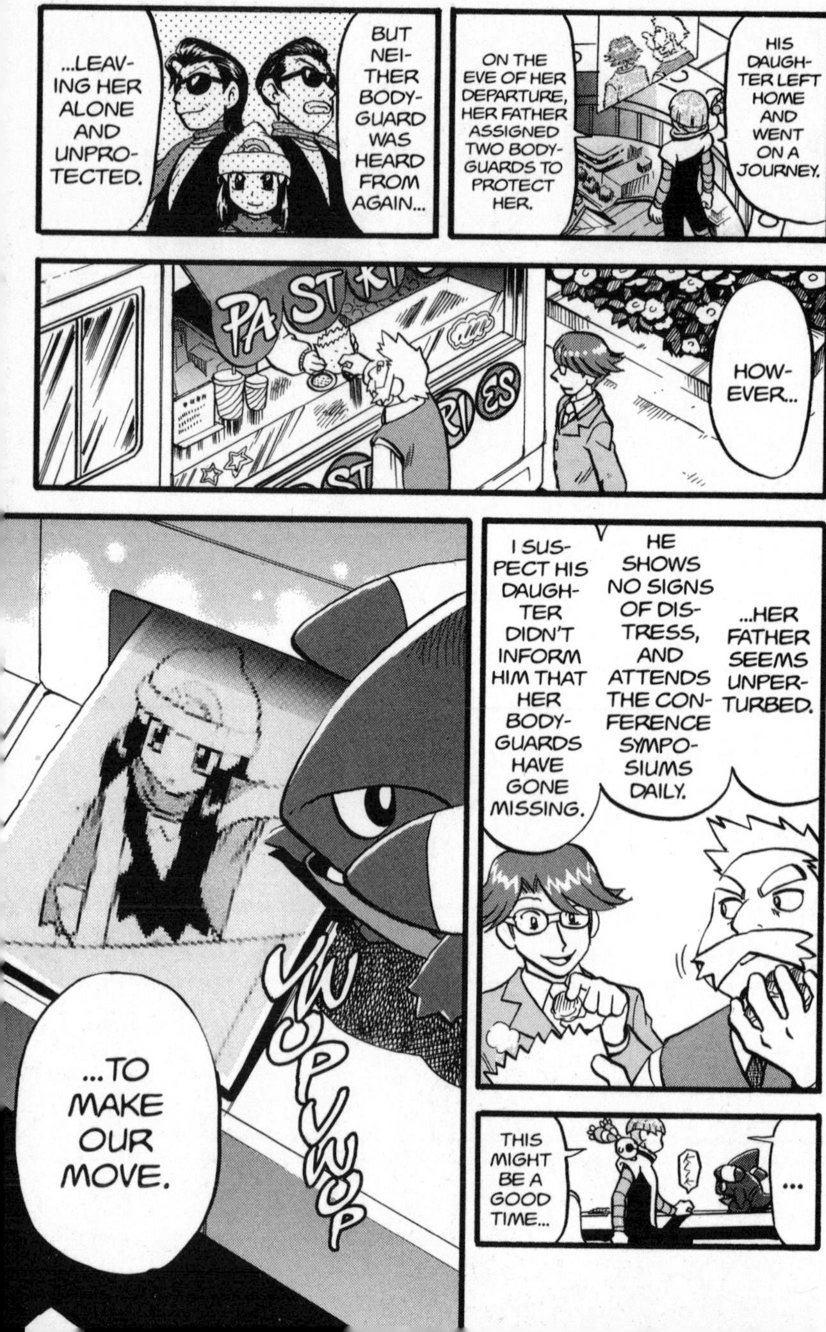

HIS DAUGHTER LEFT HOME AND WENT ON A JOURNEY.
ON THE EVE OF HER DEPARTURE, HER FATHER ASSIGNED TWO BODYGUARDS TO PROTECT HER.
BUT NEITHER BODYGUARD WAS HEARD FROM AGAIN...
...LEAVING HER ALONE AND UNPROTECTED.
HOWEVER...
...HER FATHER SEEMS UNPERTURBED.
HE SHOWS NO SIGNS OF DISTRESS, AND ATTENDS THE CONFERENCE SYMPOSIUMS DAILY.
I SUSPECT HIS DAUGHTER DIDN'T INFORM HIM THAT HER BODYGUARDS HAVE GONE MISSING.
...
THIS MIGHT BE A GOOD TIME...
WUPWUPWUP
...TO MAKE OUR MOVE.

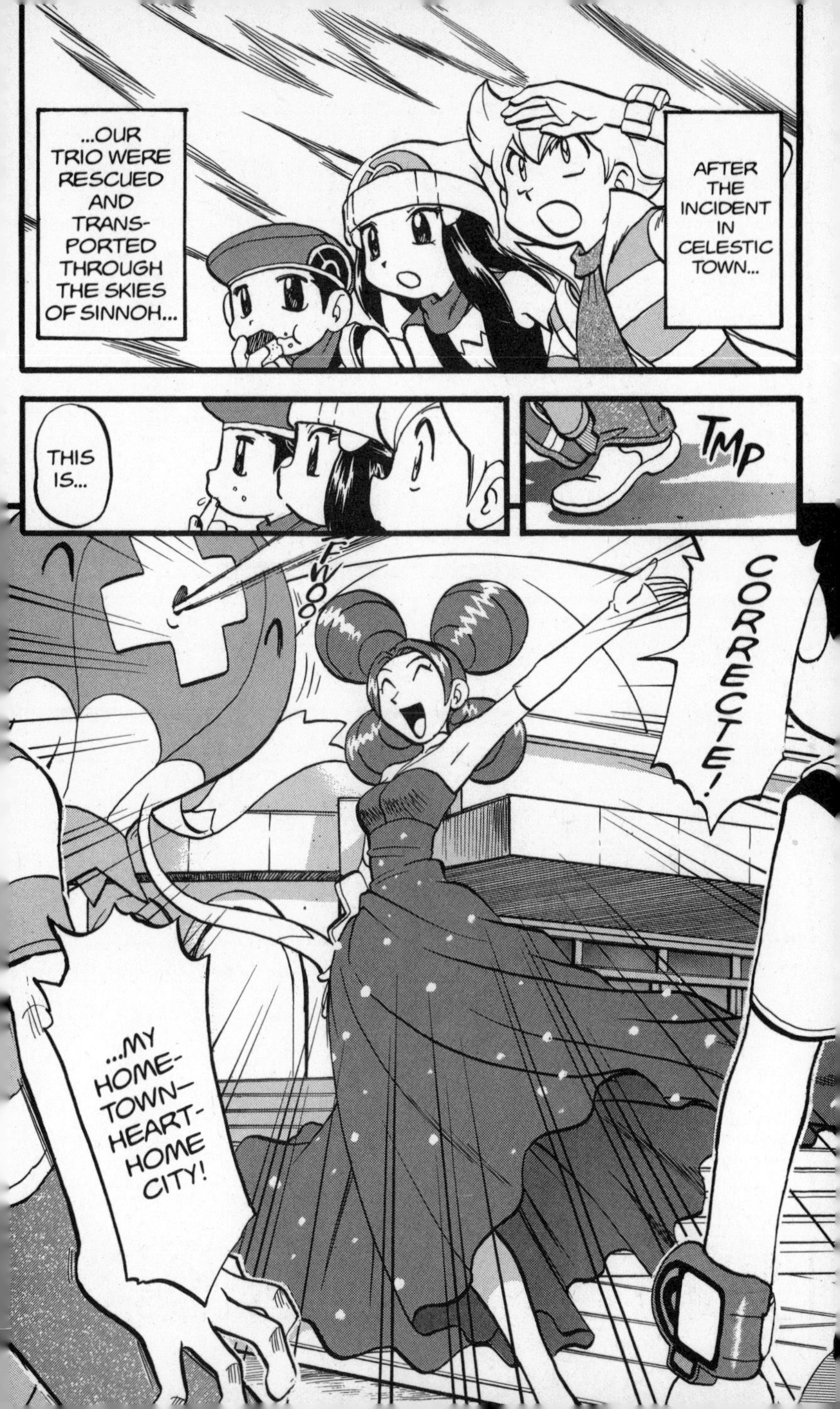
AFTER THE INCIDENT IN CELESTIC TOWN...
...OUR TRIO WERE RESCUED AND TRANS-PORTED THROUGH THE SKIES OF SINNOH...
TMP
THIS IS...
CORRECTE!
FWOOO
...MY HOME-TOWN—HEART-HOME CITY!

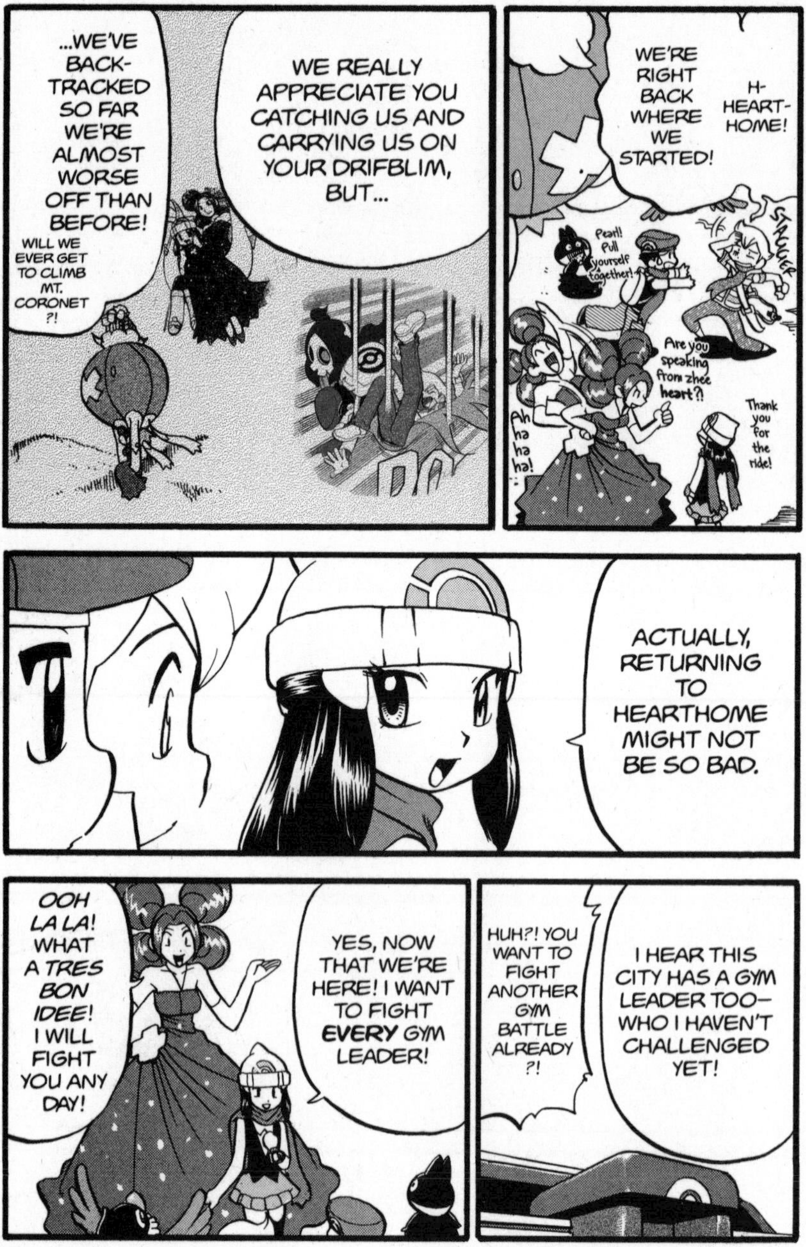
H-HEARTHOME!
WE'RE RIGHT BACK WHERE WE STARTED!
STAGGER
Pearl! Pull yourself together!
Are you speaking from zhee heart?!
Thank you for the ride!
Ah ha ha ha!
WE REALLY APPRECIATE YOU CATCHING US AND CARRYING US ON YOUR DRIFBLIM, BUT...
...WE'VE BACK-TRACKED SO FAR WE'RE ALMOST WORSE OFF THAN BEFORE!
WILL WE EVER GET TO CLIMB MT. CORONET ?!
ACTUALLY, RETURNING TO HEARTHOME MIGHT NOT BE SO BAD.
I HEAR THIS CITY HAS A GYM LEADER TOO—WHO I HAVEN'T CHALLENGED YET!
HUH?! YOU WANT TO FIGHT ANOTHER GYM BATTLE ALREADY ?!
YES, NOW THAT WE'RE HERE! I WANT TO FIGHT EVERY GYM LEADER!
OOH LA LA! WHAT A TRES BON IDEE! I WILL FIGHT YOU ANY DAY!

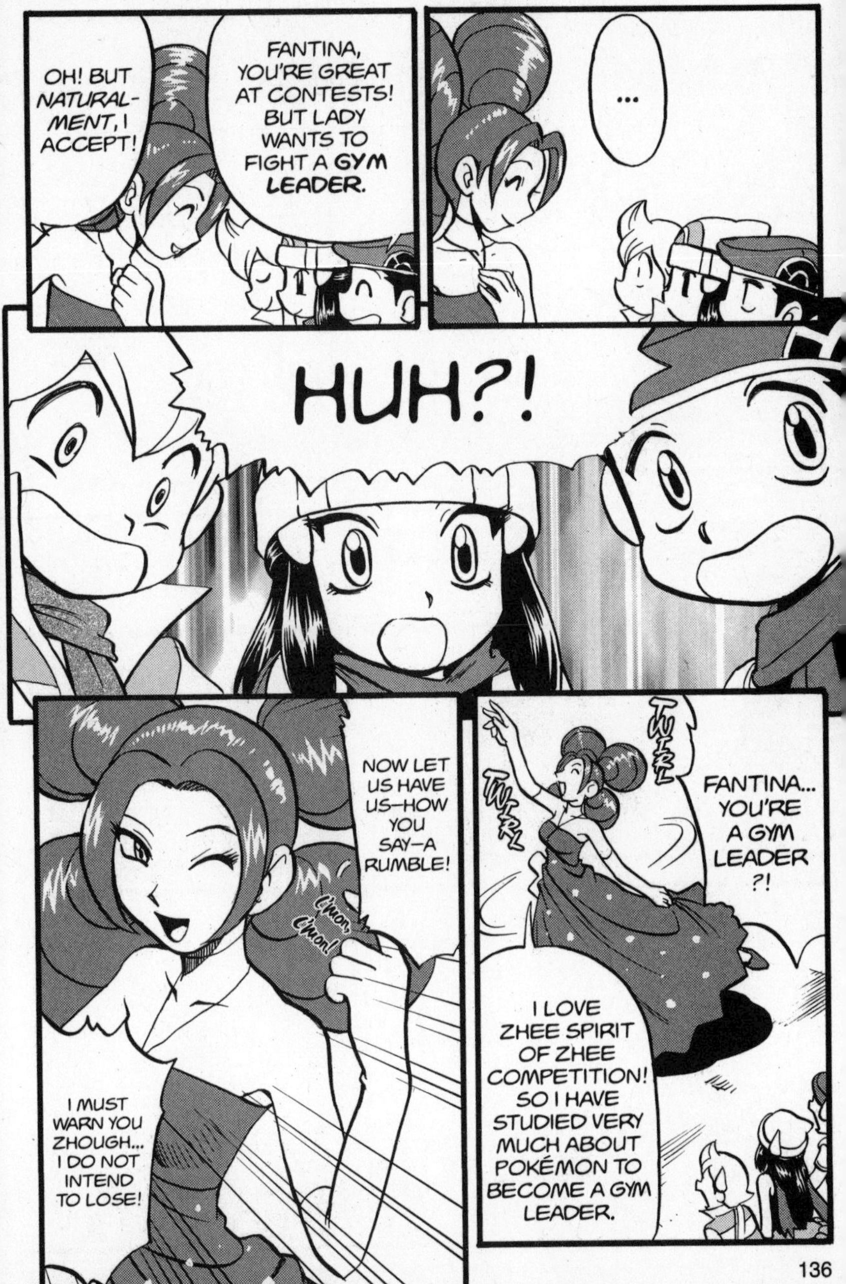
...
FANTINA, YOU'RE GREAT AT CONTESTS! BUT LADY WANTS TO FIGHT A GYM LEADER.
OH! BUT NATURAL-MENT, I ACCEPT!
HUH?!
TWIRL
TWIRL
FANTINA... YOU'RE A GYM LEADER ?!
I LOVE ZHEE SPIRIT OF ZHEE COMPETITION! SO I HAVE STUDIED VERY MUCH ABOUT POKÉMON TO BECOME A GYM LEADER.
NOW LET US HAVE US—HOW YOU SAY—A RUMBLE!
C'mon, c'mon!
I MUST WARN YOU ZHOUGH... I DO NOT INTEND TO LOSE!

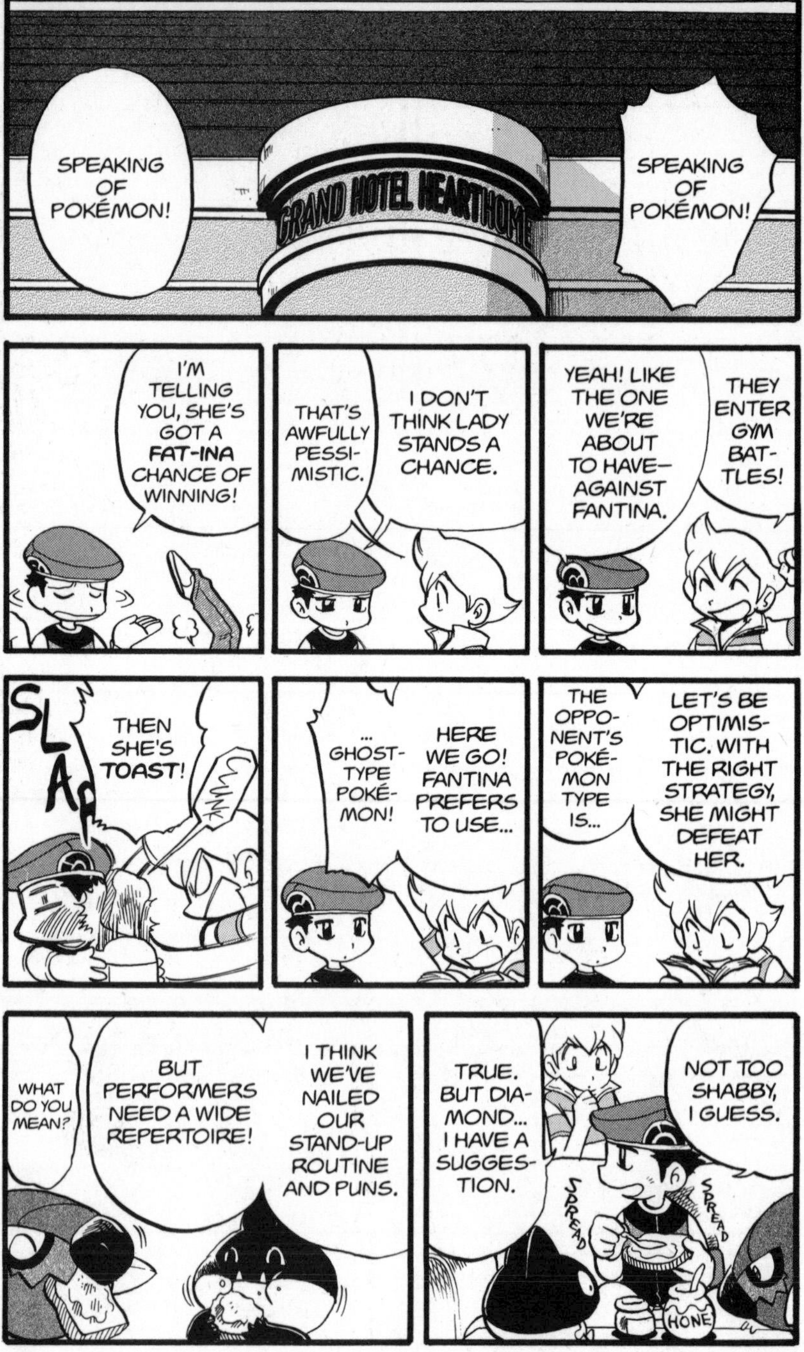
SPEAKING OF POKÉMON!
GRAND HOTEL HEARTHOME
SPEAKING OF POKÉMON!
THEY ENTER GYM BAT-TLES!
YEAH! LIKE THE ONE WE'RE ABOUT TO HAVE—AGAINST FANTINA.
I DON'T THINK LADY STANDS A CHANCE.
THAT'S AWFULLY PESSI-MISTIC.
I'M TELLING YOU, SHE'S GOT A **FAT-INA** CHANCE OF WINNING!
LET'S BE OPTIMIS-TIC. WITH THE RIGHT STRATEGY, SHE MIGHT DEFEAT HER.
THE OPPO-NENT'S POKÉ-MON TYPE IS...
HERE WE GO! FANTINA PREFERS TO USE...
...GHOST-TYPE POKÉ-MON!
THEN SHE'S **TOAST**!
SLAP
NOT TOO SHABBY, I GUESS.
TRUE. BUT DIA-MOND... I HAVE A SUGGES-TION.
SPREAD
SPREAD
HONE
I THINK WE'VE NAILED OUR STAND-UP ROUTINE AND PUNS.
BUT PERFORMERS NEED A WIDE REPERTOIRE!
WHAT DO YOU MEAN?

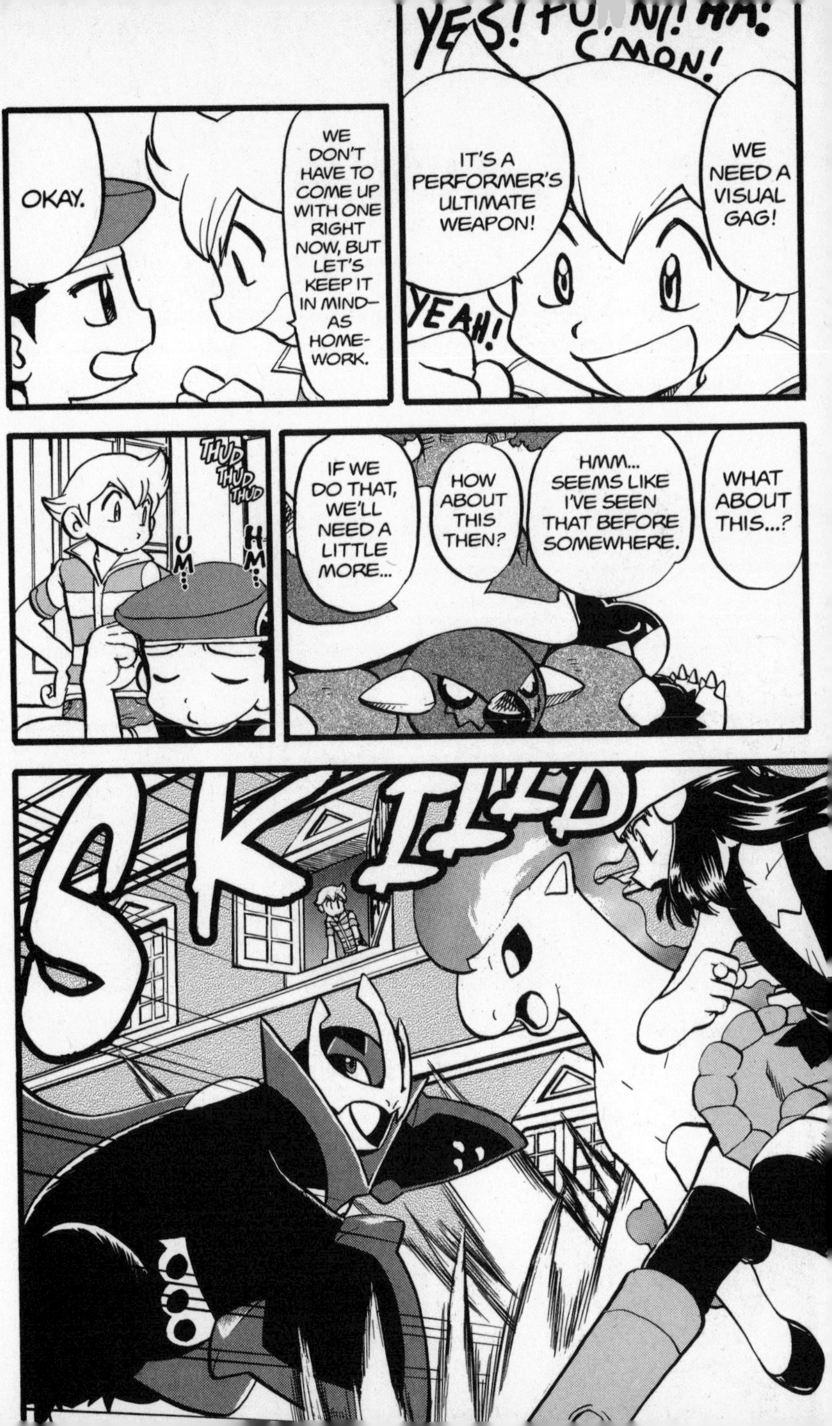
YES!
C'MON!
WE NEED A VISUAL GAG!
IT'S A PERFORMER'S ULTIMATE WEAPON!
YEAH!
WE DON'T HAVE TO COME UP WITH ONE RIGHT NOW, BUT LET'S KEEP IT IN MIND— AS HOMEWORK.
OKAY.
WHAT ABOUT THIS...?
HMM... SEEMS LIKE I'VE SEEN THAT BEFORE SOMEWHERE.
HOW ABOUT THIS THEN?
IF WE DO THAT, WE'LL NEED A LITTLE MORE...
THUD THUD THUD
HM...
UM...

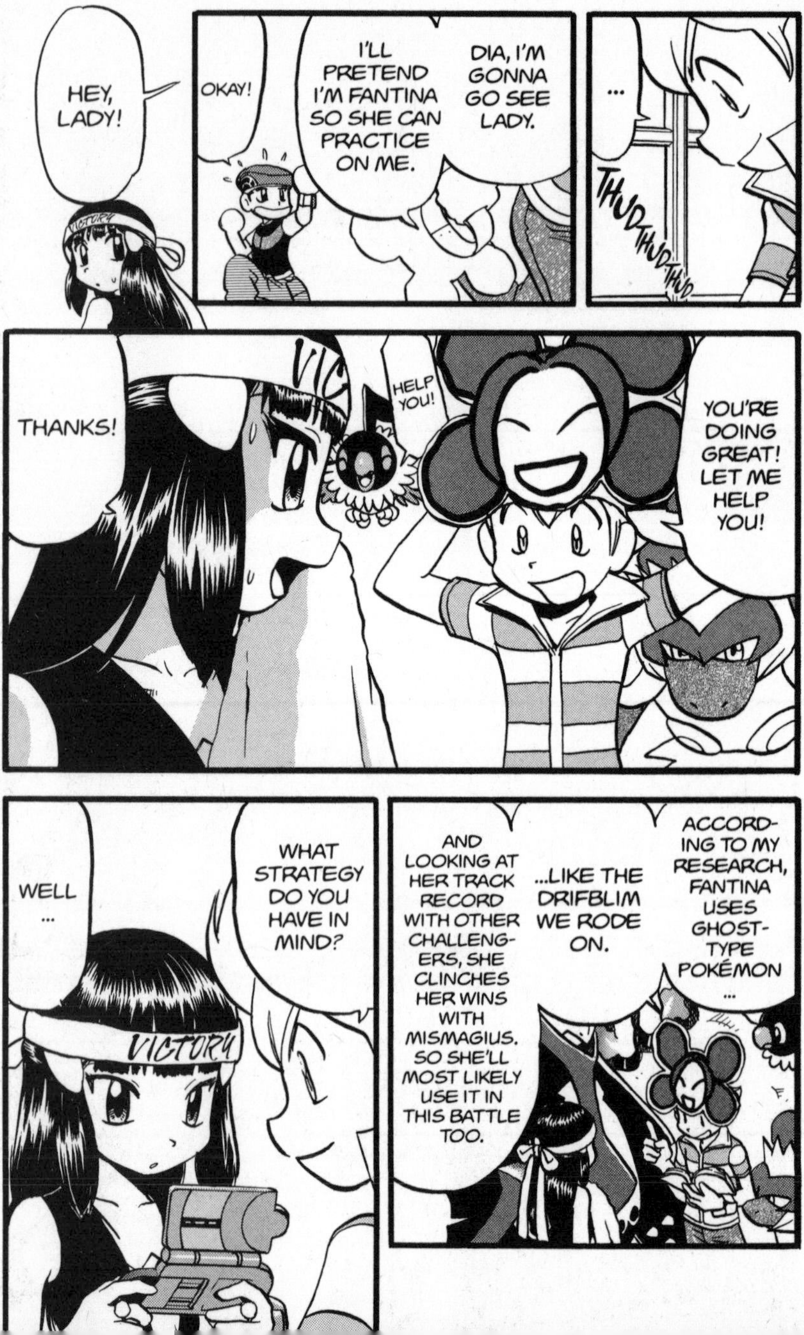
...
THUD-THUD-THUD
DIA, I'M GONNA GO SEE LADY.
I'LL PRETEND I'M FANTINA SO SHE CAN PRACTICE ON ME.
OKAY!
HEY, LADY!
VICTORY
YOU'RE DOING GREAT! LET ME HELP YOU!
HELP YOU!
THANKS!
ACCORDING TO MY RESEARCH, FANTINA USES GHOST-TYPE POKÉMON...
...LIKE THE DRIFBLIM WE RODE ON.
AND LOOKING AT HER TRACK RECORD WITH OTHER CHALLENGERS, SHE CLINCHES HER WINS WITH MISMAGIUS. SO SHE'LL MOST LIKELY USE IT IN THIS BATTLE TOO.
WHAT STRATEGY DO YOU HAVE IN MIND?
WELL...
VICTORY

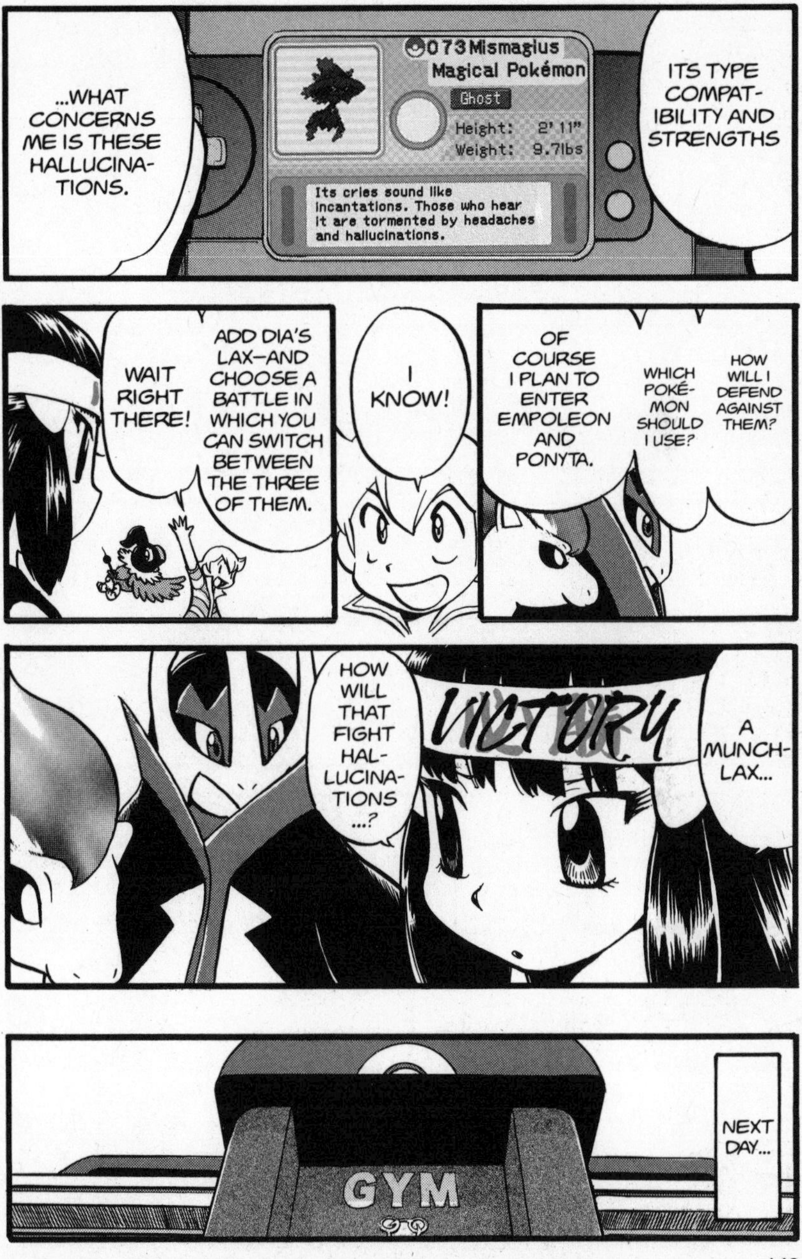
ITS TYPE COMPATIBILITY AND STRENGTHS
073 Mismagius
Magical Pokémon
Ghost
Height: 2' 11"
Weight: 9.7lbs
Its cries sound like incantations. Those who hear it are tormented by headaches and hallucinations.
...WHAT CONCERNS ME IS THESE HALLUCINATIONS.
HOW WILL I DEFEND AGAINST THEM?
WHICH POKÉMON SHOULD I USE?
OF COURSE I PLAN TO ENTER EMPOLEON AND PONYTA.
I KNOW!
ADD DIA'S LAX—AND CHOOSE A BATTLE IN WHICH YOU CAN SWITCH BETWEEN THE THREE OF THEM.
WAIT RIGHT THERE!
A MUNCHLAX...
VICTORY
HOW WILL THAT FIGHT HALLUCINATIONS...?
NEXT DAY...
GYM

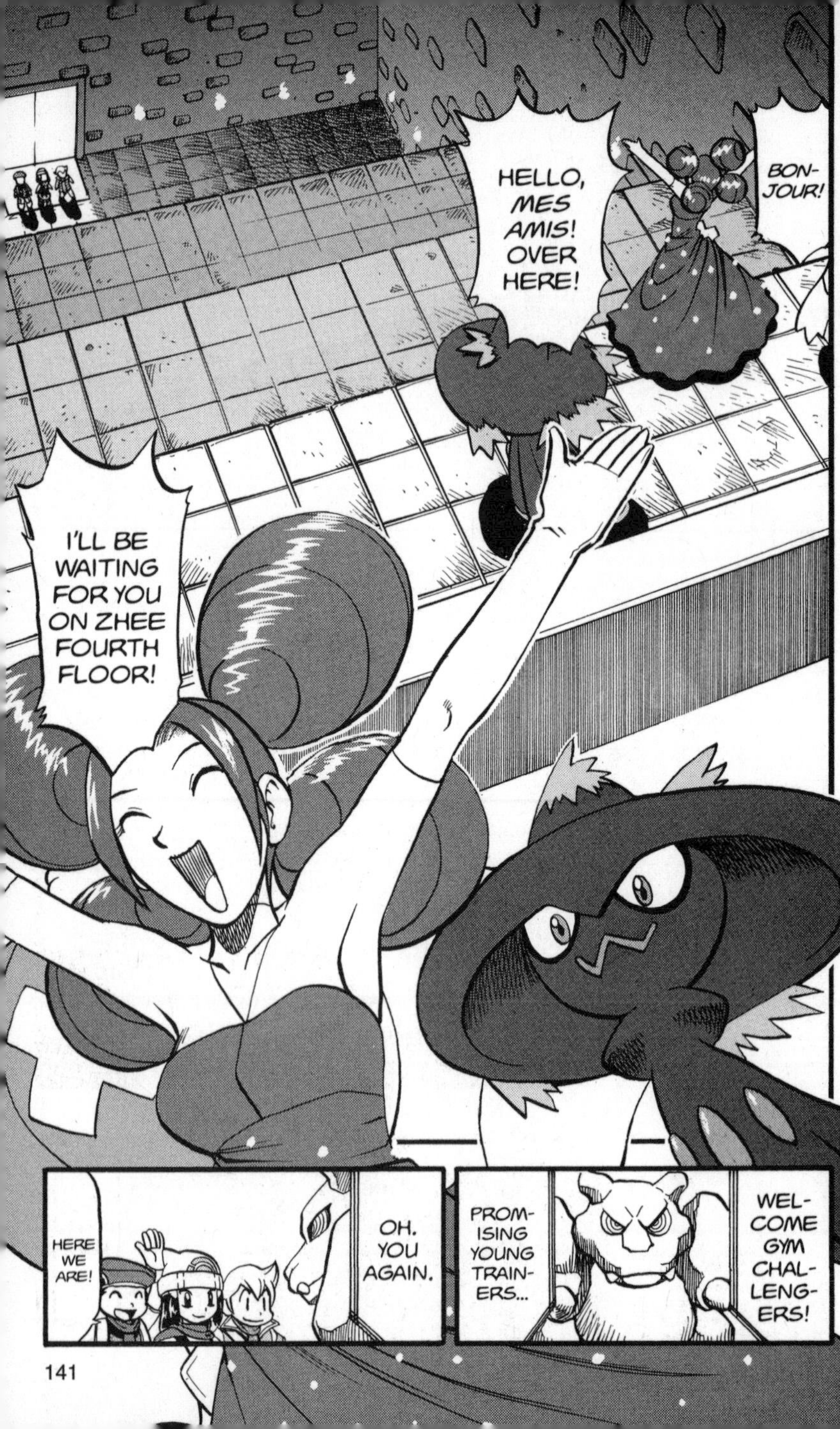
BON-JOUR!
HELLO, MES AMIS! OVER HERE!
I'LL BE WAITING FOR YOU ON ZHEE FOURTH FLOOR!
WEL-COME GYM CHAL-LENG-ERS!
PROM-ISING YOUNG TRAIN-ERS...
OH. YOU AGAIN.
HERE WE ARE!

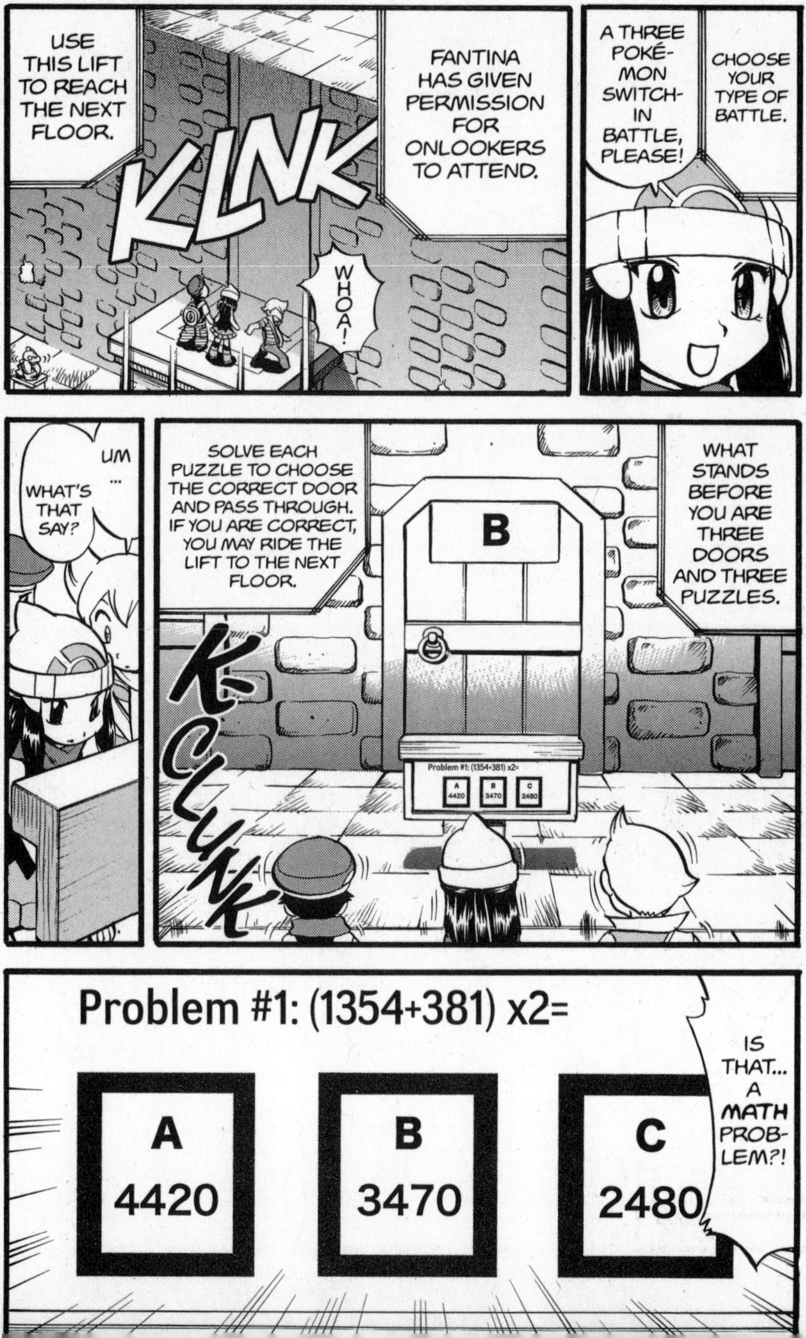

CHOOSE YOUR TYPE OF BATTLE.
A THREE POKÉ-MON SWITCH-IN BATTLE, PLEASE!
FANTINA HAS GIVEN PERMISSION FOR ONLOOKERS TO ATTEND.
USE THIS LIFT TO REACH THE NEXT FLOOR.
KLNK
WHOA!
WHAT STANDS BEFORE YOU ARE THREE DOORS AND THREE PUZZLES.
SOLVE EACH PUZZLE TO CHOOSE THE CORRECT DOOR AND PASS THROUGH. IF YOU ARE CORRECT, YOU MAY RIDE THE LIFT TO THE NEXT FLOOR.
B
Problem #1: (1354+381) x2=
A 4420
B 3470
C 2480
K-CLUNK
UM ...
WHAT'S THAT SAY?
Problem #1: (1354+381) x2=
IS THAT... A MATH PROB-LEM?!
A 4420
B 3470
C 2480

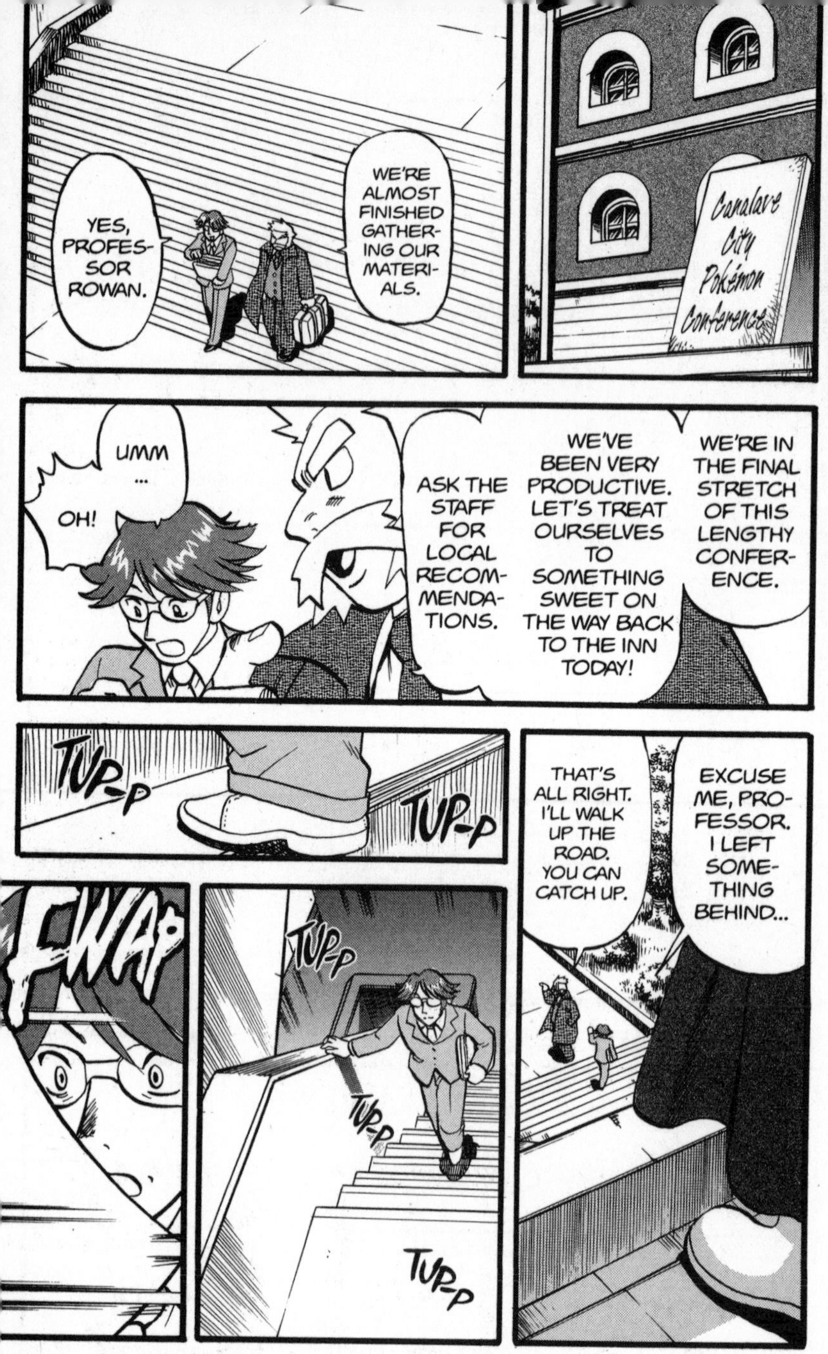
Canalave City Pokémon Conference
WE'RE ALMOST FINISHED GATHERING OUR MATERIALS.
YES, PROFESSOR ROWAN.
WE'RE IN THE FINAL STRETCH OF THIS LENGTHY CONFERENCE.
WE'VE BEEN VERY PRODUCTIVE. LET'S TREAT OURSELVES TO SOMETHING SWEET ON THE WAY BACK TO THE INN TODAY!
ASK THE STAFF FOR LOCAL RECOMMENDATIONS.
UMM ... OH!
EXCUSE ME, PROFESSOR. I LEFT SOMETHING BEHIND...
THAT'S ALL RIGHT. I'LL WALK UP THE ROAD. YOU CAN CATCH UP.
TUP-P
TUP-P
TUP-P
TUP-P
TUP-P
FWAP

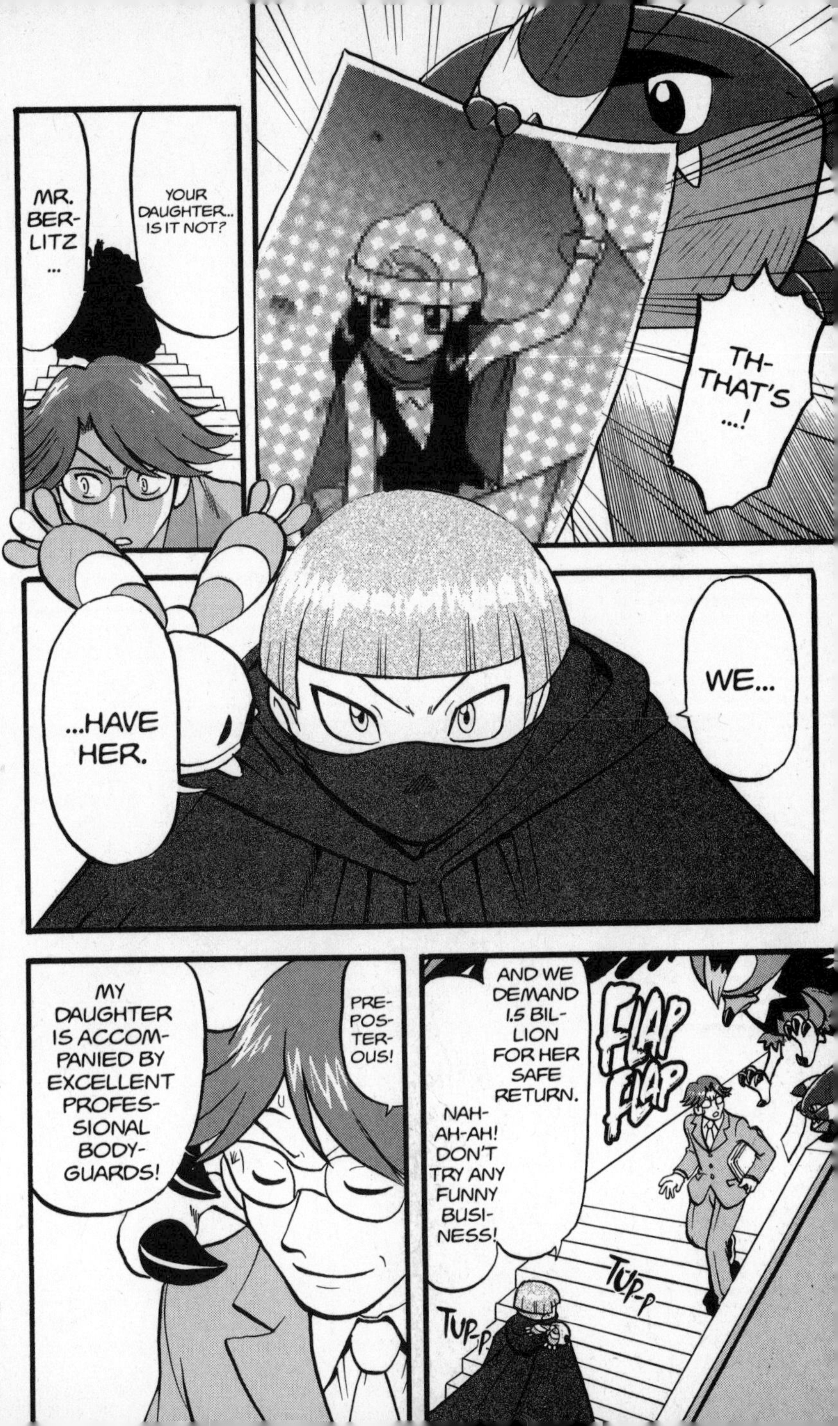
TH-THAT'S ...!
YOUR DAUGHTER... IS IT NOT?
MR. BER-LITZ ...
WE...
...HAVE HER.
AND WE DEMAND 1.5 BIL-LION FOR HER SAFE RETURN.
FLAP FLAP
NAH-AH-AH! DON'T TRY ANY FUNNY BUSI-NESS!
TUP-P
TUP-P
PRE-POS-TER-OUS!
MY DAUGHTER IS ACCOM-PANIED BY EXCELLENT PROFES-SIONAL BODY-GUARDS!

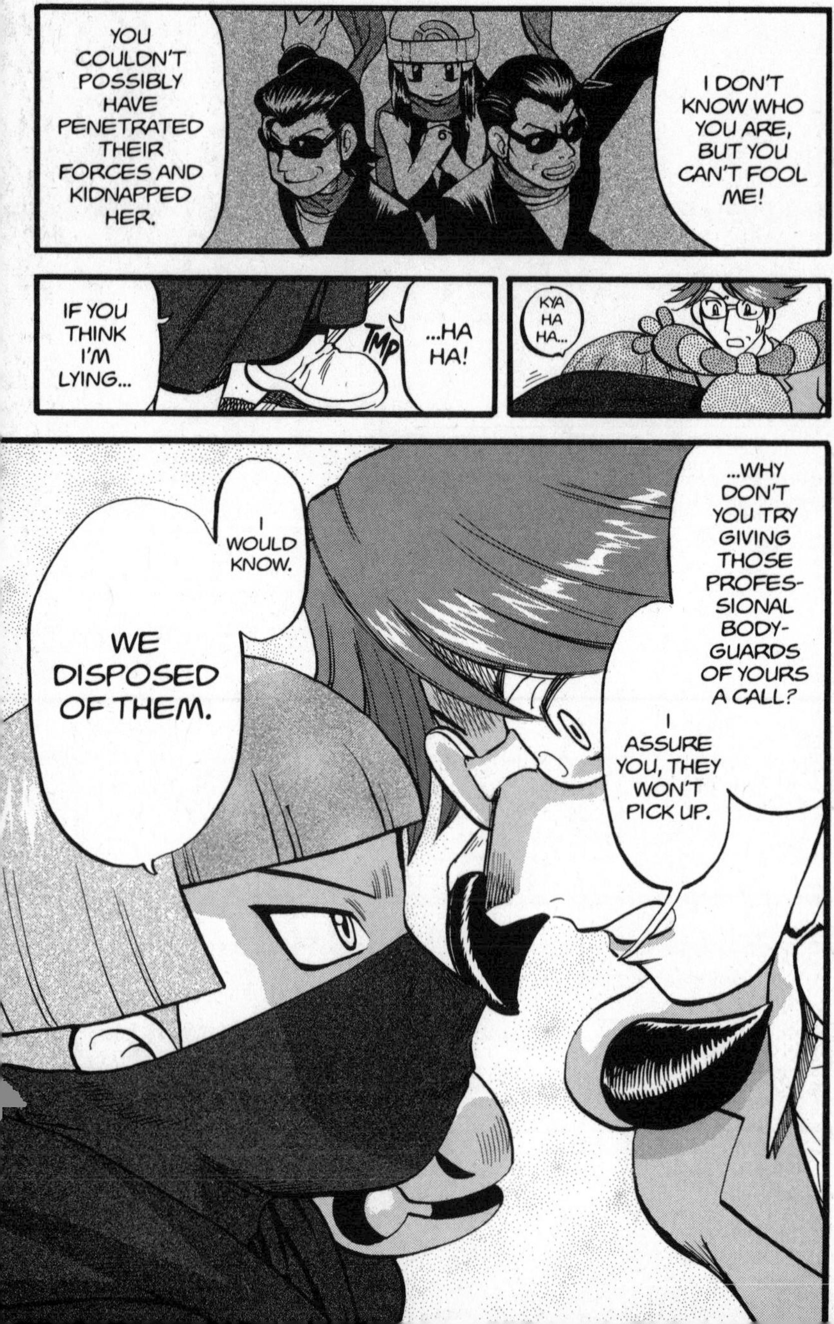

I DON'T KNOW WHO YOU ARE, BUT YOU CAN'T FOOL ME!
YOU COULDN'T POSSIBLY HAVE PENETRATED THEIR FORCES AND KIDNAPPED HER.
KYA HA HA...
...HA HA!
TMP
IF YOU THINK I'M LYING...
...WHY DON'T YOU TRY GIVING THOSE PROFES-SIONAL BODY-GUARDS OF YOURS A CALL?
I ASSURE YOU, THEY WON'T PICK UP.
I WOULD KNOW.
WE DISPOSED OF THEM.

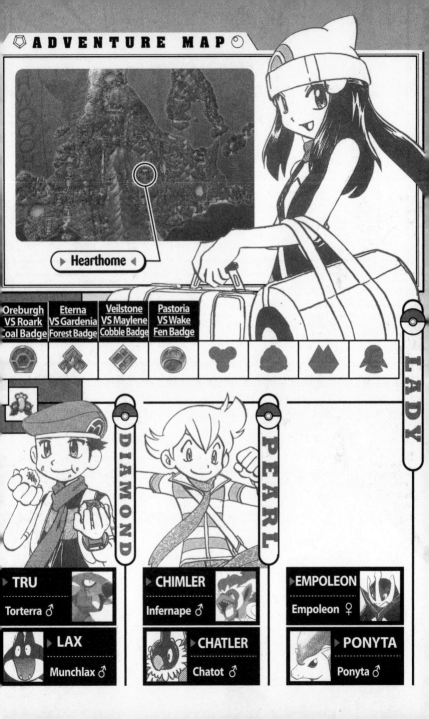

ADVENTURE MAP

▶ Hearthome ◀

Oreburgh VS Roark Coal Badge	Eterna VS Gardenia Forest Badge	Veilstone VS Maylene Cobble Badge	Pastoria VS Wake Fen Badge				

LADY

DIAMOND

PEARL

▶ TRU

Torterra ♂

▶ LAX

Munchlax ♂

▶ CHIMLER

Infernape ♂

▶ CHATLER

Chatot ♂

▶ EMPOLEON

Empoleon ♀

▶ PONYTA

Ponyta ♂

35

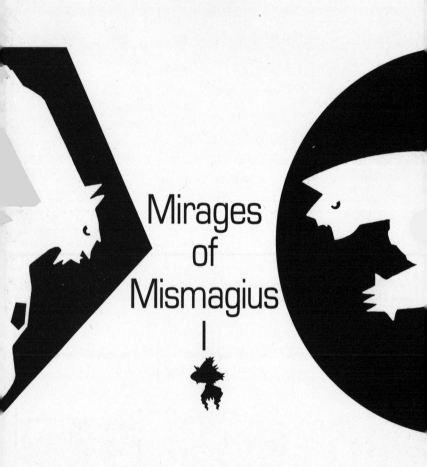

Mirages
of
Mismagius
I

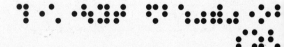

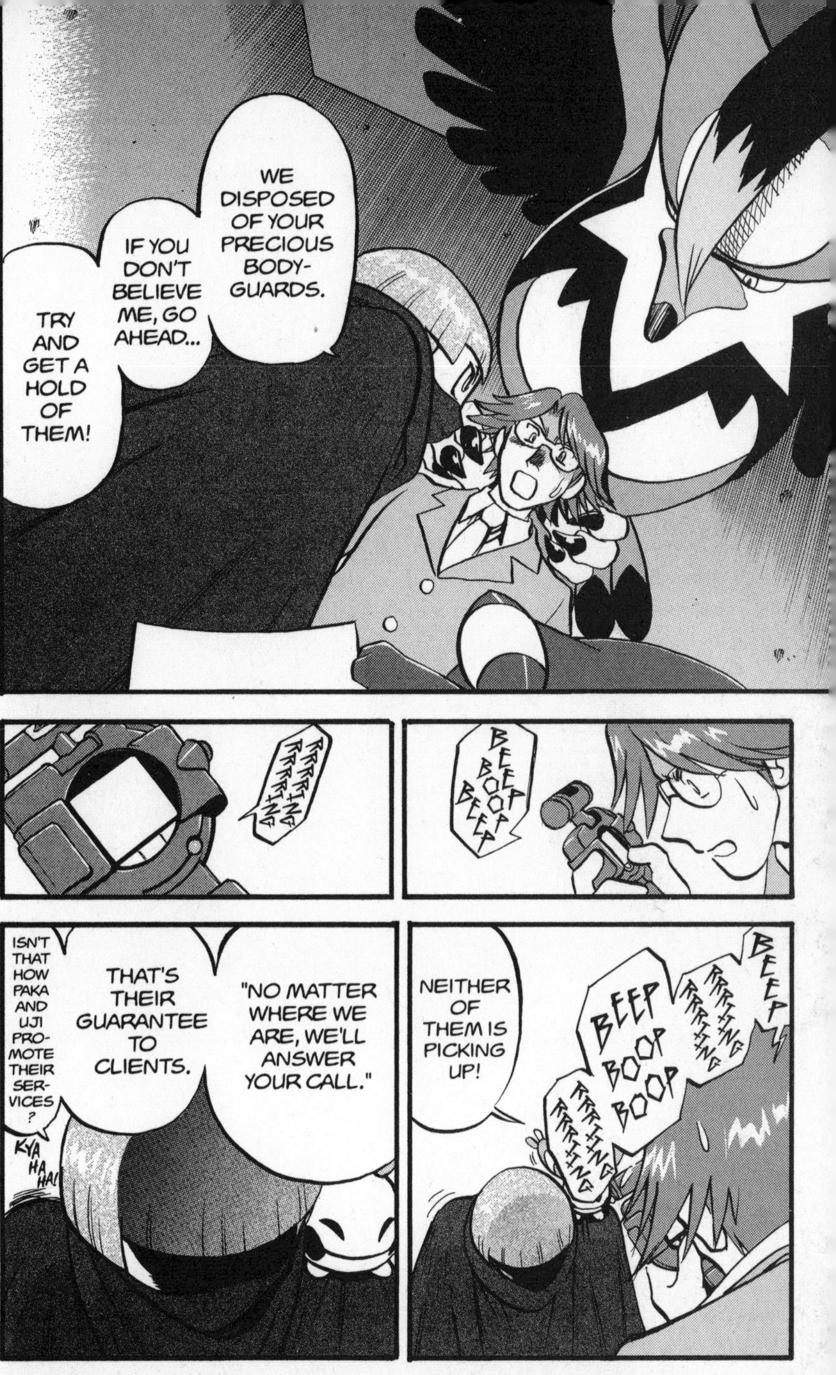

WE DISPOSED OF YOUR PRECIOUS BODY-GUARDS.
IF YOU DON'T BELIEVE ME, GO AHEAD...
TRY AND GET A HOLD OF THEM!
BEEP BOOP BEEP
RRRRING RRRRING
BEEP
RRRRING RRRRING
BEEP BOOP BOOP
RRRRING RRRRING
NEITHER OF THEM IS PICKING UP!
"NO MATTER WHERE WE ARE, WE'LL ANSWER YOUR CALL."
THAT'S THEIR GUARANTEE TO CLIENTS.
ISN'T THAT HOW PAKA AND UJI PRO-MOTE THEIR SER-VICES?
KYA HA HA!

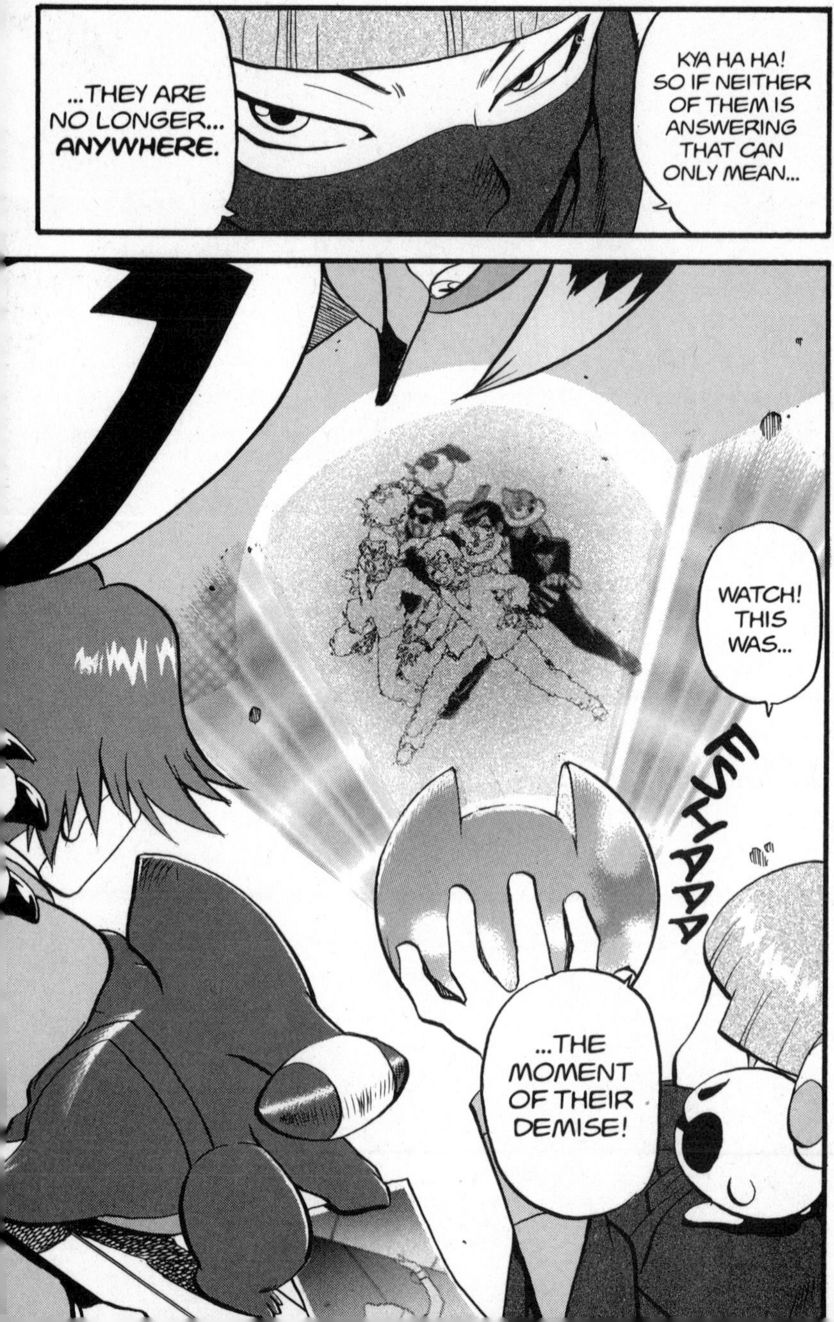
KYA HA HA! SO IF NEITHER OF THEM IS ANSWERING THAT CAN ONLY MEAN...
...THEY ARE NO LONGER... **ANYWHERE.**
WATCH! THIS WAS...
FSHAAAA
...THE MOMENT OF THEIR DEMISE!

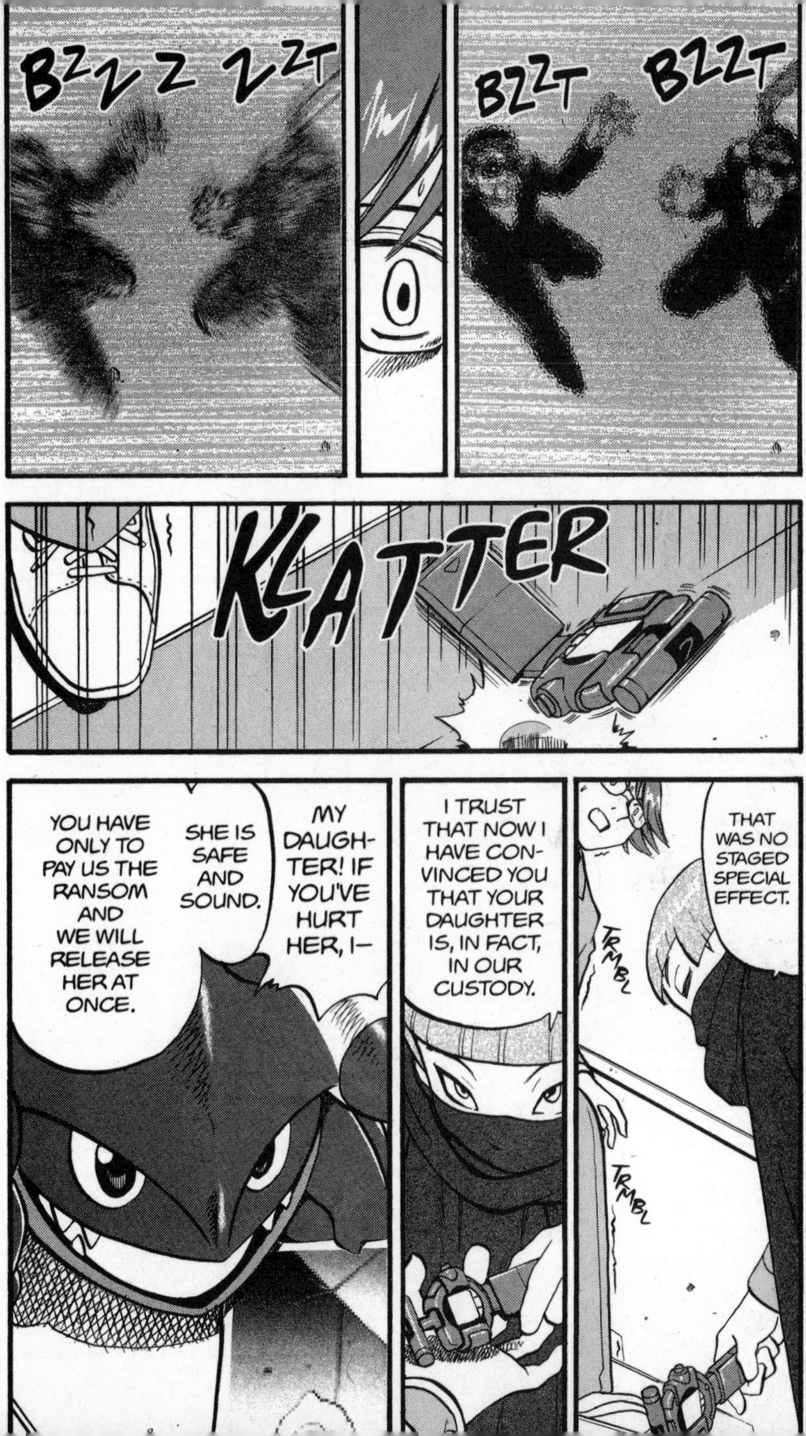
BZZT
BZZT
BZZZZZT
KLATTER
THAT WAS NO STAGED SPECIAL EFFECT.
TRMBL
TRMBL
I TRUST THAT NOW I HAVE CONVINCED YOU THAT YOUR DAUGHTER IS, IN FACT, IN OUR CUSTODY.
MY DAUGHTER! IF YOU'VE HURT HER, I—
SHE IS SAFE AND SOUND.
YOU HAVE ONLY TO PAY US THE RANSOM AND WE WILL RELEASE HER AT ONCE.

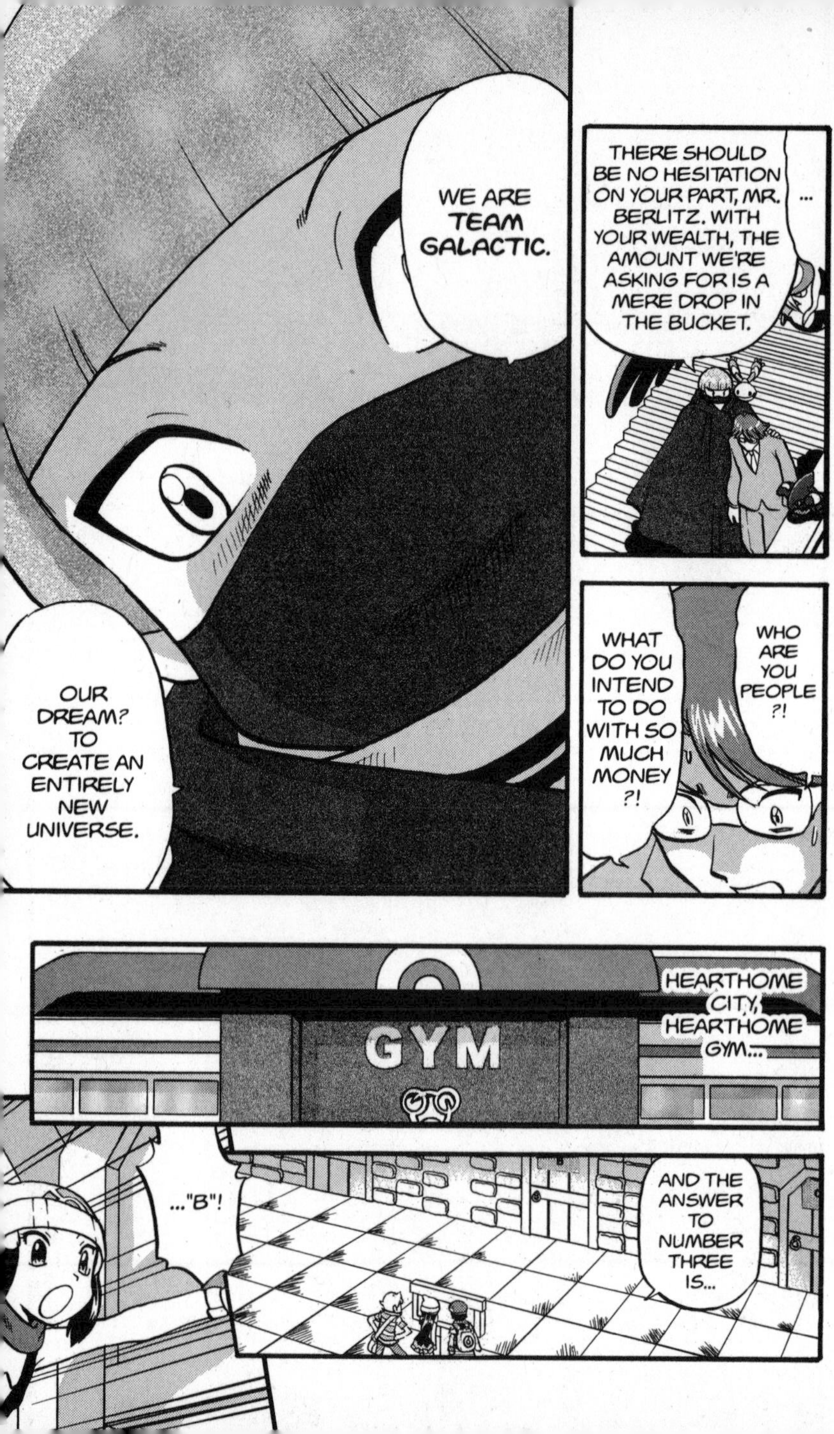
...
THERE SHOULD BE NO HESITATION ON YOUR PART, MR. BERLITZ. WITH YOUR WEALTH, THE AMOUNT WE'RE ASKING FOR IS A MERE DROP IN THE BUCKET.
WHO ARE YOU PEOPLE ?!
WHAT DO YOU INTEND TO DO WITH SO MUCH MONEY ?!
WE ARE TEAM GALACTIC.
OUR DREAM? TO CREATE AN ENTIRELY NEW UNIVERSE.
HEARTHOME CITY, HEARTHOME GYM...
GYM
AND THE ANSWER TO NUMBER THREE IS...
..."B"!

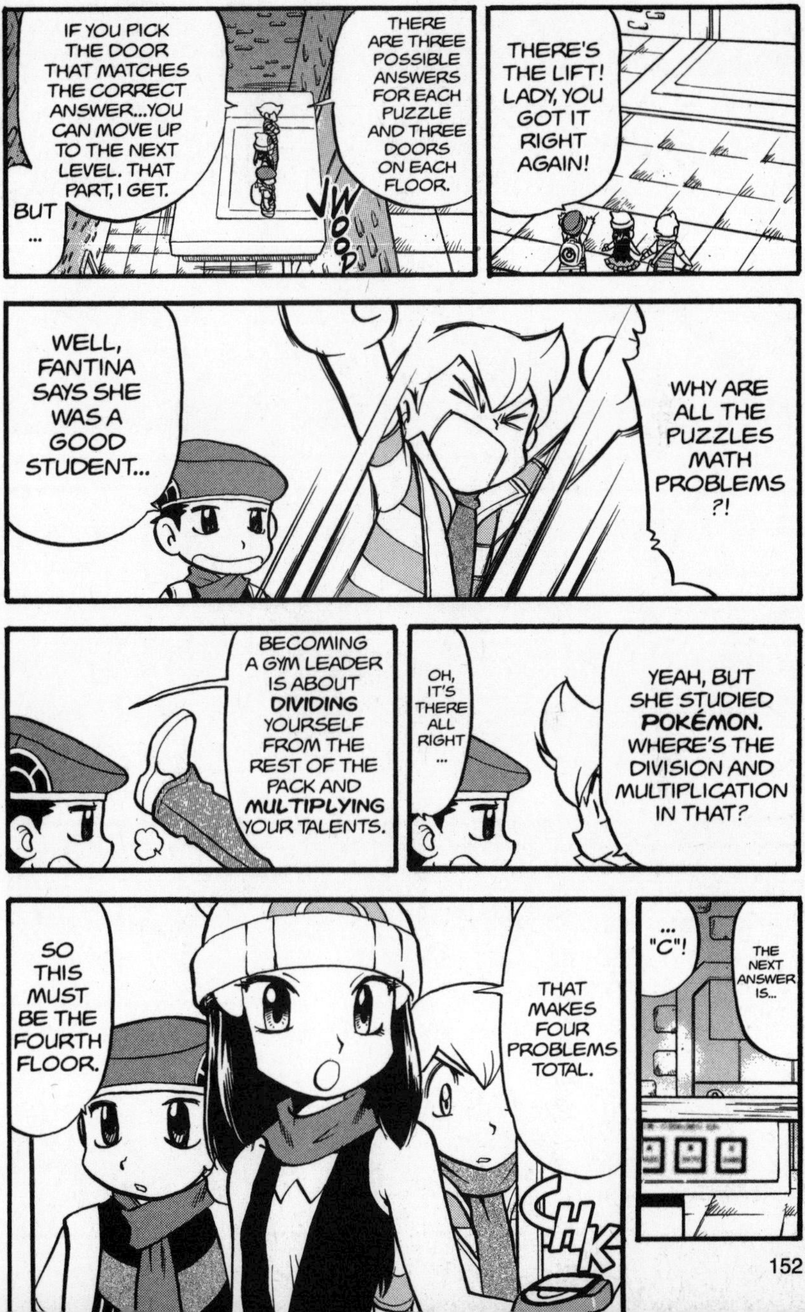
THERE'S THE LIFT! LADY, YOU GOT IT RIGHT AGAIN!
THERE ARE THREE POSSIBLE ANSWERS FOR EACH PUZZLE AND THREE DOORS ON EACH FLOOR.
VWOOP
IF YOU PICK THE DOOR THAT MATCHES THE CORRECT ANSWER...YOU CAN MOVE UP TO THE NEXT LEVEL. THAT PART, I GET.
BUT ...
WHY ARE ALL THE PUZZLES MATH PROBLEMS ?!
WELL, FANTINA SAYS SHE WAS A GOOD STUDENT...
YEAH, BUT SHE STUDIED **POKÉMON.** WHERE'S THE DIVISION AND MULTIPLICATION IN THAT?
OH, IT'S THERE ALL RIGHT ...
BECOMING A GYM LEADER IS ABOUT **DIVIDING** YOURSELF FROM THE REST OF THE PACK AND **MULTIPLYING** YOUR TALENTS.
THE NEXT ANSWER IS...
... "C"!
THAT MAKES FOUR PROBLEMS TOTAL.
SO THIS MUST BE THE FOURTH FLOOR.
CHK

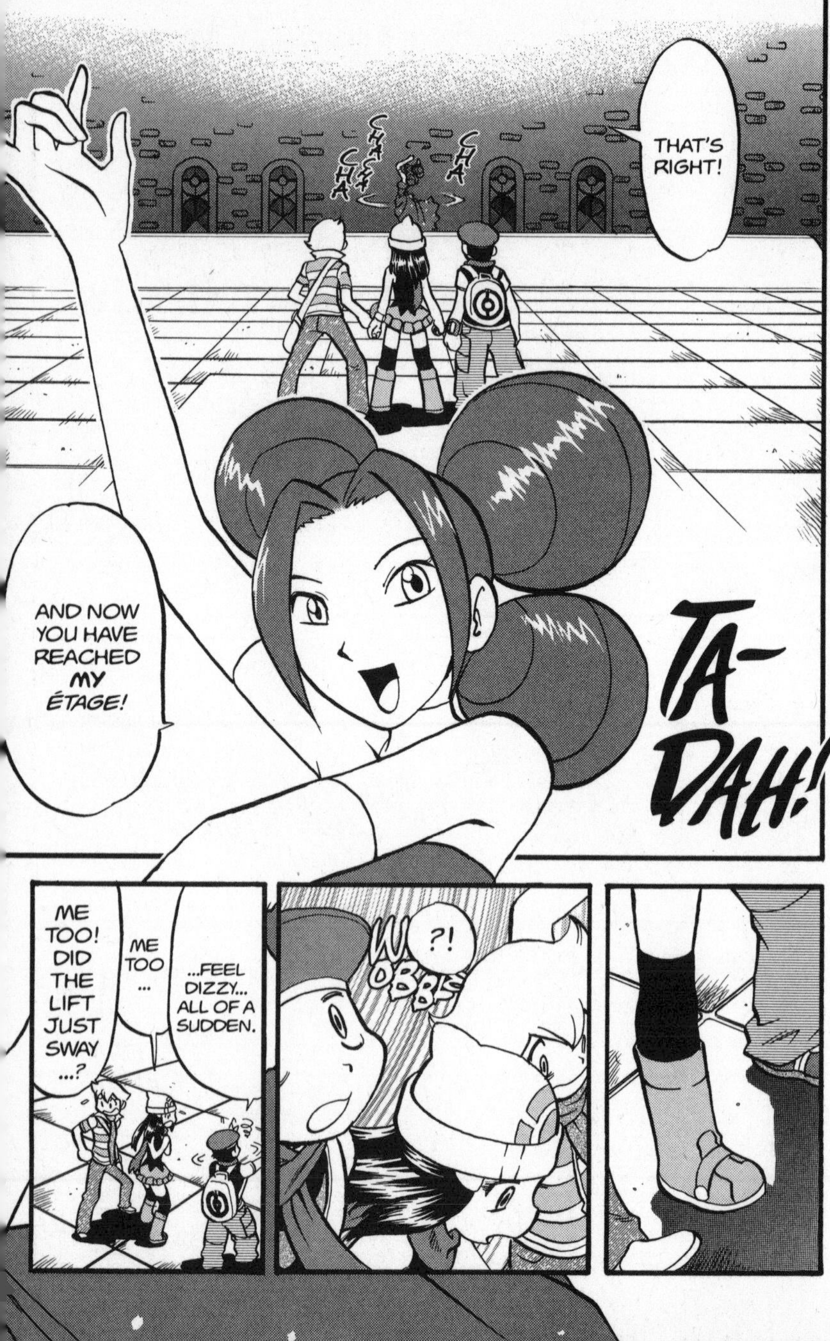
THAT'S RIGHT!
CHA CHA
CHA CHA
AND NOW YOU HAVE REACHED **MY** *ÉTAGE!*
TA-DAH!
?!
WOBBLE
...FEEL DIZZY... ALL OF A SUDDEN.
ME TOO ...
ME TOO! DID THE LIFT JUST SWAY ...?

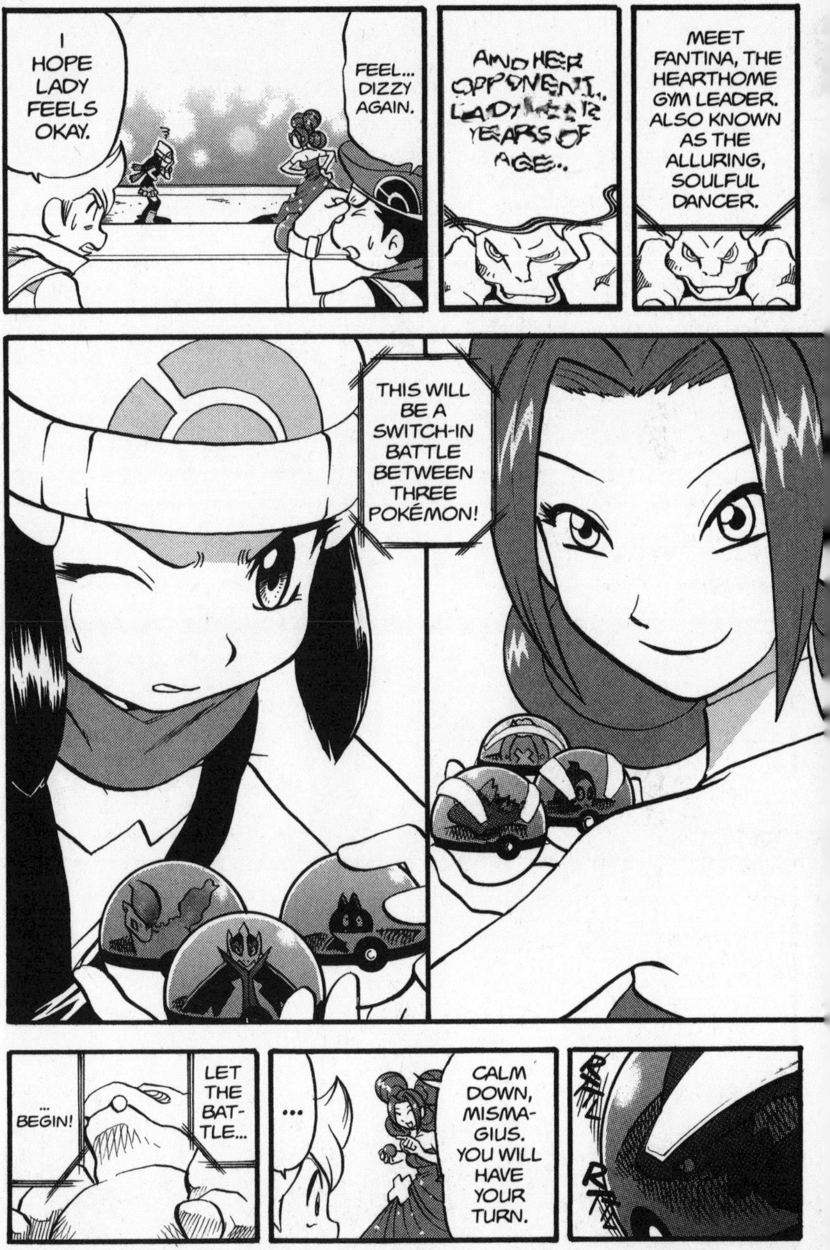
MEET FANTINA, THE HEARTHOME GYM LEADER. ALSO KNOWN AS THE ALLURING, SOULFUL DANCER.
AND HER OPPONENT... LADY [redacted] YEARS OF AGE..
FEEL... DIZZY AGAIN.
I HOPE LADY FEELS OKAY.
THIS WILL BE A SWITCH-IN BATTLE BETWEEN THREE POKÉMON!
CALM DOWN, MISMA-GIUS. YOU WILL HAVE YOUR TURN.
...
LET THE BAT-TLE...
... BEGIN!

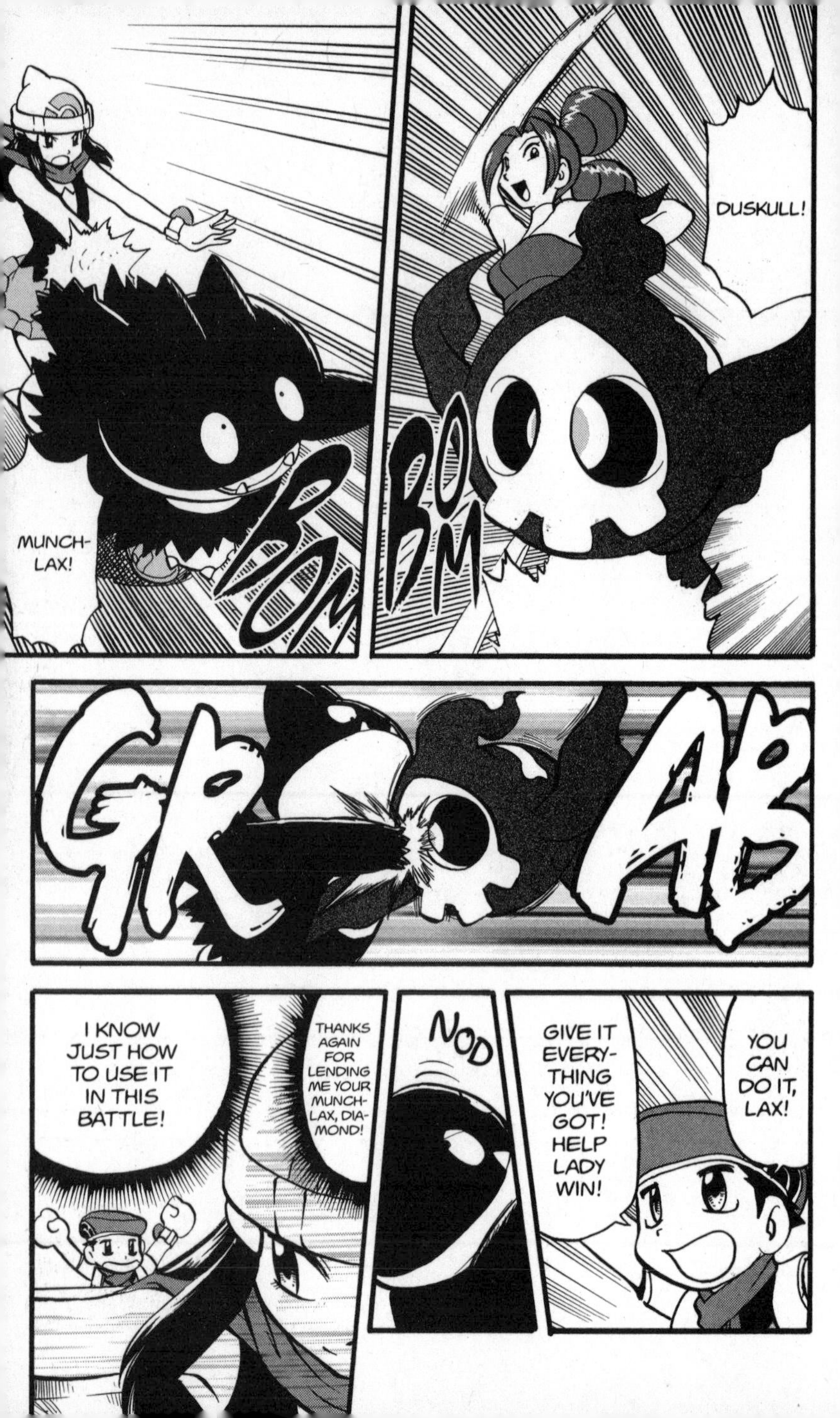
DUSKULL!
BOOM
MUNCH-LAX!
BOOM
GRAB
YOU CAN DO IT, LAX!
GIVE IT EVERY-THING YOU'VE GOT! HELP LADY WIN!
NOD
THANKS AGAIN FOR LENDING ME YOUR MUNCH-LAX, DIA-MOND!
I KNOW JUST HOW TO USE IT IN THIS BATTLE!

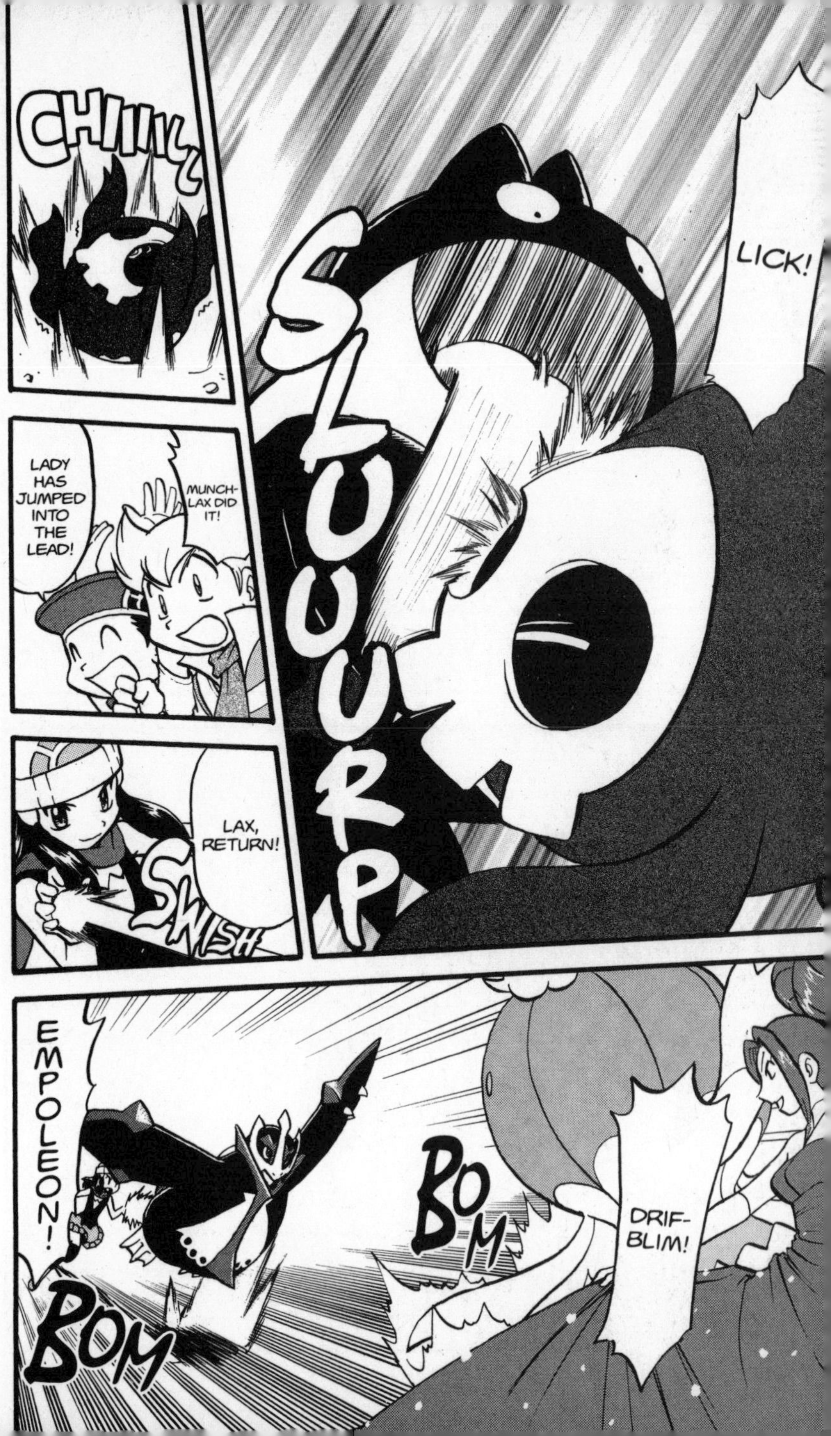
LICK!
SLUUURP
CHIIIILL
MUNCH-LAX DID IT!
LADY HAS JUMPED INTO THE LEAD!
LAX, RETURN!
SWISH
DRIF-BLIM!
BOM
EMPOLEON!
BOM

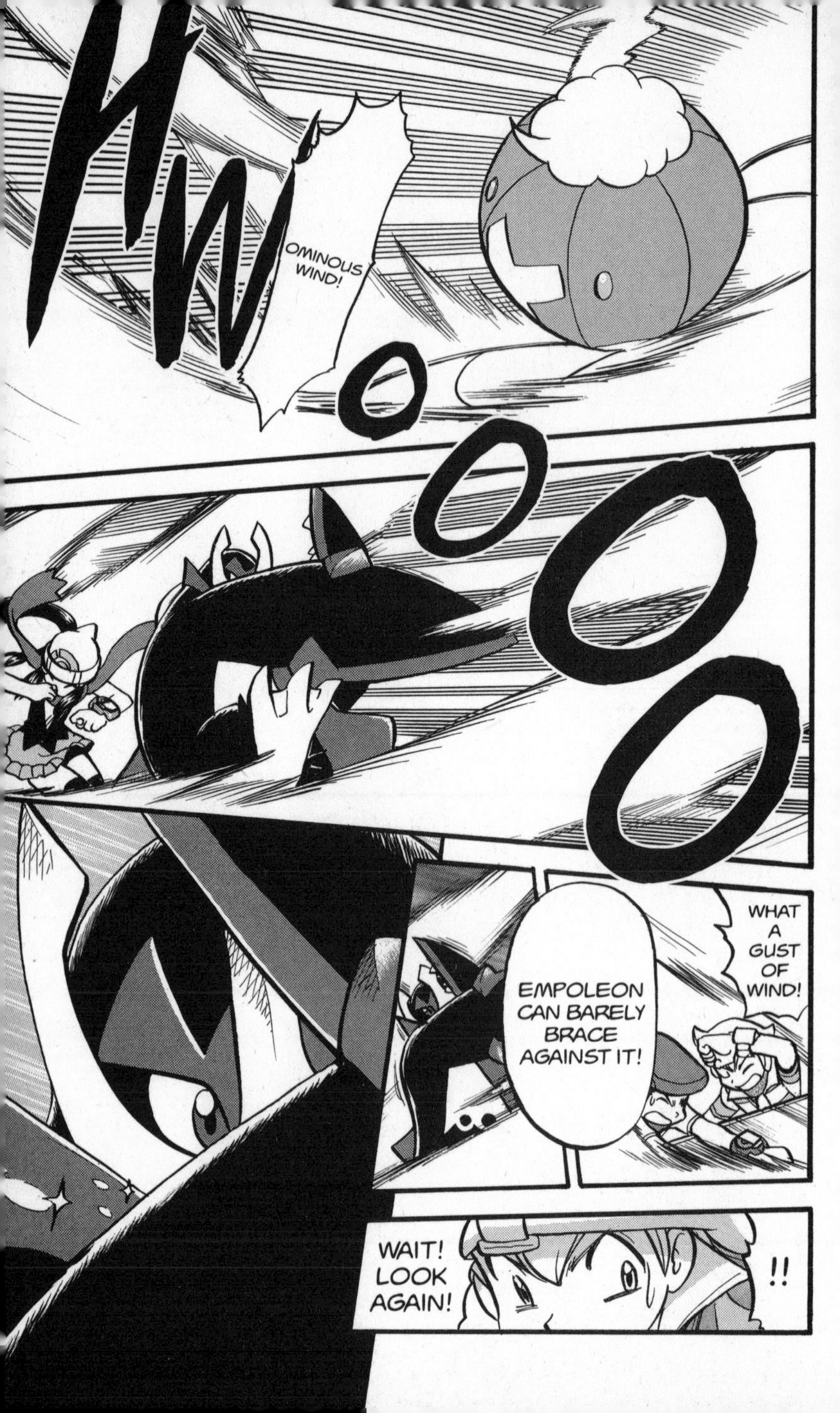
HWOOOOO
OMINOUS WIND!
WHAT A GUST OF WIND!
EMPOLEON CAN BARELY BRACE AGAINST IT!
!!
WAIT! LOOK AGAIN!

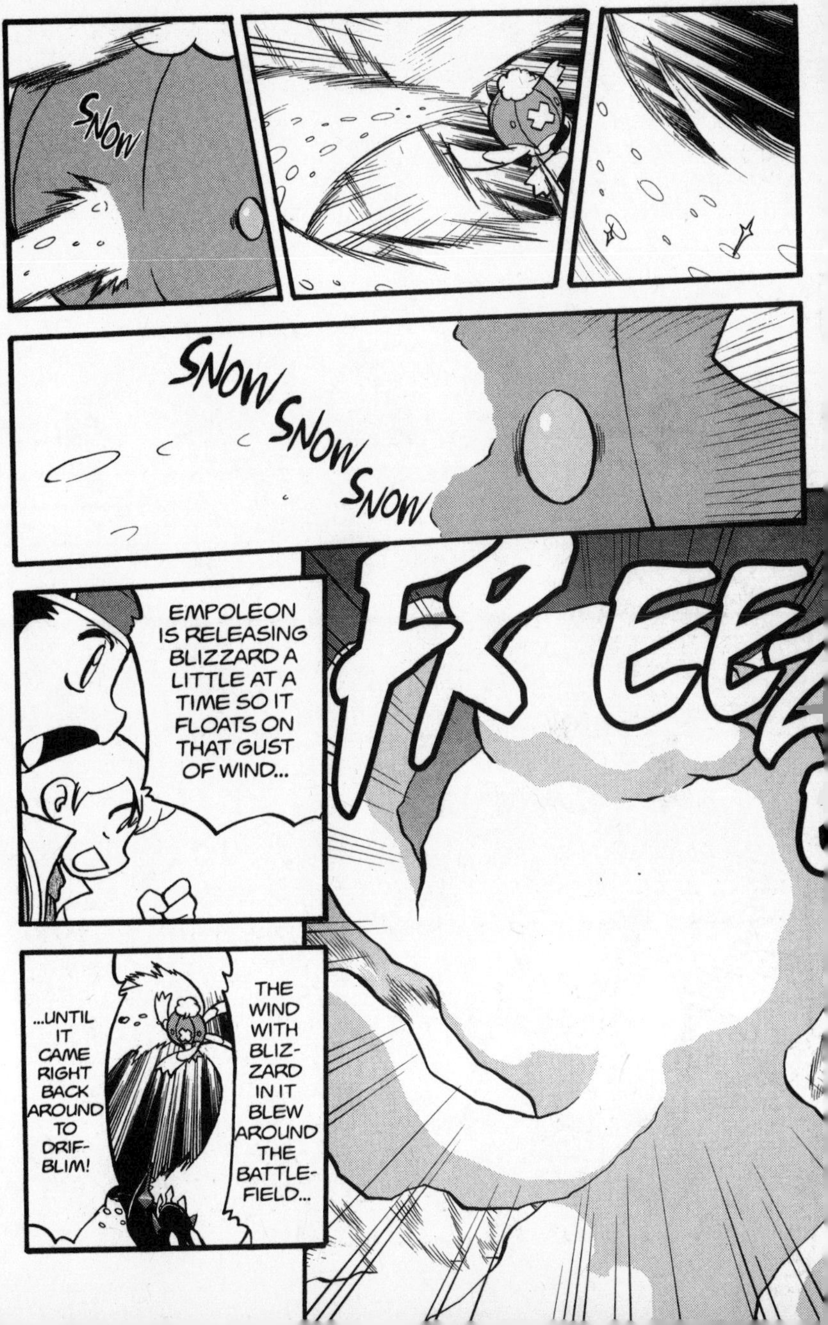
SNOW
SNOW SNOW SNOW
FR EEZ
EMPOLEON IS RELEASING BLIZZARD A LITTLE AT A TIME SO IT FLOATS ON THAT GUST OF WIND...
THE WIND WITH BLIZ-ZARD IN IT BLEW AROUND THE BATTLE-FIELD...
...UNTIL IT CAME RIGHT BACK AROUND TO DRIF-BLIM!

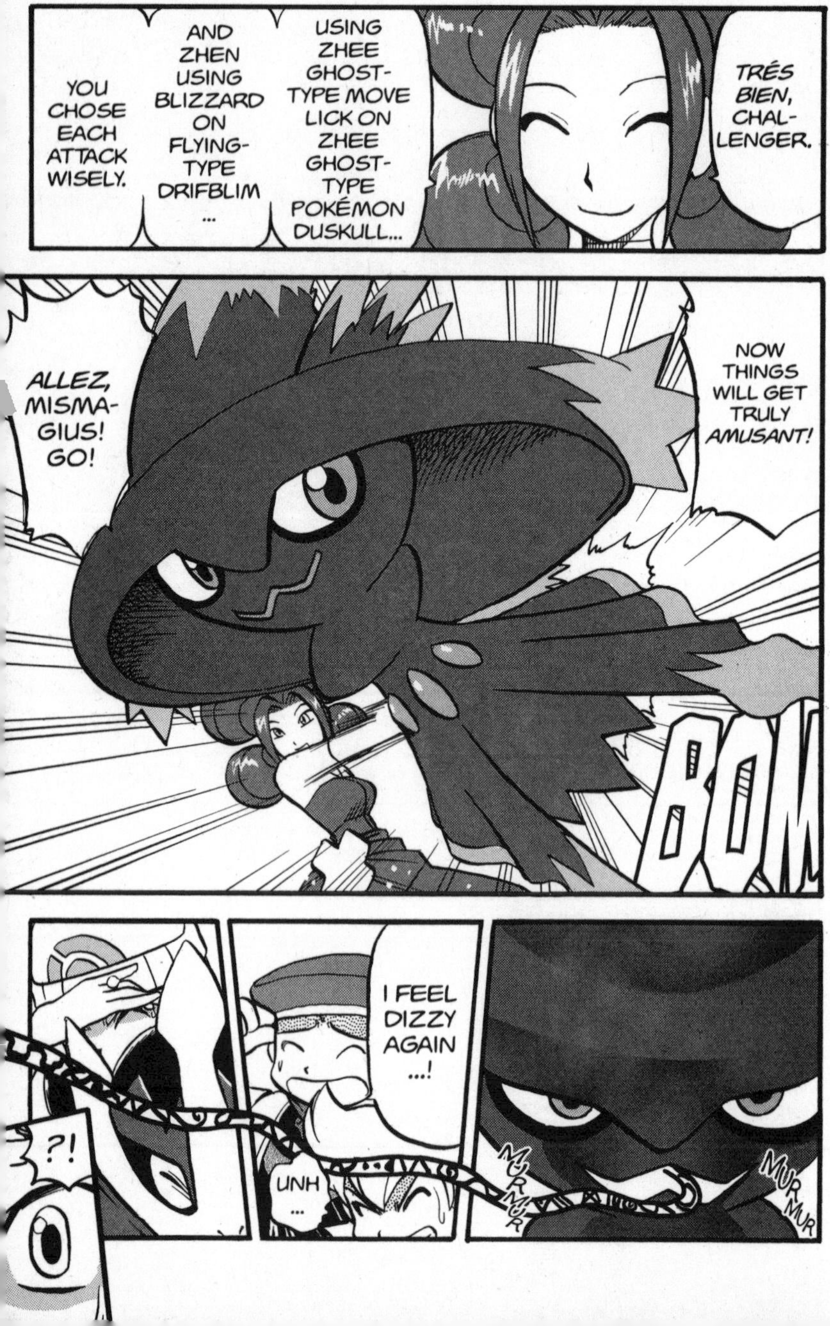
TRÉS BIEN, CHALLENGER.
USING ZHEE GHOST-TYPE MOVE LICK ON ZHEE GHOST-TYPE POKÉMON DUSKULL...
AND ZHEN USING BLIZZARD ON FLYING-TYPE DRIFBLIM ...
YOU CHOSE EACH ATTACK WISELY.
NOW THINGS WILL GET TRULY AMUSANT!
ALLEZ, MISMAGIUS! GO!
BOM
MUR MUR
MURMUR
I FEEL DIZZY AGAIN ...!
UNH ...
?!

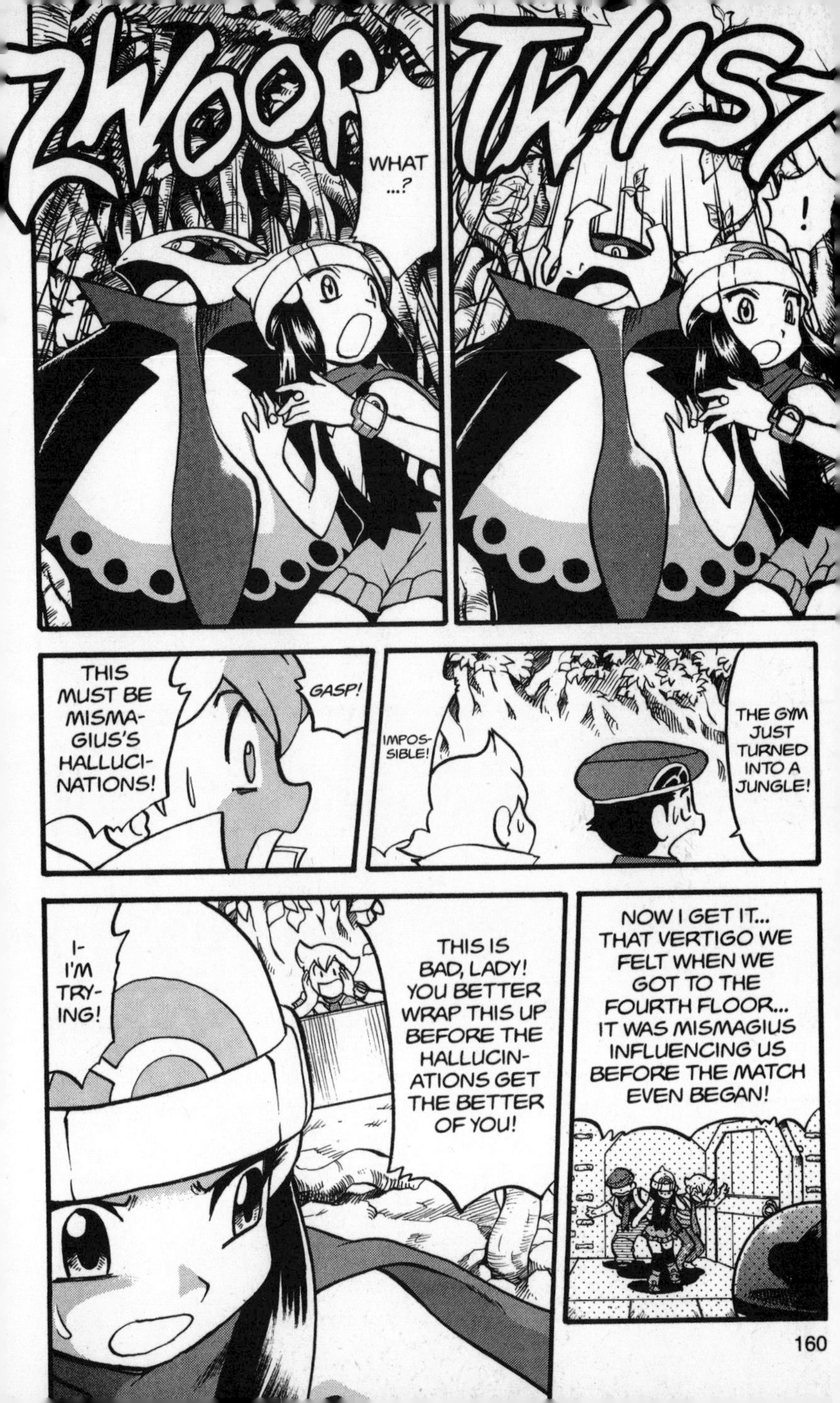
TWIST
!
WHOOP
WHAT ...?
THE GYM JUST TURNED INTO A JUNGLE!
IMPOSSIBLE!
GASP!
THIS MUST BE MISMAGIUS'S HALLUCINATIONS!
NOW I GET IT... THAT VERTIGO WE FELT WHEN WE GOT TO THE FOURTH FLOOR... IT WAS MISMAGIUS INFLUENCING US BEFORE THE MATCH EVEN BEGAN!
THIS IS BAD, LADY! YOU BETTER WRAP THIS UP BEFORE THE HALLUCINATIONS GET THE BETTER OF YOU!
I- I'M TRYING!

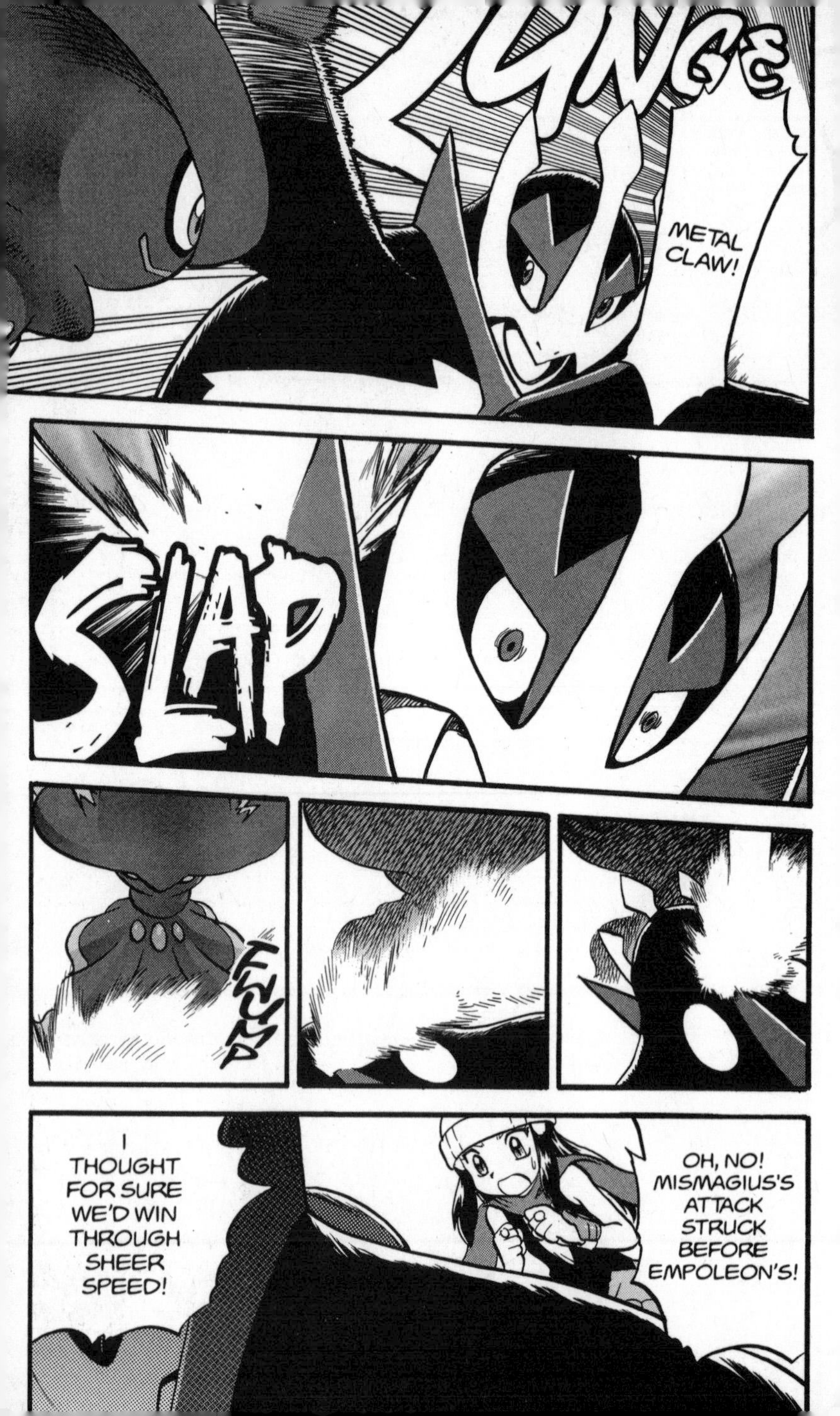
LUNGE
METAL CLAW!
SLAP
FWUMP
OH, NO! MISMAGIUS'S ATTACK STRUCK BEFORE EMPOLEON'S!
I THOUGHT FOR SURE WE'D WIN THROUGH SHEER SPEED!

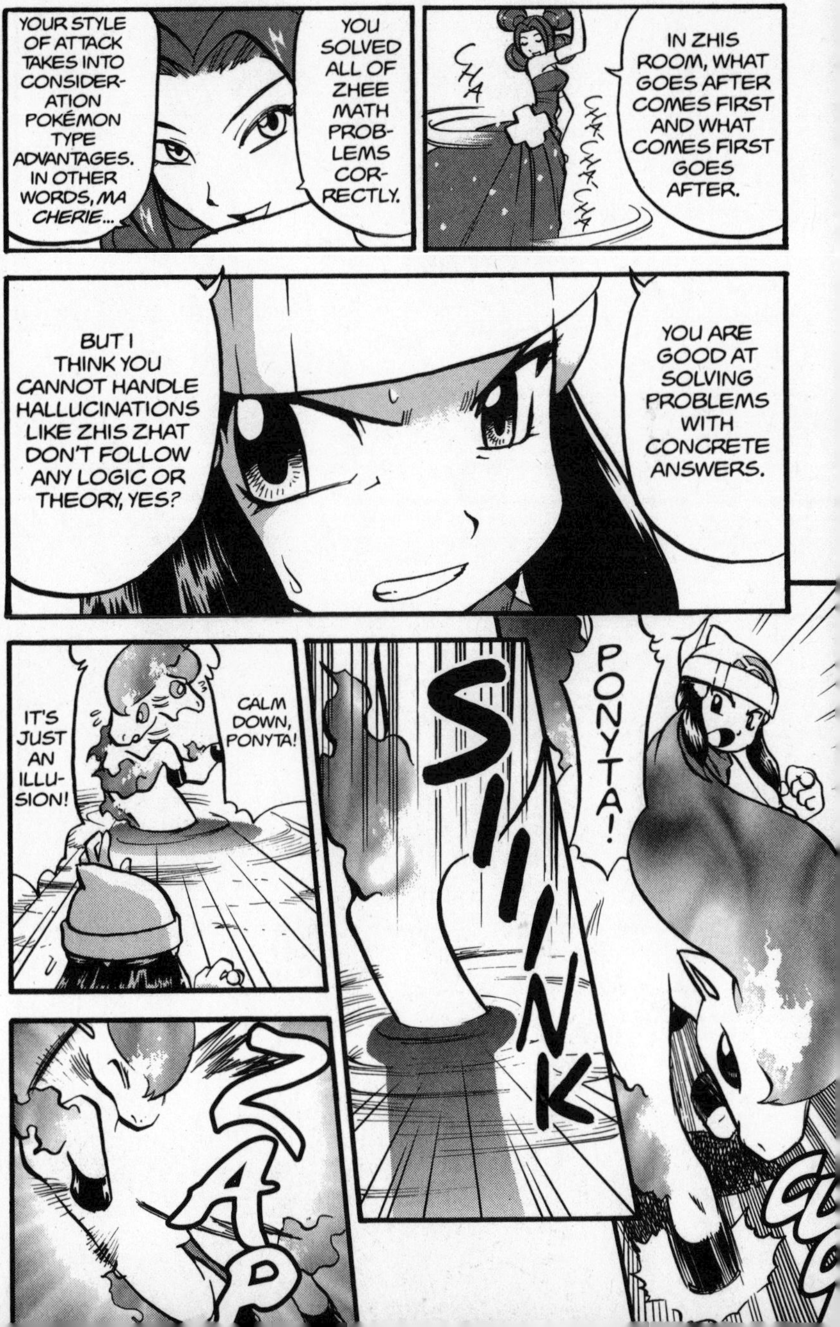

CHA
CHA CHA CHA CHA
IN ZHIS ROOM, WHAT GOES AFTER COMES FIRST AND WHAT COMES FIRST GOES AFTER.
YOU SOLVED ALL OF ZHEE MATH PROBLEMS CORRECTLY.
YOUR STYLE OF ATTACK TAKES INTO CONSIDERATION POKÉMON TYPE ADVANTAGES. IN OTHER WORDS, MA CHERIE...
YOU ARE GOOD AT SOLVING PROBLEMS WITH CONCRETE ANSWERS.
BUT I THINK YOU CANNOT HANDLE HALLUCINATIONS LIKE ZHIS ZHAT DON'T FOLLOW ANY LOGIC OR THEORY, YES?
PONYTA!
SIIINK
CALM DOWN, PONYTA!
IT'S JUST AN ILLUSION!
ZAP

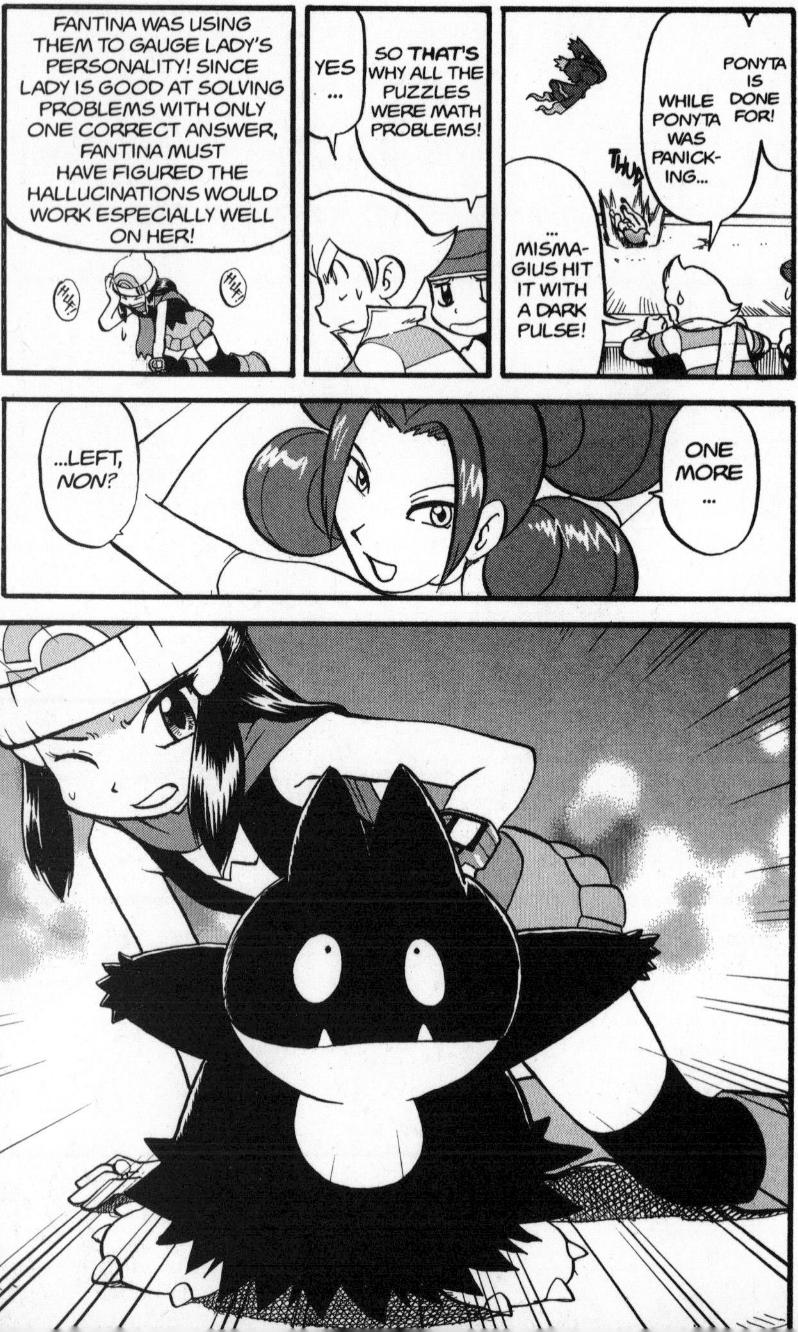
PONYTA IS DONE FOR!
WHILE PONYTA WAS PANICK-ING...
THUD
...MISMA-GIUS HIT IT WITH A DARK PULSE!
SO THAT'S WHY ALL THE PUZZLES WERE MATH PROBLEMS!
YES ...
FANTINA WAS USING THEM TO GAUGE LADY'S PERSONALITY! SINCE LADY IS GOOD AT SOLVING PROBLEMS WITH ONLY ONE CORRECT ANSWER, FANTINA MUST HAVE FIGURED THE HALLUCINATIONS WOULD WORK ESPECIALLY WELL ON HER!
HUF!
HUF!
ONE MORE ...
...LEFT, NON?

36

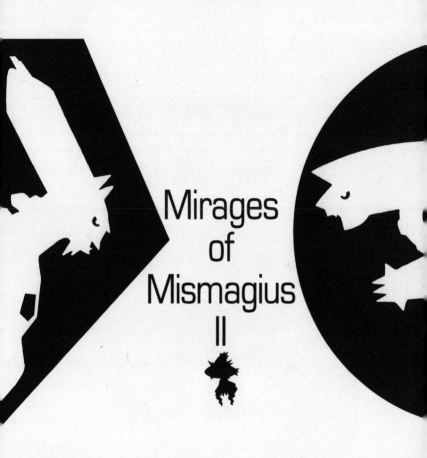

Mirages
of
Mismagius
II

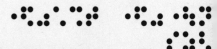

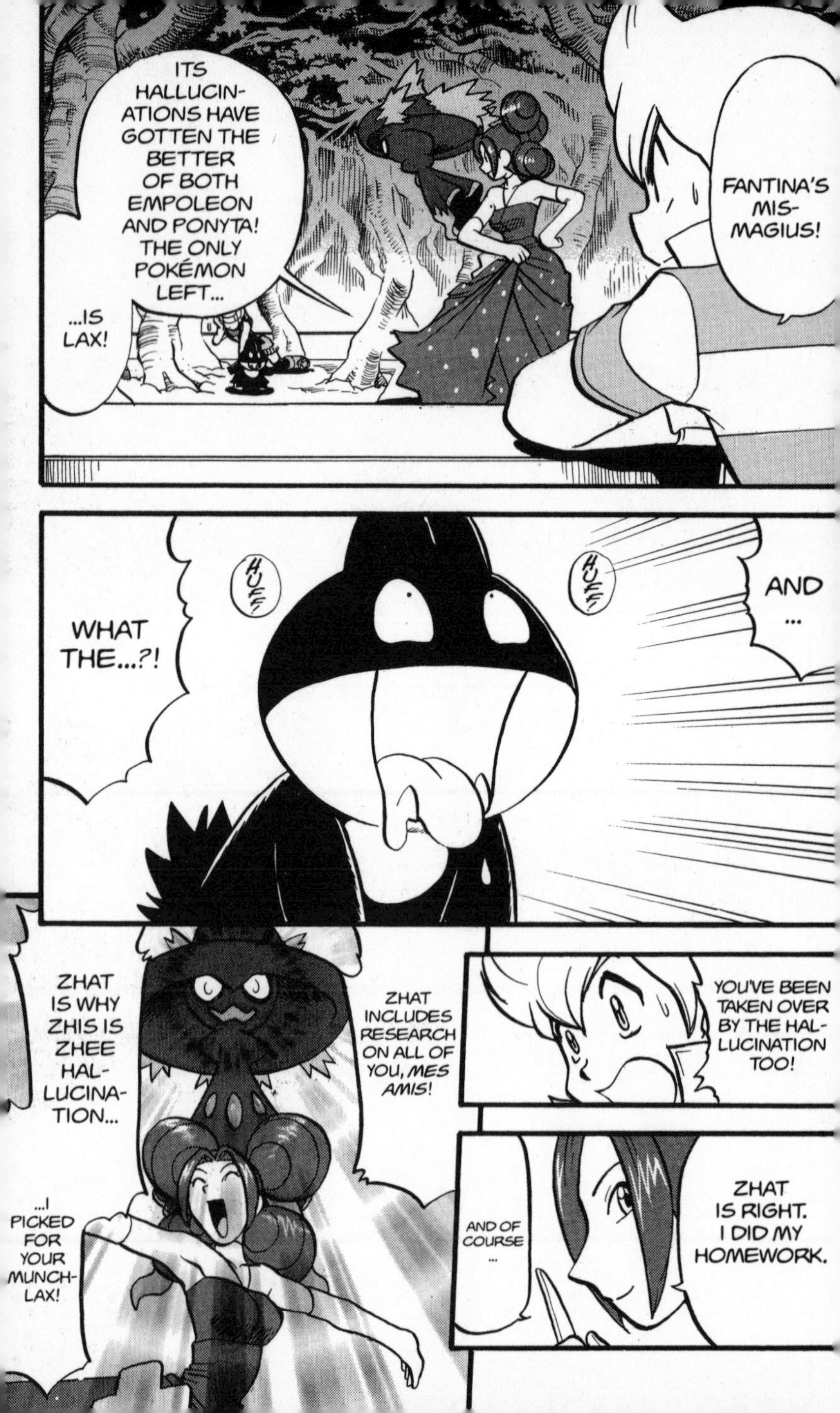
FANTINA'S MISMAGIUS!
ITS HALLUCINATIONS HAVE GOTTEN THE BETTER OF BOTH EMPOLEON AND PONYTA! THE ONLY POKÉMON LEFT...
...IS LAX!
AND ...
HUFF
HUFF
WHAT THE...?!
YOU'VE BEEN TAKEN OVER BY THE HALLUCINATION TOO!
ZHAT IS RIGHT. I DID MY HOMEWORK.
AND OF COURSE ...
ZHAT INCLUDES RESEARCH ON ALL OF YOU, *MES AMIS*!
ZHAT IS WHY ZHIS IS ZHEE HALLUCINATION...
...I PICKED FOR YOUR MUNCHLAX!

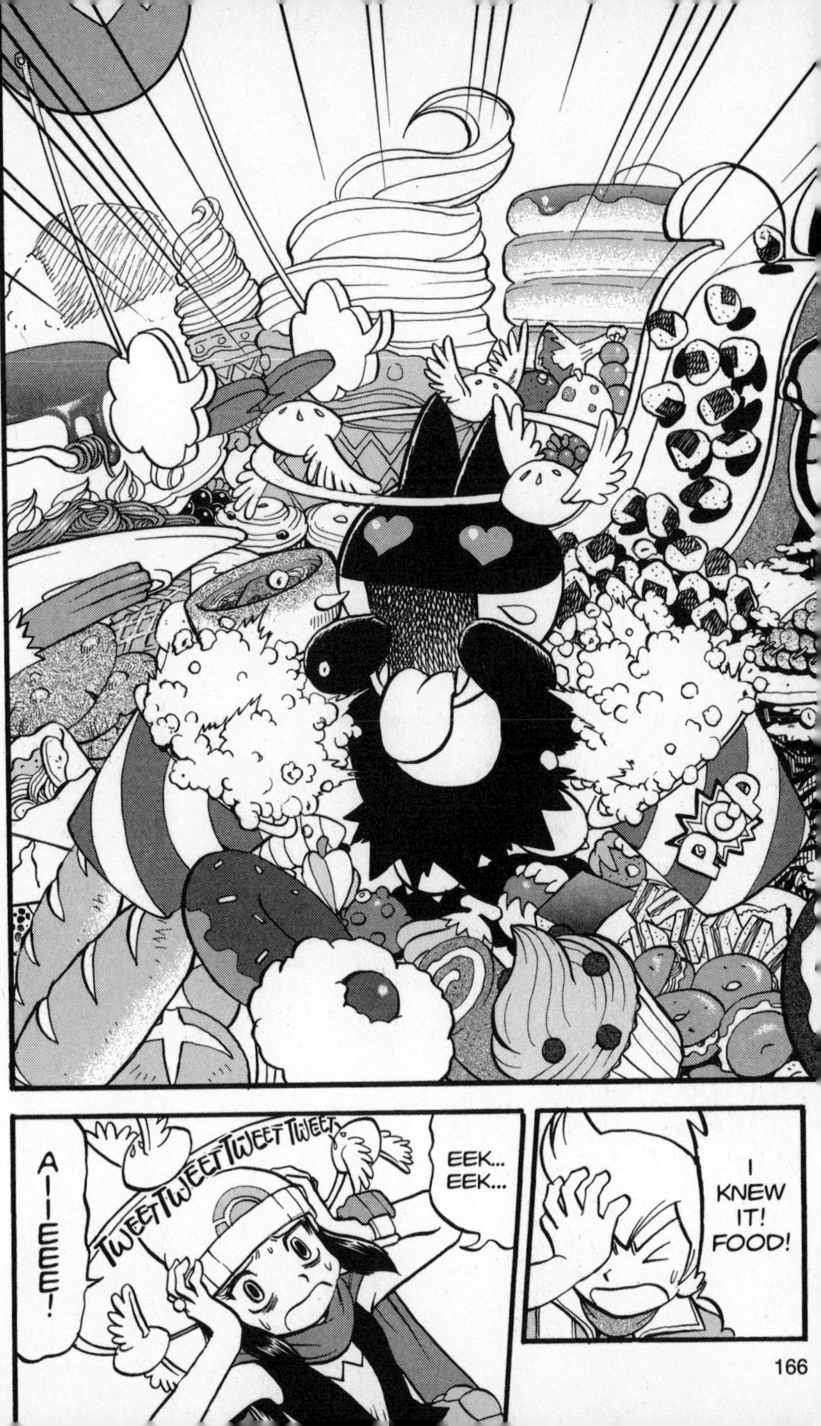
POP
I KNEW IT! FOOD!
TWEET TWEET TWEET TWEET
EEK... EEK...
AIIEEE!

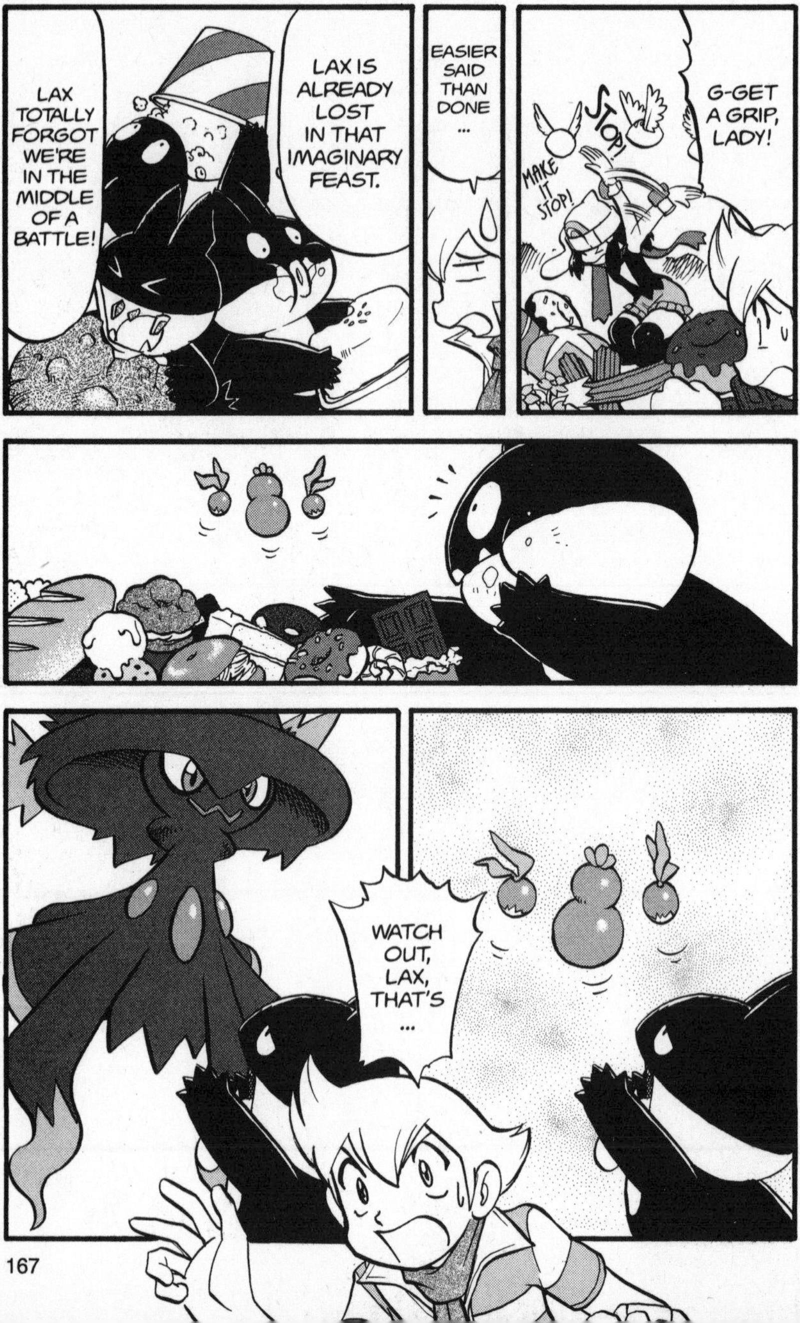
G-GET A GRIP, LADY!
STOP!
MAKE IT STOP!
EASIER SAID THAN DONE ...
LAX IS ALREADY LOST IN THAT IMAGINARY FEAST.
LAX TOTALLY FORGOT WE'RE IN THE MIDDLE OF A BATTLE!
WATCH OUT, LAX, THAT'S ...

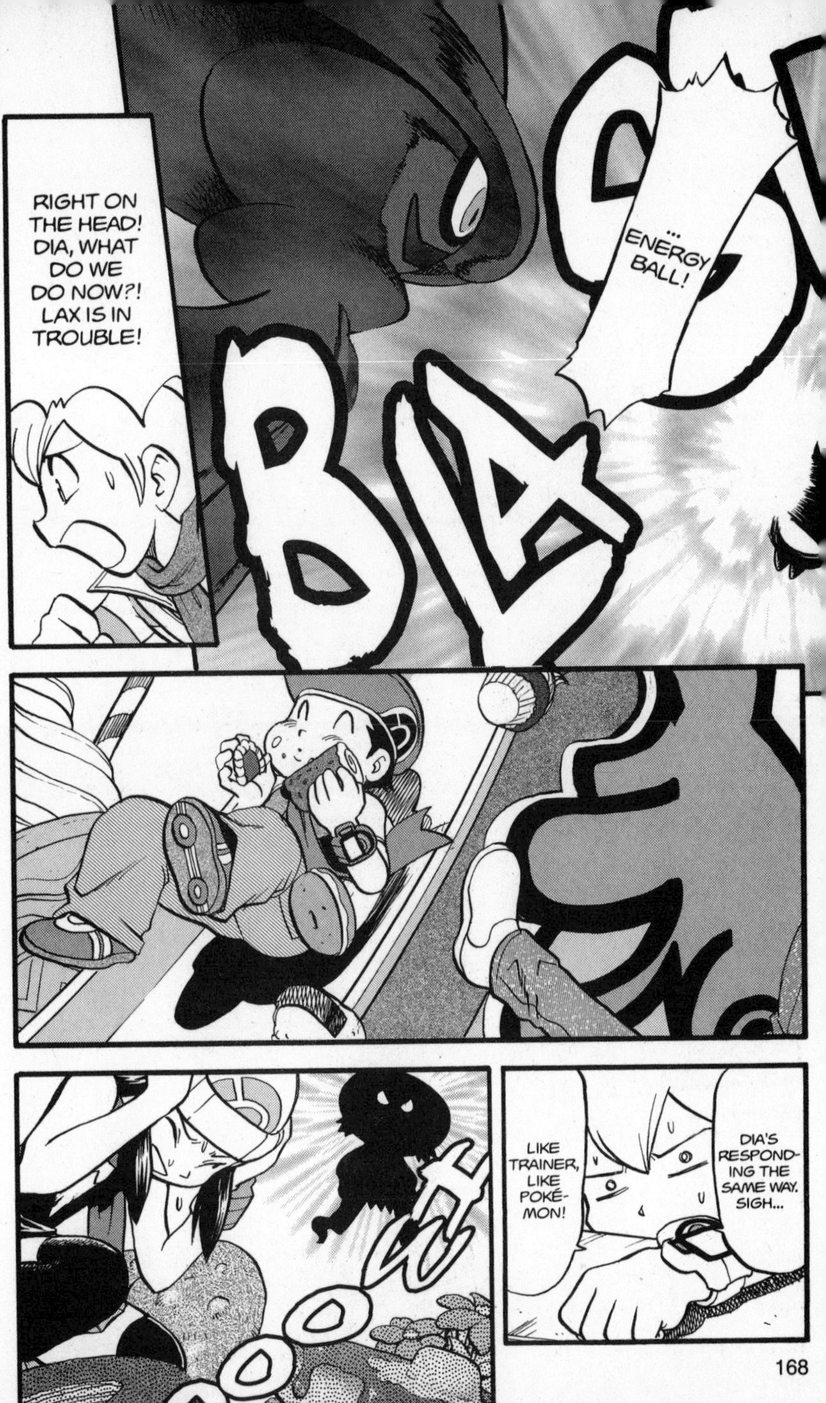
... ENERGY BALL!
RIGHT ON THE HEAD! DIA, WHAT DO WE DO NOW?! LAX IS IN TROUBLE!
DIA'S RESPONDING THE SAME WAY. SIGH...
LIKE TRAINER, LIKE POKÉMON!

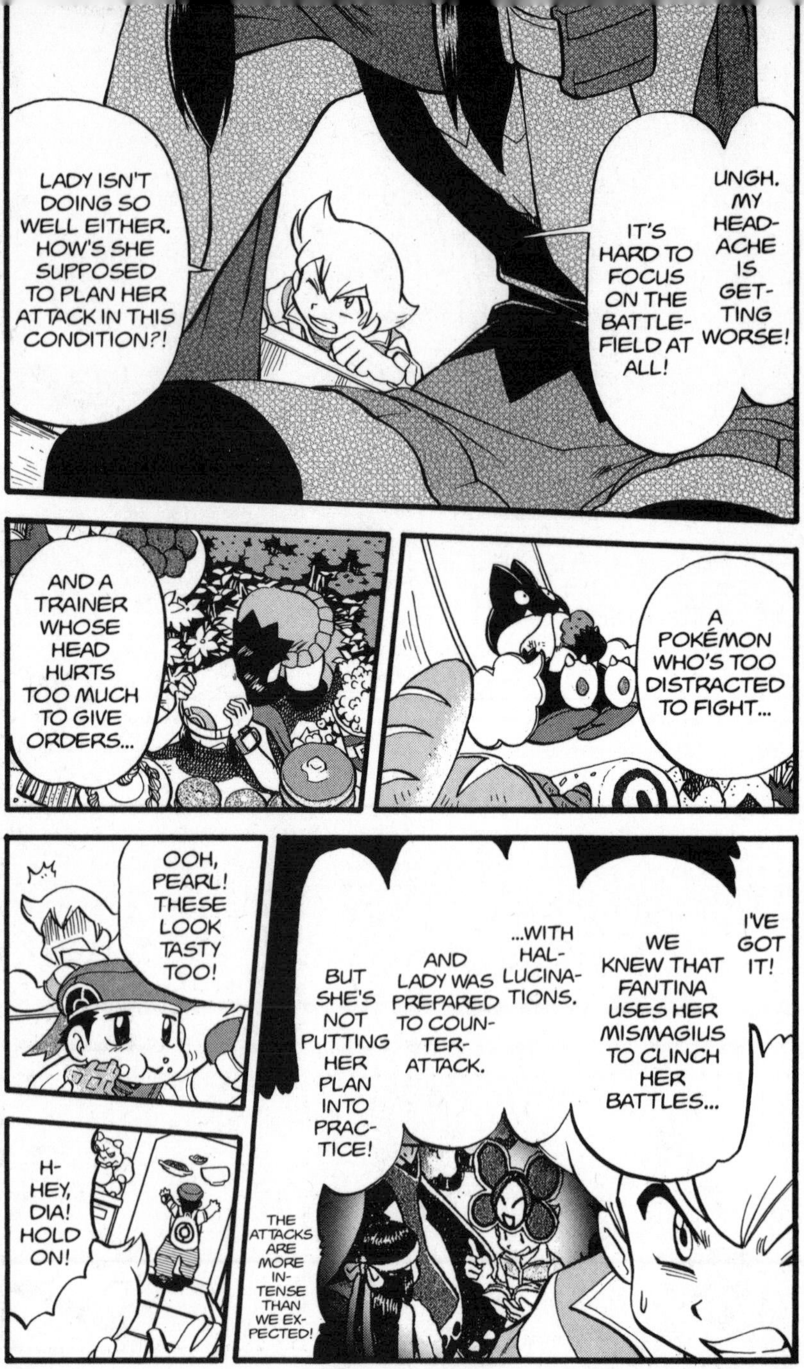
UNGH. MY HEADACHE IS GETTING WORSE!
IT'S HARD TO FOCUS ON THE BATTLEFIELD AT ALL!
LADY ISN'T DOING SO WELL EITHER. HOW'S SHE SUPPOSED TO PLAN HER ATTACK IN THIS CONDITION?!
A POKÉMON WHO'S TOO DISTRACTED TO FIGHT...
AND A TRAINER WHOSE HEAD HURTS TOO MUCH TO GIVE ORDERS...
I'VE GOT IT!
WE KNEW THAT FANTINA USES HER MISMAGIUS TO CLINCH HER BATTLES...
...WITH HALLUCINATIONS.
AND LADY WAS PREPARED TO COUNTERATTACK.
BUT SHE'S NOT PUTTING HER PLAN INTO PRACTICE!
THE ATTACKS ARE MORE INTENSE THAN WE EXPECTED!
OOH, PEARL! THESE LOOK TASTY TOO!
H-HEY, DIA! HOLD ON!

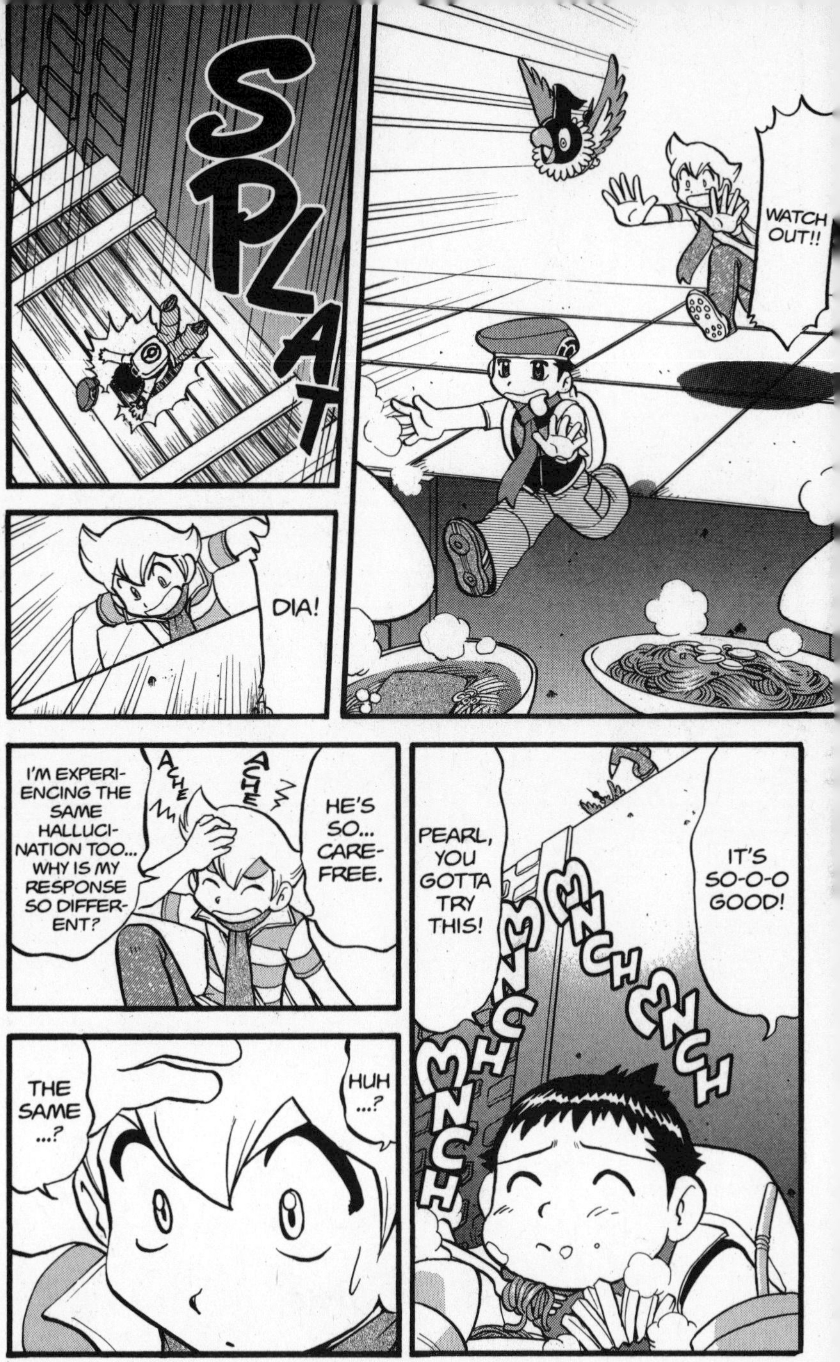

WATCH OUT!!
SPLAT
DIA!
IT'S SO-O-O GOOD!
PEARL, YOU GOTTA TRY THIS!
MUNCH MUNCH
MUNCH MUNCH
HE'S SO... CAREFREE.
ACHE
ACHE
I'M EXPERIENCING THE SAME HALLUCINATION TOO... WHY IS MY RESPONSE SO DIFFERENT?
HUH ...?
THE SAME ...?

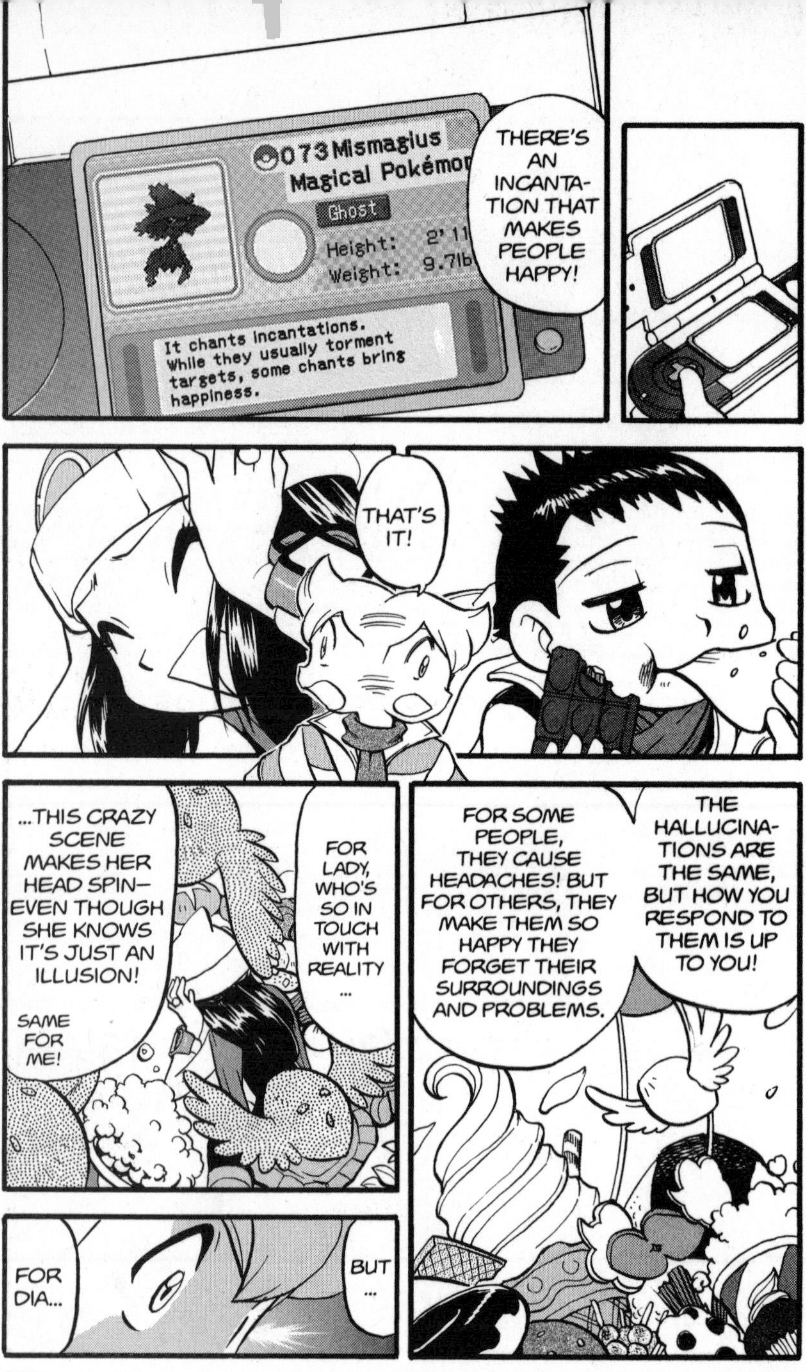
THERE'S AN INCANTATION THAT MAKES PEOPLE HAPPY!
073 Mismagius
Magical Pokémo
Ghost
Height: 2' 11
Weight: 9.7lb
It chants incantations. While they usually torment targets, some chants bring happiness.
THAT'S IT!
THE HALLUCINATIONS ARE THE SAME, BUT HOW YOU RESPOND TO THEM IS UP TO YOU!
FOR SOME PEOPLE, THEY CAUSE HEADACHES! BUT FOR OTHERS, THEY MAKE THEM SO HAPPY THEY FORGET THEIR SURROUNDINGS AND PROBLEMS.
FOR LADY, WHO'S SO IN TOUCH WITH REALITY ...
...THIS CRAZY SCENE MAKES HER HEAD SPIN—EVEN THOUGH SHE KNOWS IT'S JUST AN ILLUSION!
SAME FOR ME!
BUT ...
FOR DIA...

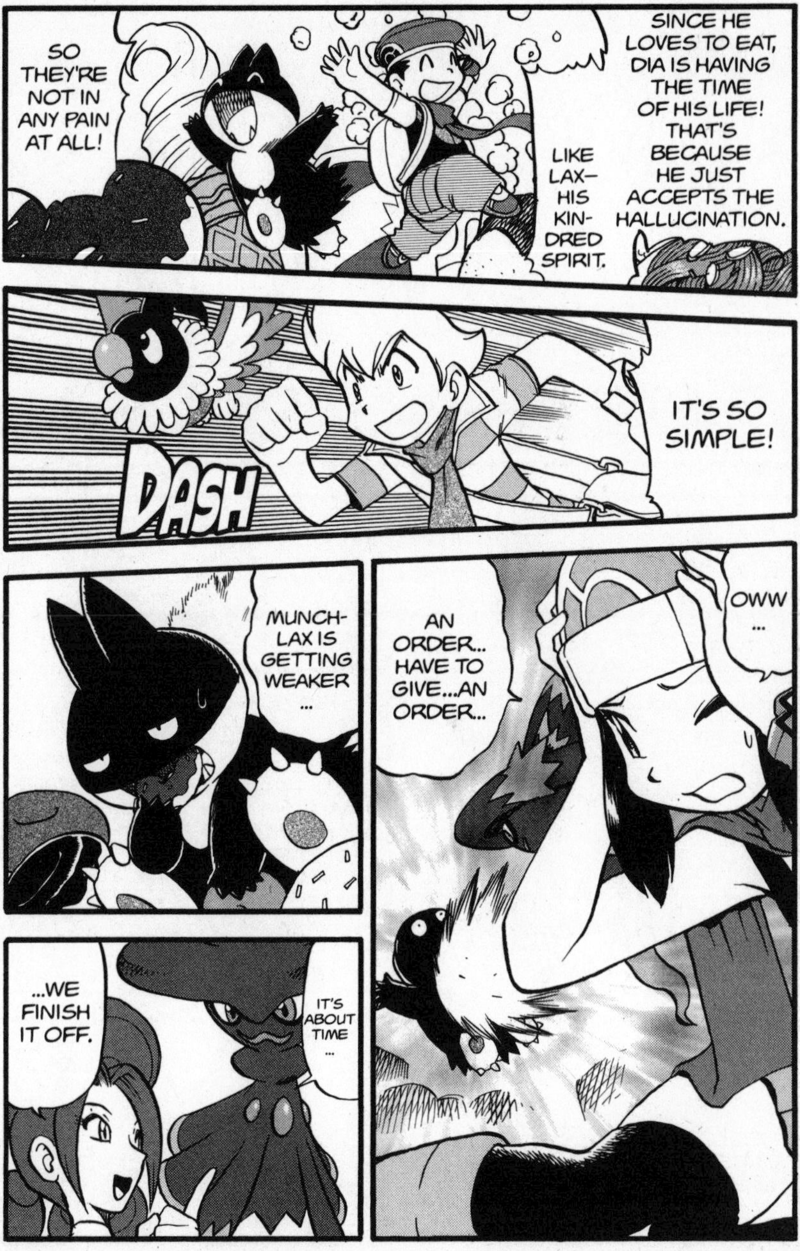
SINCE HE LOVES TO EAT, DIA IS HAVING THE TIME OF HIS LIFE! THAT'S BECAUSE HE JUST ACCEPTS THE HALLUCINATION.
LIKE LAX—HIS KIN-DRED SPIRIT.
SO THEY'RE NOT IN ANY PAIN AT ALL!
IT'S SO SIMPLE!
DASH
OWW ...
AN ORDER... HAVE TO GIVE...AN ORDER...
MUNCH-LAX IS GETTING WEAKER ...
IT'S ABOUT TIME ...
...WE FINISH IT OFF.

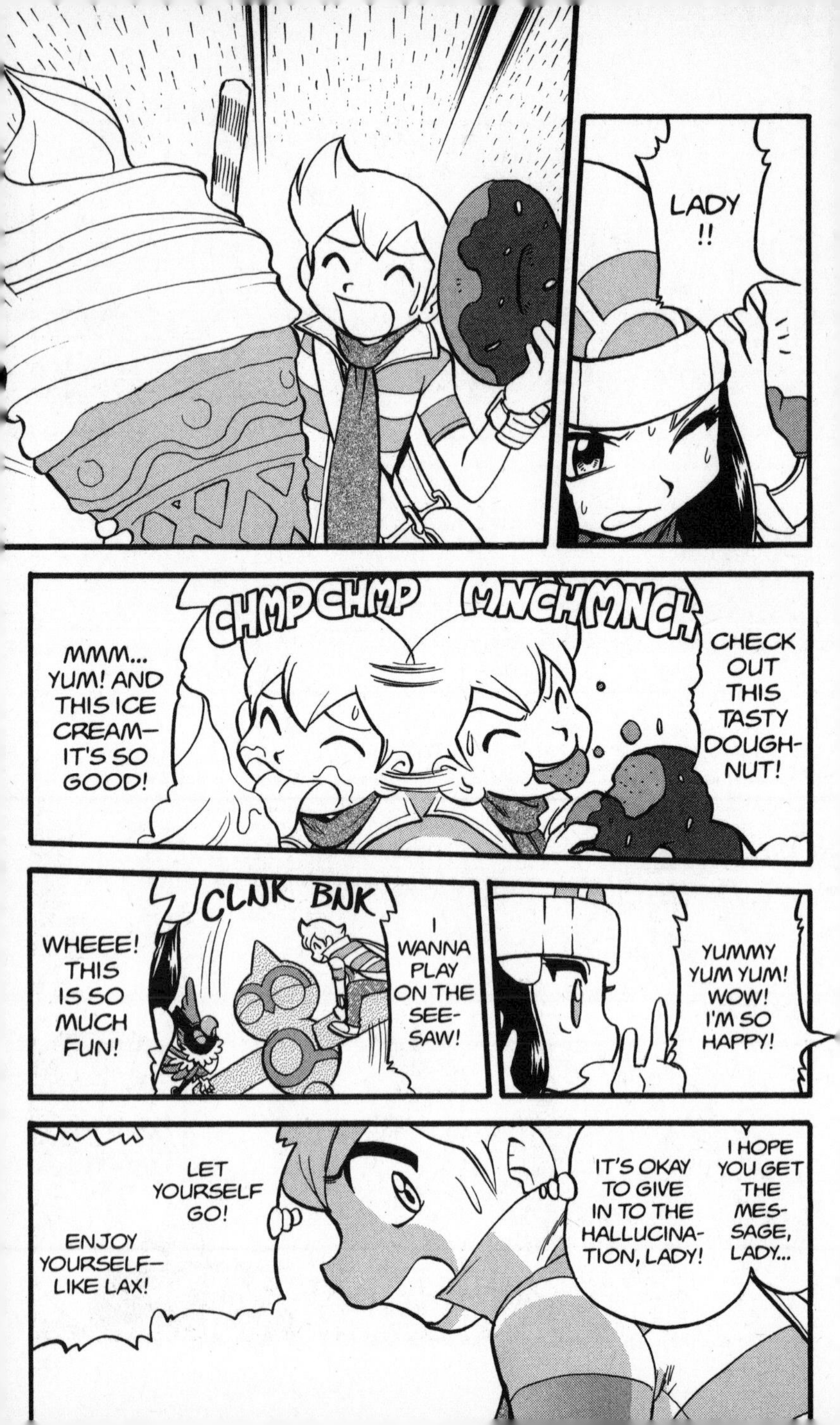
LADY !!
MNCHMNCH
CHMPCHMP
CHECK OUT THIS TASTY DOUGHNUT!
MMM... YUM! AND THIS ICE CREAM—IT'S SO GOOD!
YUMMY YUM YUM! WOW! I'M SO HAPPY!
CLNK BNK
I WANNA PLAY ON THE SEE-SAW!
WHEEE! THIS IS SO MUCH FUN!
I HOPE YOU GET THE MESSAGE, LADY...
IT'S OKAY TO GIVE IN TO THE HALLUCINATION, LADY!
LET YOURSELF GO!
ENJOY YOURSELF—LIKE LAX!

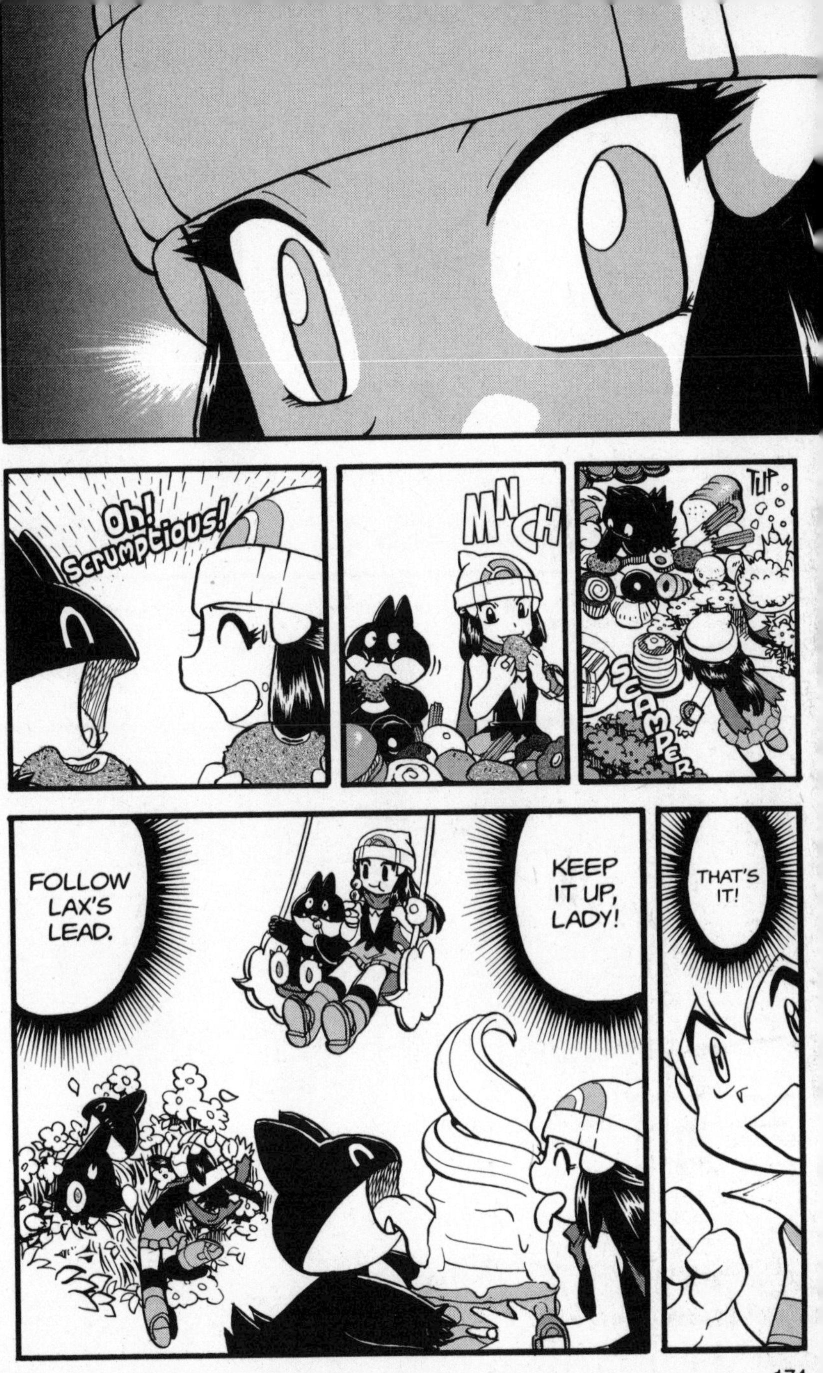
TUP
SCAMPER
MNCH
Oh! Scrumptious!
THAT'S IT!
KEEP IT UP, LADY!
FOLLOW LAX'S LEAD.

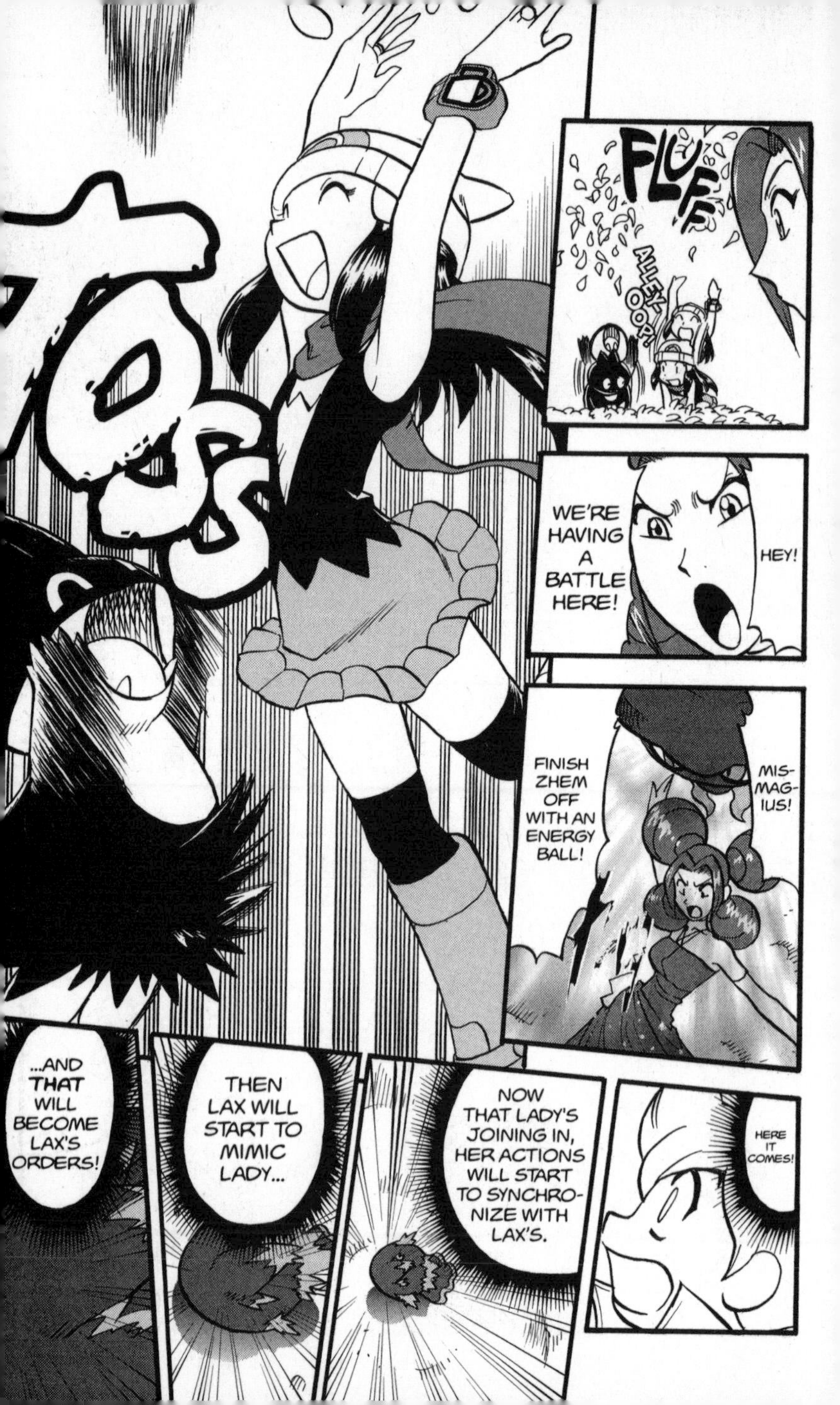
FLUFF
ALLEY-OOP!
HEY!
WE'RE HAVING A BATTLE HERE!
MIS-MAG-IUS!
FINISH ZHEM OFF WITH AN ENERGY BALL!
HERE IT COMES!
NOW THAT LADY'S JOINING IN, HER ACTIONS WILL START TO SYNCHRO-NIZE WITH LAX'S.
THEN LAX WILL START TO MIMIC LADY...
...AND THAT WILL BECOME LAX'S ORDERS!

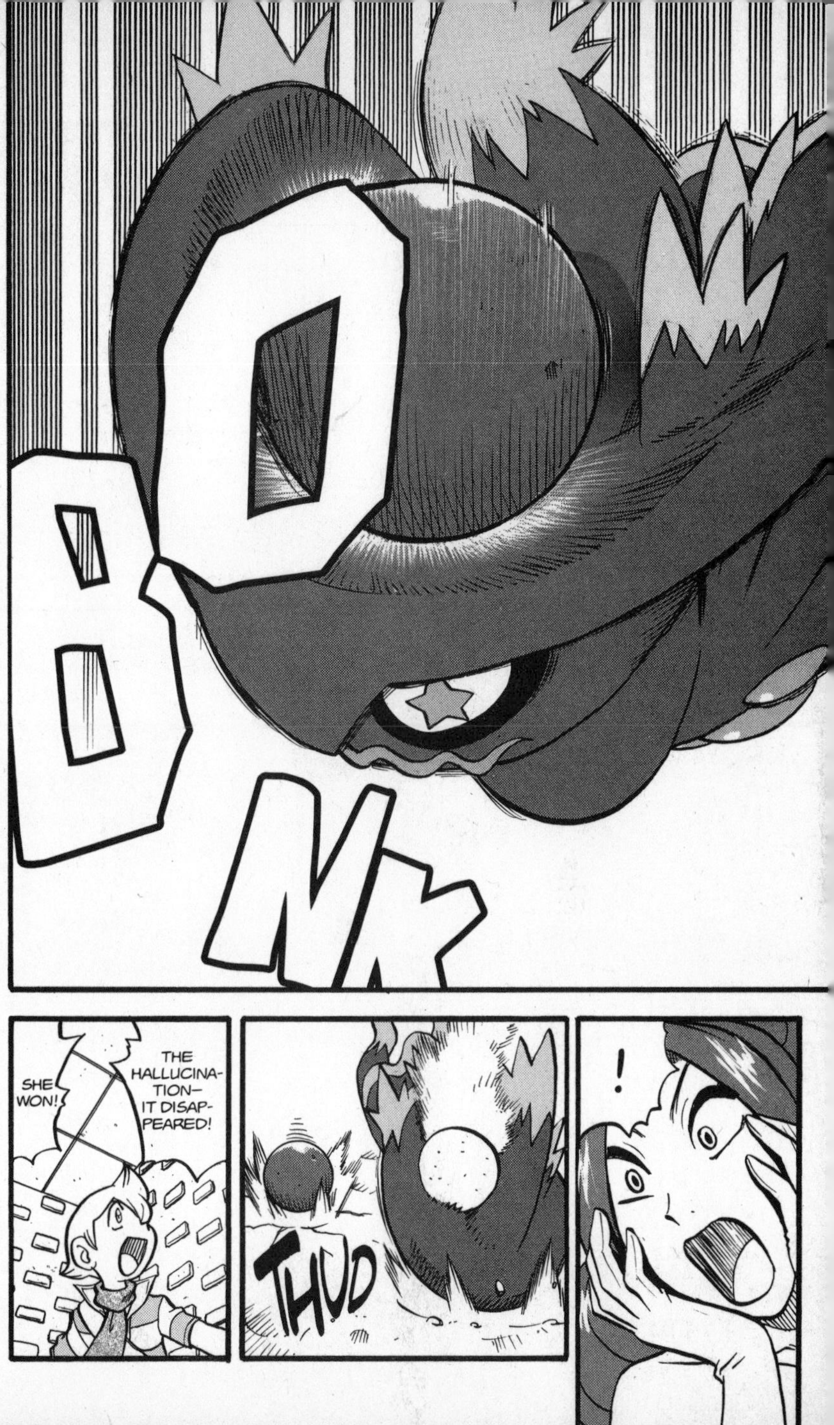
BONK
!
THUD
THE HALLUCINATION—IT DISAPPEARED!
SHE WON!

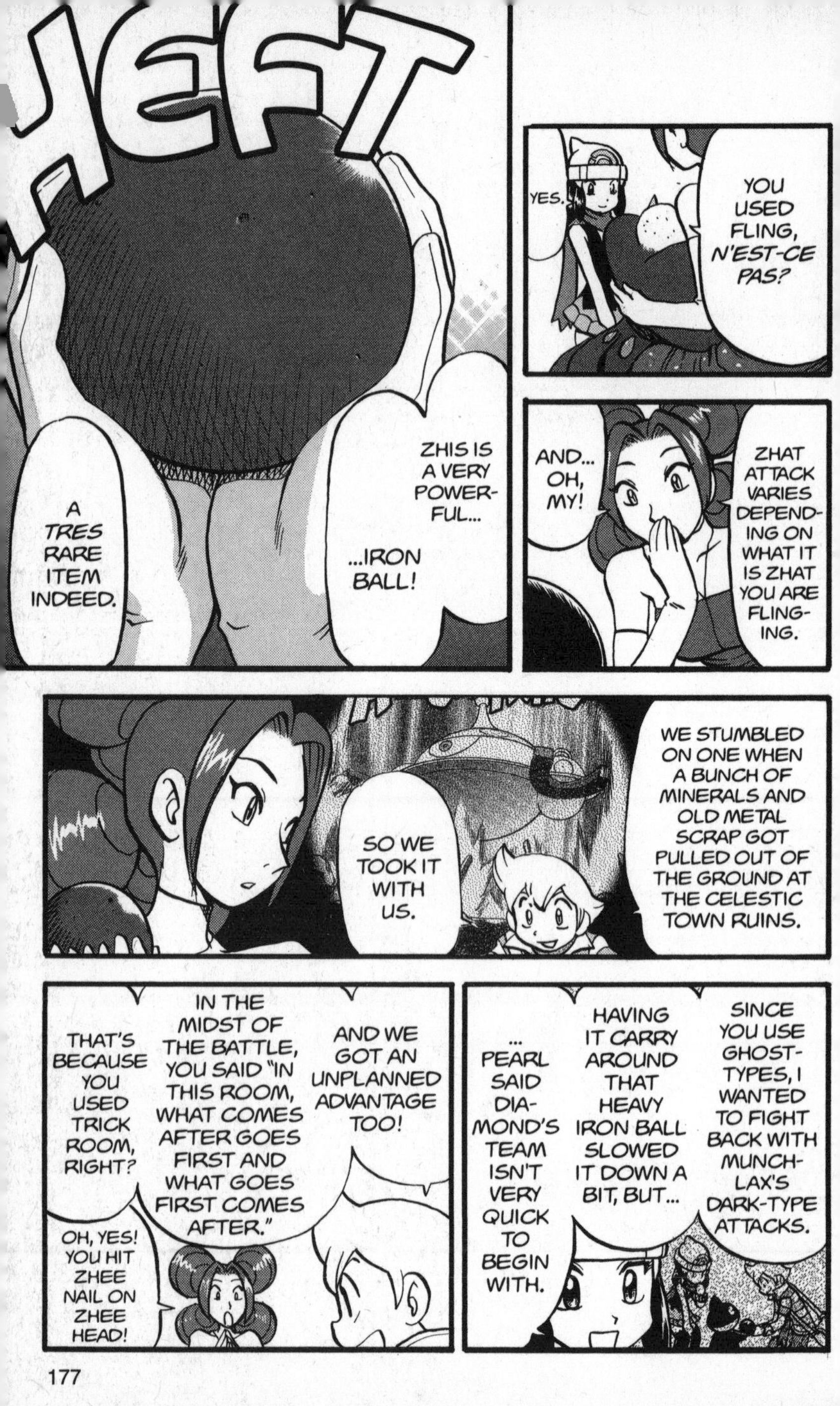
YOU USED FLING, N'EST-CE PAS?
YES.
ZHAT ATTACK VARIES DEPENDING ON WHAT IT IS ZHAT YOU ARE FLINGING.
AND... OH, MY!
HEFT
ZHIS IS A VERY POWERFUL... ...IRON BALL!
A TRES RARE ITEM INDEED.
WE STUMBLED ON ONE WHEN A BUNCH OF MINERALS AND OLD METAL SCRAP GOT PULLED OUT OF THE GROUND AT THE CELESTIC TOWN RUINS.
SO WE TOOK IT WITH US.
SINCE YOU USE GHOST-TYPES, I WANTED TO FIGHT BACK WITH MUNCHLAX'S DARK-TYPE ATTACKS.
HAVING IT CARRY AROUND THAT HEAVY IRON BALL SLOWED IT DOWN A BIT, BUT...
...PEARL SAID DIAMOND'S TEAM ISN'T VERY QUICK TO BEGIN WITH.
AND WE GOT AN UNPLANNED ADVANTAGE TOO!
IN THE MIDST OF THE BATTLE, YOU SAID "IN THIS ROOM, WHAT COMES AFTER GOES FIRST AND WHAT GOES FIRST COMES AFTER."
THAT'S BECAUSE YOU USED TRICK ROOM, RIGHT?
OH, YES! YOU HIT ZHEE NAIL ON ZHEE HEAD!

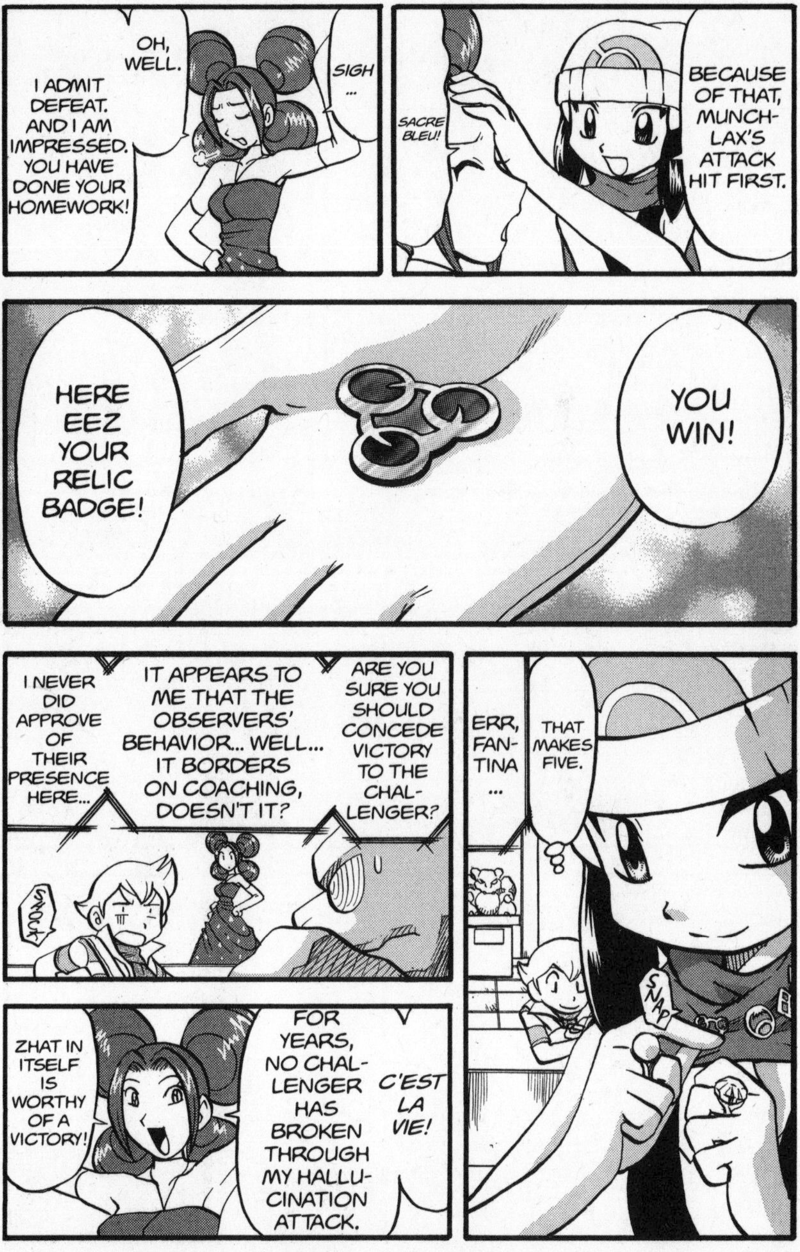
BECAUSE OF THAT, MUNCHLAX'S ATTACK HIT FIRST.
SACRE BLEU!
SIGH...
OH, WELL.
I ADMIT DEFEAT. AND I AM IMPRESSED. YOU HAVE DONE YOUR HOMEWORK!
YOU WIN!
HERE EEZ YOUR RELIC BADGE!
THAT MAKES FIVE.
ERR, FANTINA...
SNAP
ARE YOU SURE YOU SHOULD CONCEDE VICTORY TO THE CHALLENGER?
IT APPEARS TO ME THAT THE OBSERVERS' BEHAVIOR... WELL... IT BORDERS ON COACHING, DOESN'T IT?
I NEVER DID APPROVE OF THEIR PRESENCE HERE...
SHOCK
C'EST LA VIE!
FOR YEARS, NO CHALLENGER HAS BROKEN THROUGH MY HALLUCINATION ATTACK.
ZHAT IN ITSELF IS WORTHY OF A VICTORY!

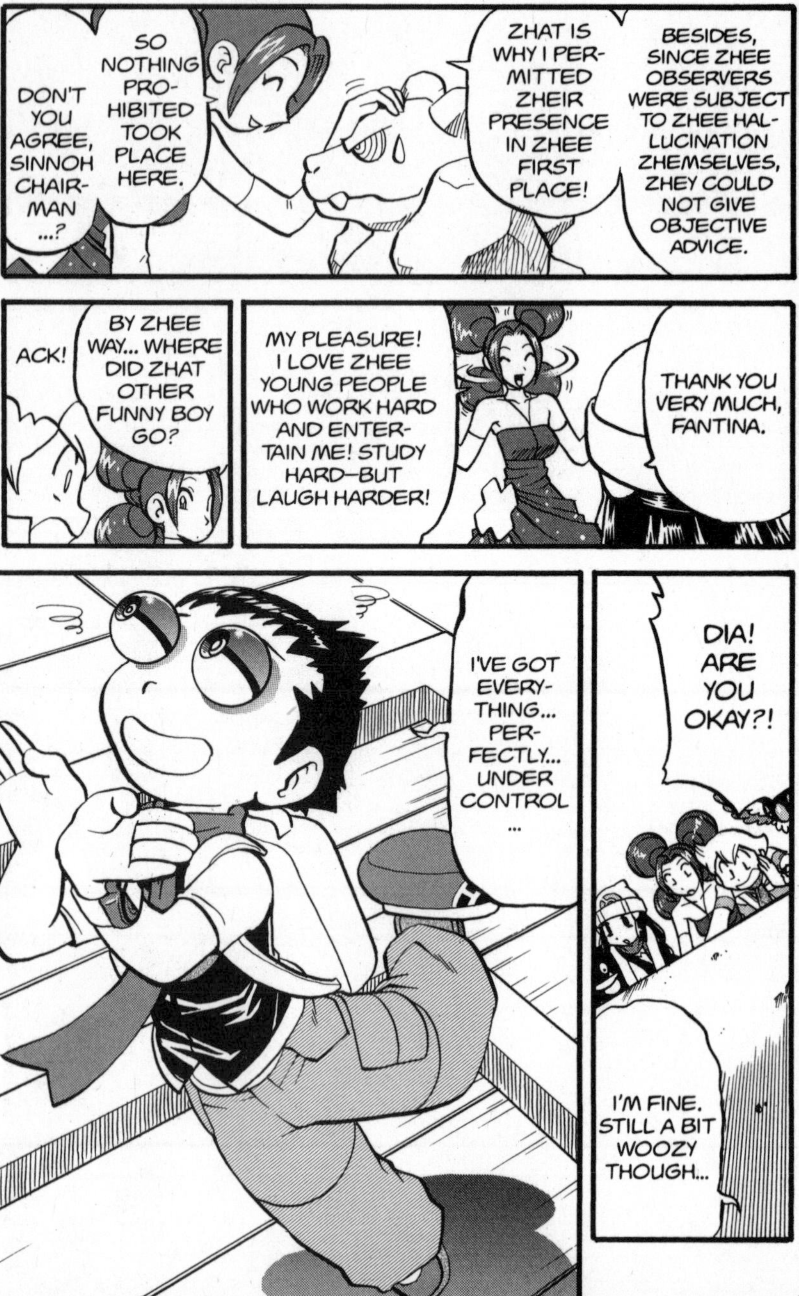
BESIDES, SINCE ZHEE OBSERVERS WERE SUBJECT TO ZHEE HALLUCINATION ZHEMSELVES, ZHEY COULD NOT GIVE OBJECTIVE ADVICE.
ZHAT IS WHY I PERMITTED ZHEIR PRESENCE IN ZHEE FIRST PLACE!
SO NOTHING PROHIBITED TOOK PLACE HERE.
DON'T YOU AGREE, SINNOH CHAIRMAN ...?
THANK YOU VERY MUCH, FANTINA.
MY PLEASURE! I LOVE ZHEE YOUNG PEOPLE WHO WORK HARD AND ENTERTAIN ME! STUDY HARD—BUT LAUGH HARDER!
BY ZHEE WAY... WHERE DID ZHAT OTHER FUNNY BOY GO?
ACK!
DIA! ARE YOU OKAY?!
I'M FINE. STILL A BIT WOOZY THOUGH...
I'VE GOT EVERYTHING... PERFECTLY... UNDER CONTROL ...

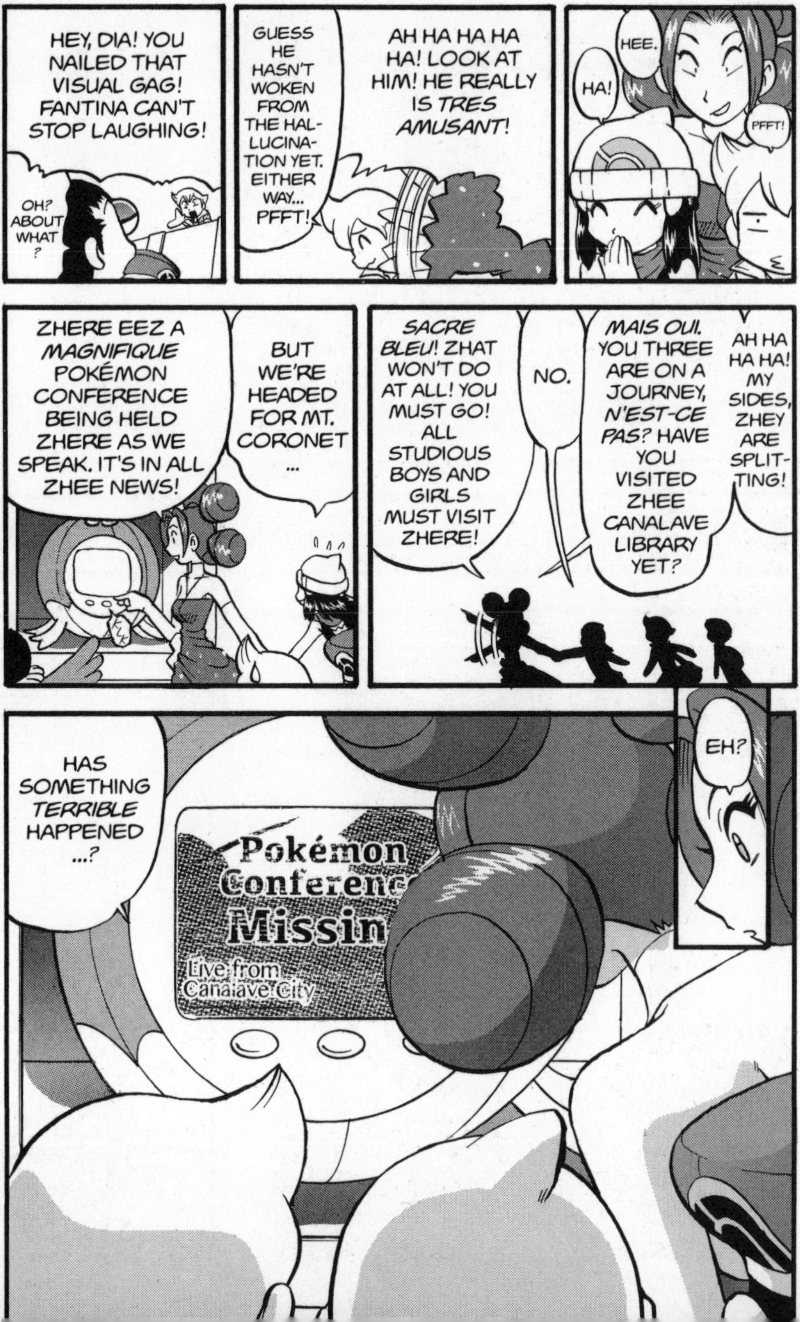
HEE.
HA!
PFFT!
AH HA HA HA HA! LOOK AT HIM! HE REALLY IS *TRES AMUSANT*!
GUESS HE HASN'T WOKEN FROM THE HALLUCINATION YET. EITHER WAY... PFFT!
HEY, DIA! YOU NAILED THAT VISUAL GAG! FANTINA CAN'T STOP LAUGHING!
OH? ABOUT WHAT?
AH HA HA HA! MY SIDES, ZHEY ARE SPLITTING!
MAIS OUI. YOU THREE ARE ON A JOURNEY, *N'EST-CE PAS?* HAVE YOU VISITED ZHEE CANALAVE LIBRARY YET?
NO.
SACRE BLEU! ZHAT WON'T DO AT ALL! YOU MUST GO! ALL STUDIOUS BOYS AND GIRLS MUST VISIT ZHERE!
BUT WE'RE HEADED FOR MT. CORONET...
ZHERE EEZ A *MAGNIFIQUE* POKÉMON CONFERENCE BEING HELD ZHERE AS WE SPEAK. IT'S IN ALL ZHEE NEWS!
KLK
EH?
HAS SOMETHING *TERRIBLE* HAPPENED...?
Pokémon Conferenc Missin
Live from Canalave City

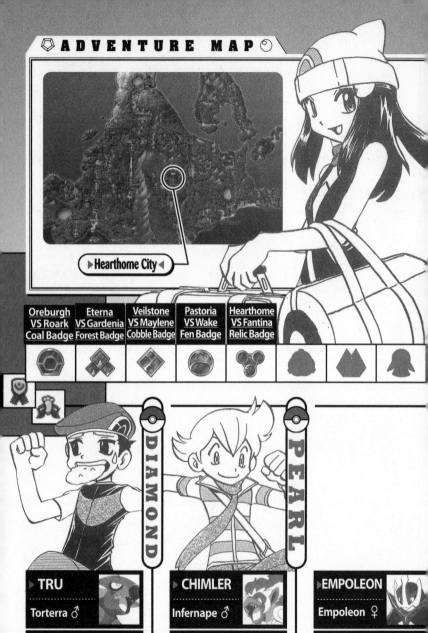

▶Hearthome City◀

Oreburgh VS Roark Coal Badge	Eterna VS Gardenia Forest Badge	Veilstone VS Maylene Cobble Badge	Pastoria VS Wake Fen Badge	Hearthome VS Fantina Relic Badge			

DIAMOND

PEARL

▶TRU
Torterra ♂

▶CHIMLER
Infernape ♂

▶EMPOLEON
Empoleon ♀

▶LAX
Munchlax ♂

▶CHATLER
Chatot ♂

▶PONYTA
Ponyta ♂

37

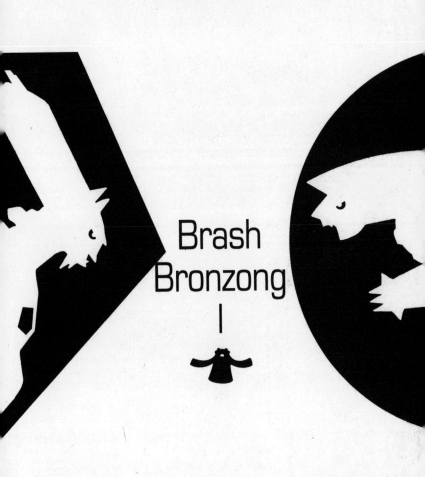

Brash
Bronzong
I

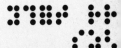

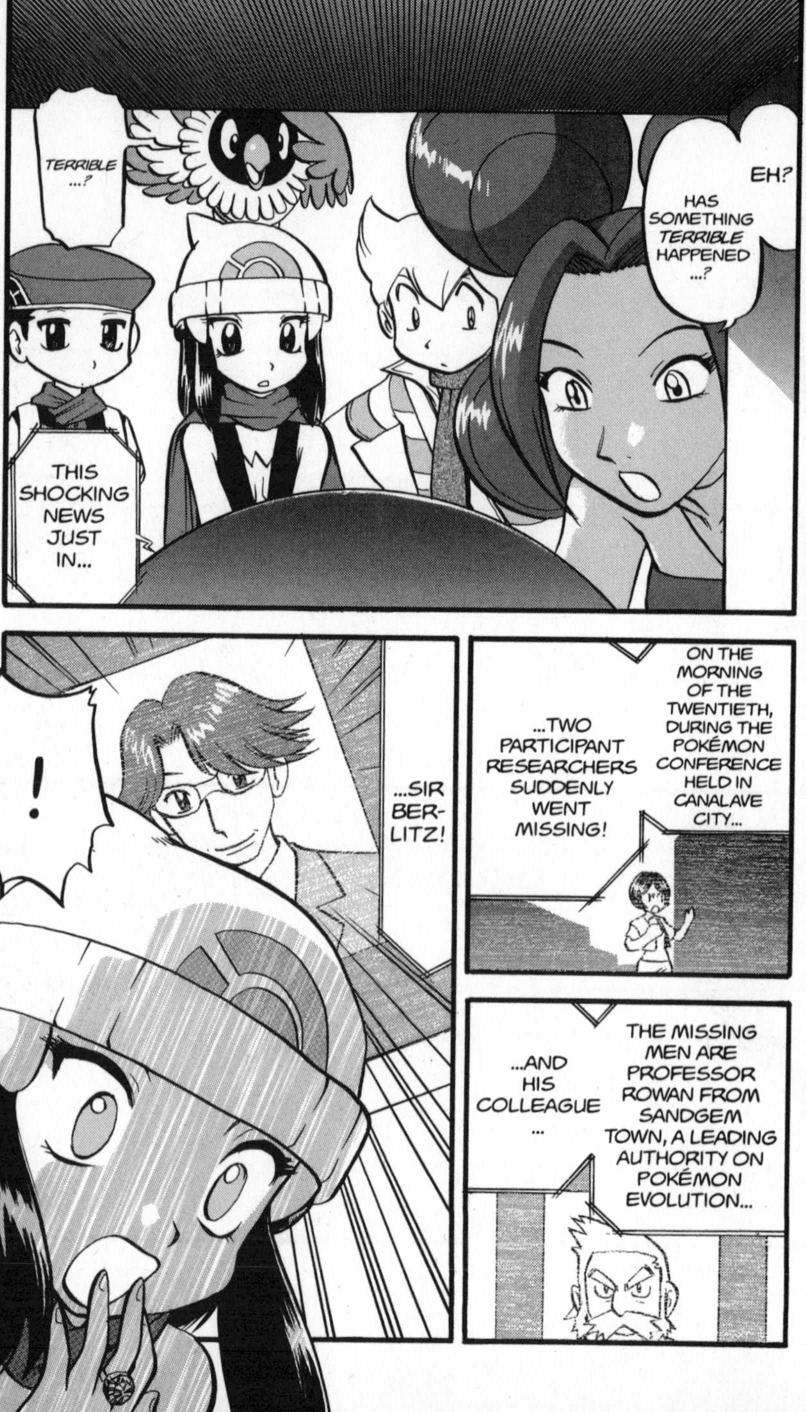
EH? HAS SOMETHING *TERRIBLE* HAPPENED ...?
TERRIBLE ...?
THIS SHOCKING NEWS JUST IN...
ON THE MORNING OF THE TWENTIETH, DURING THE POKÉMON CONFERENCE HELD IN CANALAVE CITY...
...TWO PARTICIPANT RESEARCHERS SUDDENLY WENT MISSING!
THE MISSING MEN ARE PROFESSOR ROWAN FROM SANDGEM TOWN, A LEADING AUTHORITY ON POKÉMON EVOLUTION...
...AND HIS COLLEAGUE ...
...SIR BER-LITZ!
!

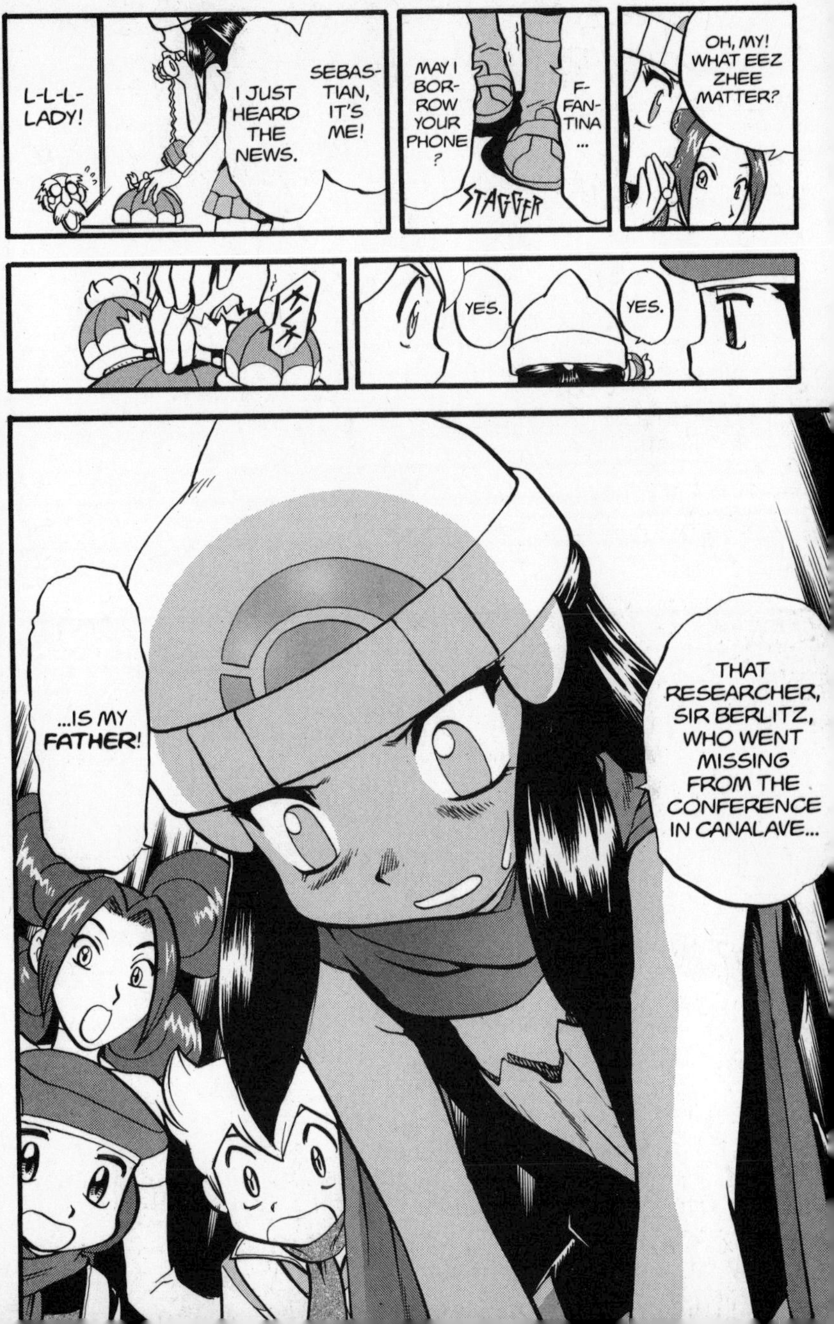
OH, MY! WHAT EEZ ZHEE MATTER?
F-FAN-TINA...
MAY I BOR-ROW YOUR PHONE?
STAGGER
SEBAS-TIAN, IT'S ME!
I JUST HEARD THE NEWS.
L-L-L-LADY!
YES.
YES.
THAT RESEARCHER, SIR BERLITZ, WHO WENT MISSING FROM THE CONFERENCE IN CANALAVE...
...IS MY FATHER!

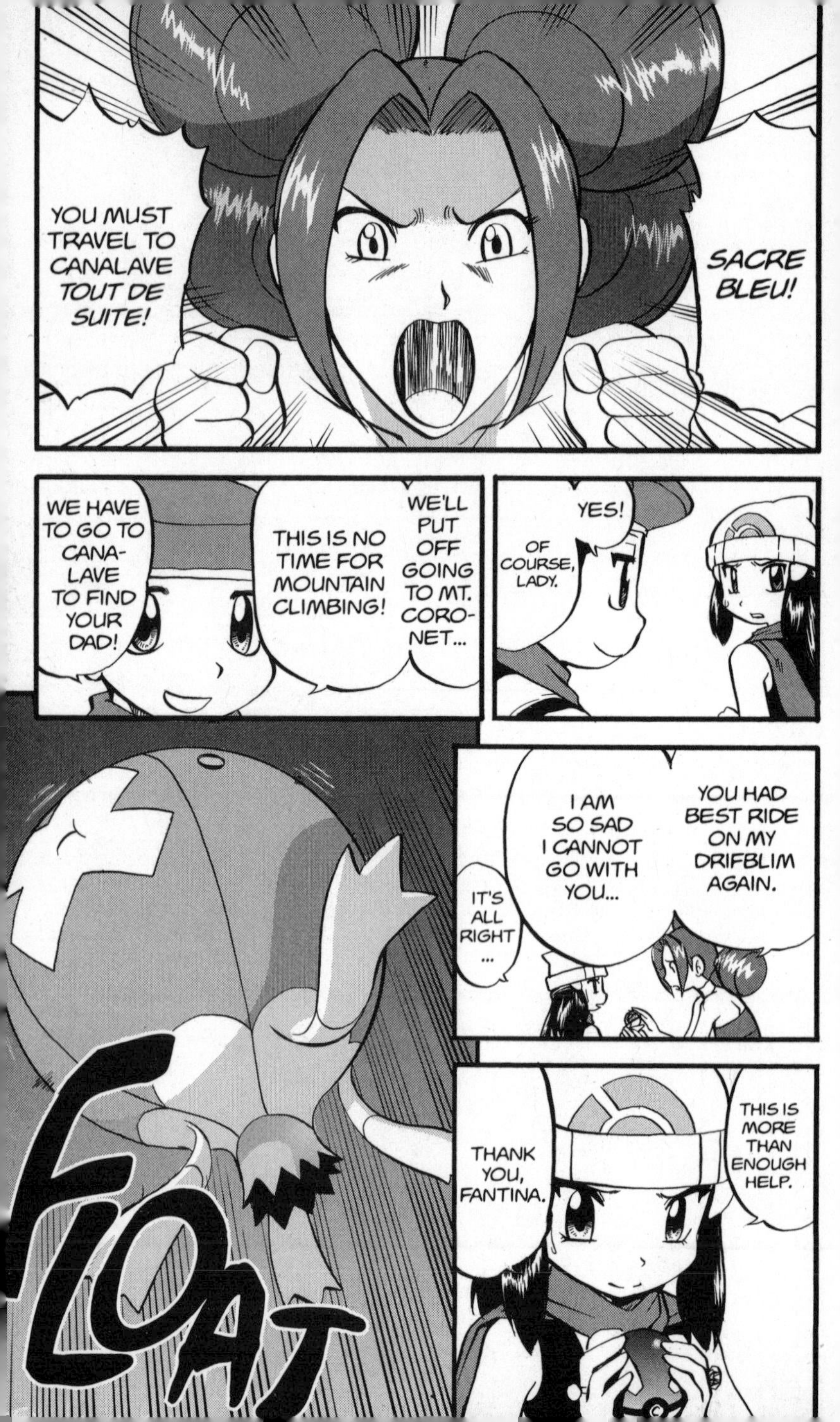
SACRE BLEU!
YOU MUST TRAVEL TO CANALAVE TOUT DE SUITE!
YES!
OF COURSE, LADY.
WE'LL PUT OFF GOING TO MT. CORONET...
THIS IS NO TIME FOR MOUNTAIN CLIMBING!
WE HAVE TO GO TO CANALAVE TO FIND YOUR DAD!
YOU HAD BEST RIDE ON MY DRIFBLIM AGAIN.
I AM SO SAD I CANNOT GO WITH YOU...
IT'S ALL RIGHT...
THIS IS MORE THAN ENOUGH HELP.
THANK YOU, FANTINA.
FLOAT

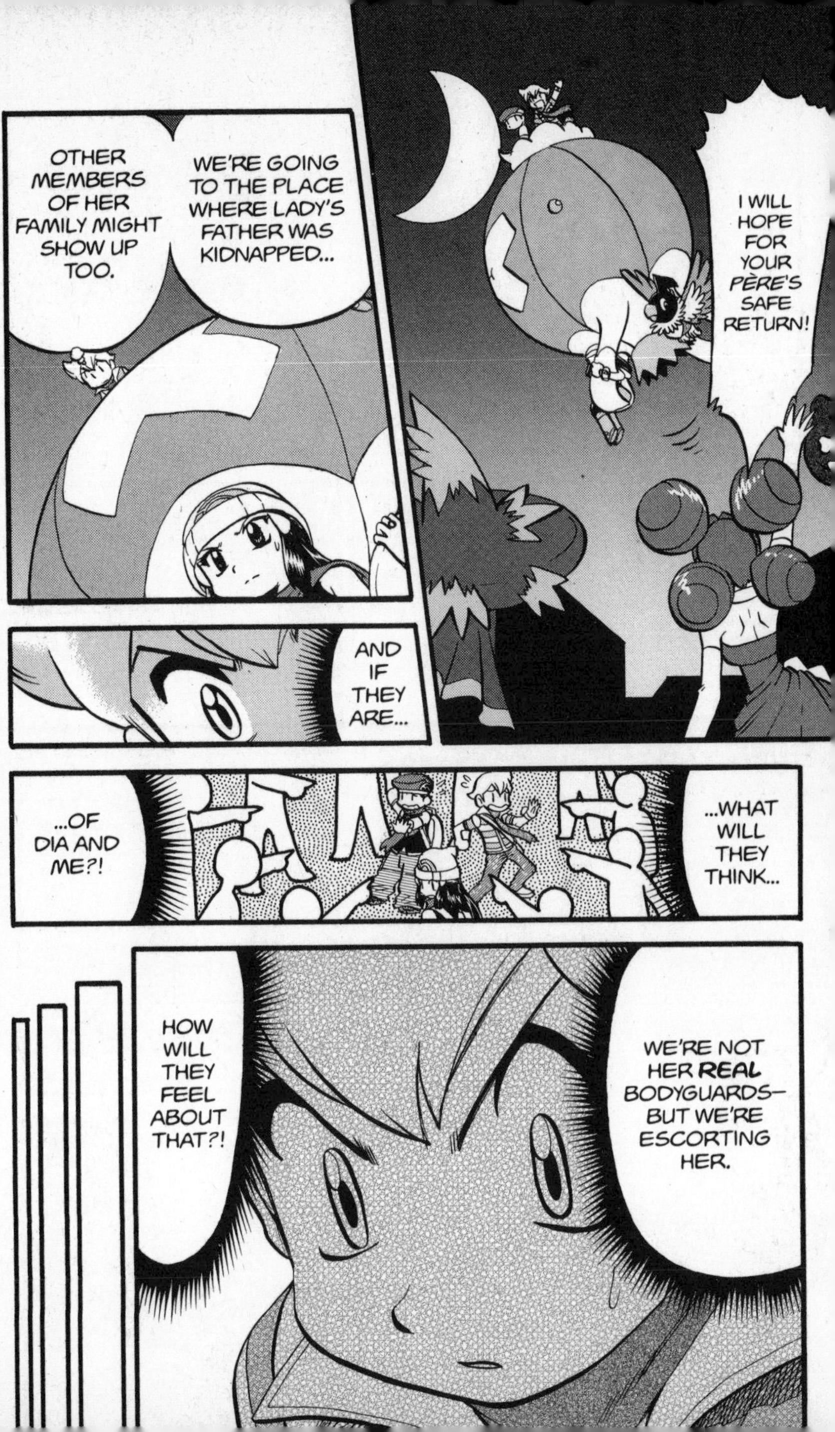
I WILL HOPE FOR YOUR PÈRE'S SAFE RETURN!
WE'RE GOING TO THE PLACE WHERE LADY'S FATHER WAS KIDNAPPED...
OTHER MEMBERS OF HER FAMILY MIGHT SHOW UP TOO.
AND IF THEY ARE...
...WHAT WILL THEY THINK...
...OF DIA AND ME?!
WE'RE NOT HER **REAL** BODYGUARDS—BUT WE'RE ESCORTING HER.
HOW WILL THEY FEEL ABOUT THAT?!

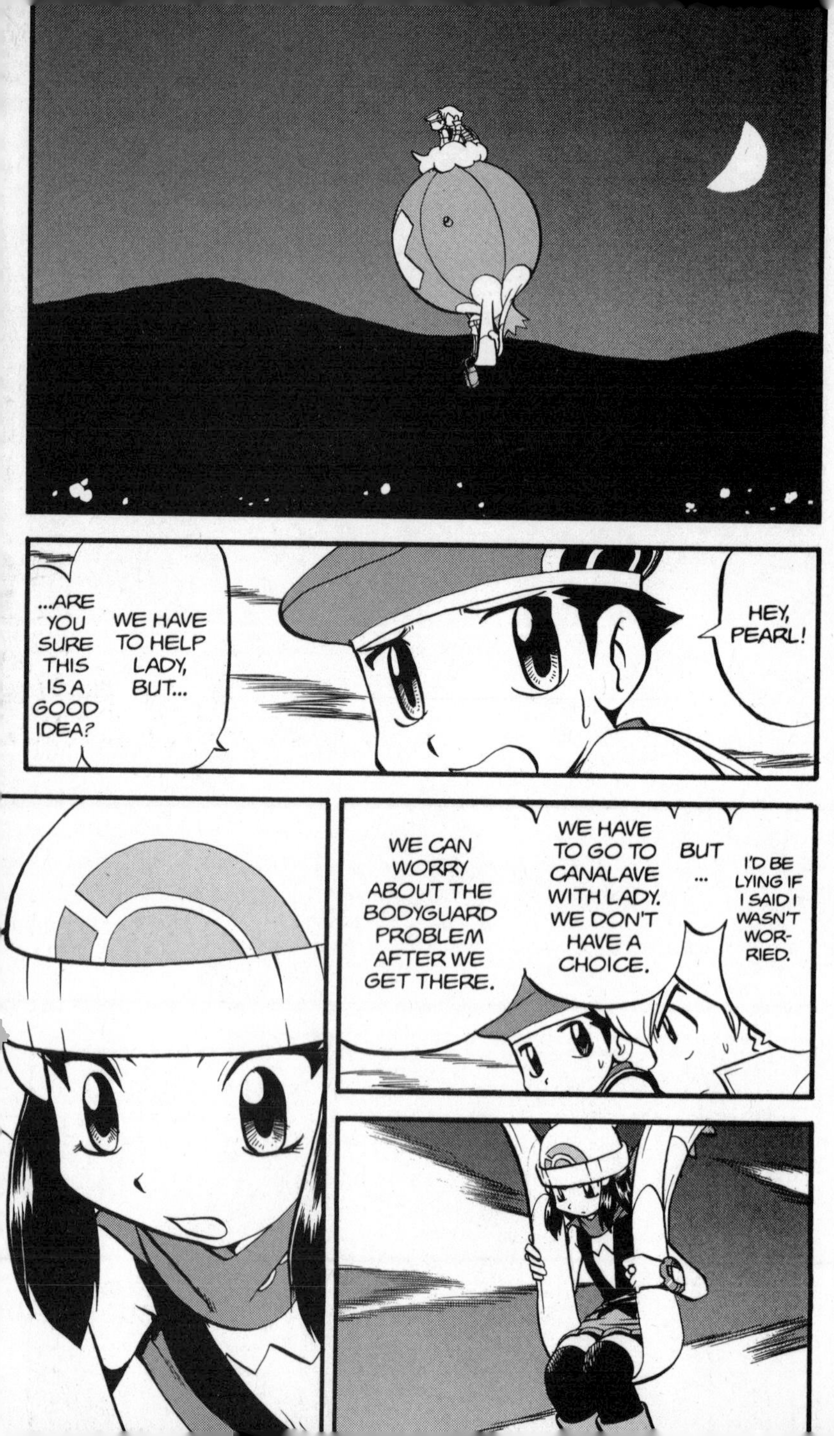
HEY, PEARL!
WE HAVE TO HELP LADY, BUT...
...ARE YOU SURE THIS IS A GOOD IDEA?
I'D BE LYING IF I SAID I WASN'T WOR-RIED.
BUT ...
WE HAVE TO GO TO CANALAVE WITH LADY. WE DON'T HAVE A CHOICE.
WE CAN WORRY ABOUT THE BODYGUARD PROBLEM AFTER WE GET THERE.

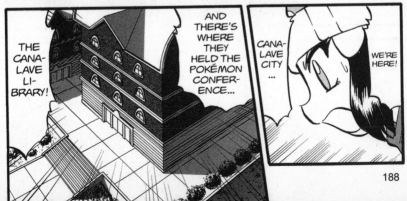

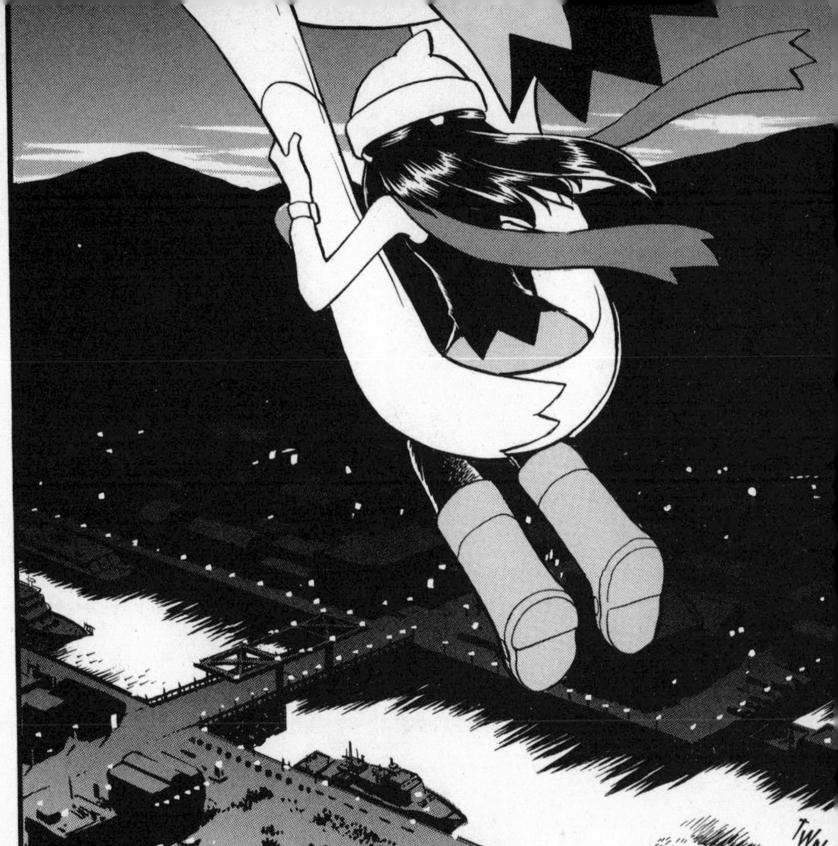
TWNKL

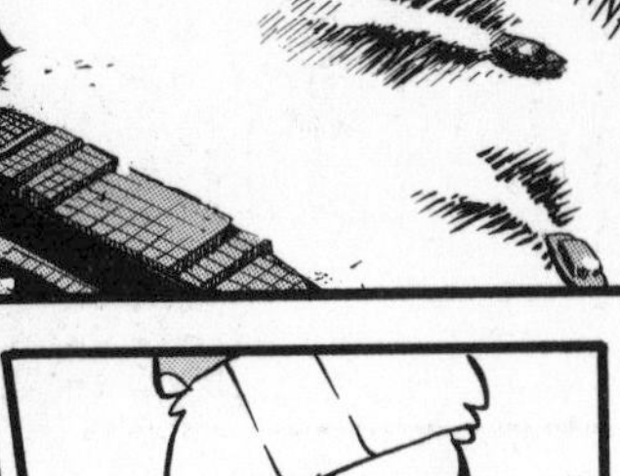
WE'RE HERE!
CANA-LAVE CITY ...

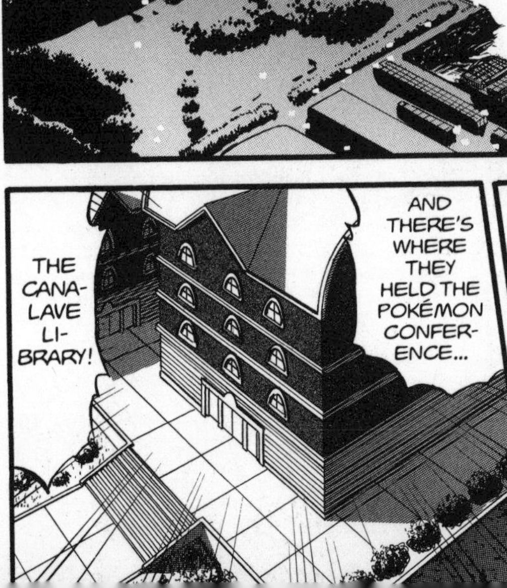
AND THERE'S WHERE THEY HELD THE POKÉMON CONFER-ENCE...
THE CANA-LAVE LI-BRARY!

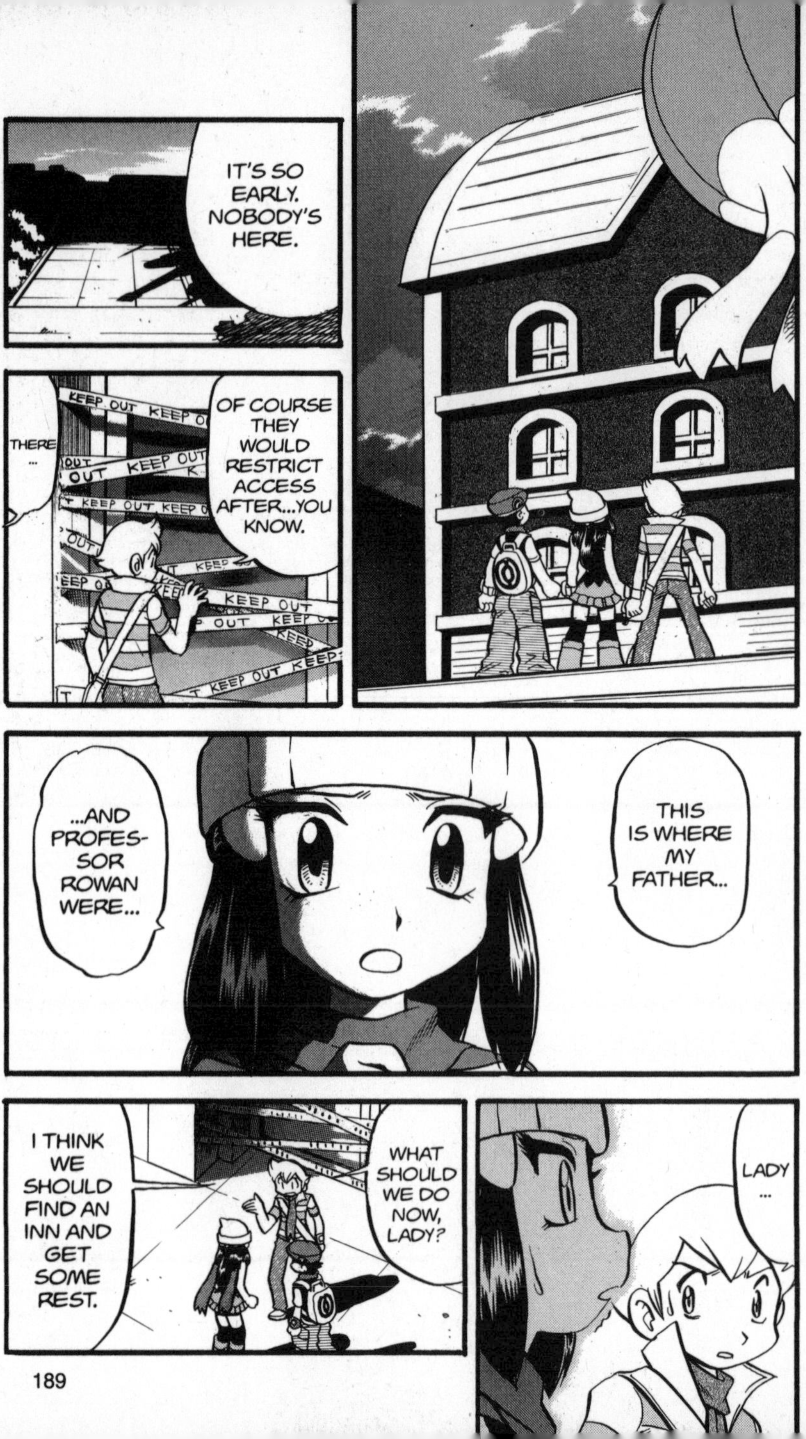
IT'S SO EARLY. NOBODY'S HERE.
KEEP OUT KEEP OUT
OF COURSE THEY WOULD RESTRICT ACCESS AFTER...YOU KNOW.
THERE...
THIS IS WHERE MY FATHER...
...AND PROFESSOR ROWAN WERE...
LADY...
WHAT SHOULD WE DO NOW, LADY?
I THINK WE SHOULD FIND AN INN AND GET SOME REST.

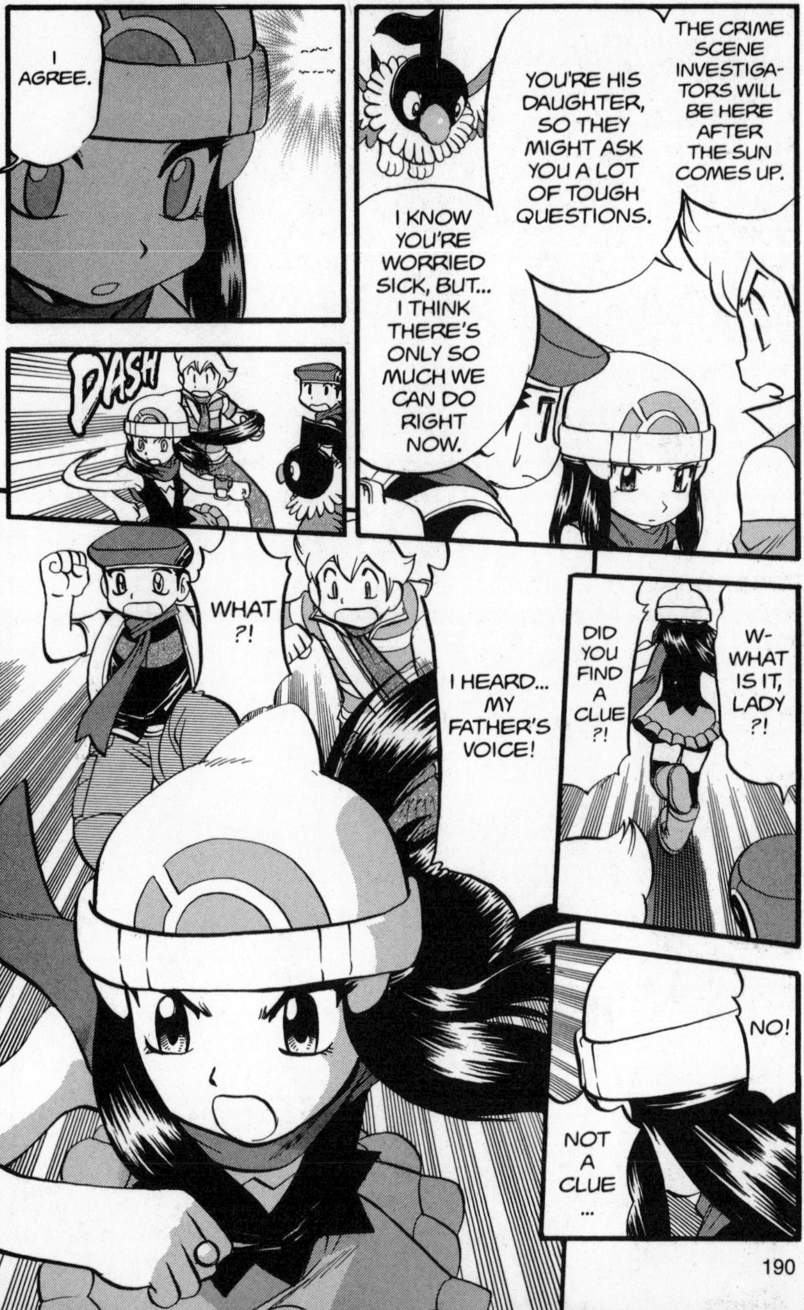
THE CRIME SCENE INVESTIGATORS WILL BE HERE AFTER THE SUN COMES UP.
YOU'RE HIS DAUGHTER, SO THEY MIGHT ASK YOU A LOT OF TOUGH QUESTIONS.
I KNOW YOU'RE WORRIED SICK, BUT... I THINK THERE'S ONLY SO MUCH WE CAN DO RIGHT NOW.
I AGREE.
DASH
W-WHAT IS IT, LADY?!
DID YOU FIND A CLUE?!
NO!
NOT A CLUE...
I HEARD... MY FATHER'S VOICE!
WHAT?!

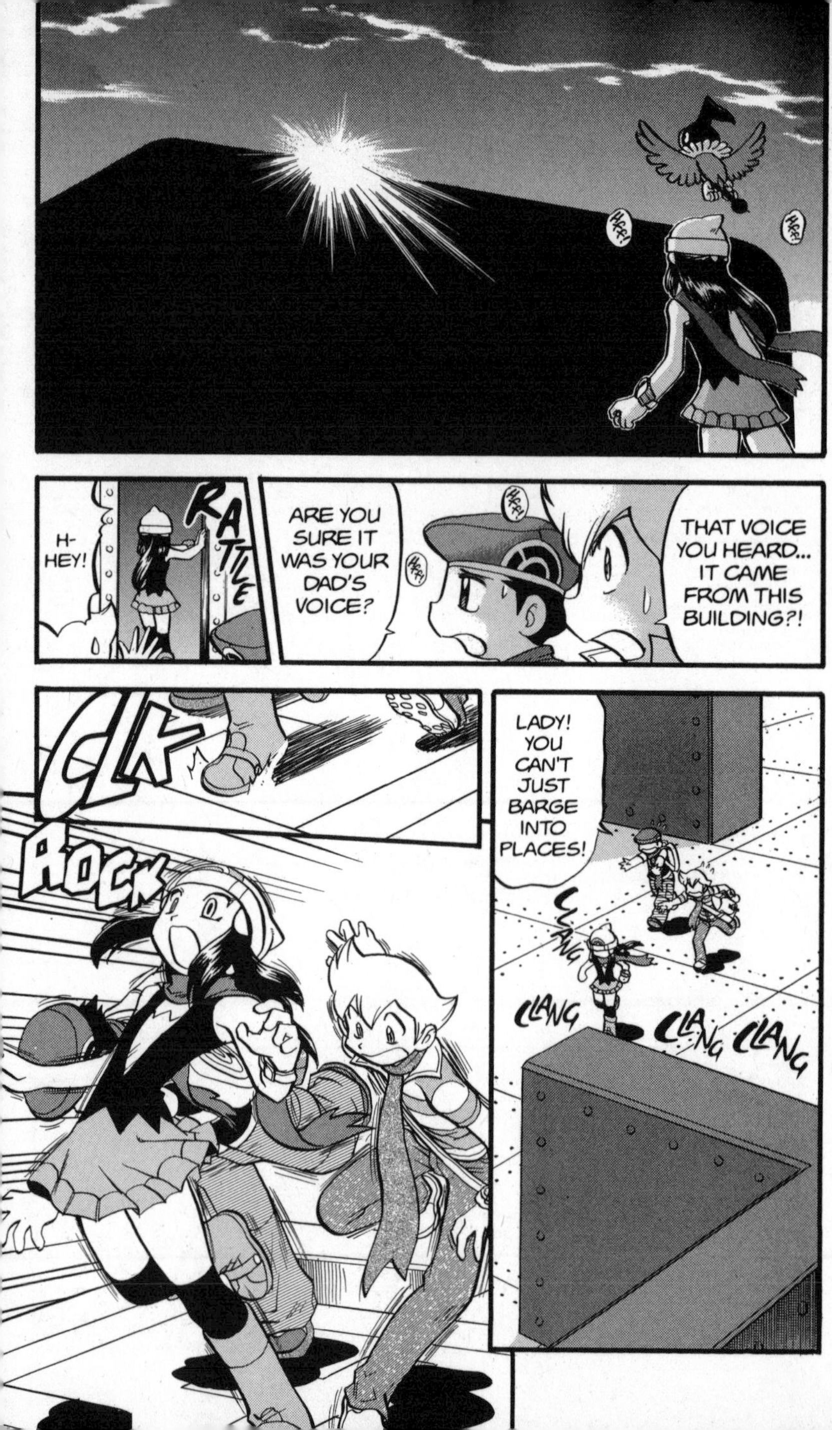
HFF!
HFF!
THAT VOICE YOU HEARD... IT CAME FROM THIS BUILDING?!
HFF!
HFF!
ARE YOU SURE IT WAS YOUR DAD'S VOICE?
RATTLE
H- HEY!
LADY! YOU CAN'T JUST BARGE INTO PLACES!
CLANG
CLANG
CLANG
CLANG
CLK
ROCK

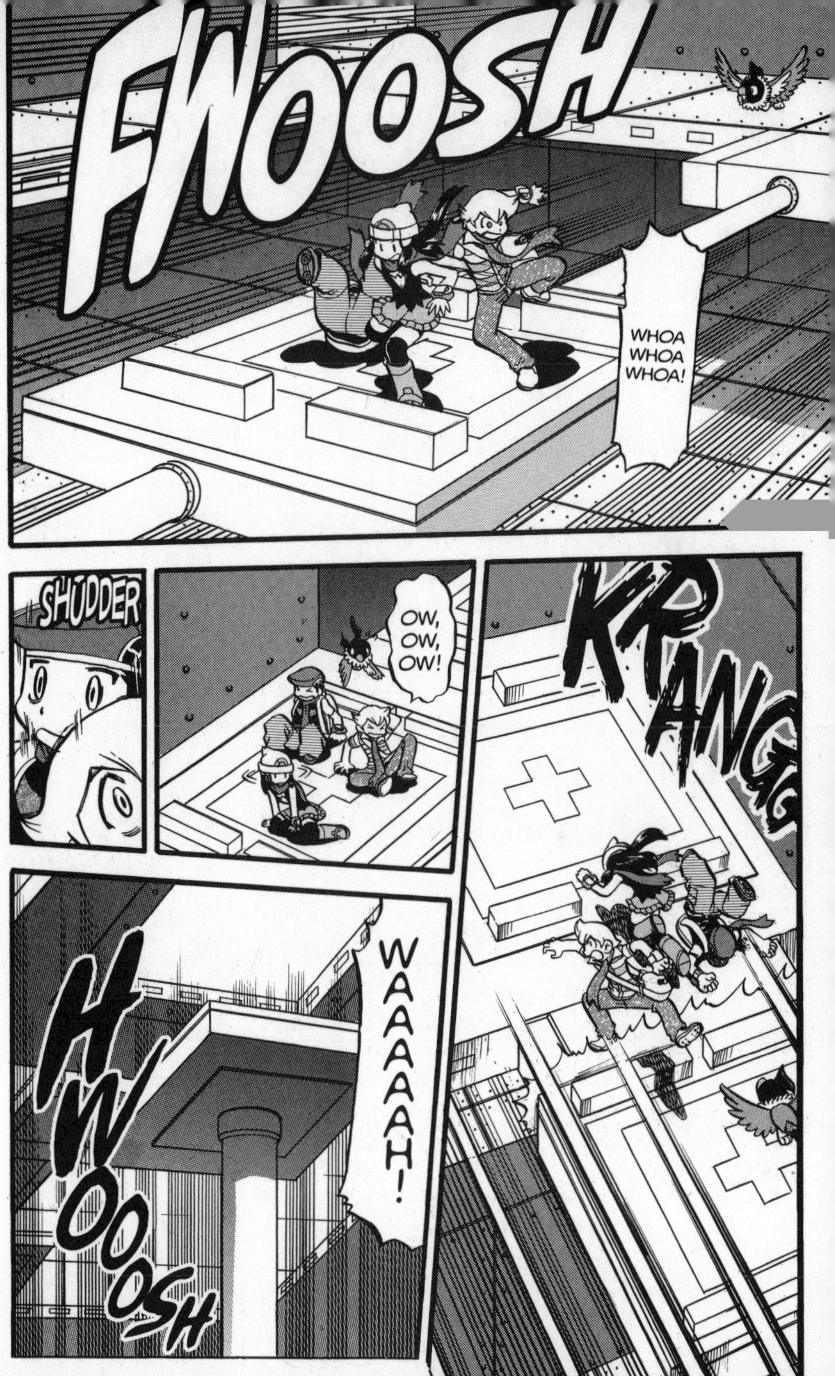
FWOOSH
WHOA WHOA WHOA!
KRANGG
OW, OW, OW!
SHUDDER
WAAAAAH!
HWOOOSH

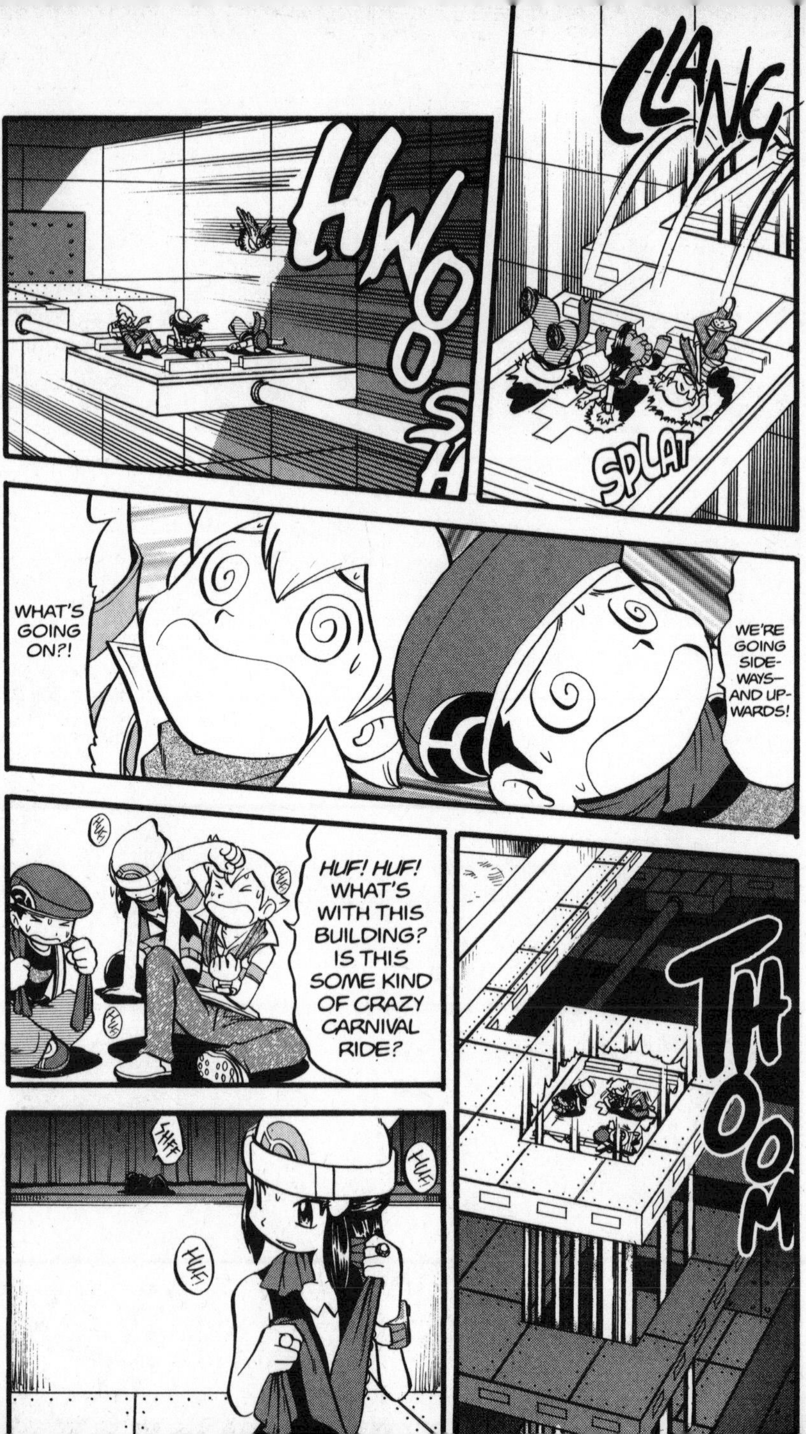
CLANG
SPLAT
HWOOSH
WE'RE GOING SIDE-WAYS—AND UP-WARDS!
WHAT'S GOING ON?!
THOOM
HUF! HUF! WHAT'S WITH THIS BUILDING? IS THIS SOME KIND OF CRAZY CARNIVAL RIDE?
SNIFF
HUF!
HUF!

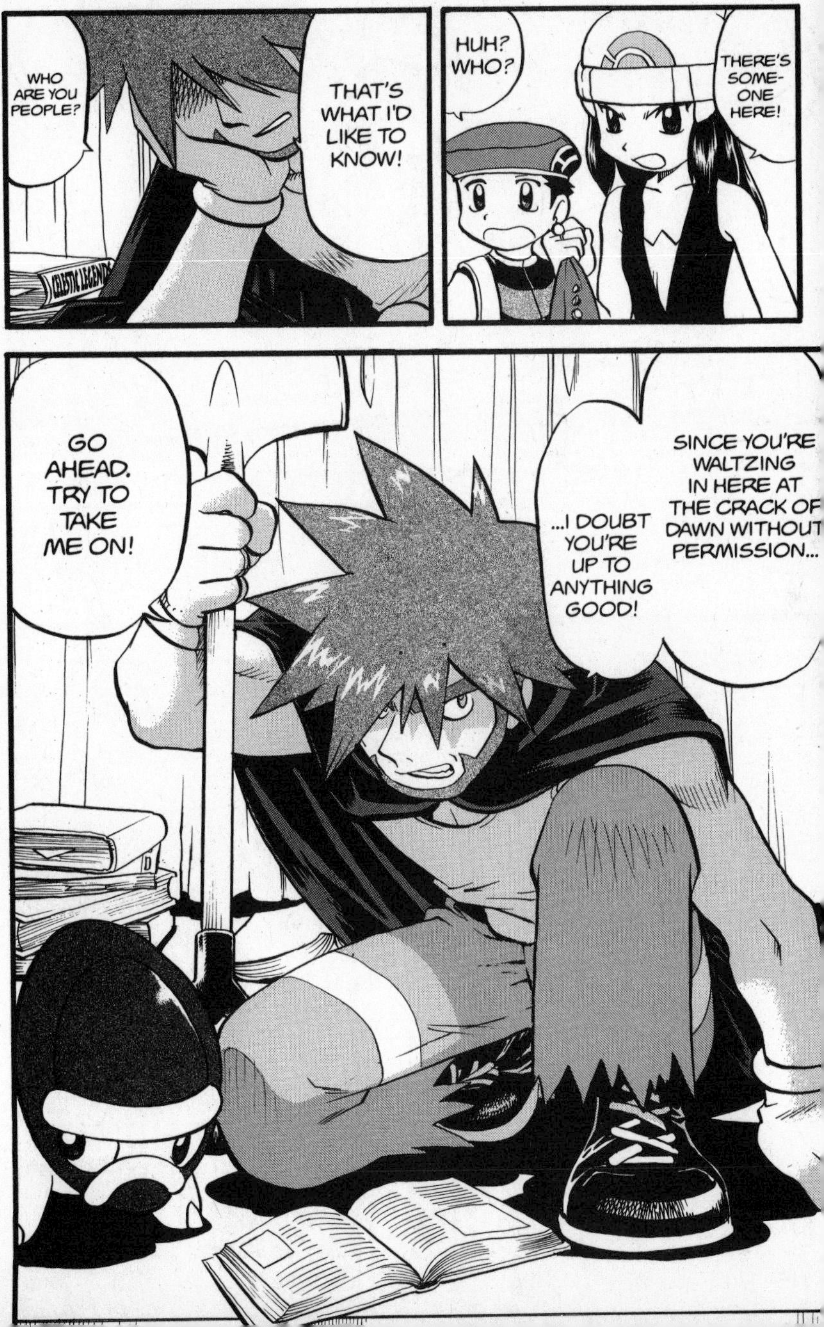
THERE'S SOME-ONE HERE!
HUH? WHO?
THAT'S WHAT I'D LIKE TO KNOW!
WHO ARE YOU PEOPLE?
CELESTIC LEGENDS
SINCE YOU'RE WALTZING IN HERE AT THE CRACK OF DAWN WITHOUT PERMISSION...
...I DOUBT YOU'RE UP TO ANYTHING GOOD!
GO AHEAD. TRY TO TAKE ME ON!

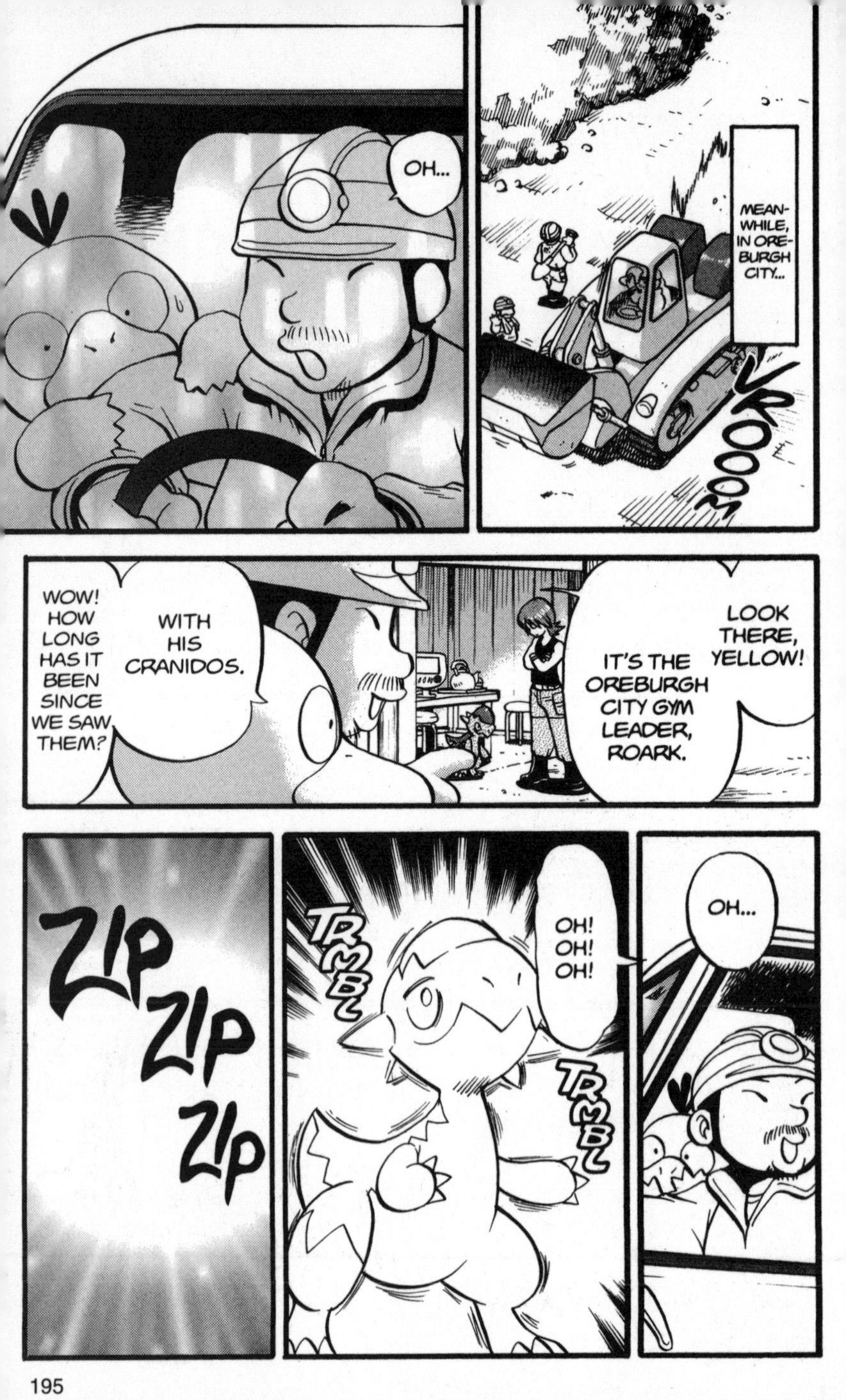
MEAN-WHILE, IN ORE-BURGH CITY...
VROOOOM
OH...
LOOK THERE, YELLOW!
IT'S THE OREBURGH CITY GYM LEADER, ROARK.
WITH HIS CRANIDOS.
WOW! HOW LONG HAS IT BEEN SINCE WE SAW THEM?
OH...
OH! OH! OH!
TRMBL
TRMBL
ZIP ZIP ZIP

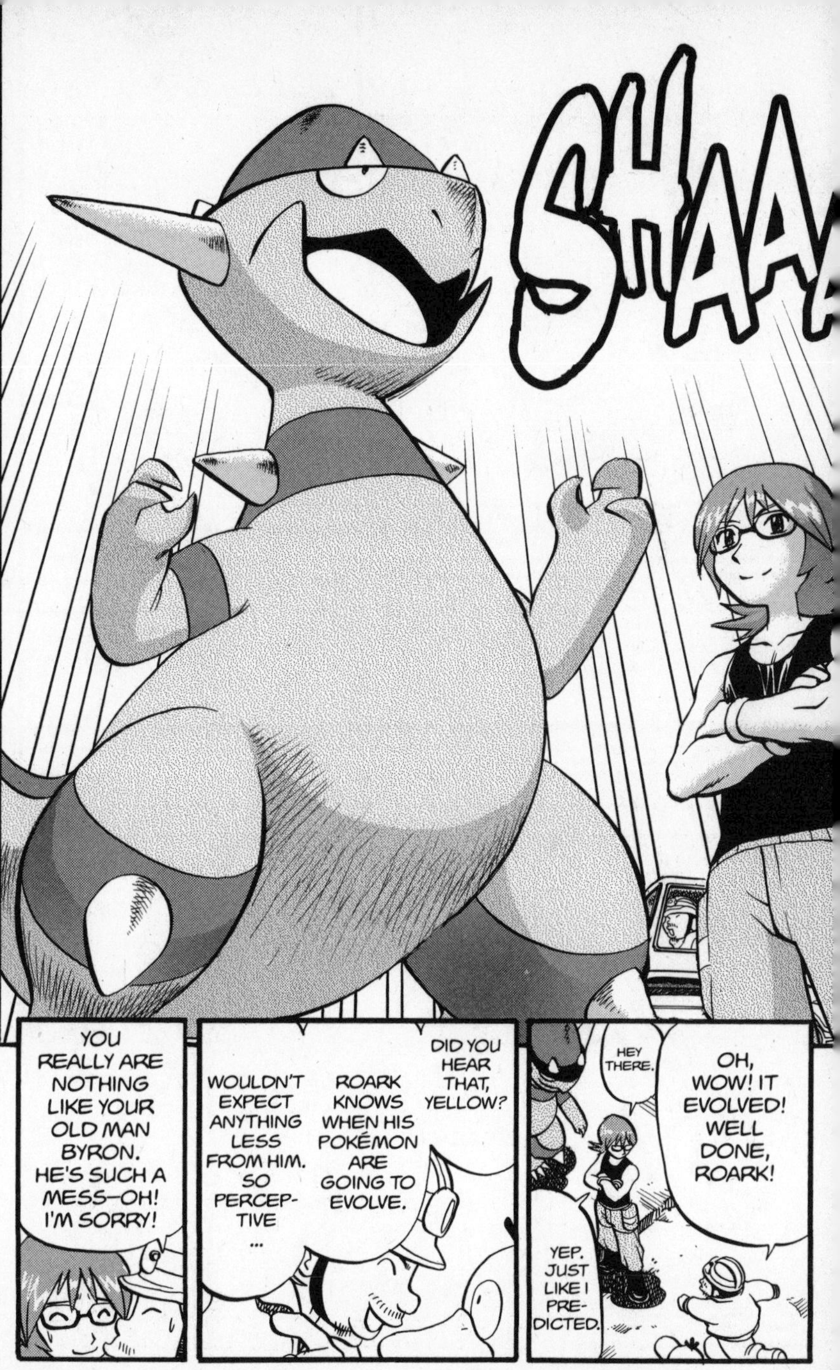
SHAA
OH, WOW! IT EVOLVED! WELL DONE, ROARK!
HEY THERE.
YEP. JUST LIKE I PREDICTED.
DID YOU HEAR THAT, YELLOW?
ROARK KNOWS WHEN HIS POKÉMON ARE GOING TO EVOLVE.
WOULDN'T EXPECT ANYTHING LESS FROM HIM. SO PERCEPTIVE ...
YOU REALLY ARE NOTHING LIKE YOUR OLD MAN BYRON. HE'S SUCH A MESS—OH! I'M SORRY!

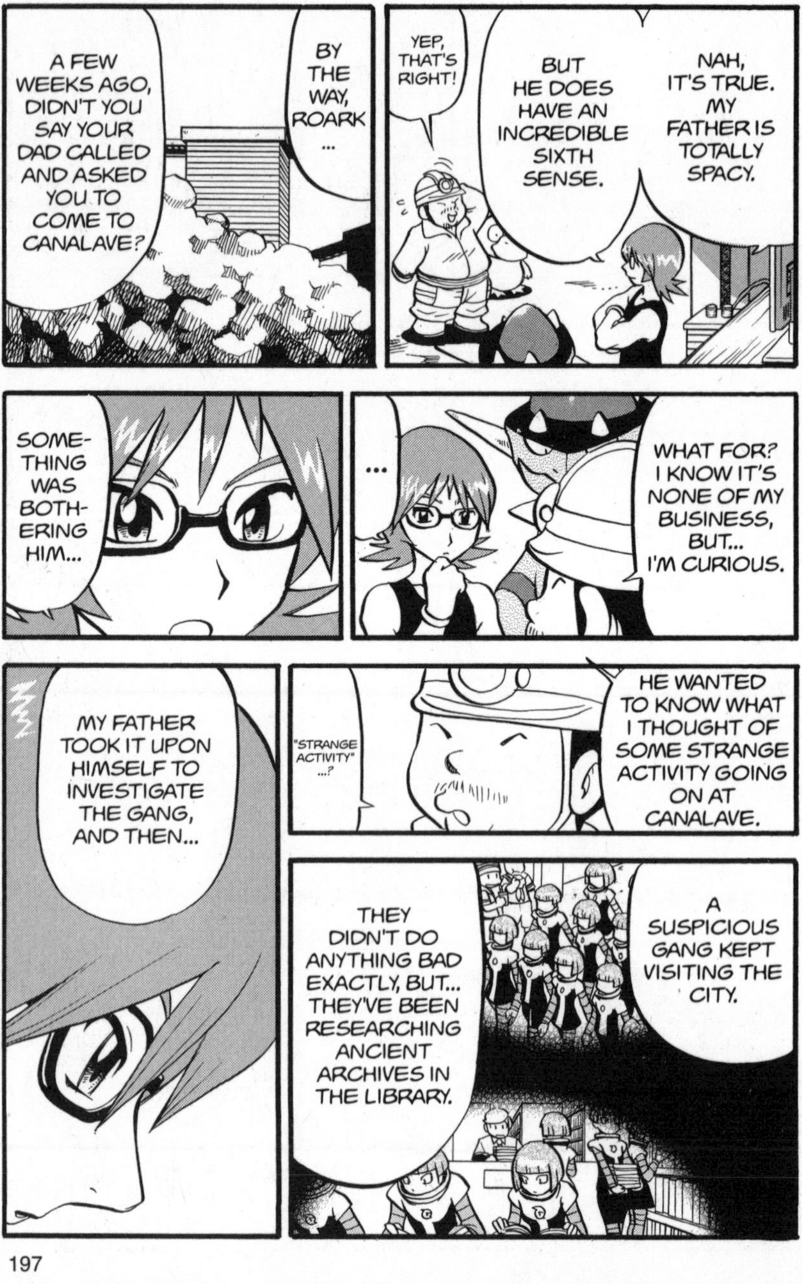
NAH, IT'S TRUE. MY FATHER IS TOTALLY SPACY.
BUT HE DOES HAVE AN INCREDIBLE SIXTH SENSE.
YEP, THAT'S RIGHT!
BY THE WAY, ROARK...
A FEW WEEKS AGO, DIDN'T YOU SAY YOUR DAD CALLED AND ASKED YOU TO COME TO CANALAVE?
WHAT FOR? I KNOW IT'S NONE OF MY BUSINESS, BUT... I'M CURIOUS.
...
SOME-THING WAS BOTH-ERING HIM...
HE WANTED TO KNOW WHAT I THOUGHT OF SOME STRANGE ACTIVITY GOING ON AT CANALAVE.
"STRANGE ACTIVITY" ...?
A SUSPICIOUS GANG KEPT VISITING THE CITY.
THEY DIDN'T DO ANYTHING BAD EXACTLY, BUT... THEY'VE BEEN RESEARCHING ANCIENT ARCHIVES IN THE LIBRARY.
MY FATHER TOOK IT UPON HIMSELF TO INVESTIGATE THE GANG, AND THEN...

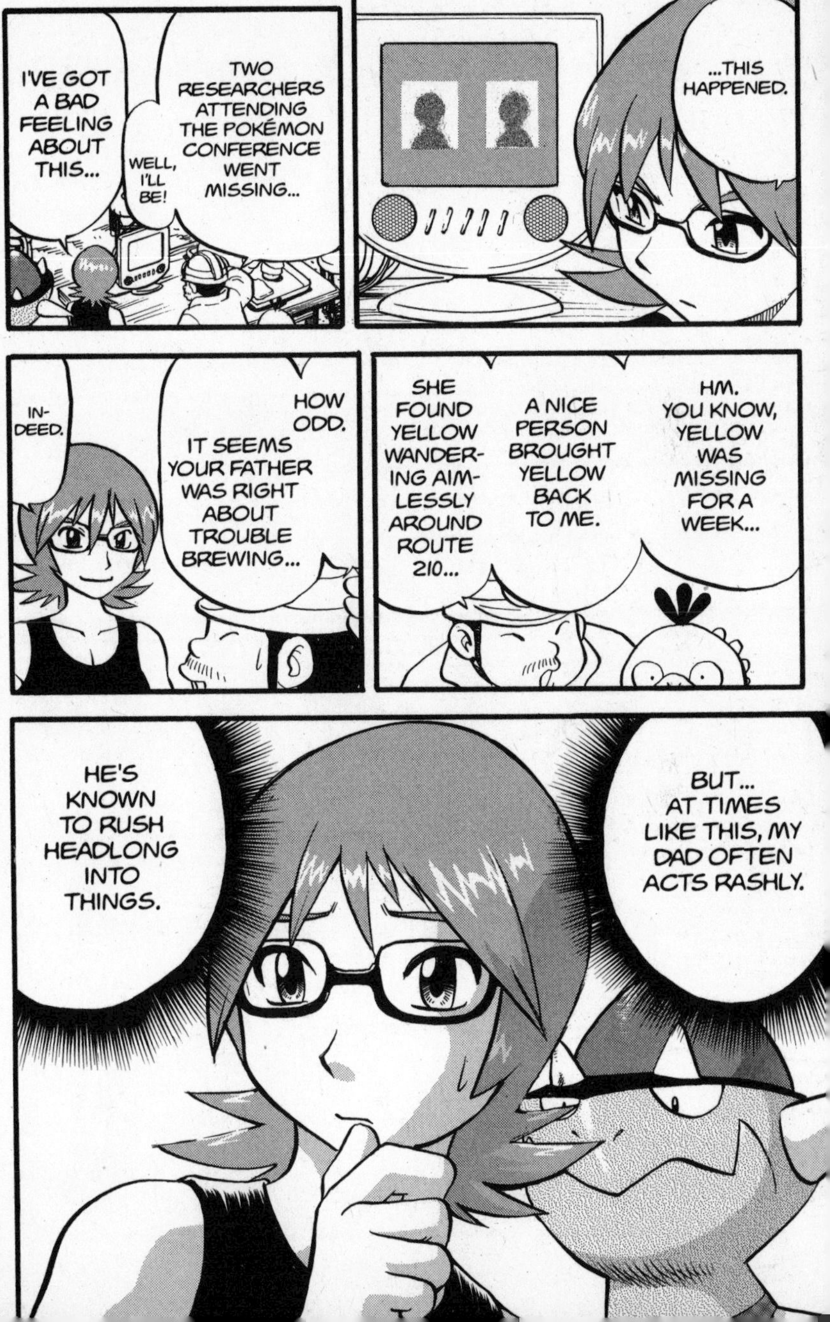
...THIS HAPPENED.
TWO RESEARCHERS ATTENDING THE POKÉMON CONFERENCE WENT MISSING...
WELL, I'LL BE!
I'VE GOT A BAD FEELING ABOUT THIS...
HM. YOU KNOW, YELLOW WAS MISSING FOR A WEEK...
A NICE PERSON BROUGHT YELLOW BACK TO ME.
SHE FOUND YELLOW WANDERING AIMLESSLY AROUND ROUTE 210...
HOW ODD.
IT SEEMS YOUR FATHER WAS RIGHT ABOUT TROUBLE BREWING...
INDEED.
BUT... AT TIMES LIKE THIS, MY DAD OFTEN ACTS RASHLY.
HE'S KNOWN TO RUSH HEADLONG INTO THINGS.

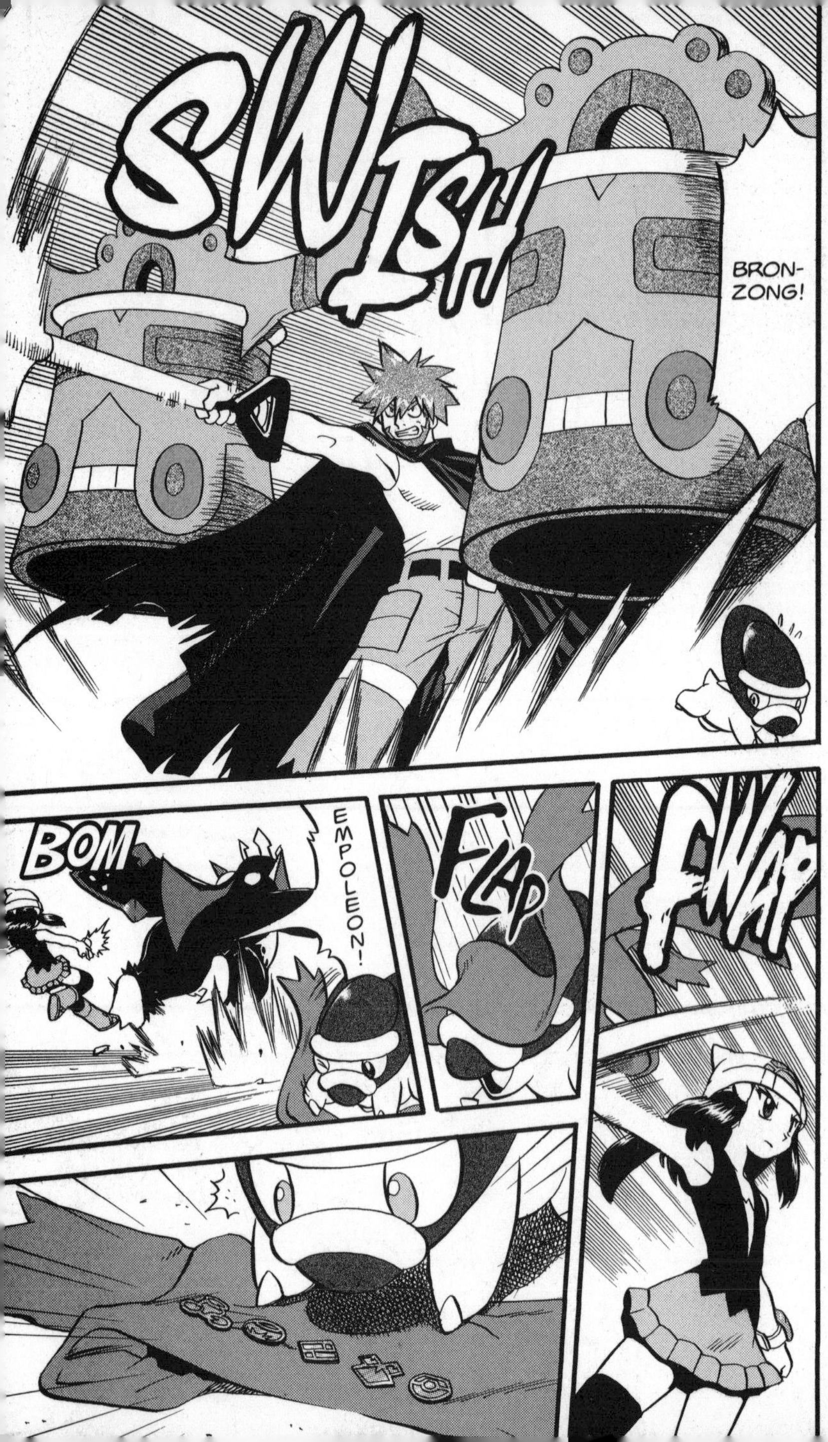
SWISH
BRON-ZONG!
FWAP
FLAP
EMPOLEON!
BOM

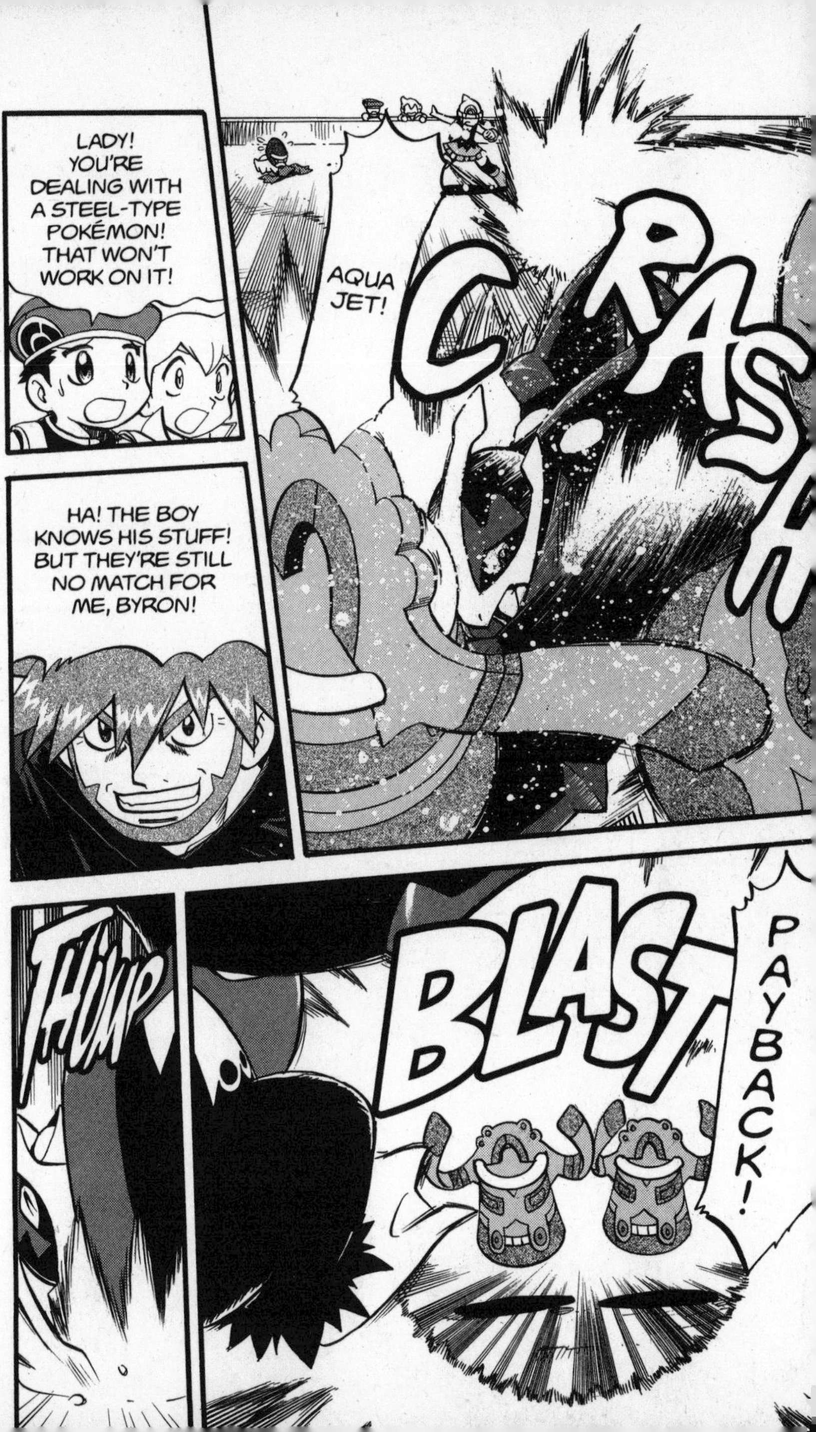
AQUA JET!
CRASH
LADY! YOU'RE DEALING WITH A STEEL-TYPE POKÉMON! THAT WON'T WORK ON IT!
HA! THE BOY KNOWS HIS STUFF! BUT THEY'RE STILL NO MATCH FOR ME, BYRON!
PAYBACK!
BLAST
THUMP

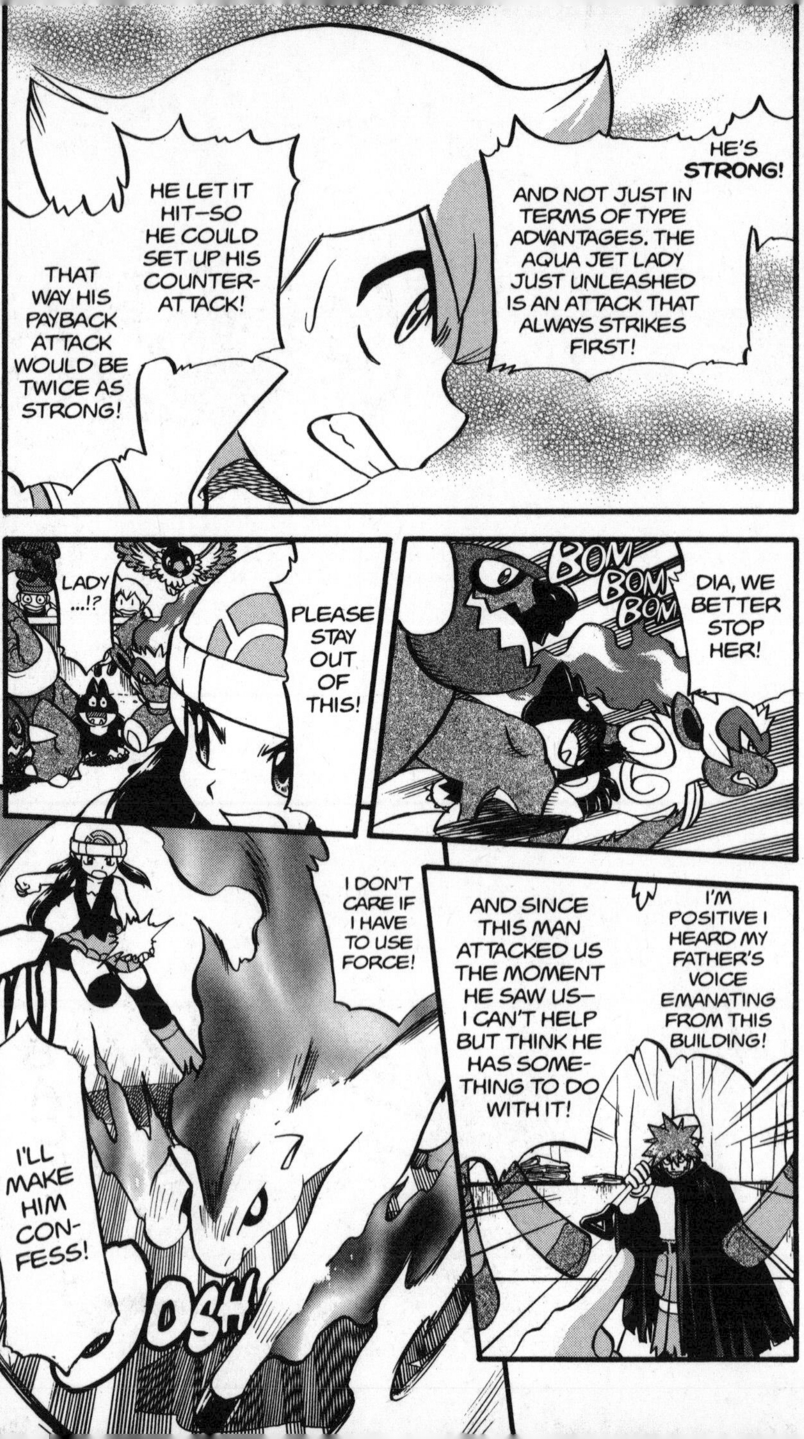
HE'S STRONG!
AND NOT JUST IN TERMS OF TYPE ADVANTAGES. THE AQUA JET LADY JUST UNLEASHED IS AN ATTACK THAT ALWAYS STRIKES FIRST!
HE LET IT HIT—SO HE COULD SET UP HIS COUNTER-ATTACK!
THAT WAY HIS PAYBACK ATTACK WOULD BE TWICE AS STRONG!
DIA, WE BETTER STOP HER!
BOM BOM BOM
PLEASE STAY OUT OF THIS!
LADY ...!?
I'M POSITIVE I HEARD MY FATHER'S VOICE EMANATING FROM THIS BUILDING!
AND SINCE THIS MAN ATTACKED US THE MOMENT HE SAW US— I CAN'T HELP BUT THINK HE HAS SOME-THING TO DO WITH IT!
I DON'T CARE IF I HAVE TO USE FORCE!
I'LL MAKE HIM CON-FESS!
OSH

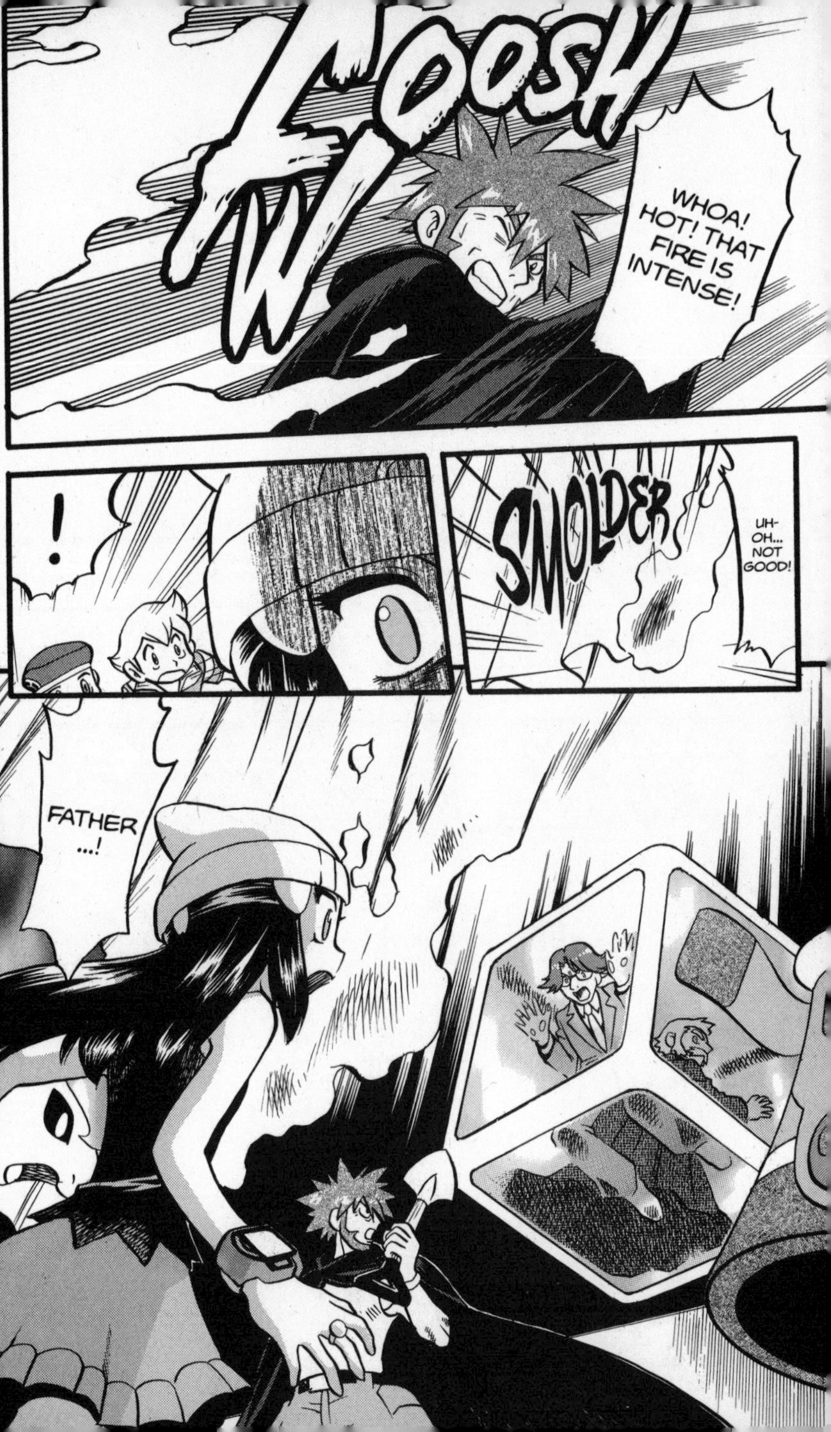
WHOOSH
WHOA! HOT! THAT FIRE IS INTENSE!
SMOLDER
UH-OH... NOT GOOD!
!
FATHER ...!

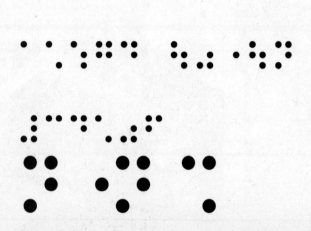

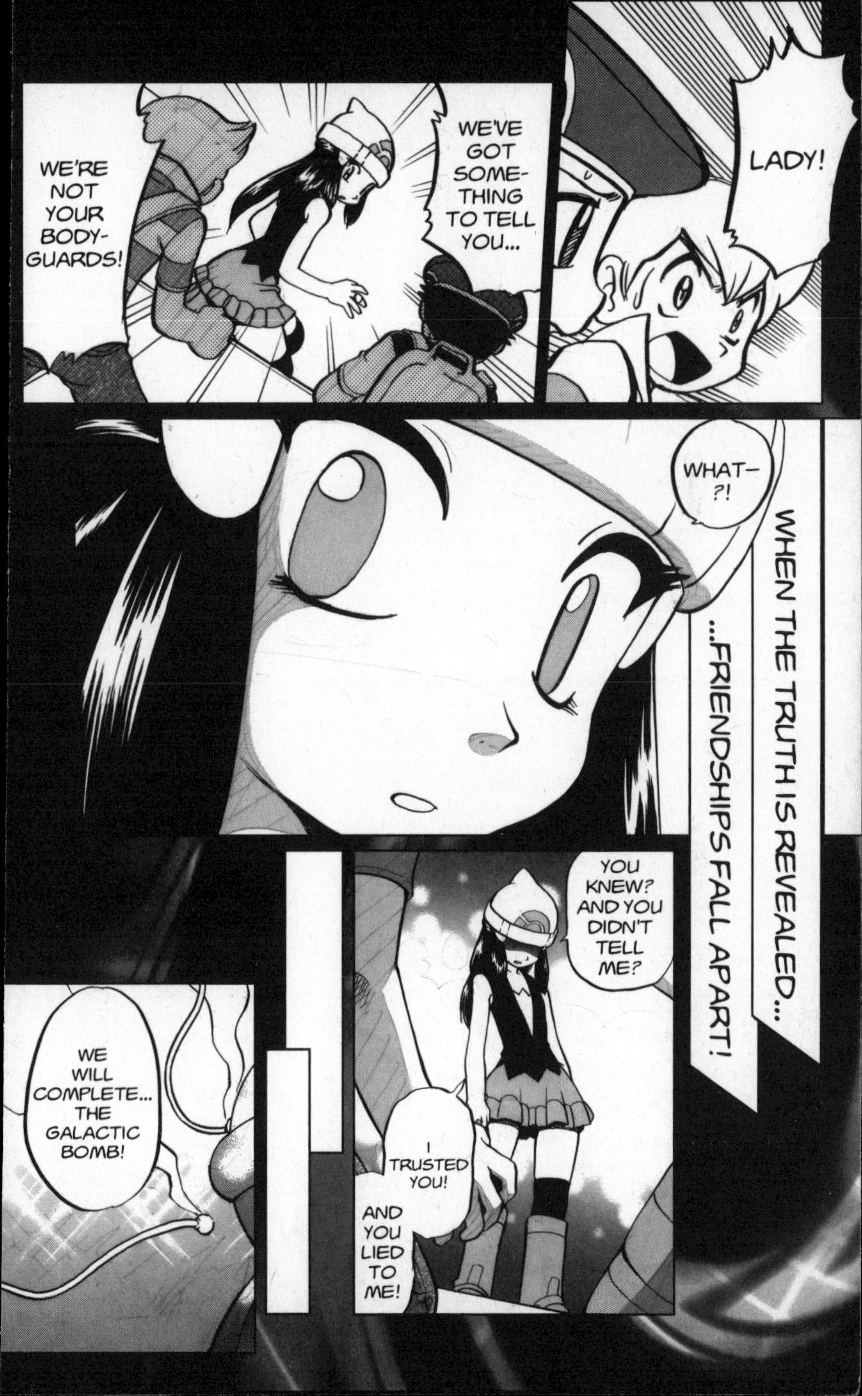
LADY!
WE'VE GOT SOMETHING TO TELL YOU...
WE'RE NOT YOUR BODYGUARDS!
WHEN THE TRUTH IS REVEALED...
...FRIENDSHIPS FALL APART!
WHAT—?!
YOU KNEW? AND YOU DIDN'T TELL ME?
I TRUSTED YOU!
AND YOU LIED TO ME!
WE WILL COMPLETE... THE GALACTIC BOMB!

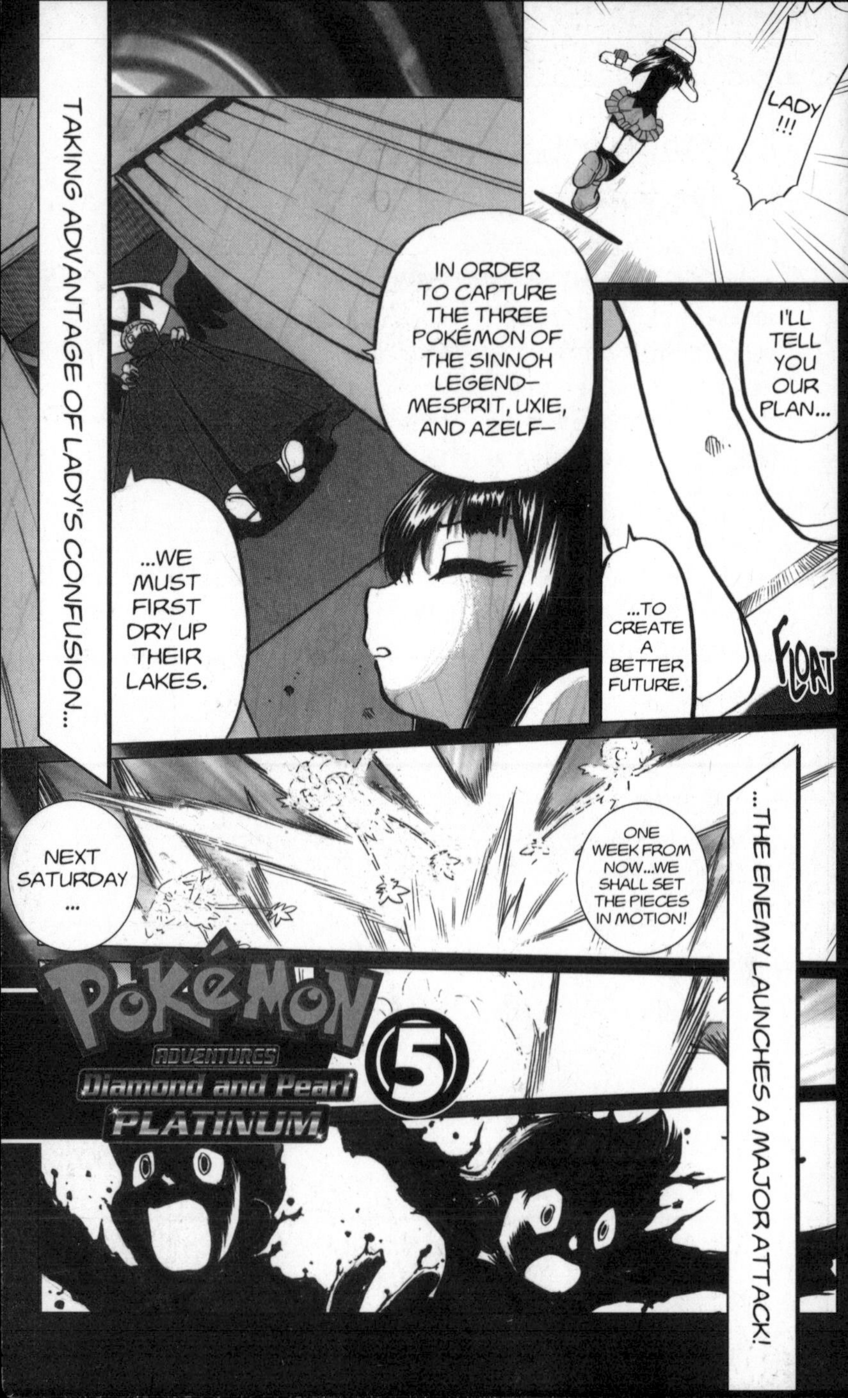
LADY !!!
I'LL TELL YOU OUR PLAN...
...TO CREATE A BETTER FUTURE.
FLOAT
TAKING ADVANTAGE OF LADY'S CONFUSION...
IN ORDER TO CAPTURE THE THREE POKÉMON OF THE SINNOH LEGEND—MESPRIT, UXIE, AND AZELF—
...WE MUST FIRST DRY UP THEIR LAKES.
...THE ENEMY LAUNCHES A MAJOR ATTACK!
ONE WEEK FROM NOW...WE SHALL SET THE PIECES IN MOTION!
NEXT SATURDAY ...
POKÉMON
ADVENTURES
Diamond and Pearl
PLATINUM
5

Message from
Hidenori Kusaka

Cyrus is the mysterious creepy archvillain of the *Pokémon Adventures* series. This first direct confrontation between Cyrus and our trio of heroes is the highlight of this volume! Despite their fears, they face him with their heads held high. Hope you enjoy the story!

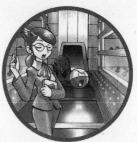

Message from
Satoshi Yamamoto

I bet the preview in the last volume worried a lot of readers. So far, best friends Diamond and Pearl have been the perfect team...but now they're fighting! And what will happen to Lady? The bonds between our three friends will be sorely tested in volume 4 as we reach the climax of the Diamond and Pearl story arc!

More Adventures Coming Soon...

Lady feels betrayed when she finally discovers the truth about Diamond's and Pearl's identities. Is the trio's journey—and friendship—over?! And how can our three heroes save three Legendary Lake Pokémon from Team Galactic... when each Legendary Pokémon is in a *different lake*?!

Meanwhile, what is Team Galactic secretly manufacturing in an abandoned factory...?

Plus, meet Shieldon, Gliscor, Lucario, Vespiquen and many more Sinnoh Pokémon friends!

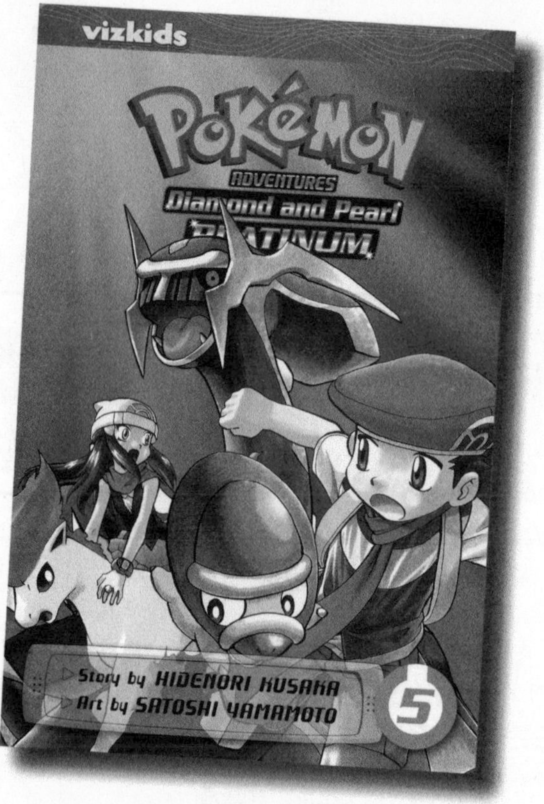
vizkids
POKéMON
ADVENTURES
Diamond and Pearl
Story by HIDENORI KUSAKA
Art by SATOSHI YAMAMOTO
5

AVAILABLE NOW!

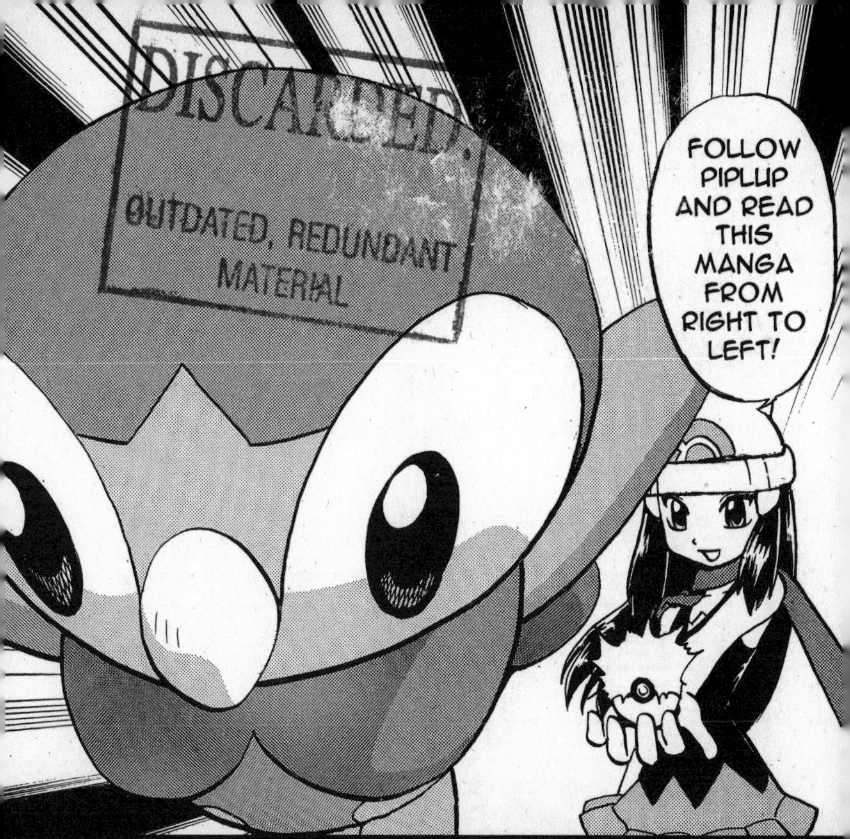
FOLLOW PIPLUP AND READ THIS MANGA FROM RIGHT TO LEFT!

THIS IS THE END OF THIS GRAPHIC NOVEL!

To properly enjoy this VIZ Media graphic novel, please turn it around and begin reading from right to left.

This book has been printed in the original Japanese format in order to preserve the orientation of the original artwork. Have fun with it!

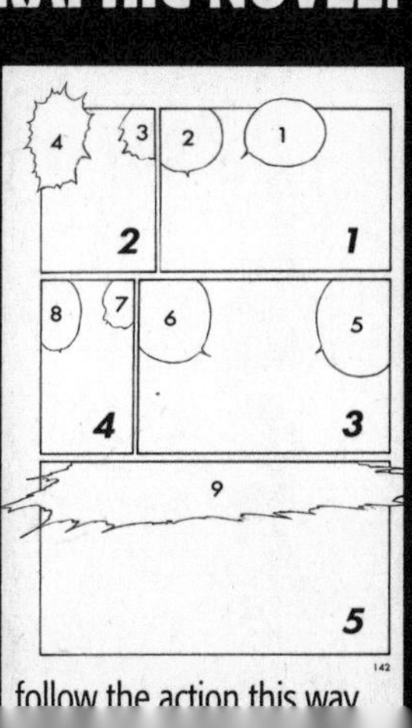
follow the action this way

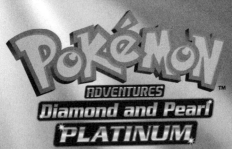

POKÉMON ADVENTURES:
DIAMOND AND PEARL/
PLATINUM
Volume 4
Perfect Square Edition

Story by **HIDENORI KUSAKA**
Art by **SATOSHI YAMAMOTO**

© 2012 The Pokémon Company International.
© 1995-2012 Nintendo/Creatures Inc./GAME FREAK inc.
TM, ®, and character names are trademarks of Nintendo.
POCKET MONSTERS SPECIAL Vol. 4 (33)
by Hidenori KUSAKA, Satoshi YAMAMOTO
© 1997 Hidenori KUSAKA, Satoshi YAMAMOTO
All rights reserved.
Original Japanese edition published by SHOGAKUKAN.
English translation rights in the United States of America, Canada, the United Kingdom,
Ireland, Australia and New Zealand arranged with SHOGAKUKAN.

Translation/Katherine Schilling
Touch-up & Lettering/Annaliese Christman
Design/Yukiko Whitley
Editor/Annette Roman

The stories, characters and incidents mentioned in this
publication are entirely fictional.

Printed in the U.S.A.

Published by VIZ Media, LLC
P.O. Box 77010
San Francisco, CA 94107

10 9 8 7 6 5 4 3
First printing, February 2012
Third printing, November 2016

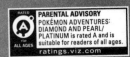

PERFECT SQUARE

VIZ media
www.viz.com